JUMPING TO CONCLUSIONS

JUMPING TO CONCLUSIONS

Christina Jones

WINDSOR
PARAGON

First published 1999
by HarperCollins*Publishers*
This Large Print edition published 2013
by AudioGO Ltd
by arrangement with
the Author

Hardcover   ISBN: 978 1 4713 1236 6
Softcover   ISBN: 978 1 4713 1237 3

British Library Cataloguing in Publication Data available

Printed and bound in Great Britain by
TJ International Ltd

ACKNOWLEDGEMENTS

To Susan Watt and all at HarperCollins with very grateful thanks.

To Sarah Molloy, my agent, for actions above and beyond the call of duty.

To Jane Wood and Selina Walker for all their help and friendship.

To everyone at Blackwells who employed me as a bookseller—I knew it would pay off one day.

To my cousins, Jill and Glen Hutchinson, for becoming pillars of Milton St John society.

To my mate, Tina Maloret in Jersey, who always wanted to be a fictional wicked lady.

To Lucinda Walker for her help with the chocolate croissants and for being a star.

To Rob and Laura, as always, for their love and unflagging support through the bleak bits.

*For my eternal butterfly-chasers with undying love:
Katie and Jeremy, Boris and Jemima, Allie and Trev,
Dominic and Moz, Vinnie and Jack and Miranda.
And especially for Sebastian, who simply broke
my heart*

April

CHAPTER ONE

On what had to be the hottest April afternoon on record, Jemima flicked the Beetle's indicator to leave the A34, and was almost immediately plunged into a maze of high-banked Berkshire roads. The faded three-legged signpost, lurching drunkenly amidst a tangle of burgeoning honeysuckle, suggested that Milton St John, Upton Poges and—yes, Tiptoe for heaven's sake, were now within her reach. Not for the first time as Floss chugged sluggishly through the heat haze, Jemima questioned her sanity.

Still beggars couldn't be choosers, and if she didn't make this move, she'd definitely be the former. Nearly homeless, completely jobless, and practically penniless, the choice was definitely Hobson's.

She'd had to leave Oxford after the hoo-ha over the party-thing. No question. No one could hang around after something like that. Even if her landlord hadn't slapped on an eviction notice, she'd have had to leave. And as she'd intended living in Milton St John from July anyway, the knock-on effect had just precipitated events.

It'd be okay, she told herself, edging Floss in the direction of the village. It would all be just fine. This would tide her over until the shop opened. Give her a breathing space. She'd found somewhere else to live—almost. And she had a new job—practically. And if the two things could just marry nicely together then there wouldn't be a problem, would there?

Immediately after the party débâcle, Jemima had donned dark glasses, convinced that everyone in Oxford *knew,* and bagged a table in Littlewoods cafeteria which was the last place Petra would go— so she knew she'd be safe. Buying a coffee with what remained of her small change, she'd scoured *The Newbury Weekly News,* confident of finding short-term work and accommodation before the summer opening of her bookshop in Milton St John. She'd felt, having hit rock bottom, there was only one way to go. Ten minutes later she wasn't convinced. She had never wanted to read the words Norland Nanny again. Neither was she particularly keen on Cosy Companion, or Housekeeper Handyman. Hotels all seemed to want honours degrees, and was she really cut out for a Genteel Gentleman Seeking Similar Soulmate?

Jemima had pushed the newspaper away across the mock woodgrain Formica and tried to avoid the eye of the table-clearer by draining her empty coffee cup for the umpteenth time. Maybe she'd opt out completely and become a New Age Traveller for three months; Floss wouldn't look out of place in a convoy of ancient and dilapidated vehicles. Or perhaps she'd get a job swabbing decks on a cruise liner. Or maybe she could be a chalet maid at Butlins for the summer season . . . She had sighed heavily. It was pretty galling to discover at almost thirty that you weren't actually qualified to do anything except sell books.

The table-clearer had been hovering menacingly with a clutched J-cloth by this time, and Jemima had grabbed at the paper again in self-defence. Then she'd seen it. Tucked away at the foot of the column and rendered almost illegible by coffee dribbles.

Self-contained one bed furnished flat in vicarage. Suitable professional person. Non smoker. Downland views. Charming Berkshire village. Apply St Saviours, Milton St John . . .

Much to the table-clearer's amazement, Jemima had punched the air. Milton St John! Hallelujah! *Milton St John!* It must have been meant! The euphoria lasted all of thirty seconds. Yes, but—a *vicarage?* Wouldn't she be struck down by a thunderbolt? Regular church-going had never been at the top of her must-do list. Perhaps it wouldn't matter . . . Perhaps God would turn a blind eye.

Deciding not to probe her religious conscience any further, she'd flashed a smile at the lady in the overall and natty hat, belted out into Cornmarket Street, and scribbled a letter to the Vicarage in a quiet corner of W H Smith.

Stunned at the speed with which Mrs Hutchinson—the Vicar's wife with the flat to let—had responded to her application, Jemima was pretty sure that there was something doubtful about the whole thing. Surely clergymen were supposed to be unworldly? Why on earth would they want to let out part of their Vicarage? And why—when she must have been besieged by replies from people bursting with the right qualifications like regular employment and hefty savings accounts—had the Vicar's wife invited Jemima who had neither, to view the flat?

5

*   *   *

With her thoughts miles away and her brain filled with the gauzy beauty of the downlands, Jemima brought Floss to a jerky halt at another overgrown junction. Although she had visited Milton St John four times previously to view the shop, she'd always approached the village from the main Upton Poges road. This time, coming in from the Lambourn end, she'd almost missed the turning. Which, she thought as she peered through the windscreen, was hardly surprising.

'Milton St John,' she said firmly to herself, 'here we come. And even if the Hutchinsons are Satanists, or Moon Children of the Sun, or Born Agains with hairy legs and acoustic guitars, I'll just join in with gusto. Anything for a roof over my head.'

*   *   *

Milton St John was at its most beautiful. The large houses swathed in Virginia creeper; the cottages with their overblown gardens; the fat brown stream curling closely beside the curve of the High Street; and all of it sheltered from the glare of the sun by a colonnade of horse chestnut trees.

Jemima stopped Floss on the lay-by outside the empty bookshop and felt a flutter of excitement mingled with pride. It was hers. Almost. The papers had been signed, the lease paid for, and the solicitors would soon hand over the keys. The shopfitters had finished, and the decorators were in. The publishers' reps had been to see her in Oxford, the suppliers had all been contacted, and the initial orders were placed. It wouldn't be long now before the signwriter inscribed '*Jemima Carlisle—Books*' in gold lettering on the dark green fascia. She had considered having something witty like Bookends, or Between the Lines, or even Page Turners, but eventually decided against it. It was a bookshop and it was hers. That was all it needed to say.

Locking Floss, she walked past the Cat and Fiddle, the Village Stores, and Maureen's Munchy Bar, and headed towards St Saviour's Church. There was a duck pond too, which she hadn't noticed on her earlier visits, and a small school, and a playing field. Everything in Milton St John appeared to be arranged along either side of the winding, dust-grey road. The Vicarage, on the opposite side of the street to the church, was almost totally obscured by bushes and looked slightly sinister in the throbbing heat.

'I knew it,' Jemima muttered to herself. 'They're going to be weirdos. They're probably only advertising because they want a fresh supply of sacrificial virgins for their orgies. Well, that counts me out.'

The sun burned Jemima's back through her loose linen interview jacket. Her ankle length paisley skirt wrapped itself limply against her legs, and perspiration was gathering beneath her spectacles, making the bridge of her nose itch. No wind stirred the pastel froth of the gardens or disturbed the embryo leaves on the trees. Milton St John slumbered. There was no traffic, no children, no sound. Despite the heat, Jemima shivered and wished she hadn't reread The Midwich Cuckoos

7

quite so recently.

St Saviour's Vicarage reverberated to a rather fruity Westminster chime as Jemima tugged on the bell-rope. She just knew that the door was going to be hurled open by a seven-foot monster with a bolt through his neck. She tugged again. The chimes echoed on for ever. Trickles of sweat snaked down her backbone.

'Can I help you?' a voice eventually echoed from behind a wildly overgrown lilac bush. 'If you're the van driver collecting the clothes for the jumble sale, they're all in the—oh . . .'

No monster, no neck bolt, and no—as far as Jemima could see—acoustic guitar. Gillian Hutchinson was slender, pale-skinned, and wearing a silver-grey dress in some diaphanous material. True, she didn't look like a proper vicar's wife— no brogues, no tweeds, no twin-set—but Jemima's spirits edged up a little.

'I've—um—come about the flat . . .'

'Good heavens! Is it that time already? Have you been waiting long? Sorry, I was listening to the National build-up on the radio.' She smiled at Jemima's frown. 'The National. The Grand National . . .?'

Of course. Jemima smiled back. No wonder Milton St John was deserted. Everyone breathing would be glued to the Grand National.

Gillian smiled even more. 'You poor thing—you must be baked to a crisp. So unseasonable! More like July. Come in and have something long and cool. I'm Gillian Hutchinson and I'm really sorry—' the laugh was gentle, '—but I can't for the life of me remember your name.'

'Jemima Carlisle.'

'Jemima! Of course!' Gillian Hutchinson linked her arm through Jemima's and started to lead her through the very welcome shade of a shrubbery at the side of the Vicarage. 'I was in the summerhouse—that's why I didn't hear the bell. When can you move in?'

'What?'

'Oh, I'm useless at this sort of thing. I know you're supposed to ask me questions, and I'm supposed to say there are dozens of other people interested in the flat, but there aren't of course, and—' she surveyed Jemima with pale green eyes, '—you'll be doing me a huge favour if you say yes.'

The sacrificial virgins were beginning to surface again. Or was it drugs? Jemima's imagination powered into overdrive as she squinted at Gillian. Surely her eyes shouldn't be that bright? Her pupils that dilated? That was it! Drugs. She peered anxiously at the glorious borders in the back garden. All those tall glossy plants? Were they . . .? She wished she'd taken more notice of the drugs scene at the Oxford parties she'd attended. Having smoked a spliff once and been very sick, she didn't feel qualified to make an informed judgement.

'The summerhouse,' Gillian announced, tossing back her very un-vicar's wife fair hair. 'My bolt hole. Grab a pew. Sorry. Both very poor jokes under the circs. Glen would have a purple fit.'

'Glen?' Jemima searched around for somewhere to sit that wasn't awash with notebooks and typing paper and eventually perched on the edge of a deck chair. It wobbled alarmingly. 'Is that Mr Hutchinson?'

'The *Reverend* Hutchinson,' Gillian corrected,

9

sweeping reams of scribbled-on paper to the floor. 'My darling husband—for his sins. Now, where shall we start? Ooh yes, drinks.'

As Gillian opened a well-stocked fridge and clinked white wine, soda and ice into long glasses, the radio suddenly spurted into life.

'And it's another complete disaster!' The commentator's voice ricocheted round the make-shift office. *'It looks as though we have a major problem here, don't you agree, John? Yes! Oh, this could be catastrophic! I think there's going to be a delay to the start—if not a complete abandoning of the race—'*

The running—or not—of the Grand National was the last thing on Jemima's mind. She looked around the summerhouse in some confusion. It certainly appeared to be an office complete with word processor and fax machine, while at the same time housing all the usual garden paraphernalia—and every inch of it was buried under scribbled on papers, screwed up scraps of notepad and a million empty cigarette packets.

'Everyone in the village has backed Dragon Slayer.' Gillian handed Jemima her glass and lounged elegantly against the fax machine. 'What's your money on?'

'Nothing. I didn't even realise it was the Grand National today.'

'What?' Gillian looked scandalised. 'Oh, no—listen . . .'

'. . . and unless they can clear the course,' the commentator had run out of clichés and was into second-guessing, *'I think it'll be another débâcle. What can you see from your end, John?'*

From the silence it was apparent that John

couldn't see anything. The commentary crackled again. *'Sorry, John. Gremlins in the link line . . . Not our day . . . And back here at the start everyone is getting very nervous . . .'*

'Poor darlings,' Gillian purred. She raised her glass. 'Cheers. Here's to a long and happy friendship.'

'But, don't you want to know a bit about me? And aren't I supposed to look at the flat? I mean, I know I sent references but—'

Gillian drank half her spritzer in one go. 'And they were wonderful! God had simply answered my prayers—I knew that as soon as I read your letter. I couldn't believe it. I had no idea who was taking over the bookshop—the jungle drums had completely seized up on that one. And then—there you are! We've got so much in common! I'm a writer, you see.' Gillian scrabbled for a cigarette and inhaled joyously.

'Oh, right.' Jemima, still sipping through enough ice cubes to sink the *Titanic,* was trying to keep up. At least it explained the office.

The racing commentator was speaking in hushed tones now—the way they do after a disaster. Something nasty was happening at Aintree. Jemima really didn't care. 'I don't know if I made it clear that I'm here a bit ahead of schedule. I've sunk every penny into the shop so I'll need to earn some money before it opens. I won't actually be gainfully employed until July.'

'I gathered that. It won't be a problem. There's plenty of temp work in the village if you're not picky about what you do. The Cat and Fiddle could do with another barmaid, and Maddy Beckett runs a cleaning firm—she's constantly on the look-out

11

for casuals and if the worst came to the worst, you could always help me with Leviticus and Ezekiel.'

Jemima racked her brains and wished that she'd concentrated more on her religious education classes at school. 'Er—Deuteronomy—um—Numbers—and oh, Genesis.'

Gillian looked slightly doubtful. 'Oh, yes, well done. Now what were we talking about—ah yes, Leviticus and Ezekiel.'

'You write religious tracts?'

Gillian's laugh sent another wodge of papers cascading to the floor. 'Whatever gave you that idea? I write romance.'

'But Leviticus and Ezekiel?'

'Leviticus and Ezekiel are my sons.'

God Almighty. Jemima spluttered through the wine. 'Oh, lovely. Er—how old are they?'

'Twins. Eight. Strange age.' Gillian stubbed the cigarette out in a plant pot and smiled indulgently. 'They're really looking forward to you moving in with us.'

'*And yes, we have confirmation of a delay.*' The radio trumpeted into life again. '*Ten minutes at least to clear the course . . .*'

Gillian groaned. 'Animal rights protesters I'll bet! Silly woolly green liberals! That could be the end of my fiver.'

Jemima, whose sympathies lay entirely with the protesters, tried very hard not to think about gambling. Gambling immediately led her to thoughts of her father. At least he wouldn't be able to remortgage the family home to raise this year's stake. The house had been repossessed in January. This year, Vincent's stake would probably be a loan from someone with shifty eyes who he'd met in a pub. Someone with bad teeth and bad breath and a betting shop stoop. Someone else to come thundering on Vincent's bedsit door demanding payment.

Her father had always convinced himself that his gambling was for his family's benefit. Vincent Carlisle had never used his own money—even when he'd had any. For years he'd been borrowing from the small building company he ran, until the coffers ran dry and the auditors moved in.

'The flat is in the Vicarage attic,' Gillian continued, still obviously tuned in to the Aintree developments. 'And you've got your own front door, and I don't mind if you want your lover to stay over or anything—Glen and I are very broad-minded.'

That at least wouldn't be a problem. 'I haven't got a lover.'

'Really?' The green eyes widened. 'We'll have to remedy that! Does that mean you're taking the flat?'

Before Jemima could answer, the radio got all excited. *'There are some developments here at Liverpool! It seems as though they've cleared the last of the protesters away from Bechers, so we may have a start very soon, eh, John?'*

'Yes!' John at last broke through and seemed determined to get his fair share of air-time. *'It looks like they'll be off at any moment—although the jockeys have been circling at the tape for some considerable time now—and unlike the heatwave in the south, we seem to have got a typical north-west gale blowing. Everyone is very cold. The delay could have unsettled a lot of preparations . . .'*

'As long as it doesn't unsettle Dragon Slayer

or darling Charlie.' Gillian refilled the glasses, lit another cigarette, and hitched the floaty silver dress above her slender knees as she perched on the desk. 'So, where were we? Oh, yes—you'll be taking the flat?'

'No—well, not no exactly. But we haven't discussed rent or the deposit, and I haven't seen it and you really don't know anything about me.'

'And they're off! The Grand National is underway at last! Several slow starters but they're heading for the Melling Road for the first time and . . .'

Gillian's eyes were glazed as she sucked feverishly on her cigarette. Jemima, who didn't want to listen, stared through the summerhouse window and wondered if planning to open her own bookshop was possibly not the brightest idea she'd ever had. She'd been employed as a bookseller for eleven years at Bookworms in Oxford, and no one had expected them to close so abruptly. Maybe she should have sunk her savings into something safer, something more high-tech and millennium-friendly, like mobile phones or computer software.

'And there's a faller! Two—no three—down at that one! All horses up on their feet! Two jockeys still on the ground! They're heading for Valentine's now . . . and the leaders are up and over! All over! No, there's another faller! Dragon Slayer and Charlie Somerset have gone at Valentine's! The favourite is out of the National!'

'Fuck it,' said Gillian.

*   *   *

Half an hour later Jemima felt as if Jeremy Paxman had invaded her soul. Gillian Hutchinson had left

14

no corner of her life undisturbed.

She'd completely understood that Jemima couldn't stay on in Oxford under the circumstances—or—heaven forbid—doss-down in Vincent's mangy bedsit. She'd dismissed Jemima's fears about her venture and declared that opening the bookshop in Milton St John was the best thing that had happened to the village for years. In fact, she announced, Milton St John in general was exactly what Jemima needed to shake off the cobwebs of her previous existence.

Jemima, on her part, was delighted with the low rent, loved the description of the flat, was scared rigid at the thought of Leviticus and Ezekiel—not to mention the Vicar—and found herself warming to Gillian more with every minute. She still couldn't quite believe that she'd told Gillian all about the party-thing. She'd never mentioned a word of it to anyone else. Still, Gillian, being a vicar's wife, was bound to be ultra discreet, wasn't she?

'Come on then.' Gillian once again linked her arm through Jemima's. 'Let me show you the flat. It's really sweet. I'm sure you'll love it.'

'But won't Mr Hutchinson want to interview me too?' Jemima queried as they climbed the vicarage stairs. The house was centuries old; homely, untidy, and exquisite. 'Surely he'll need to be assured that I'm suitable?'

'Goodness,' Gillian puffed at the top of the third flight of stairs, 'he already knows that you are. We've discussed you endlessly since we got your letter. It'll be you he's worried about—and now you've told me about what happened in Oxford I'm sure you'll be well able to hold your own with the twins. Nobody's actually bitten them before. It

15

might do them good. Here we are . . .'

Gillian unlocked a battered oak door and ushered Jemima into the flat. Large leaded windows looked down on the village street from one side, and the tiny church and sprawling shrubbery from the other. All around, the chalky Downs dipped and rose like a petrified ocean and just faintly, in the distance, unseen cars swished in the searing heat. The rooms were pale and airy beneath vast sloping ceilings, and Jemima knew she had found her new home.

'Oh, goody,' Gillian said, looking at Jemima's face. 'You can't imagine how grateful I am. When do you want to move in? You do like it, don't you?'

'I love it.' Jemima was still doing lightning fiscal calculations. She had just enough money saved for the deposit. As long as Gillian was right about the amount of temporary work in the village, she should be able to afford the rent until the bookshop got going. She looked at the glorious view again and decided that she'd sell her soul if necessary.

'Does a twelve-month lease sound right?' Gillian asked vaguely. 'I'm sorry that I'm not more business like. We've never let the flat before. It used to belong to the boys' Nanny and went with the job—but she's retired and—'

'Twelve months sounds perfect,' Jemima said, wondering if the Nanny had been pensioned off suffering from nervous exhaustion. Having had very little contact with children, and not being sure that she even liked them, she was still a little daunted by the sound of Leviticus and Ezekiel. 'You can always get rid of me, if I'm not a suitable tenant.'

'The boys'll do that,' Gillian said happily. 'Now, are you sure we've covered everything?'

16

'Yes—except I'm not a regular church-goer. And I do tend to lapse into "Oh, God!" and "Jesus!" occasionally.'

'If that's all you come out with after spending time with the twins you'll deserve to be canonised. Shall we say you'll move at the end of the month? The first of May sounds like a good day for starting afresh, doesn't it?'

It did. That would give her four weeks. Just enough time to work out her eviction notice in Oxford. Jemima had nodded again, trekked down the twisting staircases, was kissed fondly by Gillian, and found herself once more on Milton St John's sun-baked main street. Gleeful shrieks echoed from the village green and people were chatting animatedly outside the Cat and Fiddle and the Village Stores. A ginger cat washed itself leisurely on the vicarage wall.

Jemima took another look at her empty shop, visualising the shelves crammed with colourful jackets, the window displays, the comfy chairs and low tables for the browsers, and was beaming as she unlocked Floss's door. The air of brooding unreality had completely vanished and Milton St John had become far more *Thrush Green* than *Midwich Cuckoos.* She only hoped she'd feel the same way about it after May Day.

CHAPTER TWO

This had been, without doubt, the worst day of his entire career, Charlie Somerset thought as he pushed the Aston Martin to its limits along the M6.

17

Tearing away from Liverpool in the April dusk, wanting to put as many miles between him and the humiliation as possible, the speedometer was flickering at 120.

Running away? He'd never run away from anything in his life—except maybe one or two irate husbands. What the hell was the matter with him? So, he'd fallen—so what? All jump jockeys fell—it was par for the course. Half the jockeys in the Grand National had been unseated at sometime during that afternoon's four and a half miles. The fact that his horse, Dragon Slayer, was reputed to have superglue on his hooves; had never so much as stumbled in his glittering seven-year career; and had been red-hot favourite to win Aintree's Blue Riband, merely seemed to compound his felony in the eyes of the race-going public. The gamblers of the nation were baying for his blood.

He braked sharply behind a BMW dawdling at 90 in the outside lane and irritably flashed his lights. And it hadn't been only the punters, Charlie thought miserably. Torquemada and Medusa had been waiting for him afterwards.

Kath Seaward, Dragon Slayer's trainer, had been skin-strippingly scathing in her criticism. Almost worse was the reaction from Tina Maloret, the horse's owner. She'd looked at him disdainfully, as though he'd sailed from Dragon Slayer's saddle at Valentine's simply to embarrass her. Tina Maloret, with her yard-long legs which had so recently wrapped themselves sinuously round him; and her collagen-enhanced lips which regularly attached themselves to various parts of his body with more suction than a Dyson vacuum cleaner, had glared at him with contempt in her eyes.

18

He groaned at the memory, finally intimidating the BMW into taking refuge in the centre lane.

Tina had been banking on basking in the limelight this afternoon; counting on it to accelerate her catwalk career. 'Supermodel Wins National!' She had probably already written her own press release. He groaned again, this time more loudly because the Aintree bruises were beginning to make their presence felt, and the year-old injury to his leg, sustained in a crashing fall at Newbury, had decided to come out in sympathy.

Sympathy had been in pretty short supply today, Charlie thought, switching on the radio. What he needed now was a refreshing blast of Aerosmith to cheer him up.

'. . . *so we can confirm that there were no fallers at the notorious Becher's Brook on the first circuit, and only three at the Canal Turn—all up on their feet. Horses and jockeys all okay. And now they're coming up to Valentine's for the first time! Barbara's Basket, the rank outsider, is still leading the field! Satchwa, King Rupert, and red-hot favourite Dragon Slayer, are tucked nicely into the middle of the chasing pack as they approach Aintree's third major challenge of the afternoon! Valentine's will sort out the men from the boys . . .*'

Oh, God! Not a bloody re-run! Charlie started station surfing. He certainly didn't need 5 Live's commentator to remind him . . .

*   *   *

Satchwa had been bumping along beside them, having scrabbled amateurishly through the early fences, already tired. Charlie had eased Dragon

19

Slayer away from the heaving flanks, feeling buoyant, and not a little smug. Dragon Slayer, over sixteen hands, almost jet black, proud and fearless, was as confident as himself, instinctively saving any real burst of energy for later when it mattered. This truly was the ride of his life. He'd never sat on a horse half so good. Mentally thanking Kath's regular jockey, Matt Garside, who had missed the ride because of injury, Charlie felt a surge of excitement. This was going to be his race. Dragon Slayer was a winner. He could feel it. He knew that all he had to do on this first circuit was sit tight and steer away from any danger.

King Rupert, chestnut and rangy, was just visible from the corner of his eye, but he wasn't a threat. Not yet, anyway. Both Charlie and Dragon Slayer knew Aintree's Grand National course well, but, confident as they were, this was still no time for complacency. King Rupert was second favourite, a Gold Cup winner and a known stayer. They'd have to look to their laurels on the run-in.

Still, so far, so good. They'd soared over the heart-stopping height of Becher's, Dragon Slayer planting his huge hooves exactly right for the take-off, the power in his bunched hindquarters leaving daylight above the brushwood, and landing with feet to spare. With only minimal encouragement from Charlie, Dragon Slayer was instantly right-legged into his stride, bowling immediately towards the Canal Turn; horse and rider in perfect harmony. No problems here. Charlie could hear horses crashing through the soft tops of the fence behind him, and the cursing of his fellow jockeys. He chuckled. He'd been lucky to get this ride on such a superb horse, he knew. And

Kath Seaward was no push-over: she trained the best and expected even better.

Valentine's coming up . . . Charlie concentrated even harder on keeping Dragon Slayer away from Satchwa's weaving backside, on holding his middle ground, on timing the take-off. This was his big chance after being laid-off for so long after last year's fall. This was his chance to prove to Kath Seaward that he was a natural replacement for Matt Garside in all his races until he was fit, and that he deserved his previous status of champion jockey. It was also his chance to reaffirm the belief of Drew Fitzgerald, the trainer who employed him as a stable jockey, that next year, with the right horse, they'd win at Cheltenham and Aintree. And, of course, there was Tina . . .

He could see the jaunty hindquarters of Barbara's Basket—having his fifteen minutes of fame—blundering wildly across the course ahead with as much finesse as he'd smashed through the obstacles. Six—no, seven horses in front of him, all non-stayers. This was going so well . . . He could hear the distant halloo screams of the crowd all around him, and felt the rhythmic thud of hoof on turf. Dragon Slayer's motion was easy and assured. As long as they could take King Rupert on the run-in they were home and dry. Charlie began to relax.

'Stay out of trouble,' Kath had ordered in the parade ring. 'Keep him covered for the first circuit. No heroics. He jumps well and will want to be up with the leaders. You'll have to keep him in check and conserve your energy for the second circuit and the run-in. I expect you to keep him on his feet. He's never fallen. That's why he's favourite. Stay in the saddle and give him his head two from home. I expect you to be in the first three at the elbow. Okay?'

Charlie had agreed, the adrenaline already pumping round his veins. He'd touched his cap to Kath, and then he'd looked down at Tina, high-cheeked and beautiful, with the long red coat swishing against black boots and the black swansdown hat feathering around her blonde hair—a fashion statement on this course where nobody made them—and grinned.

She'd smiled back, the tip of her tongue protruding between her tiny teeth. 'You'd better win, darling. I can't wait to congratulate you . . .'

Charlie had felt the rush of lust through his body at the memory, and in that instant, knew everything was going wrong.

Dragon Slayer, totally in tune with Charlie's thoughts, gave an almost imperceptible start. The long, confident stride faltered slightly. Charlie, cursing himself for falling into the amateur's trap of letting his mind stray, tried hard to get back on course. Satchwa was thumping along just in front of him, still swerving from left to right. King Rupert and several others, as yet unseen, were gaining on him from behind.

The fragile telepathic bond with Dragon Slayer had been broken in that one second's concentration lapse. Powering down the course, the rails merely a blur, Charlie was sitting on an unguided missile. Dragon Slayer had received the wrong signals and had no idea how to interpret them.

Barbara's Basket had already bashed over Valentine's—a terrifying slow-motion scramble of horse and humanity—which miraculously didn't result in a fall. The rest of the horses in front of him were already pouring raggedly over the obstacle like a liquid rainbow. Dragon Slayer was careering towards the fence, still twitchy, knowing what he had to do, but his brain totally at odds with Charlie's.

Immediately in front of them Satchwa, already exhausted, simply didn't jump at all, and crashed through the fence. Charlie, watching all this as if in slow motion, was hurtling towards certain disaster with every speeding stride.

'Shit . . . shit . . . shit . . .'

He gathered Dragon Slayer up, trying to steady him, but it was far, far, too late. Wrong-footed . . . Wrong-footed . . . They took off awkwardly, Dragon Slayer's legs clawing frantically in mid-air. The landing was a thump of pain.

'It's okay . . .' Charlie muttered with watering eyes as Dragon Slayer's huge black neck smacked him on the nose. 'We've made it. Stay on your feet . . . Oh, Christ!'

Charlie could feel the world slip away from him as Dragon Slayer stumbled, pecked, and then bent gracefully at the knees. Amid the crescendo screams of half a dozen other horses and riders cursing and panting around him, Charlie shot from the saddle and catapulted over Dragon Slayer's head.

Instinctively relaxing his muscles, he hit the ground. The force knocked all the breath from him with a solar-plexus punch. Whatever had happened to his body, his brain was working at fever-pitch. Seven horses ahead of him; maybe the same number with him; that still left at least twenty to hurl themselves over the top of Valentine's . . .

23

Twenty odd horses to land on top of him . . . Ten tons of death.

Curling into the tightest ball, protecting his head with his arms, the noises were terrifying. The thunderous echo of the approaching cavalry charge was like a tidal roar. The shouted curses and laboured breathing were magnified a million times. Every set of crashing, slashing hooves landing inches away from him seemed determined to crush him.

Charlie prayed. A faller now, on the leeward side of Valentine's, and it would be all over. Half a ton of rocket-propelled racehorse would break every bone in his body. It had happened like that to his father. An amateur steeplechase at Fairyhouse had meant that Barnaby Somerset, privileged only son complete with silver spoon, had lived what was left of his life in a wheelchair. Twenty years earlier, Charlie's paternal grandfather had been luckier. He'd been thrown during a Boxing Day meet and killed outright.

Was that to be his fate, too? A million memories fast-forwarded through Charlie's brain. Was this like drowning? Past life played in a split-second of slow motion? A selective re-run of previous generations? Was this the third time that the Somerset breeding, the expensive education, the cosseted upbringing in a minor stately home, would lead to death by horse?

Riding had been in his blood at birth; handed down at conception along with the fox-red hair and the classical bone-structure. It had made no difference how much his mother had begged him to do something different—become a barrister—a doctor . . . He hadn't had the brains, anyway, and he had to ride. He had to. He'd been born to ride. And if he rode to his death—then wasn't that how it had been planned?

Charlie sucked in gulps of air. It tasted of blood.

Oh, God—Dragon Slayer? Was he all right? He'd die anyway if Dragon Slayer was fatally injured. He opened one eye, dreading the sight of the huge black flanks heaving, the long legs threshing, or worse . . .

Oh, thank Christ . . . Nothing. There was nothing. Just grass and mud and a ton of scattered branches.

It seemed like a lifetime later, or maybe a millisecond, Charlie wasn't sure. The drumbeat echo beneath him was growing fainter as the National field charged on towards the next fence. The banshee wail of the crowd was swelling again somewhere in the stratosphere. No other fallers . . . Oh, thank you, God . . .

He tentatively moved his arms and legs. At least they were still there and seemed to be operational.

'Okay, love?' A St John Ambulance lady—pretty, actually, despite the austere uniform, Charlie thought groggily—was bending over him. 'Walking wounded? Or do you need a stretcher?'

'The horse?' Charlie winced. His face ached. His lips were still bleeding. 'My horse—he's all right?'

'Just approaching the Chair I shouldn't wonder,' the St John Ambulance lady said, helping Charlie to his feet. 'Seems to enjoy the jumping much more now you're not on his back. He's fine, love. Now let's nip up into the meat wagon and get you back to the doc.'

Charlie had bumped miserably back to the Aintree course doctor in silent humiliation.

25

Kath Seaward was waiting for him outside the medical room door after his check-up.

'What the fuck were you doing?'

Charlie winced. His swollen lips made speaking difficult. 'I'm fine, thanks. No bones broken. No concussion. Passed fit to ride. How's Dragon Slayer?'

'We're not talking here!' Kath jerked her head at the posse of press. 'Not bloody here!'

The press, however, suddenly swooshed away in a jumble of Pentax and Nikon. The noise was deafening, the commentator's strangled screams lost against a wall of sound. With a lump in his throat Charlie watched the run-in on the massive Star Vision screen.

King Rupert, his jockey crouched low with exhaustion on his sweating neck, beat the still-weaving and completely unfashionable Satchwa by a short head.

Shit.

Kath Seaward kept walking; a tall, gaunt figure in a ground-trailing trench coat, a maroon beret rammed on to dyed black hair. Kath swore more, smoked more, drank more neat whisky, and loved her horses more passionately, than any trainer Charlie had ever ridden for. She was one pretty scary lady.

'So?' She turned on him viperously. 'What went wrong?'

'Dragon Slayer?' Charlie mumbled again, running his tongue across his crooked teeth. They were still there. It was some small consolation. 'He's not hurt?'

'Decided he'd had enough after the first circuit. Jumped the Chair like a stag. Cleared the water

26

jump and then buggered off back to the start like a lamb. The horse,' she glared at Charlie, 'managed to keep his brain between his ears, Somerset. Unlike you.'

It was so near the truth that Charlie closed his eyes. One of them felt as though it wasn't going to open again.

'So? Any explanations? Anything that might, just might, keep the racing press—not to mention the punters—from ripping me to bloody shreds?'

'None. I lost it. He pecked on landing and—'

'And you should have stayed in the fucking driving seat!' Kath lit a cigarette and blew a plume of ferocious smoke towards him. 'Jesus Christ! You had the bloody easy part! You've gone soft. You eat too much and drink too much—and you never wake up in your own bed!'

'That's hardly fair. I've stayed off the booze and I've been really careful—'

'Careful!' Kath spat the words round the filter tip. 'You need a proper regime, Somerset! You need to think and act like a bloody jockey—not a sodding playboy! Oh, fuck off out of my sight! Tell bloody Drew Fitzgerald he can keep your services in future! When I need a replacement jockey I'll engage a fucking professional!'

Charlie, literally cap in hand, had stood alone and watched her go. He felt like crying. There was a sting of truth in Kath's invective. He did overeat and he drank too much and he'd tried really hard to give up smoking again . . . But he'd always been lucky. He'd always managed to starve enough before important races to beat the weighing room scales. Maybe the excesses had taken their toll. Maybe it was time to give up . . . He wiped a muddy

27

glove across his face and groaned as it caught on his mouth.

Sod it. He'd wanted this race so badly. The entire world was on the other side of the course congratulating the winner. King Rupert and Tony McCoy loomed large on the screen.

'Thanks for nothing.' Tina Maloret stalked towards him, two spots of colour accentuating the cheekbones. 'Pity your bedroom performance isn't echoed on the racecourse. Maybe you should think of abandoning being a jockey and think about becoming a gigolo. Not,' the eyes, now level with his own, flashed with venom, 'that you're first past the post there either!'

Charlie exhaled. There was nothing he could say. He understood her anger. Tina would calm down later. He knew he'd be able to charm her into giggling submission but Kath . . . Kath was a different proposition. She'd trusted him and he'd let her down. He'd done his career no good at all. And Drew . . . Oh, God. What the hell was Drew going to say?

'Tina—' he moved towards her. His lips felt like Mick Jagger's. 'It happens. The whole race is a gamble. At least Dragon Slayer wasn't hurt—'

'If he had have been you wouldn't be standing there now!' The swansdown on her hat billowed like thunder clouds. 'Kath would have killed you and I'd have danced on the remains!'

'So there's not a lot of point in asking if we're still on for later?'

Her contemptuous laugh sliced through the stillness of the April afternoon. 'Jesus! You take the biscuit. Not a hope, Charlie. Not a bloody hope.' She span away from him on the high shiny boots. 'In fact, I'll be ecstatic if I never clap eyes on you again.'

*　　　*　　　*

Wrenching the Aston Martin off the A34 in the darkness, Charlie felt slightly better. The high-banked lanes of Berkshire meant home at last. Home, where he could bolt the door, muffle any media intrusion—why the hell they wanted to re-run the damn race every half an hour anyway, he had no idea—play some loud music, and get very, very drunk.

Home was a half-timbered black and white cottage on the edge of Drew Fitzgerald's Peapods yard. Charlie had previously lived in the stable staff bungalow, but had bought the cottage when Drew and Maddy had decided to extend the bungalow into a hostel for the lads. The residential elevation had come at about the same time as he'd traded in his Calibra for the classic Aston Martin. A time when the future looked extremely rosy. Charlie groaned. The way today had gone, he'd be down-grading the Aston Martin to a bicycle and begging a bed in the hostel—if he was very lucky.

Lights were on in most of Milton St John's houses. No doubt everyone was dolling themselves up for a night of sorrow-drowning at the Cat and Fiddle. The pub's regulars had spent the last few days daubing sheets with *Congratulations Kath, Charlie and Dragon Slayer,* and *Milton St John wins the Big One.* Charlie slowed the Aston Martin to a thirty mile an hour crawl. The entire village had been rooting for Kath and Dragon Slayer. Homes would have been remortgaged on the gamble. He'd

29

be the least popular man in the world tonight.

It was even more galling to know that the celebrations for King Rupert, trained as he was at neighbouring Lambourn, were likely to spill over into the village. It would probably end in a riot.

He carefully negotiated the curve in the road past the pub, past Bronwyn Pugh's Village Stores, the Munchy Bar, and the empty bookshop. Just as he drew level with St Saviour's Church, a shadowy figure hurried from the graveyard's darkness and ducking under the lych gate, stepped straight out in front of him.

Charlie stood on the brakes. The Aston Martin slewed across the road.

'Bloody hell!' This was all he needed, today of all days; some glue-sniffing kid walking under the wheels. He rolled down the window. 'For Christ's sake! Look where you're going! I could have killed you!'

The figure, still enveloped in blackness, hesitated for a moment, then walked back across the road towards him. Oh God, Charlie thought. Please don't let it be someone wanting to top themselves because they backed Dragon Slayer . . . Or even worse, someone who wanted to punch his lights out for the same reason . . .

'I'm so sorry . . . I wasn't concentrating. I had other things on my mind. I didn't mean—oh, Charlie! I didn't know it was you!'

Charlie felt a flood of relief. Gillian Hutchinson, the Vicar's wife, was hardly likely to deliver a swift upper-cut. She leaned towards the car, long pale hair escaping, a black cloak making her practically invisible in the gloom. Charlie thought she looked like Meryl Streep in that French Bloke's Woman

30

film that one of his ex's had adored and he'd slept through three times.

'Sorry,' she said again. 'I was miles away. And commiserations, anyway. I listened on the radio and I was so worried when you fell. They said Dragon Slayer was okay, but they said you were being bundled off in the ambulance. Were you hurt?'

'Pride mainly.' Charlie was very fond of Gillian. Gillian was the most un-typical vicar's wife in the world. 'I hope you didn't back us.'

'Of course I did. Never mind—there's always next year. In fact, I'm counting on you winning next year.'

'I shouldn't count on anything.' Charlie straightened up, easing the ache of the bruises. 'We'll have to wait and see what Drew says. He'll probably disown me.'

'Drew'll be fine about it.' Gillian tried to push her hair away from her face. 'He's an ex-jockey. He understands these things. Was Kath very vicious?'

'Made Vlad the Impaler look like Mother Teresa.'

Gillian laughed. 'Yes, I can imagine. Poor you. Oh, I suppose I really ought to be getting back— the boys have probably burned down the Vicarage by now. Sorry again for startling you. You must be dying for a long hot soak and a glass or two of something.'

Charlie nodded. He wondered for a moment whether there were dire ecclesiastical penalties for suggesting that a vicar's wife would be more than welcome to scrub his back. 'Are you sure you're okay?'

'Fine, really. I was just trying to gain a bit of spiritual guidance about the tangles in my life . . .'

31

She sighed and pulled the softness of the cloak round her slender figure. 'God didn't appear to be listening. It's so difficult trying to juggle everything and the parish duties—oh, you've got tons of problems of your own. You don't want to listen to mine.'

Charlie decided he wouldn't have minded at all. The idea of the willowy Gillian curled in one of the armchairs in his sitting room, while he sat on the floor at her feet and they shared a bottle of red, was far from unpleasant. 'Anything I can help with?'

'Not immediately. Not unless you could help me lose a lot of money.'

Charlie blinked. 'Keep backing me for what's left of the season. That should lose you enough.'

'Hardly!' Gillian laughed again. 'Oh, it's far too complicated to explain—I've got myself into this awful mess. Still, I've got one piece of good news. I've managed to let the Vicarage flat.'

'Brilliant. So the *Weekly News* came up trumps. Or did you resort to advertising?'

'What? In the window of Maureen's Munchy Bar?' Gillian pulled a face. The Munchy Bar was the last-but-one addition to Milton St John's small crescent of shops. 'No, thank goodness. Can you imagine the applicants?'

'Yeah. Bathsheba Cox spearheading the queue. I hear she's desperate to get her hands on the Vicar.'

'Don't. Not funny. She's gunning for the boys as it is. She's the witch of the village as far as they're concerned—even more scary than Bronwyn Pugh—and that's saying something . . . She certainly doesn't approve of me or them.'

'So who's your new tenant?' Charlie wasn't particularly interested, but was still pretty keen on inviting Gillian back home for the bottle of red and some mutual shoulder-sobbing, so felt the niceties should be observed.

'Jennifer—no, Jemima. The owner of the new bookshop.'

'Oh, boring.' Charlie wasn't convinced Milton St John needed a bookshop. When did anyone in the village ever have time to read a book? Still, it was bound to be managed by some elderly cat-loving spinster. She'd probably be ideal for cocoa-sharing in the Vicarage.

Gillian snuggled deeper into the cloak. The heat of the day had not lasted past sunset. 'The shop's not opening for ages yet so Jemima's going to be looking for something temporary to keep her going. She's absolutely sweet, Charlie. You'll adore her. It was very clever of you to recommend the local paper. I hope Drew and Maddy are as lucky with their advert for a gardener.'

'So do I.' Charlie felt the chance to invite Gillian back to the cottage was slipping away. 'Maybe Jessica could do some gardening at Peapods in her spare time?'

'*Jemima!*' Gillian corrected with a giggle. 'Just because you hope she looks like that buxom lass on that television garden make-over show. You are totally insatiable. Thank goodness I'm the Vicar's wife or you'd be propositioning me next!'

'As if . . .' Charlie blinked as the doors of the Cat and Fiddle were suddenly thrown wide open, illuminating the Aston Martin in a spotlight of smoky beams. He switched on the ignition. 'If you don't mind I'll make myself scarce. I've got a feeling that they're probably erecting a gibbet in the Snug as we speak.'

It was nice, he thought as he drove towards the sanctuary of Peapods, to see that Gillian was laughing as she headed for the Vicarage. Laughter, after sex, was his stock in trade. Still, if Tina meant what she said, both would be in very short supply in the future. The car bumped across the cobbles and Charlie switched off the headlights. No need to let them know at Peapods that he'd returned. He didn't want to talk to Drew Fitzgerald about the National fiasco. Not tonight. What had Gillian said? There was always next year? Charlie sighed. Twelve months was a hell of a long time to wait.

CHAPTER THREE

'. . . so,' Jemima turned away from the window and looked at her father, 'I was going to have to find myself somewhere to live in Milton St John by July, anyway. It's just going to be sooner now, rather than later. And, of course I'd relied on the money from Bookworms and—er—Petra—to enable me to stay on in Oxford and do exotic things, like paying the rent and buying food. I'll have to find a temporary job pretty quickly.' She grinned. 'Still, at last I'm all packed and on my way. I just thought I'd call in to say goodbye.'

'It's lovely to see you.' Vincent Carlisle patted her shoulder. 'But surely there were other bookshops in Oxford? Wouldn't they have taken you on as temp until July? I don't mean to sound critical, love. But, surely, making yourself homeless at your age . . . For God's sake, you don't want to end up like me, do you? One of the other

34

bookshops might have been only too delighted to . . .'

'Believe me, I tried all forty-three of them. None of them needed staff. They said they'd keep me on file. Probably under r for rubbish . . .'

Vincent pulled a face. 'Well, then I'm proud of you, Jem, love. Really. Getting down there early and getting on with it. You've made the right decision.'

'The decision was made for me,' Jemima said. 'First by Bookworms going bust, and secondly by the party-thing. Being made redundant from one job and sacked from another—and both on the same day—and then being served with an eviction notice, doesn't give you many options to play with.'

She winced as always over the party-thing. She'd told Gillian Hutchinson about it, but she'd never tell Vincent. The memory of that day still kept her awake at night. With a very scary bank loan ploughed into her new venture, two months' rent arrears on her flat, and an overdraft which would be the envy of any emerging third world nation, she'd hoped to keep her salary going until she'd worked her notice out in July. The decision to close Bookworms ahead of schedule was a hammer blow. The party-thing was simply a death knell.

Fortunately Vincent was enraptured about Milton St John and didn't dwell on the reasons for her being rail-roaded out of the dreaming spires. 'I can't wait to see you standing behind your own counter, in your own shop, with your name over the door. And Milton St John must be full of really wealthy people just dying to buy books locally. You could be the next Christina Foyle.'

Jemima was still staring out of the window. She

35

loved her father dearly and would never tell him that her shop's location had been the one reason why she hadn't made an immediate decision to take it.

Milton St John was a gorgeous village, and the very low rent on the Vicarage flat was a boon. The shop premises were the only ones she'd seen with a lease she could remotely afford, and the only place she'd visited that didn't have a rival bookshop within a ten mile radius. It all made sound economic sense, but her gambling-addict father and the horseracing hub of southern England seemed like a pretty lethal combination.

She'd thought about it long and hard, and come to the conclusion that as he wouldn't actually be living there, she'd at least be able to steer him away from temptation when he did decide to visit. As she wasn't remotely interested in racing, any new friends she'd make in the village were also bound to be outsiders. She was pretty sure it wouldn't be a problem.

'Got time for a cuppa before you go?'

Jemima watched him shuffle across to the kitchen portion of the bedsit and wanted to cry. Yes, Vincent had brought this on himself. She knew it, he knew it, and her mother, Rosemary, who had stuck with Vincent through everything until the repossession notice was slapped on the house, probably knew it best of all. Rosemary had decamped while she still had a shred of dignity and had found a living-in job in a south coast hotel. She and Vincent had been divorced now for six months. Jemima didn't blame her mother for not staying. But, it still broke her heart to see him living in this squalor; to see his grey, gaunt face. It would have taken someone with a far harder heart than hers to rejoice in seeing this destitution.

She'd shuddered, as she always did, as she'd pulled up in Floss outside the ramshackle tenement building. The cracked and grimy windows were like blind eyes, and the all-pervading smell of cabbage and garlic and cat's pee seemed to sink into her skin even before she'd crossed the graffiti'd entrance hall.

Vincent placed a couple of none too clean mugs on a rickety table. 'Sorry it's black. I—um—don't buy milk. I've been a bit strapped for cash recently. I had a bit of a setback in the National. Got a red-hot tip in the pub for the favourite, Dragon Slayer. Piled everything on it, plus a bit I didn't actually have. The bugger fell . . .' He shrugged at his daughter. 'I'm still having to pay back my debts.'

'Dad! I thought you'd given it all up. I thought you were going to GamAn? I thought—'

'I have given it up. Honest. But, you know, the National—well, it's sort of different, isn't it?'

Jemima picked up her mug and stared out of the bleak window. It was no good nagging him. Nor would it help giving him a hand-out—even if she had one—because he'd only try and treble it on a nine-way accumulator or something equally disastrous.

'Anyway,' Vincent was already bouncing back, 'I must say I'm pleased that you'll be living in the Vicarage. Oh, not that organised religion has played a huge part in our lives—but it sounds very Jane Eyre. Do you remember when you did it for A level? I spent hours going over and over it with you?'

Jemima gave a small smile. She remembered.

37

'And,' Vincent continued, 'you never know. You might meet your Mr Darcy there.'

'Rochester.'

'No, no, love—Rochester's in Kent. Milton St John is definitely in Berkshire.'

Jemima gave up pretending to be angry and hugged him. 'You'll be good while I'm away won't you? Promise me? No gambling?'

'Cross my heart,' Vincent beamed. 'And there is one thing, love, before you go . . .'

Jemima's heart sank. He was going to touch her for a sub, she knew he was.

'Oh, it's not money,' he looked quite affronted. 'I know you're as skint as I am. No, I just wondered what exactly did happen at that party . . . You've never actually told me.'

'And I'm not telling you now, either.' Jemima kissed his cheek. 'Now, take care of yourself and I'll be in touch as soon as I'm settled.'

He was still watching her from the grimy window as she slammed Floss's door and eased away from the wind-blown debris in the street outside. She waved and swallowed her tears. She'd get him out of there if it was the last thing she did . . .

Deciding to get on to the A34 via the ring road was a horrible mistake. It meant driving through Summertown. Still, she thought, steering her way along the Banbury Road, maybe that was the best way to cope with nightmares. Face up to them. Maybe, as she headed off to start her new life in Milton St John, remembering the worst day of her life in Oxford would lay the ghosts once and for all . . .

*   *   *

38

'Where the hell have you been?' Petra Martin's painted-on eyebrows had drawn together across the bridge of her hooky nose and then recoiled in horror. 'I was expecting you at six.'

'Sorry,' Jemima had panted, dropping her patchwork shoulderbag and shrugging out of her battered denim jacket in the hi-tech High Street office. 'It was the Bookworms closing-down do—it went on longer than I expected. We all cried a lot and swapped phone numbers and things. Laura and I are going to ring each other twice a week and visit each other in the summer and—' she tugged her black dress, white apron and flat shoes from the cupboard, 'I can still be at Boar's Hill in ten minutes. It's not a problem.'

'You're not going to Boar's Hill.' Petra's voice had dripped ice. 'Not any more.'

'Why not?' The two glasses of Bookworms sherry and all the tears had given Jemima a headache. 'I'm not that late, and I'm sure you said it was early evening canapés and cocktails for a few chums at Sir Neville and Lady Murtagh's before they swanned off somewhere glitzy to celebrate their silver wedding and—'

Petra had drummed black cherry nails against the side of her computer. 'It was. It still is. I've sent Barbara instead.'

'Why? I'm not that late and I like standing around looking invisible and obsequious and handing out anchovies on rye and diluted Domestos.'

'Don't be flippant!' The eyebrows had arched towards each other, remembered just in time, and slunk apart. 'Barbara is solid and respectable-looking and soirees are far more her sort of thing. They suit her bunions. You're going to North Oxford to replace Magenta and you won't,' Petra had indicated the black dress and pinny with sharp jerks of her head, 'be needing those.'

'Oh, God.' Magenta, six foot tall, gorgeous, black and stick-thin, did the more exotic bookings. Jemima who was none of those things and painfully shy into the bargain, had blinked. 'What's wrong with her?'

'She's gone sick.'

'Oh, poor Mags. How sick?'

'Long term. She's pregnant.' Petra's bee-sting lips had welded themselves together at this folly. 'You should fit into her outfit if you use safety pins but you'll have to hurry. The address is on the sheet and—'

'What is it?' Jemima had started to panic. 'I won't strip or do kissograms or anything tacky.'

'Tacky?' Petra's voice had soared an octave. '*Tacky?* Petra's Parties has *never* done tacky!'

'Well, no, maybe not tacky exactly,' Jemima back-pedalled remembering the rent arrears. 'But there was that thing with the snake . . .'

Petra hadn't met her eyes. 'The python was a one-off. Anyway, this is nothing like that at all. It's a straightforward twenty-first for,' she'd scanned her screen, 'Simon Hampton-Hyde. His parents have organised it and will give you full details on arrival. Just hurry!'

Jemima had grabbed Magenta's bag, the Hampton-Hydes' address, and hurried. She'd paused at the door. 'Oh—I wondered if you might be able to give me more hours now? With Bookworms closing and everything—especially as Magenta will obviously be out of action for a while—I wondered if I could work full-time until the summer?'

Petra had looked as though the black death was a more likely option. 'We'll see. Probably. Possibly. It just depends how you do with this one. Now scoot.'

Floss had scooted through Oxford's Saturday evening traffic, nosing her way along the Banbury Road in the rapidly fading light of the April evening. Jemima had turned up Thames Valley FM and sung along with Herman's Hermits, getting the words wrong.

The houses in this lush part of Oxford were old, spacious and luxurious. She'd sighed. Years ago, in her embryo bookseller days, this had been her dream. A home amongst Oxford's upper echelons of academia—if possible with some gloriously bohemian lecturer who just happened to look a bit like Val Kilmer . . .

She'd flicked Floss's indicators and given a small sad smile at the foolishness of fantasies. Maybe with the Bookworms redundancy cheque—however woefully inadequate—and extra hours for Petra, she might, just might, if she was very lucky, hang on to her three-roomed basement until she left Oxford in July.

Mr and Mrs Hampton-Hyde had been hovering anxiously in their driveway as Jemima scrambled from the car. The anxiety had immediately given way to full-blown panic.

'You're late.' Mrs Hampton-Hyde, plump and wearing far too much turquoise eye shadow, had bustled towards her. 'And you're not black.'

Jemima had carefully locked Floss's battered door. 'No. That was Magenta. She's indisposed. I'm

41

a replacement.'

'We don't want a replacement.' Mr Hampton-Hyde, sucking the ends of his moustache, took in Jemima's five foot five, nine stone, and layers of shaggy brown hair. His eyes had skimmed over the trailing skirt, DMs, and baggy denim jacket. He seemed riveted by the glasses. 'They never said anything about specs. We chose Magenta from the catalogue especially. She looked like Naomi Campbell. Simon is especially fond of Naomi Campbell. You haven't even got long hair. Simon is especially fond of long hair.'

Mindful that she was now virtually unemployed, Jemima had continued to smile. 'Never mind. I'll try really hard to be an adequate substitute. Now, where do you want me?'

'Dinette. But I'm going to have to ask for at least a partial refund. We especially wanted Magenta.'

Jemima had hurtled through a rather dark hallway frantically overdone with banners and balloons and into a garishly yellow and blue room hung with Mediterranean plates and very frilly curtains.

Mrs Hampton-Hyde had been only inches behind her. 'You can change in here. Simon and his chums are still at the Dew Drop. I hope he won't be disappointed. We'd so hoped to give him a Naomi look-alike. Hurry up and get dressed—Clifton and I will be waiting in the lounge.'

Propping her glasses on top of her head and slapping on her make-up, Jemima had felt the first stirrings of unease. Surely she was only there to hand over the birthday cheque? Slice the cake? Pop open the champagne? The usual twenty-first rituals. Or had Petra gone into the white slave trade? Just what was Magenta supposed to be doing for Simon Hampton-Hyde? Were his parents going to gift wrap her and hand her over after the jelly and ice cream? Would they now look shame-faced and mutter, 'Here you are, son. I know it's not exactly what you wanted but make the most of it . . .'?

Having shed her jacket, skirt, boots and patchwork cardigan, Jemima had dived into Magenta's bag. Casting aside a pair of black fishnet tights, a pair of impossibly high black stilettos and a scrap of purple tulle, she'd poked desperately into the corners. Empty. With a groan, she'd dug her mobile phone from her handbag and punched out Petra's number.

'Petra's Parties. How may I—'

'Petra. It's Jemima. Look, I know you're going to kill me but I've only got half the costume. There's no skirt . . .' Jemima had shaken out the wisp of tulle. 'No, I mean there's no anything, really. Was there another bag? What? You are joking? Not on your life—what? Yes, of course I need the job—you know I need the job—what? No, I don't. I wear far more than this on the beach—what? Petra? Petra!'

Jemima had hurled the phone back into her bag and eyed the wisp of material with hatred.

'I've just come to see if you're ready.' Mr Hampton-Hyde had poked his head round the door. 'Oh, I say!'

Jemima had cowered in a corner. 'Don't come a step nearer. I am not—absolutely not—being seen in public like this.'

Mr Hampton-Hyde's cheeks were very pink. He'd blown on the ends of his moustache. 'You look—incredible . . . Um . . . very Marilyn Monroe. You only need blonde hair.'

43

'What I need,' Jemima had muttered, looking down at the fishnet and minuscule purple costume, 'is a vest, a sensible jumper, and a brain transplant. No, I'm sorry, but—'

'Here we are then.' Mrs Hampton-Hyde had crashed into the room wheeling something that looked like a cross between a vast cardboard meringue and a gigantic wedding hat. 'Simon and his pals have just got back. Oh—' Her eyes had narrowed. 'Isn't there any more to that costume?'

Jemima, feeling like a laboratory specimen beneath the scrutiny, had shaken her head.

'It's glorious.' Mr Hampton-Hyde's eyes had glazed. 'Simon won't even notice she doesn't look like Naomi.'

'And that's enough of that talk, Clifton.' All of Mrs Hampton-Hyde had quivered. 'Well, if that's all you've got, we'll just have to make the most of it. Don't flaunt your bosoms at the boys though—that's my advice.' She'd delved into her pocket and produced an envelope. 'We've wasted enough time already, so here's the cheque.'

Jemima had wrinkled her nose. 'You just want me to give him the cheque? Dressed like this? Then what on earth is that cake thing for?'

Mrs Hampton-Hyde had almost stamped her feet. 'Good Lord! Don't these places give you gels *any* instructions? You pop inside the cake and then when Simon comes into the room, you leap out through the top and present him with the cheque. Simple. Simple.'

'What?' Realisation had started to dawn. 'You mean . . .? In there? And then . . .?'

Mr Hampton-Hyde blushed. 'It was my idea. I'd seen it on a lot of Hollywood movies. Marilyn

44

Monroe did it all the time. I thought—'

'Then you thought wrong. I'm sorry, but I just don't do this sort of thing. I do have some integrity. Some principles. This is sexism in the extreme. Ow!' She'd glared at Mrs Hampton-Hyde. 'Take your hands off me! I won't . . .'

Mrs Hampton-Hyde had obviously been Jabba the Hutt in a previous existence. 'We're paying. And paying dearly. In you go!'

Lifted from under the armpits, Jemima had been tumbled inside the monstrous cake while the Hampton-Hydes had frantically fastened the tissue paper top. The spike heels had caught in the fishnet; the tulle had slipped from barely-covering to indecent exposure. Shivering with rage and hating Petra, Magenta and Simon Hampton-Hyde with equal ferocity, Jemima had clenched her teeth, clasped her knees and prayed for oblivion.

Loud roars of very drunk rugby-playing male laughter had echoed above her. She'd heard Mrs Hampton-Hyde's twitter and Mr Hampton-Hyde's answering guffaw.

'Out! Out! Out!'

Jemima had sat, still clutching her knees, not moving.

'I say!' Mrs Hampton-Hyde had rapped smartly on the cardboard icing. 'Come on! Leap!'

'Leap yourself,' Jemima had muttered. 'I'm not coming out of here even if you use a flame-thrower.'

'Out! Out! Out!' the voices howled.

'Bugger off!' Jemima howled back.

Clutched by half a dozen pairs of scrum-trained hands the cake had started to rock wildly from side to side. The stilettos gouged into her calves.

Jemima tumbled forwards as the cake rolled backwards. Her spectacles slipped down her nose and crunched ominously beneath her. Sounds of tearing paper were accompanied by loud cheers. Shafts of daylight had penetrated the murky cardboard gloom, and with a further hefty shove, no doubt from Mrs Hampton-Hyde, Jemima had rolled out on to the revolting blue and yellow carpet.

She'd lifted her head and stared short-sightedly into Simon Hampton-Hyde's blood-shot green eyes.

'Wow.' He'd grinned lasciviously. 'And gift-unwrapped, too. Come here, darling . . .'

Jemima had scrambled to her knees, and wrapped her arms defensively round her nakedness. Simon's rugby-player chums were whooping with red-faced delight as he reached towards her.

'Take your hands off me,' she'd hissed. 'Here's your cheque. Happy birthday. Now, if you'll excuse me, I'm going home—and don't touch me!'

Simon had pocketed the envelope without opening it and licked his lips. 'I never touch what I can't afford—and I can certainly afford you! Come here . . .'

'Leave me alone!' Jemima screeched, turning beseeching eyes towards the blurred outline of the Hampton-Hydes. 'For God's sake—stop him!'

Fuzzily, the Hampton-Hydes had remained rooted to the spot. Mrs Hampton-Hyde had even been smiling indulgently. Mr Hampton-Hyde was practically dribbling. Feeling Simon's hot hands grasping greedily through the tulle, Jemima had staggered upright on the unfamiliar heels. Instinctive self-preservation had zoomed to her rescue.

46

The baying rugby chums had fallen silent as Simon let out a howl of purple-faced rage and stuffed his fingers beneath his armpit.

'Oh, I say.' Mrs Hampton-Hyde had wobbled towards her son. 'Simon—baby, what's wrong? What say? Oh, you poor lamb! She's bitten you!'

*   *   *

And the rest, Jemima thought, as she and Floss belted along the A34 towards Berkshire and pastures new, was history. Oh, well, one thing was certain. At least it was over now. All in the past. Nothing like that would ever happen to her in Milton St John.

May

CHAPTER FOUR

'Holy shit!'

Drew Fitzgerald stared at the screen in front of him with mounting horror. Seconds earlier it had been full of names and numbers, columns of them, weeks and weeks of work. Now it was blank, black, the nothingness accentuated by a galaxy of little white sparkles.

He crashed his chair away from the desk. Give him a horse with rolling eyes and snatching teeth and hooves intent on causing fatal injuries, and he was fine. Face him with an empty screen where there should be oodles of information, or little flashing boxes blinking piously that he'd made an input error and all data will be deleted, and blind panic immediately set in.

He snatched up the telephone, impatiently punching the numbers. 'Holly? It's Drew. The bloody thing's gone again! What? No, I didn't! Or, at least, I don't think I did . . . Could you—? Brilliant. You're an angel.'

Holly, Drew's secretary, was an IT wizard. He'd leave the whole thing to her. Right now, he wanted to get as far away from the unpleasant beige box as possible. This wasn't what training racehorses was supposed to be about; if he'd wanted to spend his day behind a desk he'd have gone into insurance or something respectable. Before he'd come to train in Milton St John, before he'd had his aspirational dreams of breaking into the big time, all his paperwork had amounted to names and numbers scribbled in a diary, or on the backs of envelopes—

much to his accountant's horror—or, more often than not, was merely kept in his head.

Squinting in the glare of the sun, Drew hurried beneath the clock arch across Peapods' cobbled stable yard towards normality.

Sunday. The nearest the racing fraternity came to a day of rest, although with race meetings now taking place seven days a week, even that was never taken for granted. Still, today, was as close as he was going to get to a day off. Alister, his assistant trainer, had taken the yard's two runners to the meeting at Bath. Drew had thought it would be an ideal opportunity to use the computer to check the entries for the next few weeks. Calculate the possible income. Work out in private just how desperate the financial circumstances were. He hadn't expected the bloody computer to die on him.

The stable yard was divided into two, with thirty boxes in the main yard and a further ten through the ivy-covered gate. Forty boxes for forty potential champions. Drew sucked in his breath. Only half the boxes were occupied—and none of the current inmates, much as he adored them, were going to make his fortune.

The sun dappled over the slate roofs, throwing shadows across the cobbles. The horses had had their Sunday-morning pipe-openers, been breakfasted, and the stable lads had escaped back to the hostel to catch up on their sleep. There was no sound from the stables except the occasional rustle of hooves on bedding, and the odd contented whinny of a well-fed horse. Drew breathed in lungfuls of the yard's air and felt more at peace. The equine smell was the same the world over. Mingled with dusty straw, and the spicy warmth of bran mash—Peapods' Sunday special treat—the indefinable essence of horse, as always, quickened his pulse. This was his life-blood. He'd survive somehow. He'd have to.

Sensing him, the horses poked long noses over their half-doors and snorted pleasurably. He spoke to each one as he passed, patting, pulling ears. It was only his second year as a trainer in Milton St John, and his first had brought a rash of successes. Beginner's luck, he now thought ruefully. But at the time, the wins had convinced him that he would soon be up among the best trainers in the country. That early success had, contrarily, been one of his major problems. He simply hadn't capitalised on it. There hadn't been a winner out of Peapods for far too long.

Any owner with a half-decent horse was going to try for the big yards first. It was only natural. Why would they choose him if they could afford Diana James-Jordan, Emilio Marquez or John Hastings? And that was just the flat-racers. And only in Milton St John. If you started considering Newmarket, or the star-studded National Hunt yards in Lambourn . . . Drew sighed again.

He clicked through the five-bar gate that divided the yard, and was plunged into shadow. The cool darkness was welcome after the scorch of the sun. He headed for the two boxes on the end of the row near the garages. Dock of the Bay, the best flat-racing hope of the yard, had gone to Bath. Solomon, Drew's own horse who was now fourteen and had been granted honorary retirement since they'd galloped to a swan-song victory together in the Czechoslovakian Pardubice, the toughest horse-race in the world, flapped his huge head towards the empty neighbouring box.

'He'll be back soon, you old softie.' Drew unbolted the door and stepped inside. 'I know you miss him.'

He stroked the hard bony nose and scooped a handful of horse nuts from his pocket. Solomon pushed his muzzle into Drew's shoulder and, still crunching, blew flecks of gritty foam across his face. Drew patted Solomon's withers, loving the warmth and the feeling of life. There had to be some way out of this mess. Some way of attracting new owners to the yard. Maybe a mixed yard had been too ambitious. Maybe he should have specialised. He hadn't known enough to be sure which way to go. And now he had a fair selection of also-rans in each category, but nothing that was going to set the racing press on fire.

Dock of the Bay was nearing retirement and there was nothing remotely as good to take his place. It would soon be the Derby. And Ascot. And then, by the end of the summer, National Hunt would be well into its stride—and he had no potential champions there either.

Solomon shifted in the gloom, pressing closer, still looking for titbits. Drew fed him the last of the nuts. He needed a winner, something to hurtle him into the limelight so that the owners would come knocking on his door. He needed all forty of the boxes filled with horses who were potential winners.

Solomon grated his large yellow teeth in Drew's ear. 'Yeah, I know you'd win for me.' Drew kissed his nose. 'You're a star, sweetheart.'

'I'm glad someone recognises my potential.'

Drew jumped and turned toward the yard. Charlie Somerset was leaning over the door.

'Christ! Don't do that!'

'Thought Solomon had turned into Mr Ed, did you?' Charlie joined him in the box, using his shoulder to push Solomon out of the way. 'Shift over, you great baby. So? What's up?'

'Nothing.'

'Crap. You always tell Solomon everything—even before you tell Maddy.'

'The computer's died. It always pisses me off that I can't control it. Holly's on her way over to sort it out.'

'And?'

Drew exhaled. 'And you know as well as I do that we can't survive like this.'

Charlie shrugged. 'No. It's a real shame we haven't got some hotshot for the Classics hidden away—but I suppose it's too late for that. What we need,' he ducked beneath Solomon's head, 'is something extremely media-friendly for next year's jumps. You know, a new Norton's Coin. Small stable takes on the big boys and wins. That sort of thing. You could try asking around—there might be some hairy point-to-pointer with Cheltenham potential eating its head off in one of the yards.'

'Yeah. And there might not be. Still, I suppose I could wander round the village and ask. I might catch someone at home this morning. And I certainly don't want to hang around here while Holly lectures me on pressing the wrong buttons.'

'Not,' Charlie grinned, 'a problem I encounter much myself.'

Drew laughed. Apart from being his jump jockey, Charlie was possibly his closest friend in Milton St John. And that raised another problem: if he gave up with National Hunt and specialised in

55

flat- racing, then there would be no job at Peapods for Charlie.

'Where do you intend starting?'

'Kath Seaward. She's got everyone's ear.'

'Jesus.' Charlie backed out of the box. 'Don't mention me then. I'm still persona non grata at Lancing Grange.' He frowned at Drew as he bolted Solomon's door. 'Where's the car?'

'I'm not taking the car. I'm walking. I think better when I walk.' Drew knew this would flummox Charlie who seemed to be welded to the Aston Martin. 'And don't tell me you're driving to the Cat and Fiddle? It's only a hundred yards away.'

'Nah.' Charlie slid into his car's luxurious interior and pushed his dark red hair away from his eyes. 'I'm off to London. Tina Maloret thinks she might have forgiven me.'

Drew winced. Charlie would probably be knackered for the rest of the week. 'So we won't be seeing you around for a while?'

'Hope not.' Charlie revved the Aston Martin into life. 'If I'm not back by next weekend send in the Red Cross. Or that nice St John lady from Aintree . . .'

St Saviour's bells shattered the Sunday silence, pealing across the roofs of the cottages and reverberating round the downland hills. Charlie leaned from the window. 'That reminds me—have you heard? About Gillian Hutchinson? The Vicar's wife?'

'Nothing remotely salacious, no.'

Charlie revved the car and started to pull away. 'She's rented the Vicarage flat to the woman who is opening the bookshop. A real grunge granny, according to the lads. I shan't bother checking her out.'

'I'm sure she'll be grateful. I'd heard the flat had been taken. At least Gillian Hutchinson's been luckier than me. I haven't had a single reply to the gardener advert.'

Drew felt a pang of pity for the newcomer at the Vicarage. Maddy and her friends had been delighted that there was to be a bookshop in the village, but honestly—when did trainers and jockeys ever have a spare minute to read anything other than form books or the racing papers? The bookshop seemed destined to be a spectacular failure. He knew the feeling.

Yelling to Maddy that he was going to Lancing Grange, he followed the Aston Martin's exhaust fumes out of the yard.

* * *

'It's far too bloody hot for May!' Kath flapped the tails of her checked shirt, looking, Drew thought, more like a demented scarecrow than ever. 'Thank God my season'll be all but over in a couple of weeks. This baked ground will knacker any progress. Still, apart from that nasty business with Ned Filkins at Christmas, and the effing *débâcle* at Aintree, we've had a damn good year so far.'

Kath Seaward's problems with her ex-travelling head lad were well known. His sacking had made the tabloids. And the air around Lancing Grange had been electric for days after the Grand National. Kath, it was rumoured, had put out a Mafia contract on Charlie Somerset.

Knowing that she was waiting for him to spring to the defence of his stable jockey, Drew didn't take

Kath's bait. She was a master tactician on and off the racecourse. A wrong word now could lead to a major schism; and, although the rivalries between the various racing stables in Milton St John were fierce, there was also a strong bond of local camaraderie. And anyway, as his visit to Lancing Grange wasn't simply social, he was most unlikely to get Kath's help if he started championing Charlie.

Kath leaned against a pungently steaming wheelbarrow and surveyed him from beneath the brim of her grubby Jack Charlton golfing cap. Drew, playing the same game, rested his back against the wall in the sunshine and admired her immaculate stable yard with a professional eye. The Lancing Grange boxes were ultramodern. The yard was paved with red blocks and emerald-green tubs alight with pansies stood at each corner. A state-of-the-art tack-room, food store and equine medical centre took up the whole of one side. No expense was spared for the well-being of the seventy or so National Hunt inmates.

The stable block was slightly at odds with the rest of the Grange, Drew always thought, which was a moated flint manor-house, the home of the Seawards for generations. The addition of the racing stables had been Kath's first priority when she'd inherited the estate on the death of her elder brother. A last gesture of defiance in the face of the family who had been enraged that their only daughter had not married a high-ranking army officer and produced a brood of chinless wonders. A family, Drew gathered from Milton St John gossip, who had disowned their daughter years ago when it was clear that she would far rather have been born a man.

Kath had been working as an assistant trainer in Ireland, only returning to the village and the family home after all the Seawards were resting in St Saviour's churchyard. Lancing Grange stables were all the family she needed; the horses far more precious than any baby.

'Strikes me we're getting more and more like football and cricket,' she spoke suddenly, breaking the silence and peering at him again from beneath the cap's peak. 'You used to know where you were with the seasons. There was a respectable cut-off period. Football was in the winter, like jumping; cricket and the flat took up the summer. Now,' Kath glared as if the anomaly was Drew's entire responsibility, 'it's all merged into bloody one. What with all-weather tracks and summer jumping and all that crap. And the owners expect you to enter their damn horses all year round if there's any chance of a piddly bit of money at the end of it! Bloody fools! You can't get through to them that the poor sods have worked their guts out for months—they need a break like the rest of us.'

'Tell me about it,' Drew said with heartfelt sympathy. 'You should try running a mixed yard. I don't know whether I'm supposed to be at Ascot or Chepstow half the time. And, to be honest, I haven't got enough really good horses to justify either at present. I'm only going to be able to keep both sides running for another twelve months at the most. If I don't start earning some decent money, one of them is going to have to go.'

'I'm not surprised. A mixed yard would be far too complicated for me, too. It's pretty ambitious, even for a hardened professional.' Kath knotted the tails

59

of her shirt above filthy riding breeches, exposing several inches of scrawny flesh. 'Is that why you've walked across the village on a Sunday morning? Do you want my advice? Okay then, for what it's worth, I'd say give up the jumping. You know there's more money on the flat—even if the Arabs don't currently think so. Is that what you want to hear?'

'Not really. Although it's what I've been thinking. I grabbed the opportunity to visit because I've got technology problems, and I've called Holly in to sort it out. I needed to escape before I hurled the computer through the window.' He rubbed his eyes wearily. 'I know your yard's full, so I thought you might have had to turn someone away. I just wondered if you'd been approached by anyone with a dead cert or twenty who's looking for a trainer for Cheltenham or Aintree.'

'Aintree!' Kath bristled. 'Don't know how you've got the gall to mention bloody Aintree after what Somerset did!'

Drew grinned. 'Sorry. Very insensitive of me.'

'Bloody stupid of you. And why should I put any good things your way after what Somerset did, eh? Haven't even been able to talk to the useless sod since the National,' Kath growled. 'He seems to vanish like the bloody mist every time I enter the paddock, he turns tail out of the pub every time I walk in, and his damn answerphone is always on. I nearly caught up with the bastard at the Sedgefield meeting, but—'

'He's only obeying orders. I told him to lie low as I need him fully fit for the rest of the season. I thought you might try emasculating him.'

Kath looked as though she was going to explode. 'Castration would be too good for him! I'd like to break his neck. I'd sooner pull out of races than put that cocky sod up again.'

'Still, you won't have to, will you? I know that Matt Garside is almost fully fit, and the grapevine says you've engaged Liam Jenkins for the Fontwell meeting.'

'That's as maybe.' Kath's eyes flashed. 'But Dragon Slayer should have won the National. It's all that fucking hard work wasted that breaks my heart. And letting the horse down. He was up for it, Drew. You know it. The whole bloody racing world knew it. And Somerset fucking blew it.'

Drew, not wanting to be sucked into the long-running argument, merely nodded. He peeled himself from the red-hot wall and walked across the yard. Dragon Slayer, his nearly-black head poking inquisitively over the door of his box, rolled his eyes in anticipation. 'Spoiled brat.' Drew stroked his bony nose, admiring the race-winning physique. 'I fed all my titbits to Solomon before I left.'

'He's looking for carrots.' Kath had joined him. 'And he's not having any until tea-time.' Her eyes were soft, as she fondled the horse. She produced a packet of Polos from her pocket, smiling as Dragon Slayer snuffled and crunched. 'It's not fair on him, poor baby. He loves the sport. He'd done so well at Cheltenham—and don't,' the eyes flashed again, 'tell me that there's always next year. It's a bloody lifetime away!'

'I know how you feel. I'd really like to have a shot at it myself next year, but nothing I've got in the yard at the moment will be up to scratch, that's for sure. I've got some good jumpers and a couple of out-and-out stayers—but not the magical combination of the two like this boy.' He cast covetous eyes over Dragon Slayer's seventeen hands of pure power and sighed. 'If you do hear of anyone, I'd be really grateful if you'd let me know. Failing that, I'll just have to hope some gambling-mad lottery winner decides to push their latest acquisition my way, and it turns out to be a cross between Red Rum and Arkle.'

Kath laughed. 'Dream on! No one gets those sort of horses in the real world! And—if you did—I trust you wouldn't leave it to the mercies of Somerset.'

'Charlie's a great horseman,' Drew protested. 'The best. Look, I know you're disappointed, but it was an accident. Accidents happen.'

'Yes, of course they do. Except that wasn't an accident. That was sheer bloody incompetence—and I'll prove it.' She stood with her hands on her hips and jutted her chin forward. 'Tell you what, I'll throw down a challenge now. I'll try and find an owner for you and next year we'll go for it. Aintree. The Grand National. Dragon Slayer and Matt Garside against whatever nag you can train-on and bloody Charlie Somerset. Call it your swan-song if you like. Your last tilt at the windmill before you join the prissy-flat Newmarket brigade. I'll beat you bloody hollow, Fitzgerald. A grand on it?'

Drew winced. Maddy would probably kill him. He shook Kath's thin, calloused hand. 'Okay. You're on.'

*   *   *

Walking back along the dusty curve of Milton St John's main road, Drew inhaled the silence. Sunday morning was still Sunday morning here. Maureen's

Munchy Bar was closed. Bronwyn Pugh hadn't bowed to the gods of capitalism and gone in for a seven-day opening of the Village Stores yet; the Cat and Fiddle still only opened for the pre-Sunday-lunch drinkers then shut its doors for the post-Sunday-lunch snoozers; cars were washed and lawns mowed.

A string of glossy thoroughbreds clip-clopped their way along the street, hindquarters swaying, heads up, knowing they were gorgeous, like contestants in a beauty pageant. John Hastings' last lot coming back from their Sunday-morning work-out on the gallops, Drew knew, recognising the individual horses even without the distinctive monogrammed rugs. The stable lads in the saddle grinned at him and touched their crash hats. He acknowledged them with a smile.

John Hastings was one of Milton St John's premier flat trainers. His yard would be one of Peapods' main rivals if it gave up jumping. But right now Drew's thoughts weren't on the stars of the Derby at Epsom or the King George at Ascot. He was still thinking about Kath's challenge. The National. Next year. Was it even remotely possible? Probably not. No one could expect him to compete with the likes of Jenny Pitman or Martin Pipe, could they? It wouldn't be considered decent for a yearling to come stomping up on the rails and snatch the Blue Riband, would it?

And, of course, all the yards in neighbouring Lambourn would already have their chosen prospects being coached and cosseted; and Kath had Dragon Slayer. The only other National Hunt yard in Milton St John was run by Ferdy Thornton, and he played everything so damned close to his chest that, even if he had something akin to Aldaniti or Dawn Run contentedly munching hay in his stables, no one would ever know.

Should he take Kath's advice? Peapods was doing so-so on the flat, but pretty abysmally over jumps. It made good economic sense to run with the winners, but he really didn't want to pull out of National Hunt-racing yet—not while there was still the remotest chance of winning at Aintree. And certainly not now he'd gambled away a grand which he could ill afford.

*   *   *

'I'm just off.' Holly, Drew's secretary, looked up from the computer keyboard in the Peapods office. 'I've sorted it. Major disaster averted—again. One or two of the disks had been wiped but nothing important. I've checked all the files and I've made copies. You should always do a back-up, you know.'

Drew knew. He very rarely remembered. He was just delighted to have got the bloody computer to do anything at all. He always left the technical stuff to Holly. 'Thanks a million. I'll pay you overtime.'

'Too right you will,' Holly said cheerfully, reaching for her handbag. 'And if it doesn't sound too much like grandmother and eggs, do you think you could leave inputting the data to me in future, please, Drew? It would solve an awful lot of problems. Oh, there was one bit of info that I managed to retrieve—I thought you might have missed it.'

Drew raised his eyebrows. He probably had. The damn screen had started blinking and flashing and then gone blank almost straight away.

64

Holly slung her bag on to her shoulder. 'God, Drew, you didn't even check your e-mail, did you?'

He shook his head. He wasn't sure he trusted e-mail. Letters you could open and read and answer and then file neatly away were okay. Messages that flashed instantaneously on to the screen from out of the ether were something else entirely. Anyone who was foolish enough to e-mail him over the weekend had to wait for Holly's ministrations on Monday morning.

Holly leaned back over the keyboard and started tapping. Drew looked on in admiration. Give him a dozen yearlings to break in any day.

'There—look.' Holly smiled. 'I'll stay while you read it if you like, then I'll log off again.'

Drew read the e-mail message over her shoulder, then spun round and hugged her. 'Hallelujah! Holly, I love you! I love everyone in the whole damn world!'

'I thought you'd be pleased—'

'That's the biggest understatement in the world!' Drew headed for the door. 'Where's Maddy?'

'In the garden with Poppy Scarlet and the dogs. I'll just log off now then, shall I? Right—I'll take that as a yes.' Holly was still smiling as he belted out of the office and the door crashed shut behind him.

The four dogs—all acquired when he and Maddy had visited the animal sanctuary to adopt a kitten and had returned home with them plus six maladjusted cats—greeted Drew in the dim coolness of the hall with massed thumped tails and damp noses. He patted wriggling bodies indiscriminately, pushing his way through them and out into the garden.

Whatever other delights Maddy Beckett had brought into Drew's life during the eighteen months they had lived together, and there had been many, she had transformed the Peapods garden beyond recognition. Gone were the manicured lawns, the regimented borders, the angular concrete paths of his wife Caroline's régime. The garden now tumbled with flowers, and shrubs clambered haphazardly over arches and pergolas. Wild flowers flourished beneath the chestnut trees, a canopied swing stood among rustic benches, and a fountain played down stepping-stones into the shallowest of pools, carefully covered with netting to prevent Poppy rolling in.

It was cool and green and vibrant all at the same time. It was also very hard work, and extremely time-consuming, and as Maddy had gone back to running Shadows, her cleaning agency in the village, they'd decided to advertise the post of gardener/handyman in the local paper. Drew wasn't completely sure that they could afford one.

He stood for a second at the top of the steps and watched Maddy sitting cross-legged beneath the willow tree, tickling Poppy Scarlet's tummy, giggling with their daughter. He loved them both with painful intensity. The financial problems apart, he had never been so happy. And now, he grinned, every word of the e-mail imprinted in his memory, his personal happiness would be complete.

Two years previously, miserably married, Drew had moved from his small stable in Jersey to try his hand at breaking into British racing big time. Caroline, his elegant ice-cold wife, had remained in the Channel Islands to run her own business, only visiting Milton St John when her schedule allowed.

Drew, lonely and confused about everything except his ambition to become a top-notch trainer, had been drawn to Maddy's chaotic and unself-conscious warmth. She'd lived in the cottage opposite Peapods, and Caroline had employed her as a cleaner. He and Maddy had seemed destined to bump into each other at every village function.

Friendship had developed into love, and love had led—eventually and after much moral anguish—to an affair that had shocked them both with its intensity. Neither of them had been prepared for the outcome.

He beamed happily at the memories as he leapt down the steps.

Maddy still wasn't aware of him. Her unruly auburn curls fell forward, curtaining her face. She was wearing a baggy T-shirt over her leggings again, still agonising, Drew knew, about the post-pregnancy weight that simply refused to go away. Drew told her every morning that she had never looked more beautiful, and every morning she wrinkled her nose in reply and said, 'Oh, yeah? I always thought I was fat before—but now I'm obese! And don't you dare go on about Rubens—I look like the Michelin Man with a bad hair-do! You're mad, Drew Fitzgerald, or short-sighted, or both!' And then they laughed and cuddled and tumbled back on to the bed. They did a lot of that.

Drew crossed the lawn accompanied by the dogs.

'Oh, brilliant! You're back earlier than I thought you'd be. Have you got time for a drink before lunch? It's nearly ready. Have you seen Holly? She's sorted everything out so it's safe for you to go back into the office.' Maddy scrambled to her feet, expertly tucking ten-month-old Poppy under her arm, and stood on tiptoe to kiss him thoroughly. 'What did Kath say?'

'The expurgated version?' Drew grinned, kissing her back.

'Of course. I don't want Poppy picking up any of Kath's more colourful phrases just yet.'

'Roughly translated, that she'll keep an eye open for useful horses. Oh, and that if Charlie comes within a mile of Lancing Grange she'll kill him.'

'Fairly mild then.' Maddy took Drew's hand and led him back to the shade of the chestnuts. 'Anyway you're looking pretty smug. Can you see yourself leading in a National winner already and putting a smile back on the bank manager's face? Or is it simply because Holly's rescued you from another black hole?'

'A bit of both.' Drew lifted Poppy from Maddy's arms and kissed his daughter's chubby face. She gurgled delightedly, grabbing a handful of his hair, already struggling to be put down. 'But mainly something else.'

'She walked again,' Maddy said, curling her feet beneath her beside Drew. 'Two steps before falling flat on her face. Mum said I didn't walk until I was nearly eighteen months so she must get it from your side of the family.'

'Child prodigies to a man,' Drew nodded. 'She'll be writing Shakespeare and playing Chopin before her first birthday. Hey, look at her . . .'

Using Drew's jeans as a lever, Poppy Scarlet hauled herself upright, wobbled unsteadily on her plump legs, took two paces forward, then sat down with a thump on her well-Pampered bottom. Drew and Maddy exchanged proud smiles, as they had done every day since her birth. Poppy, basking in her captive audience, promptly repeated the performance.

'So, why the Cheshire Cat grin?' Maddy asked. 'Has Kath made you an offer you can't refuse, or is it the something else?'

'Kath threw down a wager—but that isn't important at the moment. Not,' he pulled Maddy against him, 'as important as this other piece of news.'

Poppy crawled furiously towards her parents and clambered between them. Maddy kissed the dark, downy head. 'Go on then. What news?'

'I've had an e-mail from Caroline. From Jersey. The lawyers have sorted everything out to her satisfaction and given her the dates.' Drew beamed, unable to contain his excitement. 'The decree nisi will be through in June. The absolute twelve weeks later. I'll be divorced by September. We can get married straight away, Mad. Married at last! Won't that be incredible?'

CHAPTER FIVE

Two pairs of gooseberry-coloured eyes stared out from beneath straight red fringes. Jemima, in the middle of folding her T-shirts into drawers and putting her long skirts on hangers, stopped and glanced towards the doorway. The stares didn't waver.

'Hi!' Her voice squeaked alarmingly. 'I mean, hello. I'm Jemima. I guess you're Leviticus and Ezekiel?'

'Ten out of ten.' The right-hand twin scowled.

69

Whoops, Jemima thought, wrong pitch. She tried again. 'How am I supposed to tell you apart?'

'You're not.' The twins spoke together.

Jemima shrugged. 'Okay. Suit yourselves. Whenever I see you, I'll just yell "Oi, you!" and that'll cover you both.'

There was the merest flicker of matching smiles. The left-hand twin scuffed the carpet. 'We're not supposed to be up here. Mum said the flat was private now. Mum said we was to leave you in peace. Mum said we was to meet you properly at tea-time.'

His brother joined in the scuffing. 'We just wanted to have a look at you first. Do you mind wearing glasses?'

'No. Why?'

The twins stopped scuffing. The right-hand one spoke. 'There's a boy in our class—he wears glasses. Some of the kids called him specky-four-eyes.'

Jemima winced. She'd had much the same treatment at primary school. Younger and older children accepted differences without question, but at the cocky pre-teen stage children could be brutal. Along with a boy with extensive dental bracework who had been naturally called Metalmouth, and three very overweight pupils, she'd formed a sort of outsiders' club. They were still in touch with each other. 'But you don't call him names, surely?'

'Nah, course not. Glasses are cool. We beat up everyone who bad-mouthed him. He's everybody's best friend now.'

Nice kids, Jemima thought. Maybe they weren't as scary as she'd first thought. The left-hand twin gave a sudden cherubic smile. 'You're running the bookshop, aren't you?'

Safer ground. 'When it opens. Do you like reading?'

The twins exchanged glances. 'Nah. Well, *Lost Diaries* is okay. And *Colour Jets*. Telly's better.'

Slamming shut the wardrobe door, Jemima picked up a bundle of towels and headed towards the bathroom. 'Maybe you'll change your mind when the shop opens. You'll have to come and tell me which books I should stock.'

'Might do.'

Jemima turned away and grinned. So far so good. She paused again at the bathroom door. 'I have got one problem—your names.'

'We told you. We answer to each other's.'

'No, not that.' Jemima turned on the water and raised her voice. 'I mean Leviticus and Ezekiel—they're one heck of a mouthful. What do people usually call you?'

The left-hand twin wrinkled his nose. 'Bastard, mostly.'

'No—not always,' his brother corrected quickly. 'Bronwyn Pugh sometimes says "them little buggers".'

'Yeah,' a ginger head nodded. 'An' ole Bathsheba Cox told Mum we're the spawn of the devil.'

Allowing herself to laugh in the privacy of the bathroom, Jemima was straight-faced when she walked back into the bedroom. 'Well, I'm going to call you Levi and Zeke, OK? And I *can* tell you apart.'

'You can't!'

'No one can 'cept Mum and Dad!'

'Yes, I can. You,' she pointed to the left-hand twin, 'have got more freckles on your nose. They're

71

kind of splodged together. And I guess you're
Levi—'

'Just shows you don't know everything,' he
started bullishly, then sighed. 'Oh, bugger.'

'That's that sorted, then.' Jemima smiled
serenely. 'Zeke's got the splodgy nose. Now, I'm
going to have a shower. See you later.'

'S'pose so,' they muttered together, then looked
at each other and nodded. 'You're okay. See ya.'

Jemima closed the bathroom door and leaned
against it, letting her breath escape slowly. She
licked her forefinger and drew a line in the air.
'Round one to Jemima Carlisle.'

* * *

Having had very little hands-on experience with the
clergy, Vicar Glen was going to be the next hurdle.
It was one she crashed into at tea-time.

Looking mutinous, the twins were sitting side by
side at the dining-room table when Jemima came
down after her shower. Gillian, cool in something
pale and floaty, and which Jemima would bet
a month's salary—if she had one—came from
Monsoon, looked warily at them from behind a
huge willow pattern tea-pot.

'They're sulking because I said this had to be a
proper sit-to-the-table tea in your honour, rather
than pizzas on laps in front of *Grange Hill*. To be
honest, they're not all that happy with sandwiches
and cake. And they're miffed that you can tell
the difference between them. I think they were
counting on causing a fair bit of mayhem. Are you
settled in up there?'

Jemima nodded, sliding into a rather shabby

but very beautiful walnut and velvet chair. 'Everything is great, thanks.' She helped herself to two doorsteps of hacked bread as Levi and Zeke pushed butter and a pot of shop jam towards her. 'Is—er—Glen—um—Mr Hutchinson not joining us?'

'I do hope so.' Gillian looked distracted and stirred her tea fiercely. 'I told him you were here.'

'Dad's down the pub,' Zeke mumbled through a mouthful of bread and butter. 'He's always down the pub. We don't wait for him.'

Jemima concentrated on her plate. If the Vicar had a drink problem it wasn't any of her concern really, was it? It might explain why Zeke and Levi were so unruly. A mother whose head was away in the land of hearts and flowers, and a father—a man of the cloth, no less—who was joined to the barmaid's apron . . .

'Boys!' Gillian's laugh held a note of tension. 'You shouldn't say things like that. Whatever will Jemima think?'

'That Daddy's always in the Cat and Fiddle—and he is—'cepting for when he's in church.' Levi beamed jammily at Jemima across the table. 'When he does come home he's usually asleep.'

'And he snores something dreadful, but that's only 'cause he's so old.' Zeke crammed an entire slice of bread into his mouth at one go. His following, 'Can I leave the table now, Mum?' was accordingly muffled.

'You haven't had any cake.' Gillian was definitely twitchy.

'Don't want cake. We'll have crisps later.' The twins slid from their chairs and smiled at Jemima. 'See ya.' A nanosecond later the dining room

73

reverberated behind them.

You could cut the tension with the cake knife. Wondering just what sort of set-up she'd so casually drifted into, Jemima sipped her tea and stared out through the open french doors. The walled garden shimmered in the afternoon sun. Butterflies were practising for summer by flexing their wings on the green shoots of the buddleias. It was a fragile peace.

'Gillian! Are you in the dining room? Have I missed tea? I was—oh, damn and blast!'

'Glen.' Gillian's smile was stretched. 'He's probably fallen over the boys' roller-blades.' She raised her voice. 'We're in here, darling! Come and say hello to Jemima.'

With her very limited knowledge of vicars, Jemima had already conjured up a stern and severe figure in full clerical regalia. Gaunt, she decided, with a dog-collar choking a scrawny neck and cheeks criss-crossed with red-veined over-imbibing. He'd have gimlet eyes and a mouth singed by breathing hellfire and damnation. He'd probably be wearing gaiters—or was that only bishops? He'd— she stopped in mid-fantasy and gawped.

A stunning Richard Gere lookalike in jeans and a grey sweatshirt smiled sheepishly round the dining-room door. 'Sorry about the curses. It was the roller-blades—again.'

Jemima closed her mouth with a snap as Glen came into the room. He was probably older than Gillian by at least ten years, but simply oozed sexuality. Her mother would have curled up and died for him.

'Hello, sweetheart,' he kissed Gillian's cheek and then extended a slim hand towards Jemima. 'And

74

hello to you too. It's lovely to see you.'

'It's—er—lovely to be here.' Jemima blushed, and sniffed surreptitiously for any signs of alcohol, completely bemused by his golden glory.

Glen sat in Levi's vacated chair and helped himself liberally to bread and jam. 'I do hope you'll be happy in Milton St John. And after today, the awful meet-the-family bit, I promise you we'll leave you to your own devices. I'm sure we'll all be far too busy to get in each other's way.' He smiled fondly at his wife before nodding seriously at Jemima. 'Despite what you might hear in the village to the contrary, I'm very, very proud of Gillian having her own career, you know. She writes for lots of different magazines, and the money has—well—transformed our lives.'

A faint blush swept into Gillian's pale cheeks. 'Glen! I don't think Jemima wants to hear about it. Anyway, we're supposed to be above things like money and material possessions. The ladies of the parish would have a fit to hear you talking like that.'

'True.' Glen poured his tea. 'But you have to admit it is very pleasant to live comfortably instead of scrimping and saving. And I am proud of you, darling, inordinately so.' He beamed at Jemima. 'You probably won't recognise her, of course, because she writes under a pseudonym.'

Gillian dropped her cake fork with a clatter. 'Sorry! Clumsy of me. Oh, yes—I—I write as *Janey* Hutchinson for the mags and for the local Am Dram group in Upton Poges.'

'And very nicely, too.' Glen reached across and patted her hand amidst the bread and butter, as Jemima gathered the crumbs together on her

75

plate. She hadn't got a clue what was going on. She assumed that Gillian's new-found wealth, as well as funding the Monsoon frock collection, meant that Glen could spend even longer in the Cat and Fiddle. But, assuming they had more money than the clergy were used to, why on earth should Gillian have seemed so desperate to rent the attic flat?

Gillian, still appearing slightly flustered, paused in refilling the teacups and took a deep breath. 'So—how did it go? The meeting?'

'Wonderfully well,' Glen nodded heartily. 'We've practically got the whole village behind us. I only wish you'd come along and lend your support, darling.'

'I can't.' Gillian sliced cake with swift jerks. 'I'm far too busy writing. Anyway, with people like Bathsheba Cox and Bronwyn Pugh spearheading the attack you certainly don't need me.'

'Er—shall I leave?' Jemima pushed back her chair. 'I mean, if this is private—'

'Oh,' Gillian sighed. 'We're so rude. I keep forgetting you know absolutely nothing about village politics. Glen has been to the Cat and Fiddle—'

'I think the twins mentioned it.' Jemima bit her lip. 'But, I mean, everyone likes a drink—don't they? Except those who don't, I mean. At least . . . Well, drinking socially is fine . . . '

'I'm not an alcoholic.' Glen sat back in his chair, the Richard Gere eyes creased with delight. 'What *have* they been telling you? That I spend all my free time in the Cat and Fiddle?'

'Well—something like that—not, of course, that it's any of my business . . . '

'The village hall is being renovated. We're using

76

the back room of the Cat and Fiddle as a temporary replacement.' Glen was still grinning. 'As I sit on practically every Milton St John committee, I spend half my life there.'

'Oh. Right.' Jemima could feel the blush scorching her throat. She pushed back her chair and stood up. 'Look, I'm sure you have loads of things to talk about—and I really should try and find my feet. Would you object if I rounded up the twins and got them to give me a guided tour of the village?'

'Not at all. Great idea,' Glen nodded round a mouthful of cake. 'You'll probably find them on the fruit machines in the Munchy Bar. And I do hope you don't think we were being greedy over the rent on the flat. I told Gillian that I thought it was somewhat excessive. I mean, if you think we should lower it . . .'

'It's fine.' Jemima paused in the doorway. The rent had actually seemed ridiculously low, but maybe that was just the difference between Oxford and the heart of the country. Gillian appeared to be trying to communicate something to her with frantic eye-signals. Jemima, completely at a loss, resorted to what she hoped was an all-encompassing smile and slid from the dining room.

*   *   *

As Glen had predicted, she located the twins among the blinding whirrs and fizzes of the Munchy Bar's one-armed bandits. They were both losing heavily, and didn't raise too many objections to the Milton St John trek.

'Mind,' Levi said as they wandered slowly along

77

the dusty street—it was still far too hot to be energetic—'you'll probably see everyone if you just sit on that ole bench by the duck pond. Everybody comes by sooner or later.'

Jemima, used to the crowds and traffic of Oxford, was enchanted by the tranquillity. Everywhere was a mass of emerging green, with tiny pastel buds tipping the branches. The stream gurgled pleasantly. The honey-coloured houses still basked; dogs and cats scratched half-heartedly; people leaned on bicycles and chatted to other people with shopping baskets; somewhere, from an open window, a radio played.

'That's it then, really,' Zeke said kindly as they reached the end of the chestnut tree colonnade. 'It's mostly all stable yards. You see more horses than cars here. There's not much more to it, apart from the football field. It's a bit boring, don't you reckon?'

'I reckon it's paradise,' Jemima said fervently. 'No noise, no traffic . . .'

'No bloody anything.' Levi took hold of her hand. 'Still, Upton Poges is quite good.'

Zeke, not to be outdone, caught Jemima's free hand. 'An' we go to the pictures in Wantage, and Newbury's just the biggest place in the whole world!'

She smiled down at the twins. 'Thank you for being my escorts anyway. Now, I want a simple answer to a simple question.'

The matching gooseberry-green eyes zoomed in from each side. Two sets of sandy eyebrows arched inquisitively.

'I want to know,' Jemima continued, 'if they do great big ice creams at Maureen's Munchy

78

Bar? And she raised her voice above the yells of assertion, '—I want to know if I'm the only person out of us three who fancies one?'

'Nah! I can eat two!'

'Betcha can't!'

'One each,' Jemima said firmly as they approached the curve that fronted the Cat and Fiddle, the Village Stores, the Munchy Bar—and her bookshop. 'And I'm paying.'

The twins grinned gappily, the friendship sealed, and scampered off ahead to place their orders. Jemima followed at a more leisurely pace, trying not to look smug. In spite of the rather strange undercurrents at the Vicarage, she felt that she had the measure of the twins.

Levi and Zeke were already at the Munchy Bar's counter. The whole place was heaving with people. Jemima looked around with delight. Dozens of potential customers. They could all pile out of here in a couple of months' time—and straight into her bookshop.

'We've ordered Knickerbocker Glories,' Levi informed her as she eased her way through the closely-packed Formica tables to join them. 'Is that okay?'

'Lovely.' A ceiling fan was working overtime, but it was still stifling. The woman behind the counter, who Jemima guessed was the eponymous Maureen, was trying to serve everyone at the same time. 'Is there anywhere to sit?'

'On yer bum!' they chorused together, giggling.

Two middle-aged ladies, looking like cloned Mrs Mertons in floral polyester, cross-over sandals, and tight perms, glared from the nearest table.

Zeke smiled at them. 'Hello, Mrs Cox. Hello,

79

Mrs Pugh.'

The matching perms bobbed down towards their teacups.

'We hate them,' Levi said cheerfully. 'They're horrid about Mum.'

Maureen, who had a bleached beehive and sparkly eye-shadow and had obviously been informed all about Jemima by the twins, placed three overflowing sundae glasses on the counter. 'They are, too. You want to ask Gillian about Bathsheba and Bronwyn. Go to church twice every Sunday and think that gives them the right to slag everyone off for the next six days. They fancy the pants off the Vicar, of course, but that don't give 'em the right to be bitchy to Gillian.' She huffed her spectacular chest in the direction of the tightly permed heads. 'They can be venomous old cows if you gets on the wrong side of them.'

Jemima paid for the ice-creams. Milton St John's chocolate-box idyll was beginning to melt as quickly as the Knickerbocker Glories.

'Mum always says to Dad that they needs a good man,' Zeke mumbled through his ice-cream. 'We always think that's funny 'cause they're married to Ted and Bernie an' they're Dad's churchwardens an' you can't get much betterer than that.'

'Christ!' Maureen grinned, showing lipstick-stained teeth. 'Gillian's not far wrong neither. Did you see the poster they've just put up? Load of rubbish but they has tea here twice a day, so I don't object. Doubt if anyone'll read it anyway.'

Jemima hadn't seen the poster. In the crowded Munchy Bar it was impossible even to see the walls.

To the twins' evident delight, Maureen leaned chummily across the counter displaying a vast amount of cleavage. 'Bathsheba and Bronwyn are always crusading for summat or other. At the moment they've got a bee in their bonnet about books.' Maureen cast a wary eye at Levi and Zeke who were engrossed in their ice-creams, and leaned even closer to Jemima. 'You'd know all about them, of course. The ones with bonking an' that in. Them Fishnet Publications. Sort of sex for women. I love 'em myself.'

'Oh, right. Erotica.' Jemima spooned the cherry from the top of her Knickerbocker Glory. Bookworms had stocked Fishnets. They'd been very popular. She'd already ordered the new July ones for her own shop. 'But surely they don't have to read them?'

'They don't want anyone else to read them either.' Maureen straightened up and moved away to serve another customer. 'That's why they had the meeting in the Cat and Fiddle this afternoon— them an' all the other sad saps in the village. Waste o' time if you ask me. Poor Vicar's got enough on his plate.'

So that's where Glen had been, Jemima thought, mixing in peach ice-cream with raspberry syrup, on an anti-erotica campaign. She'd be sucked into the fray herself if she wasn't very careful. She'd chosen a wide range of books from the publishers' lists— something for everyone, she'd thought, at least until she'd got a feel for the village and her customers. It looked as though she could be heading for trouble even before she opened. Just for a moment, she wondered if she should in fact mention her Fishnets order to Glen. Perhaps not. Probably just a storm in a teacup. Hopefully, Bronwyn and Bathsheba would be campaigning about something completely

81

different by July. They'd probably never spot the slim Fishnet volumes. And to think everyone in Oxford had told her that she would find life in the country deadly dull.

Levi and Zeke, wearing identical ice-cream moustaches, were scraping the bottoms of their glasses, "'s okay if we go and have a kick-about on the field? Or do you want us to stay?'

'No, I can find my way home from here. And thanks for the tour.'

The twins squirmed through the crowds and paused at the door. 'Ta for the ice-creams too, Jemima. You're ace.'

'Jemima.' Maureen paused for a second to whisk away the empty glasses. 'That's pretty. Old-fashioned. Is it a family name?'

Jemima had always hated it. In addition to her glasses it had led to quite a few taunts during her childhood. Especially when the majority of her contemporaries had been called Tracy. 'Actually I was named after a racehorse.'

She had never quite come to terms with the fact that she had apparently been conceived during an alcoholic celebration shortly after Vincent had won a thousand pounds on Jumping Jemima in the last race at Ayr during her parents' Scottish honeymoon. It spoke volumes for her father's lack of gambling success that she was an only child.

'Bloody hell!' Maureen spluttered through her pasted-on lipstick. 'Still, it could have been worse, duck. You could have spent your life as Desert Orchid. Anyway, you're in the right place here.'

'I don't like horse-racing, either.'

Heads turned and stared. Maureen sucked in her breath. Jemima realised she'd just uttered the worst possible heresy. 'Well, that is—I don't know anything about horse-racing. And I'm not particularly keen to find out.' She wasn't going to say anything about Vincent and the gambling. That was all behind her now.

'You ought to go to a race meeting.' Maureen swept away the perspiration from her cleavage before diving off to serve a bevy of youngsters at the far end of the counter. 'You never know. You might change your mind.'

Never in a million years, Jemima thought, spooning up the last mouthfuls of melted ice-cream. The formidable Bronwyn Pugh and Bathsheba Cox were just leaving and they smiled inquisitively at her. Her natural inclination was to bob her head downwards, hiding behind her glasses and the tousled layers of her hair. It had helped a lot so far. She'd read all the articles in *Company* about assertiveness—and even practised being bolshie in front of her mirror—but the principles always deserted her in real life. Still, once she was running the shop she'd have to get over her shyness, and start greeting people with confidence. So why not have a trial run now?

She smiled back. 'Hello, I'm Jemima Carlisle. I'll be running the bookshop next door.'

'We've heard,' Bronwyn said cheerily. 'Just what the village needs. I hope you'll have plenty of Agatha Christie and Dick Francis.'

'And Catherine Cookson,' Bathsheba joined in. 'And none of that filth that masquerades as romance these days. Dame Barbara is the only one who writes romance proper, if you know what I mean.'

'I'm sure there'll be something that you'll enjoy.'

Jemima resisted the urge to fiddle with her glasses and carried on smiling. She hoped she wasn't blushing.

'We won't tolerate filth and degradation,' Bronwyn said. 'We've never had any of that in this village. Anyway, it's lovely to meet you, dear. You look like a nice respectable girl.' The gimlet eyes approved the ankle-length skirt and studious spectacles. 'Perhaps you'd like to come to our next meeting? Might be as well for you to know what we want in our bookshop. And, more important, what we don't. Ask the Vicar for details.'

'Yes . . . yes, I might. Er—thank you.'

'Well done,' Maureen puffed, wiping down the counter as the floral frocks disappeared through the doorway. 'Get 'em on your side. They can be the very devil if they takes against you.'

Jemima scraped the bottom of her glass, feeling proud of herself. This was a nice village, she thought, despite it being full of jockeys and trainers. She had been here for merely half a day and everyone had been very friendly. No doubt because the people she'd met so far were nothing to do with the racing brigade. The stable staff would probably never come within sniffing distance of the Munchy Bar or her bookshop. Obviously, Milton St John's horsy fraternity were scattered across the country's racecourses, being cruel to animals and relieving mug punters of their hard-earned cash.

'I needs six pairs of hands.' Maureen grabbed at Jemima's empty sundae glass. 'It's bloody non-stop. I only opened up last year—and they told me I wouldn't make a go of it. Now, I'm rushed off me feet—and with Maud, she's me regular help, still getting over her hysterectomy, and none of the

84

casuals ever turning up on time—if at all—I'm fair frazzled.'

Jemima jerked herself back from drifting into a daydream in which Milton St John was far more famed for its cosy, friendly and well-stocked bookshop than its racing connections.

'Sorry? Are you—um—looking for staff?'

'Looking? I'm long past looking.' Maureen's glittery eye-shadow had run into greasy creases. 'I'd take Old Nick himself if he could fry a burger.'

As her religious beliefs hovered somewhere between God being an elderly man with a flowing white beard reclining on a cloud, and some rather woolly Buddhist ethics regarding self-help and the right of everything to an uninterrupted life-span, Jemima was rather reluctant to thank any celestial deity for this job opportunity. However, it might just have something to do with her now living cheek-by-jowl with the clergy, mightn't it? She firmly interrupted this train of thought. Much more of that and she'd stop shaving her legs, buy a guitar, and be belting out 'Lord of the Dance'.

Pushing aside her vegetarian principles in the name of survival, she took a deep breath. 'Actually, I used to work in McDonald's, and I need a job, you see, until the shop is ready, and—'

'Hallelujah!' Maureen's cleavage jumped for joy. 'Grab yerself a pinny, my duck, and let me show you the ropes.'

CHAPTER SIX

The Cat and Fiddle was heaving. Having managed to secure half a pint of bitter, Vincent Carlisle held it above his head and looked hopefully around the scrum for a likely face. Not finding one immediately, he settled for a seat in the corner just beside the juke-box.

This, he decided, was just what the doctor ordered. Maybe Lambourn would have been better—and, of course, Newmarket would have been ideal—but, there was a God, after all—alive and well and flourishing in Milton St John. He quaffed half the beer and grinned at the irony. Jemima getting the flat at the Vicarage suited his plans nicely.

Not of course that he'd let her know that he was here. At least not today. She knew him too well. No, he'd leave her to issue an invitation when she was ready. When, he thought, she believed he could be trusted in the midst of so much temptation. Not, of course, that he saw it as that. One man's temptation was another's opportunity.

However, today was just a flying visit, a recce, to see how the land lay. To find out whether or not there was an outlet for his talents. Talents which would, with the right contacts, be able to restore him to the sort of lifestyle he'd lost so unfairly. And, equally important, enable him to repay Jemima.

She was a star, his daughter. Working in that burger place—despite her having been a vegetarian from the age of five when he, in a thoughtless moment, had made the link between the lambs frolicking so prettily in the fields and their Sunday lunch—*and* sending him half her money! How many kids would do that? He loved Jemima dearly, and always felt ashamed that he'd let her down. Well, not any more. Not with this God-given realm of possibilities for wealth being delivered gift-wrapped into his lap. He'd make her proud of him before the year was out, or die in the attempt.

Having decided to make the Milton St John pilgrimage, Vincent had had to face one or two pressing problems. Money was the most pressing of all. Or rather, the lack of it. His car had disappeared not long after the bank had repossessed the house, and just before the bailiffs moved in and removed the goods and chattels. No car and no money had meant that transport difficulties were pretty insurmountable—and despite the Government's promise of accessible public transport for all, no one had yet seen fit to provide a free hourly bus service from Vincent's bedsit into the heart of the downlands.

He'd compromised by walking to the outskirts of town and then hitching lifts. He'd actually quite enjoyed it. It took him back to his days as a student. The A34 had been no problem. Two lifts with reps and then a very pretty lady lorry driver from Upton Poges—Diamond or Diadem or something, the company was called—had kindly taken him from Chievely Services to the Milton St John-Tiptoe crossroads.

Vincent had managed to catch the Cat and Fiddle at the height of the lunchtime rush.

He tackled the second half of his drink with more circumspection. He'd only got a couple of pounds left in his pocket, and as yet hadn't fastened his glance on anyone who looked likely to stand the next round. He leaned back in his chair, enjoying the racing chatter, delighted to be part of the scene—albeit on the periphery. His eyes slowly scanned the crowded pub like CCTV.

Good God! Wasn't that Kath Seaward by the bar? And Ferdy Thornton? And—dear heavens! Barty Small and Emilio Marquez! Vincent all but punched the air. Four of the country's top trainers in one place! This would suit him very nicely indeed . . .

'Sorry, mate.'

Vincent looked in horror as his glass clattered sideways and his precious last few mouthfuls of beer slopped across the table. A short, middle-aged man with a creased face and no teeth, was leaning towards him.

'My fault. Bit crowded in here,' the toothless mouth flapped. 'Someone jogged me elbow. Let me get you another one. Bitter, was it? Pint?'

Vincent bit back his groan of complaint and turned it into a nod of compliance. The man left his own drink on the table and expertly wriggled through towards the bar. Short and weather-beaten, Vincent noted, bow-legged and malnourished—he had to be an ex-jockey. This could be the one . . .

Ten minutes later, a fresh pint in front of him, and his benefactor beside him, Vincent was well into his patter. No need to involve Jemima at this juncture, he'd decided. And maybe a widower would elicit more sympathy than a divorcee . . . The lack of home he'd put down to tied accommodation and redundancy, rather than repossession and bankruptcy. And his past position as director of his own building company had become handyman, gardener, jack-of-all-trades . . .

The trap set, Vincent sat back to wait for a catch.

'Ned.' The gums stretched into a smile as hands were shaken. 'Bit in your position meself. Worked as travelling head lad for Mizz Seaward for years.' A whine crept in as he motioned his head towards the trainers at the bar. 'Cow sacked me just before Christmas. Still got me home, thank the Lord—but I has to scratch a living where I can. Not welcome in many yards round here, I can tell you, thanks to her ladyship. Not that I did nothing wrong—but mud sticks, don't it? There's not much going for me in the old nine-to-five lark—but if you're looking for a bit of work, no doubt I could point you in the right direction.'

More drinks were bought. Vincent made a show of patting his pockets and proclaiming in great distress that his wallet must have been nicked at the service station.

Ned patted his shoulder. 'Never you fear, mate. I'm not short of a bob or two.' He tapped the side of his nose. 'Know what I mean?'

'Little jobs pay well round here then, do they?'

'Little jobs pay piss-poor like they does everywhere.' Ned scowled through his Guinness. 'But it pays to keep your ears open and yer mouth shut and be first in the queue at the bookies, if you get me drift. You looks like a man who likes a gamble, if you don't mind me saying?'

Vincent thought that he did mind. It was far too early to show his hand. He shrugged. 'Not really. A little flutter on the Derby, a fiver on the Grand National, that sort of thing. I'm a bit hazy when it comes to horses, to be honest.'

'Stick with me then, mate.' Ned wiped away the

Guinness traces with the back of his fist. 'There ain't nothing I don't know about gambling, nor horses come to that. You're in the right place here and no mistake. What brought you to these parts, anyway, if you're not into the nags?'

Vincent fudged a bit, playing with his beer mat, staring across the bar to where Kath Seaward and Ferdy Thornton had been joined by—hallelujah!— Matt Garside. Vincent was pretty sure that if Matt Garside had been riding Dragon Slayer in the National, and not that jerk, Charlie Somerset, all his financial problems would already be over.

'I hitched a lift. Had to go somewhere. Lorry driver dropped me off up the road. This seemed as good as anywhere. I can't stay in the shelter for more than three nights on the trot, you see.'

Ned smacked his gums together in sympathy. Vincent wondered if he hadn't gone a little over the top with the sob story. Apparently not.

'Well, Vince mate, this could be your lucky day. I've heard that they're looking for a gardener for Peapods. Fitzgerald's place. Heard of him, have you? Drew Fitzgerald?'

Vincent was on the point of nodding enthusiastically, and then remembered and shook his head. Christ! Drew Fitzgerald! A racehorse trainer! He could be working for a racehorse trainer! His eyes gleamed at the thought of all that inside information.

Aware that Ned was watching him, he assumed his hangdog expression again. 'I don't think so. He wants a gardener, you said?'

''s right. Should suit you down to the ground.'

Vincent, who knew less about gardening than he did about particle physics, tried to look positive.

90

Ned drained his Guinness and was standing up for refills. 'Got a nice yard. Nice bloke, Mr Fitzgerald. Lovely family. His lady-friend potters about a bit, but she's got a kiddie now and her own business to run, and I've heard on the grapevine that they're looking for someone to keep the weeds down, mow the lawns, do a bit of repair work round the place. What do you reckon?'

Vincent reckoned it sounded like hell but continued to grin. 'I'd have to find somewhere to live, though.'

'Cottage what goes with the job.' Ned scooped up Vincent's glass. 'Not much, mind you. Just a couple of rooms—but it'd be better than sleeping rough. Good like that, is Mr Fitzgerald. Allus gives accommodation to his staff. Tell you what, we'll have the next jar and then I'll show you where Peapods is. It won't hurt to ask, will it?'

Vincent watched Ned disappear into the scrum again, his brain working overtime. This was exactly what he'd wanted: chums with a stable insider; someone with the contacts that he lacked; someone with the knowledge that could turn his gambling from disaster to success; someone who would guarantee him winnings . . . Of course, he'd only toyed with the idea of actually living in the area— God knows what Jemima would say—but this was far too good an opportunity to miss. Especially actually living in a training yard!

There was one fly in the ointment. A rather unpleasant, wriggling fly. A not knowing a dandelion from a delphinium type of fly. Still, Vincent thought cheerfully, watching all the familiar faces from television racecourses passing merely inches in front of him, he'd always been able to persuade people that he knew exactly what he was talking about. Plausibility, that was the key. Not overdoing it—he'd come up with something, he was sure of it. He always had before.

He took the frothing pint from Ned's gnarled hands and felt a surge of excitement. Everyone's luck had to change, didn't it? He had a feeling that his just had.

A shadow fell across the table, blocking out the midday sunlight. Vincent looked up, but the tall gaunt figure didn't even seem aware of him. Kath Seaward was glaring at Ned.

'I've heard that you had the bloody nerve to go crawling to Drew for his handyman job! You've got some neck! After what you did to me! No trainer in the village will have you within spitting distance of their horses! You could have killed mine—you bastard!'

Ned muttered something into his Guinness. Vincent kept his eyes studiously on the tabletop. He was beginning to think that perhaps Ned wasn't quite the right choice for a best buddy in Milton St John. What the hell had he done to Kath Seaward's horses, for God's sake? Vincent liked animals— there was no way he'd condone anything nasty . . .

'And who's this?' Kath's invective speared towards the juke-box. 'Another one of your unsavoury cronies?' She leaned towards Vincent, peering from under the brim of a dirty white cap. 'A word to the wise—this man is a bad 'un. Don't you go getting sucked into any of his schemes.'

Not a good lady to cross, Vincent decided, giving Kath his most charming smile. 'Thanks for the advice, but there's no need. This—er—gentleman and I have only just met. I'm in the village for an interview—at Peapods. He was giving me directions.'

'Make sure that's all he damn well gives you.' Kath drew her bony shoulders together. 'Because if Drew and Maddy got wind of you being in cahoots with Ned Filkins you wouldn't get a sniff of any job!'

Vincent exhaled slowly as Kath marched away, slicing through the Cat and Fiddle's throng with the determined precision of a surgeon's scalpel. He had always followed Kath's horses, always had a bit of luck with them—especially the ones ridden by Matt Garside. She was an excellent trainer. But there had been some sort of scandal in the autumn, he remembered now, when a couple of her horses hadn't run as well as expected. Major gambling coups were suspected. The racing press had been full of dope-testing, but nothing had been proved, and Lancing Grange had emerged lily-white.

Vincent cast a rather worried eye over Ned. Had he been behind that, then? This was big-time stuff. He wasn't sure that it was quite what he'd planned. Ned, however, seemed remarkably unruffled.

'Silly cow. She can't get over the fact that she entered the wrong horses for the wrong races a couple of times. Didn't get the results she wanted. Had to blame someone—couldn't accept that maybe she'd made a mistake and sent out a couple of green 'uns before they were ready. I copped the blame. Still, no point in being bitter. Life's too short. Another pint, mate? Or do you want to go and find Mr F?'

Deciding that if he had another pint he'd probably forget who he was, Vincent stood up. The Cat and Fiddle's public bar dipped and swayed slightly, and Vincent caught hold of the edge of the table. This wouldn't be any good at all. No one would employ him if he staggered and slurred. What he needed was a brisk walk and several lungfuls of good clean downland air.

Once outside and squinting in the sunlight, Vincent followed the direction of Ned's twisted finger.

'Just down there on the curve,' Ned said. 'There's a little tumbledown cottage with a green roof on this side of the road, and Peapods' drive is dead opposite. The house is through the clock arch—if there's no one about, give 'em a shout in the yard, or go into the office. Okay?'

'Yes, thanks. But—shouldn't I have an appointment?'

'In Milton St John?' Ned roared at this civilised notion. 'Good God, no. If it's an appointment, it's VAT or double glazing! Just you show your face—oh, and maybe it wouldn't be a good idea to say you'd heard about the job from me. Mizz Seaward and Mr Fitzgerald are pretty close, you know? Like I said, mud sticks and all that. Look, good luck, mate, and I'll see you back in the bar later, okay?'

Vincent nodded his agreement, and as Ned dived back into the Cat and Fiddle's fray, he took a deep breath to steady himself.

It really was a pretty village, he thought, with the winding road and the bubbling brown stream running alongside. And, whether Ned was a wrong 'un or not, Vincent wasn't going to chuck away this sort of opportunity. He was a gambler, for heaven's sake! He'd spent his life throwing everything on to the turn of a card or the tumble of a dice—or, more relevantly here, the nose of a horse. Situations like

94

this were worth their weight in gold. How he'd cope if he got the job would be something to worry about later. A minor detail. The handyman part would be fine—he could knock in nails and repair gutters—but the gardening . . . Still, there were always library books and umpteen television programmes, weren't there? Vincent whistled cheerfully. He was sure he'd manage somehow. He always had before.

His optimism almost deserted him as he walked across the cobbled yard.

Drew Fitzgerald was a prominent trainer. No mug. Surely he'd see straight through him? And if he did, then Vincent's plans for a prosperous future would be scuppered before he'd even started. And Jemima? What the hell would Jemima say? She knew he'd never gardened in his life. And surely Jemima, of all people, would know exactly why he was living and working in Milton St John? He hoped against hope that he wouldn't run into his daughter today.

These worrying thoughts were interrupted as a tall, dark-haired man in jeans and T-shirt emerged from beneath the clock arch. A slight frown was followed by a friendly grin. 'Can I help you?'

Christ! Too late now. Recognising Drew from his numerous visits to racecourses, Vincent felt hopelessly star-struck.

'Er—yes. I've come about the post you're advertising. Gardener and handyman?'

'At last! Mr Benson, isn't it? You rang this morning?'

'Carlisle. Vincent Carlisle. And I—'

Drew was grinning even more broadly. 'My fault. I probably wrote it down wrongly. God, am I pleased to see you. We'd all but given up hope of

95

finding anyone. You've brought your references?'

Vincent, who'd taken the opportunity of calling in a few favours prior to the receivership, had elicited several glowing reports of his abilities from various colleagues. They had all stressed his honesty, hard-working attitude, integrity, and team spirit, and had conveniently left out what he was capable of doing. He nodded.

'Great.' Drew was walking back beneath the clock arch again, and beckoned Vincent to follow him. 'Come along and meet Maddy. She's the expert. I'm sure you'll get on really well. I know damn all about flowers and things.'

And that makes two of us, Vincent thought, following Drew Fitzgerald into the cool gloom of the ancient archway.

CHAPTER SEVEN

Jemima pocketed the key to the bookshop, and made her way across the lay-by to the Munchy Bar. Bronwyn Pugh was opening up the Village Stores for its Monday-morning onslaught, and waved to her. Having managed to avoid the anti-erotica meetings under the pretence of Maureen being a slave-driver, Jemima waved back. As she wasn't due behind the Munchy Bar's counter until half past seven, she'd sneaked a few minutes to open up her shop and simply stand and stare.

The shelves and counters were in place, the decorators had finished the green-and-gold decor, and the furniture for the sitters and browsers was stacked in a corner hermetically sealed in polythene. She'd touched everything, closing her eyes and imagining how it would be when the shelves were stocked with colour and the sisal floor was hidden by dozens of pairs of feet. She'd also tried adding a constantly ringing till to the fantasy, but realism insisted on creeping in. She'd been a bookseller for long enough not to have too many aspirations.

A small sound system had been fitted at one end of the shop and Jemima was planning to have audio books playing quietly. The realism reminded her that the shop would probably never make her fortune, but its mere existence was the embodiment of a dream.

And as soon as she started to make a profit she'd look for a house to buy, and then contact her father and invite him to live with her. As there was no telephone in Vincent's bedsit, she'd written to him, just to let him know that she was settling in well and about her job with Maureen. He hadn't replied yet. Vincent, she knew, would love Milton St John and, with her to keep him under control, would never slide back into his old ways.

Having sorted out the next ten years of her life at least, she'd locked the door behind her and breathed in the pink pearly mist of the downland morning. Oxford and Bookworms and Petra's Parties were all in another lifetime, she thought. Her future was here in Milton St John and, horse-racing or no, she'd have to make the best of it. She knew she was lucky to have the chance.

Tucking the glossy layers of hair behind her ears, Jemima lifted her face to the sun. She'd pulled a long beige dress over the top of her T-shirt that morning and hoped that she wouldn't bake to death. The newscasters on Thames Valley FM were drawing comparisons with the summer of '76 and warning of impending water restrictions and drought.

'Doom, gloom and despondency,' Gillian had said as she'd left the Vicarage. 'It's either too hot or too cold. We get two weeks of early sunshine and every programme is full of global destruction and skin cancer. Still, being England, it'll no doubt pee down for the rest of the summer.'

Jemima had been shocked to hear a vicar's wife saying pee.

Ribbons of horses were weaving their way to and from the gallops, and Jemima watched them. They were so beautiful: strong and gleaming with health, their gentle liquid eyes and their exquisitely intelligent heads turning to stare at her. It was such a pity that their natural strength and competitive spirit brought untold misery to so many people.

The stable lads, all dressed in jodhpurs and boots and bobbled crash hats, swayed past in the saddles, high above her. Some grinned. Nearly all of them called good morning. She returned the greetings and sighed. Horse-racing was the reason for the village's existence, and these people were hopefully going to be her customers. She'd have to compromise her principles if her dream was ever going to become reality. It would be pretty dumb, she thought with a grin, to slap a 'No Horsy People' notice on the shop door in the cavalier way people did with hawkers and free papers.

She had survived two weeks in Milton St John, and apart from an early problem with the char-grilling equipment, had settled in nicely at the Munchy Bar. The hours were long and the customers were non-stop, but she was used to working hard. And it was an ideal way to get to know the villagers. *Company*'s assertiveness training was beginning to pay off. She now only hid behind her hair and her glasses in very stressful moments, and took every opportunity to introduce herself as the bookshop's owner and to start canvassing business. However, she still became paralysed with shyness when anyone asked her about herself. After all, what was there to say? The product of a broken home, a redundant bookseller, a failed waitress, a failed lover. It was hardly the sort of exciting and vibrant past life that would keep people riveted.

It had amused Maureen greatly that Jemima found it impossible to differentiate between Milton St John's racing fraternity and what she still called 'normal' villagers.

'But they were lovely!' she'd protested, after Maddy Beckett and her jockey sister, Suzy, had left a five-pound tip under their saucer. 'Maddy—the one with the red hair and that totally gorgeous baby—is engaged to a *trainer?* And that pretty girl actually *rides* racehorses?'

'They don't all have horns and hooves, duck,' Maureen had giggled. 'And those other ladies—the ones who were getting so enthusiastic about your bookshop earlier—they're both trainers.'

'No!' Jemima had stopped wiping tables. 'But the really glamorous one looked like a TV presenter, and the other one spoke like the Queen! And they were both so knowledgeable about books!'

'Diana James-Jordan and Kimberley Small.' Maureen had hardly been able to conceal her delight at the bewilderment on Jemima's face. 'Two of the top lady trainers in the country—worth a fortune between 'em. And, if you don't mind me saying, duck—it sounds a bit snobby to be surprised that they can read.'

'Oh, I didn't mean—' Jemima had blushed. 'Well, it just seems—I mean—'

'Preconceived notions don't get you nowhere,' Maureen had said wisely, whisking the squeezy mustard bottle away from a gang of stable lads. 'People's people the world over—good and bad. Rich and poor. It don't matter what job they do. Like I said, it might be a good idea for you to go to a race meeting some time, just to find out what it's all about . . .'

She already knew what it was all about, Jemima had thought. It was about gambling. And gambling led to moving house a lot, not answering the door, and hearing her mother crying when the postman arrived. Not even the friendly Maddy and Suzy, or the erudite Diana and Kimberley, could make her forget just how damaging horse-racing was.

She pushed her glasses more firmly on to her nose and walked back into the Munchy Bar.

Maureen was already frying bacon and eggs in huge quantities. 'You see to the teas, duck. We'll get the breakfasts out of the way and then we'll sort out the coffee and pastries for elevenses. Okay?'

Jemima struggled with the industrial-sized tea-pot, and wondered, as she had done every day since she'd started working with Maureen, how on earth the stable lads—who all looked as though a puff of wind would blow them away—managed to consume such vast quantities of food.

It was nearly eleven before there was any lull. Most of the tables were now occupied by the more elderly residents of Milton St John, enjoying a cup of Douwe Egberts with their Bath Olivers. In deference to them, Maureen had switched off the fruit machines and silenced the juke-box. The Formica tables were covered with lace cloths, and bud vases had been arranged dead centre. This transformation occurred again for afternoon tea at three, thus keeping both lots of customers satisfied. Jemima was most impressed by this clever strategy on Maureen's part and wondered if she'd be able to manage something similar in the bookshop.

'Jemima!' Gillian Hutchinson stage-whispered from the doorway. 'Is it safe for me to come in?'

'Coast completely clear of Glen's fan club, if that's what you mean.' Jemima laughed. 'Bronwyn said she was far too busy to stop this morning and had a take-out, and Bathsheba left ten minutes ago. Coffee?'

'Please. Black, strong. Oh, and an ashtray. I'll sit here by the door and blow outwards.' Gillian, wearing something diaphanous and pale green, drifted in and sat down. 'I'm absolutely frazzled. I think I've got writer's block with a vengeance. Have you got time to join me?'

'Course she has.' Maureen appeared from the kitchen. 'She never takes her break properly. You go and sit down, duck, and I'll bring the coffees over.'

Fanning her face, Gillian looked anxiously at Jemima's dress and T-shirt. 'Goodness—aren't you boiling in that? I thought this morning that you were rather overdressed. Haven't you got any shorts?'

Jemima smothered a smile. Shorts had never featured in her wardrobe. 'I'll be fine. The breeze from the door sort of wafts through the layers. I've been in this student-hippie look for so long now that I think I'd feel naked in anything else.'

'You and naked don't seem to go together somehow. But I simply can't understand why you want to hide that beautiful figure behind all those dowdy clothes.' Gillian stopped suddenly, shaking her head. 'Oh, I'm sorry. That was crass of me.'

Maureen arrived with the coffees. 'You tell her, Gillian. Oh, I know I'm full to bursting at the moment, but we'd have 'em queuing out of the door if she put a pair of shorts on. Pretty girl like her shouldn't be all bundled up like my Brian's granny.'

Brian, Mr Maureen, was a long-distance lorry driver working out of Upton Poges, Gillian had informed her. He only got home at weekends.

'I've always dressed like this,' Jemima protested, laughing. 'It feels right. It's like some people develop into spandex, some become designer-label freaks, some want jeans and leather jackets. Me—I just like long, loose clothes. I think they make me invisible. People don't usually bother to give me a second glance.'

Maureen had bustled back to slicing buns for the lunchtime burgers. Gillian wrinkled her nose. 'Really? They must be mad. But you've had some boyfriends?'

'Loads, thanks.' Jemima grinned. 'But they took the trouble to get to know the me behind the grunge. That was my yardstick. The ones who only wanted instant physical attraction weren't worth knowing.'

Gillian leaned forward across the table, lowering her voice. 'Do you know, I've always longed to wear something skin-tight and sparkly—a bit like Maureen. I'd never be allowed to get away with it, though. Bathsheba Cox would go all Roman and demand three weeks of Hail Marys.' She sighed. 'Of course, I adore Glen, but there are drawbacks to being spiritually pure and morally perfect.'

'God, yes, I can imagine. Er—I mean, I couldn't even attempt it. It must be hell being a vicar's wife. Oh, sod it,' Jemima took refuge in her coffee. 'You have to admit that you're hardly a typical vicar's wife, though, don't you? Is that why the blue-rinse hit squad are gunning for you?'

'That, and the fact that they're consumed with lust for my husband. Bronwyn's okay, really. It's Bathsheba who can inject the real venom. Actually, my unsuitability caused several lively diocesan debates when Glen and I first got together. The ladies of the parish wrote to complain. Luckily the Bishop, bless him, loves me so he came out on my side.'

Jemima stared out of the open doorway over Gillian's head. The early-morning warmth had blossomed into full-blown heat, and Milton St John was shimmering again. Another string of horses wound its way along the High Street towards the Munchy Bar. 'Did you meet Glen in church, then? Did your eyes meet over the altar rail at Communion? Did your hands touch during the offertory?'

'You should be the one writing romance,' Gillian said. 'No, it was far more mundane. We met in Newbury. I was a hairdresser—Glen had just been appointed curate here and came in to get his hair cut. It sort of developed from there. I thought he was drop-dead gorgeous. I went all out for him— started going to church again, joining confirmation classes, everything. Not that it was too much of a hardship. I'd always been a Christian—I think the Bible is the greatest piece of literature ever. I mean—what an opening sentence: "On the first day God created the heaven and the earth . . ." It's almost as good as Dick Francis. You'd just have to read on to find out what happened next, wouldn't you?'

'I suppose you would. I'd never thought of it like that.' The horses were much closer now. About half a dozen of them. Their hooves were muffled on the baked road. Dust rose in spurting clouds, hovered and then fell. Jemima watched, drawn again by their beauty. 'And were you already writing? Before you met Glen?'

'Oh yes, I wrote short stories and articles as a hobby. It's taken me several years to become successful.' Gillian stopped and stared into her coffee cup. 'Actually, I meant to mention it before, but if Glen ever again brings up the amount of rent that you pay—I don't think he will—but, if he should, could you not tell him exactly how much you're really paying.'

'Yes, sure. But—'

'There's a very good reason.' Gillian blushed and watched the equine procession. 'Believe me. I don't make a habit of lying to Glen, but—well, let's just say that I have more money at the moment than he thinks I have. I'd rather he didn't know the source. I'd prefer it if he believed—at least for a while—that it came from you.'

Completely mystified, Jemima hoped that she wasn't being sucked into something iffy. Still, if Gillian was selling her body or peddling cannabis to the stable lads, it really wasn't any of her concern, was it? She wondered, fleetingly, if Bathsheba and

Bronwyn may have got wind of whatever Gillian was doing, and if this was the real reason behind their spiteful behaviour. God—she'd only been in the village for two weeks and she was already developing the mindset of a village biddy!

'Drew Fitzgerald's lot.' Maureen bounced up to them and nodded her head towards the horses that were now level with the doorway. She gave Jemima a sly grin. 'And even though he's in horse-racing up to his neck, he's dead handsome, isn't he?'

Jemima had to admit that he was. Very Mel Gibson in fact. He raised a hand in greeting.

'He's Maddy Beckett's man,' Maureen said. 'The one she's going to marry now his divorce is through.'

Lucky Maddy, Jemima thought, and smiled.

The smile wasn't lost on Gillian. 'We'll convert you yet. I expect the whole village will be invited when Drew and Maddy get married. And then you'll meet lots of lovely horsy men. I simply love weddings, don't you?'

'Not really.' Her coffee break over, Jemima stood up. 'I suppose you have to. It's part of the job description, surely?'

'Oh, I know. But there are parts of being Mrs Vicar that aren't so pleasant, especially the funerals. I'm supposed to be calm and caring and offer support and sympathy—and I always end up bawling my eyes out. Thankfully people live so long round here that we haven't had too many of those. But the weddings,' she was dewy-eyed, 'all that hope for the future and undying devotion . . . everyone looking so beautiful . . . the eternal vows . . .'

'Which in two out of three cases get broken

105

within the first five years.'

'Don't be such a cynic. Don't you believe in romance?'

'Definitely not.' Jemima picked up their empty cups. 'Romance equates with broken promises and broken hearts in my book. My men are strictly for fun—no strings.'

'And you don't mind being on your own?'

'I've never been on my own.' Jemima thought of the people who had crowded in and out of her twenty-eight-and-a-half years. 'But I'm manless by choice. They've been a pleasant addition to my life—but never the reason for it.'

Gillian frowned. 'That's just because you haven't met the right one. We've got oodles of single men-friends—we'll have to introduce you to them. Milton St John is simply seething with the most gorgeous jockeys.'

'That's what I've been telling her,' Maureen joined in. 'She hasn't seen any of them yet, you know. They're all too bloody weight-conscious and starving to set foot in here—more's the pity. I keep telling her she ought to go to a race meeting—'

'No way,' Jemima said firmly. She'd been convinced that Gillian Hutchinson would be firmly in the anti-racing camp. She was rather shocked to discover she wasn't. 'I disapprove of racing on principle—and gambling in particular. Jockeys are all cruel to animals, and I'm certainly not going out with someone who comes up to my knees.'

'Ouch! Were you dropped on your head by a bookie as a baby or something? All the horsy people I know in Milton St John absolutely dote on their animals. And let me assure you that jump jockeys are perfectly normal—in every way.' Gillian

106

lit another cigarette. 'Even some flat jockeys are taller than you. I'll have to ring round and invite a selection for supper—just to get you to change your mind.'

'Specially Charlie Somerset,' Maureen's leer was lascivious.

'Definitely Charlie Somerset,' Gillian affirmed with a grin.

'Please don't even think about it.' Jemima headed for the counter. 'If you start playing Mrs Bennet and introducing me to a lot of fox-chasing, horse-bashing, bandy-legged midgets, then I'll abandon the bookshop and be off to do something simpler—like brain surgery.'

'God forbid,' Gillian muttered, flapping the hem of the floaty green dress and scattering cigarette ash over Maureen's just-wiped table. 'And don't knock what you haven't experienced.'

Jemima paused in refilling the coffee percolator. 'What? Being a brain surgeon?'

'No,' Gillian shook her head. 'The men of Milton St John.'

CHAPTER EIGHT

Charlie Somerset turned the bridle over in his hands. It comforted him. The feel of the softened leather, the smell, even the way it gleamed in the shafts of dusty sunlight splintering through the high tack-room window, gave him a feeling of security.

He'd cleaned tack since he was old enough to walk. It didn't matter whether it had been at home in the well-appointed hunting yard of the Somerset mansion, or in David Nicholson's high-profile set-up where he'd served his apprenticeship, or those glorious early years with Franklin Pettigrove when he'd been champion jockey, he'd always enjoyed cleaning tack.

Odd really, when most of the lads hated it, and he, being naturally lazy, shied away from any sort of organised labour. But cleaning tack had never seemed like work: it relaxed him and gave him time to think. And today, there were a hell of a lot of things to think about.

Peapods' tack-room, dark apart from the one window, and cluttered with bridles and bits, girths and rugs, all hanging from the overhead hooks, offered him sanctuary. Even the perpetual aroma of dried mud, mingled with sweat and wet leather and warm, foetid air, was pleasing. If he'd stayed in his cottage the phone would ring, or someone would knock on the door. This afternoon he didn't want to talk to anyone.

More than anything, he wanted something calorie-laden to eat and a pint of beer, but he knew he could afford to have neither. Kath Seaward's barbs at Aintree had penetrated deeply. She had been right. If he was ever going to achieve that ultimate jump-racing accolade, he'd have to get in shape. His new fitness regime took in boiled eggs, steamed chicken, and unadulterated pasta. If he was lucky he could even squeeze in a glass of slimline tonic.

He pushed the collection of empty coffee cups, whips, and crash hats a bit further along the bench and applied more dubbin. The small circular movements were as reassuring as smoking and, as Charlie hadn't had a cigarette for twelve-and-a-half days, it gave him something to do with his hands.

This thought led, naturally, to thoughts of Tina Maloret. Charlie sighed. The days in London with her had been as energetic and inventive as usual—and he'd probably burned off more calories than he could have hoped for with any of the expensive diet sheets that littered his cottage. He knew, as every jockey knew, that there was really only one way to lose weight. Not eat and sweat. As he and Tina had scarcely emerged from the bedroom in her West London flat, he felt he'd met the criteria pretty well.

It bothered him to realise, as he ran the bridle through his fingers and replaced the dubbin with brass cleaner, that he'd been almost glad to leave. Of course, Tina was physically gorgeous. Her angular, long-limbed body never failed to excite him. Her ferocious temper, however, didn't. She didn't suffer fools gladly, and would scream and bawl if things weren't exactly to her liking. Charlie, being peaceable and easy-going, sometimes found her tantrums hard to cope with. He'd implore her not to shout, not to express her displeasure—whether it be with a waiter, a taxi-driver or him—quite so loudly. And, despite her profession, Tina was no air-head. She took only the assignments that paid the most money, had a rock-solid shares portfolio, made sure she was in the right place at the right time, and read all the heavyweight Sunday supplements so that she could discuss politics and world affairs, or rave over the latest art exhibition or literary novel, with all the right people.

But there seemed to him to be something wrong with a lifestyle which appeared to involve an enormous amount of pleasure-seeking, and very little giving. Not just in bed, either. When they did venture outside the flat, the giddy whirl of parties and premières, clubs and trendy restaurants, seemed as shallow as Milton St John's brook. Charlie held the buckles up to the sun. He must be getting old. On that last night in London he'd thought longingly of his cottage, of Peapods, of the horses, of riding, of the village. And, most of all, of winning the Grand National.

He'd ridden in the National five times while he'd been with Franklin Pettigrove, and although he'd never finished higher than sixth, he had at least always completed the course. That was why the fall from Dragon Slayer was so galling. Surely he would never have a better chance? The horse was out of this world, the race had been his for the taking. And he'd blown it. No one, not even Drew, knew just how humiliated he had been. And no one knew how fiercely determined he was now to show that next year, he could do it. He *could* win the National.

He and Drew had discussed Kath's wager over and over again, watching the dawn breaking across Peapods' cobbles, each of them knowing that it was more than a friendly challenge between rival yards. It meant survival.

The whole business of being a jump jockey was so damn precarious. Applying more Brasso carefully to the buckles, Charlie told himself how lucky he was to still have a future, however brief its duration might be. Fortunately, his disaster on Dragon Slayer had been a seven-day wonder in the village. There was always another triumph, a further catastrophe, to become hot gossip in Milton St John. Apart from Kath Seaward, most of those

110

involved at Aintree, and nearly all those who had backed him, had forgiven him. But he still had so much to prove. It was the one prize that had so far evaded him.

Was there a chance with Drew? There was certainly no chance without him. Charlie was well aware that there were plenty of new apprentices coming up, more fit, less battle-scarred than him. Always supposing Drew found a suitable horse in time, this would be his last shot at it. And if Drew decided to cut his losses and merely run the flat-racing side of the yard in future—which looked increasingly likely—he'd never get another offer. What would be left then? A racing hack for one of the papers? A TV commentator? Without the National under his belt, they'd all seem like consolation prizes. Charlie, desperate for a cigarette, grabbed at yet another bridle.

He was still industriously polishing when Maddy, carrying Poppy Scarlet and accompanied by all four dogs, appeared in the tack-room doorway.

'Don't let me stop you. I like to see a man working.' She plonked Poppy on to his lap amidst the bridles. 'Show Poppy the ropes, Charlie. Drew needs all the unpaid labour he can get.'

The dogs snuffled noisily in the corners, tails wagging. Charlie cuddled Poppy and kissed her. He adored his goddaughter. He reckoned he'd make a brilliant father. Still, no point thinking along those lines, was there? He raised his eyebrows. 'As bad as that?'

'You bloody know it is.' Maddy cleared away more paraphernalia and sat beside him. 'Where is Drew, anyway? I thought he'd be in the yard somewhere.'

'Office, I think. Talking to Alister.'

'Oh. Right.' Maddy stretched her legs out in front of her. 'I wanted to tell him that the new gardener—Vincent—has just arrived. I've left him moving his stuff—what there is of it, poor man—into the cottage. Such a sad life—lost his wife and his home . . . Still, he knows everything there is to know about gardening—and his references were out of this world. We were lucky to get him. I've invited him to supper. He doesn't look like he's had a decent meal for weeks.'

Charlie grinned. Drew and Maddy immediately made everyone at Peapods part of their extended family. It was probably the only yard in Milton St John that kept the same stable staff for more than a season.

'Lucky bastard.' Charlie jangled the bridle just out of Poppy's reach and thought longingly of Maddy's incredible cooking. 'Tell me to shut up, Mad, but can you afford him? Vincent, I mean? I thought—'

'Don't.' Maddy pulled an agonised face and pushed her head back against the tack-room wall. 'I've promised Drew I'll pay his wages out of my Shadows money. When we advertised earlier in the season, I don't think either of us realised how dire things were going to be. It's just that I need to work full-time—and if I do then this place needs someone to look after it. I can take Poppy to work with me, but I can't take the house and the garden. Whether we can afford him or not remains to be seen.'

'You know I'd help you out if I could.' Charlie lifted Poppy high into the air, making her squeal with laughter. It was a sore point. The Somerset money was all tied up in ninety-year investment bonds or something equally unhelpful. His mother held on to the purse-strings with tightly clenched fingers. He lived, comfortably at the moment, on his racing income and his overdraft. 'Still, maybe Drew's discussing new owners with Alister?'

'And maybe he isn't.' Maddy screwed her curls into a knot on the top of her head. 'I certainly haven't been aware of the Maktoum family queuing on the doorstep. And thanks for your offer—but I know you're in the same boat. We've all been guilty of living over our limits and not giving a toss about the consequences. Anyway, what are you doing in here? Why aren't you out pillaging the village maidens?'

'Didn't feel like it. I'm getting seriously worried about myself, actually. I was indulging in lurid thoughts about fish and chips and lager.'

Maddy giggled. 'Really? You weren't having a fantasy about Gillian Hutchinson smothering you with them, were you? And you can't fool me. I know you fancy her. You're disgusting, Charlie. Really—'

'Oh, come on, Mad. The Vicar's wife! Give me some credit.' He jiggled Poppy again. He really would have to be less obvious. Even he had standards. 'Anyway, Tina does it with beluga caviar and champagne.'

'Still on then, are you? You and the stalking clothes-horse?'

'Just about. She's more or less forgiven me for spoiling her moment of Grand National glory— but it took all my powers of persuasion. Thankfully she's off on the Italian catwalks for a couple of weeks, which should give my back time to heal.'

'You honestly are incorrigible!' Maddy leaned across and squeezed his arm. 'When are you going to settle down and find yourself a wife?'

Charlie kissed the top of Poppy's head again. She smelled lovely. The recent hot weather had meant a rash of shorts and skimpy tops in Milton St John. There really were some gorgeous women about. How on earth could any red-blooded male settle for just one? 'I've never seen the point of having a wife of my own when I can have everyone else's.'

'If I thought you meant that I'd never speak to you again! Seriously though, Charlie—haven't you ever thought about it? Getting married?'

He hadn't. It had always seemed a pretty scary thing to do. 'I'm not lucky in love—unlike some. Which reminds me—when are you going to ask me to be best man?'

'What?'

'Well, Drew told me that the divorce will be through in September. Obviously you'll be getting married straightaway, and I thought I'd be the obvious choice as best man. Still, if you've chosen someone else, can I be chief bridesmaid instead?'

Maddy lifted Poppy from Charlie's arms, whistled the dogs, and stood up. 'I don't really want to talk about weddings yet. I mean, Drew and I are brilliant as we are. I can't understand why he wants to leap into another marriage as soon as his divorce from Caroline comes through.' She smiled. It didn't quite reach her eyes. 'Look, I'm going to take Poppy down to the duck pond. She likes it better than our own pool. I think ours is a bit too PC for her. If you see Drew, be an angel and tell him where we are. Oh, and that Vincent has arrived.'

Charlie watched her disappear across Peapods'

cobbles and pulled a face. He'd been certain that Maddy would be simply bursting with enthusiasm for getting married. Still, it just went to show. You never knew where you were with women—thank God.

Of course, Maddy was aware of the precarious financial situation at Peapods, and probably didn't want to cause Drew any more unnecessary expense. He hoped that's all it was. Dear God—he'd always thought that Maddy and Drew's relationship was rock solid. They were one of the few couples he knew who were truly right for each other. They had love and laughter, friendship and understanding by the bucketful.

Tiring of the bridles at last, Charlie stuffed everything back into the tack cupboard and leaned on the door until it shut. The next unfortunate lad to open it would no doubt be buried beneath an avalanche of dirty cloths and dubbin.

He wandered along the row of boxes in the first yard. The closed doors, indicating no inmates, looked like pulled teeth. The Epsom meeting was just over a week away. Drew's five entries at the early stages for the Derby Day races had all been withdrawn. Even the most optimistic owner was aware that they didn't stand a chance. It was no surprise, then, that on a midweek May day, when the flat was firing on all cylinders, both Drew and his assistant trainer were in situ at Peapods. Again, the yard had no runners.

Dock of the Bay had acquitted himself well at Bath and Windsor, and three horses were due to run the following day at Brighton. But they were small tracks, and the prize money was comparatively meagre. Racing was cutthroat business, and one where only the strong survived. Trainers were going belly-up all the time. Poor Drew, Charlie thought. And poor him if nothing else turned up.

A small boy emerged suddenly from beneath the clock arch, causing the horses to clatter in their boxes, and cannoned into him. 'Oh, bugger! Sorry! Didn't see you—I was taking a short cut and—Oh, hello, Mr Somerset, it's you.'

Charlie looked down into a pair of pale green eyes glittering up at him from beneath a ginger fringe. One of Gillian Hutchinson's sons—he hadn't got a clue which one. God—was school out already? Where the hell had the day gone? 'No problem. No damage caused. But you really mustn't run in the yard. The horses don't like it. Who's chasing you?'

'Tyler an' Nathan.' The child was darting looks over his shoulder. 'I think they might have got Ezekiel!'

Really, Charlie thought, Gillian and Glen should have more sense than lumbering the kids with those appalling names, especially in a village where their compatriots were all called Wayne and Jason. They might as well have had 'Punch me' tattooed on their foreheads at the christening.

'Why?'

''Cause we beat 'em up in the playground. They said Mum was on drugs. They said she looks like a hippie.'

Charlie thought that maybe Tyler and Nathan had a point. 'You shouldn't really be in here, though, should you? And is your brother—er, Ezekiel—here too?'

'Somewhere. Sorry.' The child grinned gappily.

116

'Jemima calls us Levi and Zeke. Cool, huh?'

Who? Ah, yes . . . Jemima. The grunge granny from the bookshop who was renting the vicarage flat. Charlie nodded. No point in not putting in a bid. 'I've heard she's really pretty.'

'God, no! She's old! I mean—as olds go I s'pose she's all right. She's working in the Munchy Bar 'til her shop's ready, and brings us crisps and Coke and stuff every night. She wears glasses.'

Charlie quite liked women who wore glasses. They always reminded him of the matron at his prep school, who had had enormous bosoms and incredible legs, and about whom everyone had fantasised. Working in the Munchy Bar was a definite no-no, though. With his current starvation regime he was giving the place a wide berth. Just the aroma of bacon and eggs would have him drooling. He'd have to wait until the bookshop opened to give her the once-over.

'Mega!' Levi grinned suddenly. 'Zeke's okay!'

The second Hutchinson twin emerged unscathed from the clock arch. 'They think we've cut through the pub car park,' he panted at his brother. 'Thick as planks—Oh, hello, Mr Somerset.'

Charlie repeated the no trespassing speech, and again began to feel extremely old. Just when had he started to become responsible? Bloody hell! Was he growing up at last?

The Hutchinson twins, promising never to run through Peapods again and looking slightly crestfallen, started to walk away across the cobbles just as Drew emerged from the office. They darted a look in his direction and then, immediately forgetting Charlie's warning, took to their heels.

'It's okay, I've read them the riot act,' Charlie

started, then looked at Drew. 'What's up?'

'I've let Alister go.'

Charlie blinked. Sacking your assistant trainer at this stage of the season was a major disaster. 'Why? What's he done?'

'Nothing.' Drew exhaled. His face was grey. 'Well, nothing wrong, poor bugger. Ferdy Thornton's offered him a job—far more than I'm paying. Alister didn't want to leave, but he's got a family to support. He asked me if I could match Ferdy's salary—I couldn't.' Drew stared across the yard. 'We've parted on good terms, thank God. I don't blame him.'

Charlie, who had never, not even at Radley, hugged another man, really wanted to hug Drew. 'Shit. I'm so sorry. Is there anything at all I can do?'

'Start learning how to train.' Drew shoved his hands in the pockets of his jeans. 'You might need to know how. I certainly can't afford a replacement.'

'No problem. I need to look to my future anyway . . .'

'I'm beginning to think I haven't got one.'

'If you want to tell Maddy, she's taken Poppy Scarlet to feed the ducks.' Charlie decided that it wasn't the best moment to inform Drew of Vincent's arrival on the Peapods payroll.

'I don't want to talk to her yet. I can't tell her.' Drew started to walk away across the yard. 'I'm going to the Cat and Fiddle for intravenous Glenfiddich. You might have to start evening stables without me.'

The air of gloom deepened. Charlie looked up at the flax-flower blue of the sky, hazy with the heat still rolling from the Downs, and wondered whether praying would help. He wasn't too hot on praying except when he was racing. Maybe he should ask Gillian if there was a set formula for making requests to God. Niggling away in the back of his mind was the stentorian voice of his religious education master: '. . . and remember, when you ask God for favours, that no is an answer, too . . .'

Charlie looked across the yard, wondering if he could join Drew in the pub and pretend that Diet Coke was gin, and frowned. There was a crowd at the end of the drive. Not more bloody kids! He started to walk up the yard towards them and suddenly grinned. That was better. Maybe God was being receptive after all.

A crowd of schoolgirls were hanging around Peapods' gate. They often did, of course. Pony-mad kids were part of racing life. But these weren't children from the village school. These were leggy, pretty, fresh-faced. Hopefully they weren't just interested in Peapods' equine residents. A doting teenage fan club would do his ego no harm at all, and would fill in the time while Tina was away. And they'd be absolutely ideal to take his mind off the slender and fragile forbidden fruit of Gillian Hutchinson.

One of the schoolgirls smiled at him. 'Charlie?'

'Yeah?'

She was pretty. Very. Olive-skinned. Long black hair in a single plait. The blue-and-white striped dress, yanked up to mid-thigh by an elasticated money belt, indicated that she'd come straight from the convent's highly-priced classroom.

'Don't you remember me?'

He shook his head. The gang of girls with her were giggling shrilly. She didn't look like a giggler,

119

though. How old was she? Fifteen? Sixteen at a push? Going on thirty. 'Sorry. Should I?'

'You taught me to ride. Years ago. When you were with Mr Pettigrove. I've been away at boarding school. I'm back to do A-levels at St Hilda's. You haven't changed at all.'

She had, though, Charlie thought, whoever she was. He'd taught quite a few of the village children to ride when he'd first arrived in Milton St John ten years earlier. She might just be seventeen, then. 'Sorry—I really don't remember your name.'

'Lucinda.' She smiled at him, turning away, tossing the plait across her shoulder. 'Lucinda Cox. It's nice to see you again.'

'And you.' Charlie beamed, although the name meant nothing to him. Presumably she was old enough to drink? It was worth a try. 'Look, I've finished here. Do you fancy a drink in the Cat and Fiddle? Talk over old times . . .'

'Why not?'

The giggling group got louder. Lucinda stared at them with disdain.

God, Charlie thought, they must teach sang-froid at St Hilda's. She smelled of soap and youth and fresh air, he noticed as he got closer. So different to Tina Maloret's unpronounceable French perfume and American cosmetics.

Lucinda Cox, Charlie decided, could be exactly what he needed.

CHAPTER NINE

There was something wrong. He wasn't in his own bed. The sheets felt soft against his skin, and they smelled of fresh air. Everything smelled of fresh air, actually. There was no sour, stale stench. Maybe he was still asleep. Maybe he was dreaming. And if he wasn't, then the noises were wrong too. There weren't any. No repetitive bass of rap music, no screaming children, no warring couples. Was he ill? In a coma? Dead?

Vincent opened his eyes. The sun, just hazy through the flowery curtains, cast a golden glow across a small well-polished oak wardrobe and matching dressing table. The bed, also oak, was flanked by twin bedside tables with brass lamps. There was a carpet on the floor. It was neat and clean and homely. Homely . . . His new home . . . Vincent rolled over on the deep feather pillows and swallowed the lump in his throat.

Last night he'd had the best meal he'd ever had in his life: sitting in Peapods' kitchen, with Drew Fitzgerald—Vincent still couldn't quite believe that part—while Maddy heaped his plate over and over again. Then they'd taken their cups of coffee outside under the chestnut trees and Maddy—who was absolutely gorgeous—had explained how she'd planned the garden, and started to develop it, and how she'd like him to continue with it—but only if he felt it was right, him being such an expert . . .

Vincent groaned and pulled the sweet-smelling sheet over his face at the memory. They were so *nice.* It seemed the worst kind of deception. He'd almost confessed all at that point. Almost, but not quite. He knew what he was going to do, and the long-term end would surely justify the short-term means. He wouldn't be taking money from Drew and Maddy under false pretences. He'd get the hang of gardening if it killed him.

He'd then endured an excruciating hour being shown round rockeries and shrubberies and perennial borders. He'd nodded and smiled and told Maddy that everything she'd done so far was just perfect and he'd be delighted to carry on with her schemes. There had been one particularly horrendous moment when she'd got very technical over various types of clematis. Vincent, who'd thought that they were a kind of small orange, made some remark about not seeing much of them except around Christmas. Maddy had looked at him in amazement, and said he must be thinking of some evergreen hardy varieties she hadn't heard of, and please, please could he get her some?

Possibly even more difficult had been Drew's twilight trip round the stables. Vincent, who had to pretend total ignorance of all things equine, had almost immediately blown his cover by being able to quote Dock of the Bay's racing form, chapter and verse. This time it was Drew who had looked at him in surprise.

'Er—I—um—looked it up,' Vincent had muttered. 'I thought I—er—ought to know a bit about it . . .'

Fortunately Drew had nodded and accepted it without further question. In fact, Vincent reckoned, if he wasn't much mistaken, Drew had had a fair bit to drink even before the wine they'd had with supper, not to mention the whisky afterwards. He

122

liked that. He liked a man who enjoyed a drink.

Anyway—he eased himself up in the bed, luxuriating in the softness—there were loads of things to do today. Maddy was going to show him the shed where the equipment was kept, and the greenhouse with the cuttings and seedlings, and the files with the maintenance history of the house. She'd like him to sort out the walled garden, she'd said. Just to break him in gently. He thought he'd cope okay. He had brought some books. One of them was bound to cover walled gardens. And a walled garden sounded almost urban. It was sure to be concrete. So, at least today's gardening wouldn't hurl too many hazards his way. And then there was Jemima . . .

Vincent sat on the edge of the bed. He could hear birds now, and the rattle of hooves on the cobbles. The stable lads were shouting, but it was cheerful, not aggressive. Even the swearing sounded chummy. He pinched himself. He, Vincent Carlisle, was *living* in a racing yard!

Now, where had he been? Ah, yes . . . Jemima. He pulled his threadbare dressing gown round him and walked into the kitchen. The cottage's four rooms were tiny, but compared to his bedsit they were palatial. And one day soon, Vincent thought cheerfully, slopping water into the kettle, he'd have a house again. A huge house, the sort of house which he deserved. Somewhere he could be proud of, and somewhere Jemima would be able to call home.

He carried his cup of tea to the window. Horses were being led out of boxes, the dogs weaving in and out of the skittering legs, while bleary-eyed stable lads were getting instructions from an equally bleary-eyed Drew Fitzgerald. Vincent chuckled. That was a hangover and a half if ever he'd seen one!

The horses clattered sideways, blowing frothily, tossing their heads. Vincent's eyes misted. He'd never seen anything more beautiful. He gulped his tea. It didn't matter what Jemima said when she found out that he was here; it didn't matter that he'd make a better concert pianist than a gardener. He was due a change of fortune, wasn't he? And this—unseen behind the flowery curtains he raised a teacup salute to Drew's first lot—was definitely it.

After a quick shower—Maddy, bless her, had not only stocked his larder but his bathroom too— Vincent dressed. Fortunately most of his clothes looked ideal for gardening. He'd brought very few with him. He'd brought very little of anything, actually, apart from the books, having made the journey from his bedsit to Milton St John by bus, which had involved four different changes. It was sheer luck, Vincent thought, that all his worldly goods divided neady into three carrier bags. Anymore and the transport situation would have been insurmountable.

Most of the stuff he'd been left with after his company had gone into receivership had been hocked for gambling stakes months before. And of course Rosemary had taken any of the furniture that remained after the bailiff's final visit. He hadn't begrudged her it. It wasn't much to show for all those years of marriage, after all. She'd stuck with him for far longer than he'd expected. He had loved Rosemary very much. He still did. Love, unlike hate, Vincent found, had a habit of hanging on.

He bent down to tie his shoes but couldn't quite see the laces. Bugger. He wiped the back of his hand across his eyes. Rosemary would never come back. He knew that. He had hurt her too many times. It was far too late to make amends to Rosemary—but Jemima . . . Oh, yes, he'd make everything wonderful for Jemima.

He had her letter in his pocket. It had arrived at his bedsit just after he'd got the Peapods job but he hadn't actually received it until three days later because Greg downstairs, who wasn't very bright and couldn't read, accosted the postman in the lobby each morning and thought all the letters were for him. If you were expecting a giro or anything, you had to get up really early to beat Greg. The bedsit residents raided Greg's room twice a week to retrieve their mail.

Anyway, he thought, closing his front door behind him and breathing in the horsy air, he'd go and see Jemima at the Munchy Bar this afternoon. It would be preferable to calling at her flat. He knew Jemima. However furious she was, she'd never blow her top in front of other people. It would be far safer to tell her his news in a crowded café rather than in the privacy of her flat where he might not be able to supply all the answers. And, he reckoned, digging his hands into the pockets of his corduroys, she'd surely see that it was all for the best. They'd be living close again, after all this time. They could be like a proper father and daughter. He sighed. He'd been a lousy husband. He only hoped it wasn't too late to make up for his paternal shortcomings.

*   *   *

125

'. . . and that's it, really,' Maddy said, trying to keep the dogs from burrowing excitedly in the borders and failing. 'You're lucky we've had such a hot spell—it's kept the weeds down. They go mad after rain, don't they?'

'Completely berserk,' Vincent agreed, peering again at the walled garden. It looked very weedy to him. All those things sprouting out of the bricks and up between the gravel. He'd be able to get rid of those. And roses? Roses, Vincent knew, had thorns. There was a big thorny thing growing up one wall with frothy bushes underneath. He'd cope with that first.

'Don't worry about the pinks,' Maddy was saying. 'They take care of themselves.'

Pinks? What pinks? Everything looked green. Still, if he didn't have to worry about them then it didn't matter if he couldn't see them, did it? There were a lot of clumpy grey things. Weeds. Definitely weeds. Vincent earmarked them for decimation.

Maddy at last managed to get the dogs under control. 'I don't know how things were done at your last place, and of course, we've never had a gardener before—but I thought once we get organised, if I leave a list of things that need doing in the office every morning, then you can sort out your own agenda. Does that sound all right to you?'

Vincent said that it sounded just the job and Maddy sighed happily. They walked along a further maze of crazy-paved paths, while Maddy muttered words like rudbeckias and ajuga and limnanthes. He wished he could write them down.

'And we keep the herb garden going here.' Maddy stopped and, crouching down, pointed at

126

a rather overgrown patch just inside the garden's crumbling arch. 'Well, I do, I mean. Drew still thinks herbs come out of Schwartz jars.'

Vincent, who was amazed to hear that they didn't, remembered to laugh.

'That's about it really.' Maddy straightened up, pushing her hands into the small of her back. 'No doubt you'll soon get the feel of the place. The mowing machine is in the shed along with everything else—and you said you were an expert on water gardens, didn't you?'

Vincent was afraid he might have done, during the interview.

Maddy grinned. 'Ours is very embryonic, of course. But if you want to extend it, then go ahead. You've got a free hand. Now, if you'll excuse me I've got to get to work. Drew is going to be at Brighton races all day, but if you need anything, Holly will be in the office. Take breaks whenever you want—and have your lunch in the hostel with the lads. They usually get a two-course meal there and then go down to the Munchy Bar.' She stopped and stretched out her hand. 'I do hope you'll be happy here, Vincent. I know how lousy things have been for you. We'll try and help however we can.'

God help him! He'd far, far rather be going to Brighton with Drew. Vincent looked into the warm and trusting green eyes and hated himself. 'Thank you. You've both been very kind. And the cottage is great. Really lovely. I'm sure everything will be just fine.'

*　　*　　*

Piece of cake, he thought, three hours later, easing

127

his aching muscles and looking with pleasure at the heaped wheelbarrow beside him. He still hadn't discovered anything pink, but the nasty little spiky grey things had all been pulled up. He had left the big thing with thorns—a sort of gigantic rose, he reckoned, rampaging its way up the wall, and dug out all the spindly truncated bushes beneath it. The walls and paving slabs were clear; he'd gouged out every last invasive sprout. Maddy, he was sure, would be delighted.

The sun was spiralling overhead, and not having stopped at all, Vincent decided it must be time for a break. Maybe it would be politic to visit the Munchy Bar now, rather than leave it until lunch-time when it was obviously going to be crowded. Emptying the wheelbarrow into the composter as instructed, Vincent had a quick wash in his bathroom—hot water and clean towels—and set off for the village.

Maybe, if Jemima didn't mind, they'd go to the Cat and Fiddle. He'd like to see Ned Filkins again. He'd like to thank him for pointing him in Peapods' direction that fateful day. He wasn't totally sure that Ned Filkins was on the straight and narrow— but he had contacts, and contacts were what Vincent needed to get his scheme off the ground. And quickly.

The Munchy Bar wasn't quite what he'd expected. For a start there was no sign of Jemima, and he'd expected it to be a bit more, well, laddish. It was all lace doilies and Miss Marple. Several tables were occupied by elderly ladies having coffee and brushing crumbs from the front of flat Moygashel chests.

Not a problem for the lady behind the counter, though, Vincent thought, as Maureen's prow-head bosoms sailed towards him.

'Yes, duck? What can I get you?'

Vincent studied the comprehensive menu. It was most impressive. Burgers and Knickerbocker Glories, however, didn't seem to be the number-one choice for the current genteel clientele. He smiled. Clever. Very clever. Running with the fox and hunting with the hounds, so to speak.

'I'm spoiled for choice,' he said, admiring not only Maureen's statuesque figure but also the sparkly eye-shadow. He liked a woman who knew how to make the most of herself. 'Lovely day, isn't it?'

'Ah.' Maureen's tower of peroxided hair nodded. 'But it'll be wet afore night, you mark my words.'

Vincent studied the cerulean sky through the open doorway Not a cloud on the horizon. 'Are you sure?'

'Sure as eggs. The cows was all lying down this morning, see. That's a sure sign.'

Vincent's brow furrowed. Didn't cows sleep lying down, then? There seemed to be an awful lot to learn. He raised an enquiring eyebrow.

Maureen chuckled. 'They can sense the rain on the wind long before we can. They secures themselves a nice warm dry patch for later. Clever buggers, is cows. Now, when you've made up your mind, you get yourself a seat and I'll be over.'

Vincent settled for a pot of tea and a slice of lardy cake and a seat by the window.

Maureen brought it across, an unseen petticoat rustling tantalisingly beneath a very tight black skirt. 'Haven't seen you in here before. New, are you? Or passing through?'

'New.' Vincent paid her with a collection of coins. It was practically all that remained of his last benefit giro. Maybe he'd have to glean a bit of info from Ned Filkins. Just to make ends meet until pay-day. 'I've just moved in.'

'Ah.' Maureen nodded. 'You'll be the new gardener up at Peapods, then. Bronwyn and Bathsheba said you'd arrived.'

Vincent blinked at this accurate information-gathering system. 'That's right—um—?'

'Maureen, duck. And you are?'

'The new gardener at Peapods.' Vincent hoped his grin was roguish. He didn't actually want his name bandied around. Not just yet.

'Get away with you!' Maureen's beehive rocked alarmingly. 'I can see you and me are going to get on just great, duck! Now, if there's anything you wants to know, you just ask me.'

Vincent sipped his tea. It was very good. Strong and hot. 'There is one thing. I believe you have an assistant working here? Jemima? Jemima Carlisle? Is it her morning off?'

'Jemima don't take time off, duck.' Questions were flickering across Maureen's sharp eyes. 'She's out the back preparing the salads. Did you want a word? Message from Peapods, is it? Maddy said she'd try and persuade her to go racing . . .'

Maddy might as well try and persuade the world to stop turning, Vincent thought. 'Something like that. Yes, if I could just see her for a minute? Would that be all right?'

'I'll send her out. Shall I say who wants her—?'

'I'd like it to be a surprise, actually.' Vincent winked.

To his delight, Maureen winked back. 'Okay,

130

duck. Whatever you want.'

Vincent bit into the lardy cake. It squelched in a most satisfactory manner. Probably a good idea to stoke up the system with a few carbohydrates. Jemima may not be a screamer, but she could put up one hell of a mental battle.

He saw her before she saw him. She looked very well. She was an extremely attractive girl—even if she wasn't aware of it. That glorious glossy hair— so exactly like Rosemary's that it caused him to bite his lip—fell forward in shaggy layers, and she was wearing a rather pretty, if shapeless, long cotton frock. There was a look of surprise on her face as she scanned the Munchy Bar. Oh, love her! She wasn't wearing her glasses. She'd never spot him. Vincent half stood up. Several elderly ladies turned to stare.

'Jemima! Over here!'

'Dad?' She scrabbled in the frock's pocket for her glasses, blinked, then smiled in delight. 'Dad! What on earth are you doing here?'

*　　*　　*

It had been every bit as difficult as he'd expected. Oh, not at first. At first, Jemima had been gratifyingly pleased to see him. She'd chattered non-stop about her flat and about the developments at the bookshop and about the people she'd met. She oozed enthusiasm for Maureen and the Munchy Bar and Milton St John in general. It was only when she stopped to draw breath and asked him about his unannounced appearance, that the rot had set in.

He'd fudged, naturally. But not for long. Jemima

131

was far too astute for any of that sort of nonsense.

'Of course I'm pleased you're here. And I'm delighted that you're working. But why didn't you tell me that you'd been offered a job? And you don't know anything about *gardening*?' she hissed across the table. 'You can cope with building and plumbing and electricals—but *gardening*. And in a racing stables? Sorry, Dad, but it won't wash.'

Vincent quickly shifted into another gear. 'Look, love, I'd rather you didn't let anyone know that I'm not actually trained in horticulture. The gardening was all part and parcel of it. And I'm learning. I've actually done rather well this morning. It's a job, Jem. A good job. With accommodation—and in the same village as you. We can be a proper family again . . .'

'But it's a racing stable! You're a gambler, for God's sake! You've already lied yourself into a job! And you could have got that sort of job anywhere! Why here? Why in a place where everyone sweats racehorse through their pores?'

'Because I wanted to be closer to you. You're all I've got left now.'

'And whose fault is that?' Jemima had drummed her fingernails on the tabletop. 'Sorry, Dad, but your addiction caused the problems. And you could have been very close to me in Oxford for the last three years, and I never even got a Christmas card from you. But then Oxford isn't exactly well-known for its horse-racing connections, is it?' She stopped drumming. 'You may well be able to fool everyone else, but you can't fool me. You're up to something, aren't you?'

Vincent shook his head and looked at his daughter. 'I really thought that you, of all people, would have some faith in me, love. You've made a fresh start—and I want to do the same. All I'm doing is hanging on to your coat-tails, don't you see?' He covered her hand with his. 'This is the only way I can prove to you that I'm a reformed character. Gambling is a thing of the past. I've learned my lesson. And how better to prove it than to set up home slap bang in the middle of temptation, eh?'

Jemima's expression softened slightly. 'Well—maybe. But if I ever get wind of you setting foot in a betting shop—'

'I have no intention of ever going inside a bookie's again.' With an air of affronted indignation, Vincent leaned back in his chair. Well, at least that was true. 'And now you'll be right on the doorstep to keep an eye on me, won't you? It's going to be wonderful, Jemima. Just wonderful. Trust me.' He leaned forward again. 'There is one thing, Jem, love?'

'Yes?'

'You couldn't see your way to lending me twenty quid, could you? Just until pay-day?

June

CHAPTER TEN

It rained for the next ten days.

'Bloody wet Sunday at Fakenham,' Matt Garside, wearing red- and-white colours, looked glumly out of the weighing-room door. 'I'm surprised Barry Manilow hasn't written a song about it.'

'Probably has.' Charlie, in dark green, joined him at the top of the steps. 'Still, we've got a good crowd.'

'I shouldn't think there's much else to do in Fakenham on a Sunday.' Matt grinned suddenly. 'Want to make a bit on the side? Tenner win, fiver second? Add a bit of interest?'

'Done.' Charlie shook hands.

'You will be.'

He and Charlie often held private wagers at the smaller meetings—especially when they were the top-rated riders on the card. As jockeys, they were not allowed to place bets with bookmakers, so it satisfied their latent gambling urges and had encouraged an exciting finish in many an otherwise unspectacular race. They usually broke even and spent the money together on very drunken evenings in the Cat and Fiddle.

'Nothing much to look at out here.' Charlie turned back into the weighing room. 'Nothing remotely fanciable.'

Matt cast his eyes over the ranks of raincoats and headscarves and sturdy shoes, and nodded. Charlie got first pick—always. At everything. Horses and women. Especially women. Two inches shorter, Matt considered his looks to be no more than average, and as they came with average brown hair and average grey eyes, he was well aware of his status as an also-ran in the pulling stakes and as a non-starter when Charlie was around.

Not for him, he thought, the delights of supermodels like Tina Maloret. He'd been riding her Dragon Slayer for a year now, and she'd given him no more than a haughty smile before the start of a race, or the coolest kiss on the cheek in the winner's enclosure. Even on the rare occasions when she visited Lancing Grange, he might as well have been invisible.

Then, when he'd been sidelined by injury and Charlie had been available to ride Dragon Slayer, within moments of meeting Tina and Charlie had been glued together like the layers in a bar of KitKat. It was bloody unfair.

Matt watched the Sunday raindrops drip into shallow puddles, and sighed. Not only did Charlie have Tina, but there was also a string of absolutely stunning local girls who continued to feature in Charlie's life as a back-up team when Tina was away. And this new one that he had in tow in Milton St John—the schoolgirl from the convent—Lucinda Something. Now, she was a real head-turner.

Still, Matt had had his moments: and there was always Jennifer at home in Devon, his on-off girlfriend from school days. And since he'd become Kath Seaward's stable jockey, he'd been able to move in fairly high-class circles. For a farmer's son, with none of Charlie's wealthy bloodstock lines, he supposed he hadn't done too badly. However, it didn't prevent him gazing at himself in the mirror sometimes and wishing that it was Charlie's face that gazed back.

He wandered back through the weighing room. The clerk of the scales was getting everything in order for the first race; registration books showing the jockeys entered at the course and their weight allowances, medical records, the number-cloths to be allocated—all the day-to-day administrative necessities for the legal side of race-riding—were arrayed on the table opposite the scales.

Matt grinned. 'If it carries on raining like this, we'll all weigh heavier when we come back than when we set out.'

'Better bloody not.' The clerk frowned. 'The job's a bugger to keep up to scratch as it is. You lot always try and pull flankers.'

Matt was still grinning when he reached the changing room. It was bedlam as ever. Twenty jockeys in various stages of undress called ribald greetings. He and Charlie always tried to get changed first. It saved fighting for space later. The valet was already laying out the colours for the second race, and hanging the postage-stamp-sized saddles—some only weighing as much as a bag of sugar—on the hook allotted to each jockey, along with all the tack, and checking at the same time that each of the weight-cloths was exactly right.

Matt reckoned the valets had the worst job in racing—toting all the equipment from course to course, taking it home covered in mud after a meeting, and producing it in pristine condition all ready for the next day. It was the behind-the-scenes people like this that kept racing going—and very few people realised it. He always gave his valet large tips.

Charlie was sitting slightly apart from the other

jockeys, leaning his head against the utilitarian green-painted wall, his eyes closed. Matt slid beside him, ignoring the surrounding elbows and knees and half-naked bodies. 'What's up?' He had to shout. The noise level was unbelievable. The jokes were blue. The language even more so.

'I'm bloody starving.' Charlie opened his eyes and gazed wistfully at the ceiling. 'And that bugger Liam Jenkins down there has got a bar of chocolate.'

'Bastard.'

Matt felt sympathetic. Naturally chunky, he spent the entire jumping season starving himself. It was one of the drawbacks of being a jump jockey—and another area where Charlie had always seemed to score points over him. While he had to watch his weight continually, Charlie was renowned for gracing picnics and barbecues, fork suppers and dinner parties, throughout the area, eating Falstaffian meals, and still managing not to tip the scales the following day. Matt, who had a season ticket to the sauna, seemed to gain half a stone if he even sniffed a pizza.

'Weighing out for the first race!' The voice echoed through the changing room.

Like schoolchildren leaving everything until the last minute on a Monday morning, there was a further burst of invective and a final mad scramble for saddles and cloths, whips and bridles.

Clutching all his gear, Matt followed Charlie on to the scales. He'd been allowed ten-and-a-half stone including his saddle and tack. It had taken a week of starvation to get there. All jockeys were generously allowed an extra pound for their body protector. The needle flickered up past the half-stone mark, wavered, and settled down. Dead on. Matt exhaled.

'Garside. Ten eight! Next!'

Ducking his head down against the penetrating drizzle, Matt ran to the parade ring. Kath Seaward, with raindrops studding her maroon beret like incongruous pearls, nodded to him. 'Okay? Up for it? This one and the rest of the card?'

'All six.' Matt nodded. 'It's a bit now-or-never.'

This meeting in far-flung Norfolk was one of the last of the jumping season. Flat-racing was well into its stride, Epsom had been and gone, and dreams and aspirations were now centred on Newmarket and Ascot—not the hazy distance of next year's Grand National.

Kath pulled the maroon beret round her ears and turned up the collar of the ground-trailing trench coat. 'Hopefully the racing press haven't read too much into Dragon Slayer being in the fourth. Fakenham is hardly Aintree trial status. Drew's remaining tight-lipped about us running him. He's turning into a right dour bugger these days. What's Somerset said about it? You must have had bloody hours to discuss things on the way up.'

Matt had travelled to Fakenham in Charlie's Aston Martin. The conversation during the convoluted journey had had very little to do with Dragon Slayer.

Matt shrugged. He knew, as Kath knew, about Drew's financial troubles. He admired Drew and was fond of Maddy. It seemed wrong to gloat. 'Charlie's main preoccupation at the moment seems to be more with his new girlfriend than why the hell we're sending out a champion chaser at a

141

minor meeting.'

'Ah. Knocking her off in Tina's absence, is he? Dangerous business. Ms Maloret will probably castrate him when she finds out. Bloody good job, too. What's she like—this latest tart? Will she distract him well into next season?'

'I've no idea. And she's no tart. She's from St Hilda's.' Matt grinned. 'And I gather she's giving him a bit of a run for his money. She's playing it very cool. He's slightly miffed that she keeps standing him up to do her A-level revision.'

Kath chuckled. 'Camping outside the classroom, is he? Doing his usual naff trick of delivering ice-buckets of Moët and tons of red roses?'

'I don't think so. For once he seems to be planning a different strategy.'

'As long as it keeps his mind off race-riding it'll be all to the good. Silly bastard.' Kath snorted her approval of Charlie's testosterone-led conversation level, patted Matt vaguely on the shoulder and stomped off towards the saddling boxes.

The first three races were over. The rain had eased away to no more than a fretful drizzle, and the diehard Sunday-afternoon punters were hauling their delayed picnics from the boots of their cars. There was always a relaxed, point-to-point atmosphere at Fakenham and the jockeys enjoyed their visits there, despite the lengthy travelling time.

Matt stood in the parade ring beside Kath and watched Dragon Slayer plod round, completely unperturbed. Charlie had won the first race while he'd finished a close second, and the positions had been reversed in the next. The third had been a bit of a disaster, with Liam Jenkins and Chris Maude stealing their thunder, leaving them scrabbling for the minor placings.

'Four double gin-and-tonics down the drain,' Charlie had muttered as they'd lugged their saddles muddily back to the weighing room. 'Thought we were going to keep a clean sheet. One of us had better head the field in the next or we'll be on Aqua Libra tonight.'

Kath was assessing Dragon Slayer with a professional eye, and Matt alone knew why she'd chosen to send him out on this seemingly easy course. The ground was always good due to the natural drainage of the sandy subsoil, the half-dozen fences were far from testing, and the tight, square track had little in the way of problems.

'Keep him up front,' Kath advised from under the damp rim of her beret. 'I want a start-to-finish lead. This is the ideal place to find out if maybe our tactics were wrong at Liverpool. This course is a dream for front-runners, and that little hill on the run-in will still give him a stamina test. Maybe—just maybe—I was wrong to cover him up in the National. And this is the best place to find out—away from too many prying eyes. Okay?'

Matt touched his cap. Charlie, again in the dark-green colours, was talking to Drew. How different they looked, he thought, to him and Kath. Drew Fitzgerald and Charlie Somerset looked like every film director's dream of racing superstars: tall and handsome. Kath was right, though, Drew seemed less affable than usual. Charlie hadn't elaborated on the problems at Peapods—but then he wouldn't. Whatever other faults Charlie had, disloyalty wasn't one of them.

Still, Matt thought, as he hauled himself high off the ground and into Dragon Slayer's saddle, all trainers had problems: if it wasn't lack of money, it was lack of good horses, or the threat of some virus wiping out a season's work.

'Remember,' Kath was looking up at him. 'Go for it. Right from the start. I want to see if he can hold it.'

*   *   *

They bucketed off side by side, Matt on Dragon Slayer and Charlie on Drew's Moonstone. It was only slightly more taxing than the gallops at home, and Matt eased into a gentle stride, keeping Dragon Slayer's nose just ahead of the other five horses in the field.

'What's the plan?' Charlie yelled across the rhythmic thumping. 'He's not a front runner.'

'He's not a faller either,' Matt grinned, easing up a notch for the first hurdle. 'Watch and learn, Charlie. Watch and learn.'

They were still steadily ahead at the start of the second circuit. Dragon Slayer was moving easily, hardly having to make any effort at all to clear the hurdles. The rest of the field weren't far behind, Matt knew, but they *were* behind—and that was good enough.

Two fences to go. Dragon Slayer was, without doubt, the best horse he'd ever ridden. The long striding motion was assured, the pricked ears indicated his sheer enjoyment, the pleasure he was experiencing transferring itself to Matt. He was a winner. Better than anything Charlie could hope to ride. Here at least he'd got the beating of Charlie.

He had been desperately upset not to have been fit enough to ride him at Aintree, and it had driven him mad to see this great horse dumped so unceremoniously out of the Grand National. Dragon Slayer could have done so much better.

The muted sounds of the commentator were growing louder, and the roar from the stands swelled in his ears. Dragon Slayer spurted forward with a burst of speed that was totally instinctive, and cleared the final hurdle with feet of daylight between his black flanks and the top of the fence. It was like sitting on air. Matt had nothing to do except steer. Dragon Slayer sailed past the winning post, hardly sweating.

Standing up in the stirrups, punching the air with his whip as though he'd just cleared the hill at Cheltenham, Matt looked over his shoulder. The remainder of the field was still labouring up the incline some twenty lengths behind him. Charlie and Moonstone were battling to stay in contention. Matt grinned in delight. Kath's instincts had been right: Dragon Slayer was a natural front-runner. They'd wipe out the field at the next National! It was what he wanted most in the entire world. He was pretty sure he'd kill to achieve it.

'Bloody superb!' Kath gave him an uncharacteristic hug in the winner's enclosure. 'We're right-on for next season. He's proved that he knows better than me—and now he's going to have a good holiday and eat his head off before we get down to the hard work after the summer. This baby,' she kissed Dragon Slayer's nose, and Matt was amazed to see tears in her eyes, 'is going to be the next star of Aintree—and so, Matthew Garside, are you.'

*　　　*　　　*

145

Charlie was silent for most of the journey home. He had hardly spoken at all by the time they'd left the flat landscape behind them and hit the first motorway.

'We didn't do that badly.' Matt was slouched down in the Aston Martin's passenger seat. Give him half a ton of horse hurling itself at a mile-high fence and he wouldn't blink. Charlie Somerset's Aston Martin on a kamikaze mission with a forty-ton lorry was something altogether different. 'We've got enough in the kitty for a reasonable piss-up.'

'Yeah.'

Matt tried again. 'Tina will be pleased with the way Dragon Slayer went today. Kath's going to ring her tonight. In Italy.'

'She's not in Italy.' Charlie clenched his hands on the steering wheel and overtook a line of boy-racers. 'She's gone on to LA. Some première thing or other.'

'Missing her, are you?'

Still travelling at over a hundred, Charlie stabbed a CD into the player. 'What do you think?'

They continued in silence—apart from the eardrum-shattering accompaniment of Aerosmith—until they pulled off the M25.

'Is everything okay with Drew?' Matt realised that he'd been gripping the edge of the seat for the last half-hour and tried to unfurl his fingers. 'He's seemed a bit—well—off lately. It's all round the village that he's going bankrupt.'

'Bollocks.' Charlie squeezed even more out of the accelerator. 'It's a bit of a blip, that's all. All yards get them, you know that. And he's completely knackered. Since Alister left to go to Mr Thornton's it's all been down to him. There's no let-up in a mixed yard—and his flat runners have been a bit of a disaster recently, haven't they?'

The understatement of the year, Matt thought. 'Er—so, under the circumstances—is their picnic still on next week?'

'As far as I know. Maddy's invited the world. You know what she's like. Who are you taking?'

'No one.' Matt eased himself up in his seat, took one look through the windscreen and slid down again. 'What about you? Will Tina be back in time?'

'Doubtful. I'll have to call on my reserve team.' Charlie screamed the Aston Martin past three cars and grinned across at Matt. 'You might not have much luck with the ladies, but you've certainly got one hell of a horse. Pity you can't take Dragon Slayer to the picnic, eh? So, what was that all about? Running him today? Kath planning a change of tactics for next year?'

'Nah. It was just a muscle-stretcher before his summer break.' Despite the pallor of his passenger-seat terror, Matt knew he was blushing. 'I mean, Drew entered Moonstone this afternoon. He's not coming on for the National, is he?'

'I fucking hope not.' Charlie indicated to leave the motorway. 'Tailed off last of six at bloody Fakenham. Hardly the stuff of Aintree dreams, is it?'

*　　　*　　　*

Even the Cat and Fiddle seemed rather subdued tonight, Matt thought. Sunday evening, the light

147

just fading with June dampness, and only the ever-thirsty stable staff lining the bar, eager as always to celebrate their one day of almost-rest.

Charlie had dropped him off at his two-up two-down house in the back-streets of the village and agreed to meet him later. The hands on the clock had already ticked away two gins. Matt, unsure whether to stay or wander off home for the delights of a thinly sliced breast of chicken and a tomato—opted for another drink. At least the gin acted as an antidote to fluid retention.

'Sorry I'm late.' Charlie crashed in through the door. 'Tina rang. Kath had told her about your incredible success this afternoon. She says well done, by the way—and she can't see why I couldn't have done that at Aintree.'

'I trust you told her that skill and judgement on the racecourse sometimes takes precedence over all-night performances in the bedroom?' Matt pushed a double gin-and-tonic across the table. 'I've divvied up our winnings. We should have enough to be satisfactorily plastered by closing time.'

'Thank God for that.' Charlie collapsed into a chair. 'I need something to lift the gloom. Lucinda is heavily into the *Canterbury Tales* and won't see me. It's the first time I've been passed up in favour of a bloke who's been dead for nine hundred years. Oh, bugger.'

'What?'

'Over there. Ned Filkins—and Drew and Maddy's new gardener, Vincent. They're real bosom buddies these days. I don't think Ned's the best companion for him.'

'Ned's not the best companion for anyone.' Matt drained his glass. 'Maybe someone should warn him

148

before it's too late.'

Charlie swirled the remainder of his gin, before swallowing it in one go. 'I've tried. Mind you, I picked a bad moment. I walked in on the mother and father of all rows.'

Matt raised his eyebrows. He loved gossip. Charlie always had some titbit. 'What? At Peapods? With Drew and Maddy?'

'Nah. Maddy and Vincent. Seems he'd completely wrecked her walled garden. You know, the one she's been nurturing ever since Mrs F took up permanent residence in the Channel Islands? He'd pulled out all the roses, and some cottage garden plants that had belonged to Maddy's gran and, well, practically everything. The whole place looked like it had been napalmed.'

'Christ.' Matt gathered up the empty glasses for refilling. 'A bit of an odd thing for a gardener to do. Did he know what he was up to?'

'That's more or less what Maddy was asking—in no uncertain terms.' Charlie grinned hugely. 'Then Vincent said that he'd discovered that all the plants had lumbago root rot or some other crap, and they had to go. He said he'd turn it into a Japanese garden, all concrete and stunted growth, until the soil was clear of infection.'

'Oh.' Matt was a bit disappointed. He'd expected more. He stood up, ready to head for the bar. 'And was Mad happy with that?'

'Dunno. She looked bloody murderous. The next day it was all down to paving slabs and stunted growth. Oh, shit—Ned's spotted you.'

'Hello, Matt.' Ned was calling to him across the pub. 'Quite a little coup you an' the ole cow struck this afternoon by all accounts. I was just telling

149

Vince here all about it, wasn't I, Vince?'

Vincent nodded. Matt greeted them both briefly and turned his attentions to the Cat and Fiddle's landlord.

Picking up the drinks and heading back to the table, he groaned.

Ned and Vincent had vacated their own table and were chattering to a thunder-faced Charlie.

'Hurry up, Matt, lad!' Ned patted the seat beside him. 'Come and sit down. Ole Vince here is a right babe-in-arms when it comes to matters of the turf. I told him, there's no one better than you and Charlie to give him a few tips.'

CHAPTER ELEVEN

'Jemima! Mum's not ready to go yet, and she says can you meet her in the summerhouse, and—Zeke poked his head round the door of the flat. 'Oh, bugger. Sorry.'

The head disappeared and the door closed. There was then a polite knock before it reopened. Zeke grinned. 'I always forget that bit. Yeah, anyway, Mum says she'll be about another ten minutes. Hey, you look really nice.'

'Thanks.' Jemima flicked her hair behind her ears and burrowed under the sofa for a stray canvas boot. 'Suitably dressed for a picnic, do you reckon?'

'Nah. Too grown-up. Anyway, picnics are for kids—not for old people. Old people grumble about dog poo and getting ants in things and they always see wasps that aren't there and complain about grit in the sandwiches and—'

150

Jemima laughed. 'Cheers. I can see I'm going to have a really nice time. At least it hasn't rained this week, which means we won't all have to sit on our pac-a-macs, will we?' She found the boot and laced it. 'There. Now, shall we go and chivvy your mum up a bit?'

*   *   *

The summerhouse was in a state of chaos. The June sun, blazing through the windows, illuminated the debris with halogen brilliance. Gillian, looking wonderful in a silver silk trouser suit, languidly cleared a space on one of the chairs. 'Sit down. I won't be a tick. Just a few bits and bobs to put away.'

'Isn't five o'clock a strange time to be going on a picnic?' Watching Gillian's leisurely tidying-up process, Jemima ran her fingers through her hair again. It hadn't quite reached an acceptable level of tousledom. 'Shouldn't we be taking our own contribution of egg sandwiches and a flask? Oh, I can't get my hair right! And you look sensational— I'm nowhere near as posh as you. What exactly should I be wearing?'

'No to the time, and no to the sandwiches, and your hair looks lovely.' Gillian paused.

'Yes?' Jemima frowned. 'But?'

'That dress—it's absolutely gorgeous. Perfect. You look very Renoir. Laura Ashley, isn't it?'

It was. It was also her best going-out frock. 'There's still a but, isn't there?'

'Not a huge one.' Gillian laughed. 'But I'd advise against wearing the black knickers under it.'

'Christ!' Jemima hurtled out of the

151

summerhouse.

Back in the sanctuary of her bedroom, she changed into white knickers, added an ankle-length cotton petticoat for good measure, and wondered how many times she'd displayed her underwear in Oxford. She had always worn the Laura Ashley—minus petticoat—to Bookworms functions. Why hadn't anyone ever had the balls to tell her before? Probably, she thought, because Gillian was rapidly becoming something she hadn't had for a very long time. A close friend. In fact, Milton St John was making a rather lovely habit of giving her things she had thought she'd have to live without. Like friends, like a social life, like a future, like a father . . .

She was delighted that Vincent was here. She had seen him three times since he'd surprised her in the Munchy Bar: twice in the Cat and Fiddle and once here at her flat when she'd cooked him a meal. She loved him to distraction, and was so pleased to see the pallor subsiding, and his muscles beginning to fill out—but she still didn't trust him an inch.

He was so damn plausible. Always had been. Gillian and Glen had thought it was wonderful that Vincent was living in the village, and couldn't understand her reservations. But how could she tell them? She had learned very quickly that in Milton St John, if you sneezed at one end of the High Street, someone immediately said 'Bless you' at the other. And Vincent *might* really have turned over a new leaf. If so, she didn't want to put any doubts in Maddy and Drew's mind. It was so long since anyone had given him a chance—and she was blowed if she was going to be the one that ruined it

152

for him.

She had ordered him back issues of all the gardening magazines, guiltily aware that she was now compounding his felony, and advised him after that first fiasco to check with Maddy on exactly what she wanted pulled up or pruned. Typically, he'd got away with that desecration—and Maddy had been into the Munchy Bar singing Vincent's praises and raving about her new low-maintenance Japanese walled garden. Jemima had warned him that he'd never get away with it twice.

At least, she thought, as she inspected the Laura Ashley in the mirror for total opaqueness from every angle, there was one good thing about tonight's picnic: she'd checked with her father and he wasn't going. Meeting a few chums, he'd said, in the pub. Much more fun. She hoped it would be. She just hoped his fun didn't involve gambling— the betting shop in the village would be closed, wouldn't it? And he didn't have transport to get to the bigger ones in the nearby town. She'd just have to trust him . . .

And his absence did have a further plus point: whatever lies he'd invented for his CV, at least she wouldn't be expected to agree with his fabrications tonight. She could enjoy a village evening out without having to worry about a thing. Grabbing her ethnic mirror-glass shoulder-bag and locking her door, she almost skipped down the staircase.

Gillian still wasn't ready. Jemima leaned against the desk and tried to read some of the sheets spewing from the printer.

'Oh! You were quicker than I thought you'd be.' Gillian switched off all the equipment, and gathering the A4 sheets together in an untidy bundle, stuffed them into a drawer. 'Stand up against the light. Oh, yes. That's much better.'

'I'm still not sure I should be going with you. I know Maddy invited me, but I think she meant me and a Significant Someone. Shouldn't this be a romantic evening out for you and Glen?'

'He wouldn't have wanted to come even if he hadn't already had a prior engagement with the Parish Biddies' Clean-Up Campaign,' Gillian said. 'It isn't his sort of thing at all. And you really don't know that many people yet, do you? It'll be a great opportunity to circulate away from the Munchy Bar.'

'And you're sure it's safe to leave the twins to their own devices?'

'Stop chucking in obstacles. Glen's having his meeting here. He's rescheduled from the Cat and Fiddle. The twins will be chaperoned by Bathsheba Cox and Bronwyn Pugh and the rest of the village's sturdy-ankle brigade.'

The invitation to Maddy and Drew's picnic had, as far as Jemima was concerned, been a mixed blessing. True, it would remove her from the Vicarage on Bathsheba's anti-sleaze campaign night which meant that, yet again, she wouldn't have to admit to ordering Fishnets, but it also meant that most of her fellow guests were going to be connected—however tenuously—with horse-racing.

Gillian delved into her bag and sprayed on scent. 'It's going to be an ideal opportunity to introduce you to some men. And don't look like that. I know what you're thinking. You've gone all wrinkly-nosed which means you're getting sniffy about the company. It'll be a complete mixture of people. They won't all be from the stables. I'm not asking you to announce your engagement to Charlie Somerset or anything—'

'Who?'

'Charlie Somerset. You mean you've never heard of Charlie Somerset?'

Jemima put on her glasses. 'I think I might have done. Isn't he a jockey?'

'He's sex on legs.' Gillian gathered up her handbag. 'But don't tell Glen I said so.'

*   *   *

'Where exactly are we going?' Jemima asked as Gillian eased her elderly Triumph away from the twisty Berkshire lanes and headed for the M4.

'Windsor.' Gillian concentrated on the road ahead.

'Really?' Jemima swivelled round. 'As in the castle?'

'Not exactly. It's not a royal command—but close—yes . . .'

Windsor. Wow! Jemima wriggled happily in her seat. Life was very definitely on the up. She stared out of the window, completely relaxed. The sensation of bowling along with her bottom about six inches off the road, made her feel silly and giddy and eighteen again—and took away the weight of responsibilities which for so long had threatened to overwhelm her.

The journey across Berkshire went very quickly. 'Heavens!' Jemima looked around with total surprise as they bumped across cattle grids. 'Is it a stately home? It's beautiful. And all these cars! It must be a very big picnic.'

'Huge,' Gillian said quickly, as they scrambled from the Triumph beneath a canopy of chestnut trees. 'Drew Fitzgerald and Maddy are well-known for their hospitality—but, of course, not all these people are their guests.'

'They're not? Is it a sort of communal thing, then?' Jemima followed Gillian in the direction of a shingle path running alongside various single-storey buildings which were labelled with notices saying 'Stables', 'Visiting Lads', and 'Permit Holders Only'. The penny took a second to drop. 'Bloody hell! It's a bloody racecourse!'

'Jemima, look, I was going to tell you, but I talked it over with Maddy, and we knew you weren't too keen on racing and we thought that you'd change your mind once you were here and—'

'You thought wrong then.'

The still-warm sun filtered in dappled patterns through the trees as crowds of other early racegoers, all decked out in their summer finery, tramped past them. Horses whinnied from behind the high walls. Jemima, incensed by Gillian's duplicity, stopped walking.

Gillian cannoned into the back of her. 'I'm sorry if I wasn't exactly truthful about the venue, but I'm sure you'll enjoy it—'

'And I'm sure I won't.'

'I had no idea that you were *this* anti.' Gillian sighed heavily. 'I thought we were friends. I thought I knew everything about you.'

'No one knows everything about anyone.' Jemima sucked in her breath. She should have explained the situation to Gillian ages ago. It was her own fault. She had always, through force of habit, kept things to herself. 'My parents divorced because of racing. We never had any money because my father was addicted to gambling. He lost his business and our home because of horses, dogs, cards, dice—two flies crawling up a window. Have you any idea what it's like to be scared of the postman? Or terrified of a knock on the door?'

Gillian shook her head. 'Oh, God. I had no inkling—'

'That's why my father lived in a sordid bedsit. And why my mother has a live-in job in a hotel. Nothing to do with the recession. Nothing to do with being made redundant. Because, thanks to my father's gambling, they lost everything and neither of them will ever be off the blacklist.'

'Oh, Jemima—you poor thing. You should have told me—'

'Well, now I have.' She swallowed. 'I would be very, very grateful if you never mentioned this to another soul. And definitely not to Drew and Maddy. I really don't think they'd want an undischarged bankrupt—not to mention an addicted gambler—living on their property and working for them.'

'Of course I won't breathe a word to anyone.' Gillian still looked pole-axed. 'I'm so sorry. But Maddy and I—well, we honestly thought it was some animal-rights thing . . .'

'It's that as well. But it's mainly the gambling.'

Gillian pulled a face. 'Then this is about as insensitive as taking an alcoholic's family on a day-trip to a distillery, isn't it?'

'On a par, yes.'

A doubt was wriggling through Jemima's mind. Vincent must have known the picnic was on a racecourse. Working at Peapods he couldn't possibly not have known. So why—in the name of all the saints—when he had a bona-fide reason to come racing, had he chosen to remain in Milton St John?

'Do you want to go home?' Gillian was pushed against her by a tide of ladies in hats. 'I'd totally understand if you did.'

'And spoil it for everyone? No, I'm here now. After all, I suppose I've been lucky so far—living in Milton St John and not getting even a whiff of a jockey. But don't expect me to enjoy it. I promise not to be po-faced for the entire evening, but it'll cost you. I'll think of something really awful for you to do in return. And don't expect me to be nice to anyone—because I won't.'

'You're an angel.' Gillian hugged her. 'Look, I need to have a little word with Drew about something—but I promise you, once I've done that if you're absolutely hating it, then we'll go home. Deal?'

'Deal.' Jemima gave Gillian one of the twins' high-fives, and feeling quite brave, followed her along the scrunchy gravelled paths.

Gillian waved their permits and invitations at a panama-hatted steward as they passed through the towering wrought-iron gates. Windsor, Jemima thought as she gazed around, especially on this glorious June evening, didn't look anything like she'd imagined a racecourse to look. A steel band was playing calypso music beneath the trees, the air was filled with the seduction of philadelphus and honeysuckle, there was a background scent of trampled grass and hot horse, and, somewhere, someone was frying onions.

And everyone, Jemima had to admit, looked very

respectable. She'd imagined it would be dirty, grey, bleak. She'd imagined racegoers to be shabby and furtive. This was beautiful.

Gillian pointed to a small ring where sleek, long-legged horses stalked round wearing their rugs and a haughty demeanour. 'Those are the runners for the first race.'

'Aren't they gorgeous? They look like supermodels at a Calvin Klein show. What a pity they've got to be mistreated.'

'Shush!' Gillian steered Jemima firmly in the opposite direction. 'I think you'll soon realise that ill-treatment is not one of the priorities of either training or race-riding. I can understand your reluctance to have anything to do with gambling— but trainers and jockeys love their horses. Cruelty doesn't come into it. Not anywhere. Animals don't react to cruelty, only to respect, love and understanding—and believe me, racehorses are the most spoiled brats in the animal kingdom.'

Jemima wasn't convinced. She continued to stare over her shoulder at the circling horses. 'What are they doing, then?'

'Waiting to go into the parade ring. The first race is a selling handicap. That means that the winner is put up for auction immediately after the finish. Sometimes owners end up buying their own horses back at amazingly inflated prices.'

'What on earth for?'

'Because they hadn't expected them to win and realise that they might have a potential money-spinner on their hands.' Gillian touched Jemima's elbow. 'And sometimes because they simply can't bear to part with them. Drew's is the one with the red-and-gold rug. Suzy's riding him—

Maddy's sister. You've met her in the Munchy Bar, haven't you? Anyway, you'll probably get to meet Suzy again later. She lives with Luke Delaney who—'

'Even I know who Luke Delaney is!' Jemima retorted. 'You can't watch a chat show, game show, or anything else on the telly these days without seeing Luke Delaney, superstar jockey.'

Gillian laughed. 'Oh, goody. You've managed to mention a jockey's name without turning to stone. I doubt if I'll have you placing Waterfalls or Each Way Multiples with friendly Joe Grimshaw down in the Silver Ring by the end of the evening, or even actually watching a race, but you never know. God moves in mysterious ways indeed, and no one is more aware of that than I am.'

Gillian had stopped walking and Jemima trampled on her heels. 'You said a picnic! Not a Commem Ball!'

The gaily striped marquee with its own bar, a huge covered food table, and a collection of white filigreed tables and chairs arranged on the roped-off lawn, looked awesome. Gillian smiled encouragingly. 'This *is* a picnic—Milton St John style. Just a bit more comfortable than grass and rugs. No, don't you dare run away!'

'What good timing!' Maddy was relaxing in her chair, her auburn hair in a loose cluster of curls on top of her head. 'We're just going to refill the glasses. Food will be dished up in about an hour and carry on for the rest of the evening.' She stood up and hugged a rather bemused Jemima. 'How nice to meet you again. I'm so glad you came. Gillian said you didn't really like racing. It's Jemima, isn't it? Vincent's daughter?'

160

Oh, God. Jemima, having hugged Maddy back, nodded.

'You should have told me when I was in the Munchy Bar that your father had applied for the gardening job. You must have thought I was being very superior.' Maddy giggled. 'And I can promise you that I'm not. He's very talented, isn't he? Kimberley Small and Diana James-Jordan want to talk to him about developing Japanese gardens for them.'

Jemima tried not to laugh out loud. He had the luck of the devil, her dad.

Maddy indicated the chairs beside her. 'Do come and sit down, both of you. I'll go and get the drinks. Gillian, be an angel and tell Jemima who everyone is—'

Gillian groaned, staring at the crush by the bar. 'Looks like I've got the short straw. Are you ready for this?'

Jemima shook her head. 'I'll never remember their names. Still, as I'm unlikely to ever meet them again, I don't suppose it matters. Go on then, do your who's who of Milton St John.'

'The blonde girl in the linen shift-dress is Maddy's best mate Fran who, according to Mad, got back to size ten five minutes after she had her baby so now she hates her. Her husband Richard is riding in the first race—as is Suzy, Mad's sister, and Luke Delaney who—'

'I said I know about Luke Delaney.'

'Yes. Sorry. I forget about his publicity machine. Next to Fran are Kit and Rosa Pedersen. They're friends of Drew's from Jersey, and his business partners.'

'They look nice. And who is Maddy talking to?'

161

Jemima stared at the tall fair-haired man with his arm round the shoulders of a very pretty dark girl in a vivid pink-and-orange sundress.

'Rory and Georgia Faulkner, mates of hers from Upton Poges. They had a whirlwind wedding after a whirlwind romance and still can't keep their hands off each other.'

'Ah, sweet. Aren't they handsome? Oh, goodness—so is he!' Jemima, forgetting to be disinterested, sat up and blinked at a totally devastating man with silky dark red hair, in tight, rather grubby white jeans and a navy polo shirt. 'Who on earth is he?'

'Charlie Somerset. Told you, didn't I?' Gillian sighed wistfully. 'Charlie has more notches on his bedpost than anyone has a right to have. He's completely incapable of being faithful. But he does it so beautifully that everyone still adores him afterwards. Georgia once called him a serial cheater.'

'Really?' Georgia—wasn't she the newlywed? 'Did she go out with him, then?'

'Charlie tries it on with everyone. Even Maddy went out with him once—when Drew and she had separated. Don't you think he's absolutely stunning?'

'No,' Jemima said shortly.

'Liar.'

Maddy returned from the bar with the drinks then, sitting down between Jemima and Gillian. 'I think nearly everyone's here except Matt, of course—he'll be along later. And Charlie's date for this evening—she's just gone in search of the loo. So, has Gillian done a suitable character assassination on the assembled guests so far?'

'Brilliant, thank you.' Jemima sipped her wine.

Racegoers swept past in waves, eager to get their bets on before the selling stakes. The disembodied voices of the bookies could just be heard echoing from the enclosures. Jemima cringed. She recognised the language. Vincent had used the words frequently, and she had to concentrate hard on the steel band which was strolling between the flower-beds playing 'Island in the Sun', to block out the raucous shouts of 'Five to two against!'

Gillian leaned forward. 'Is Drew around, Mad? I'd like to have a word with him.'

'With Blue Ruin in the saddling boxes, I expect. Go and have a look, and take Jemima with you. Introduce her properly.'

Jemima panicked. It felt safe enough sitting here. All these people seemed—well—normal. And Maddy was, as she had been in the Munchy Bar, just lovely. And hopefully no one would mention Vincent any more. But she didn't, truly didn't, want to know anything more about racecourses, or horses, or racing, or, well, anything.

Gillian drained her glass and stood up. 'Come on, Jemima, you'll love Drew—good Lord! Who on earth is that?'

The girl shimmying towards the tent had brought even the most eager punters to a standstill. Tall, slender and tanned, with long black hair in a single plait down her back, she was wearing tight denim shorts cut to display the pert cheeks of her bottom to their best advantage. Her full brown breasts spilled out of a minuscule black bikini top. The air around her was heavy with CK One.

'Oh, she's Charlie's current wild child. Tina Maloret is still in the States—and you know what

163

he's like.' Maddy waved a lazy hand. 'Come over here, Lucinda, and join the rest of the party. Of course, you already know Gillian, but have you met Jemima yet?'

Lucinda beamed hello at them both.

'Bloody hell!' Gillian grabbed Jemima's arm. 'It's Lucinda! Little Lucinda! Bathsheba Cox's schoolgirl daughter! I'm sure we can capitalise on this. Charlie Somerset, I love you! Come on—let's find Drew.'

Unable to free herself from Gillian's grasp, Jemima was dragged rather reluctantly across the grass.

*   *   *

Drew had just finished saddling Blue Ruin for the first race, and smiled and shook her hand as Gillian introduced them. He had a lovely smile, Jemima thought. Warm and friendly and sexy all at the same time. And he was even more Mel Gibsony close up than he'd been when she had seen him riding past the Munchy Bar. It was all so confusing. He seemed far too nice to be cruel to animals—and far too charming to realise what heartache he caused gamblers and their families.

She had never been this close to a racehorse before either. Blue Ruin was beautiful. So huge, with fabulously gentle eyes, and strong glossy muscles—and those fragile ankles! How on earth could they support the weight of a galloping horse? They looked as though they'd snap like a twig.

'Tell me something,' Gillian tapped Drew on the arm. 'Lucinda Cox. How long has she—er—been with Charlie?'

164

Drew followed his horse with a critical eye. 'She's a recent acquisition, I think. Why?'

'Does Bathsheba know?'

'Christ, I shouldn't think so.'

'Oh, goody. It's always handy to have a few aces up one's sleeve. Just let her start laying the law down about immorality and impropriety in future. People in glass houses and all that. Still, it wasn't Charlie's sex life I actually wanted to discuss with you—fascinating though it is.' Gillian paused. 'I want your advice.'

'I thought I was supposed to come to you for spiritual guidance?'

'Spiritual guidance I can handle.' Gillian leaned her elbows on the flaking white rails of the pre-parade ring and indicated to Jemima to squeeze in beside her. 'This is financial. I want to make an investment. I—er—need to lose some money, and not with a bookmaker. A lot of money.'

'You've come to the right place then,' Drew said bitterly. 'All contributions gratefully received. I've no doubt that you're well aware of Peapods' financial crisis—which is one of the reasons why Kit and Rosa are over from the Channel Islands. They're trying to work out a strategy for our survival.'

'Oh God, yes, I know and I'm so sorry. But I'm looking at more of an investment for me than a rescue package for you. Although, it might amount to the same thing.'

'I doubt it.' Drew shrugged. 'I don't think I can be much help. If you were going to ask me to divert some of your cash to a bank in Jersey, you've left it too late. I'm afraid the Chancellor has tied up all the offshore loopholes.'

Jemima, still feeling confused and pretty sure that she shouldn't be listening to this, moved away.

'I wasn't,' Gillian said, making a grab for Jemima. 'Please hang on a minute. It's okay. I need you to be here too, actually. I want to invest my money in bloodstock. I want to buy a horse.'

Jemima blinked.

Drew seemed equally as stunned. 'Gillian, exactly how much does Glen get on the offertory plate? Have you any idea how much a horse costs?'

'Not really. Look, I don't particularly want to go into details, but I've earned far more than Glen thinks I've earned by—well, writing. I don't want it appearing on the bank statement. I love racing and I love horses—and I've been thinking about this for ages. I want to buy a horse and I want you to train it for me.'

'If you're serious, then of course I'd be delighted. Do you want me to put in a bid for the winner of this seller tonight, then?'

'Goodness, no! I want to do it properly. I want you to take me to the sales.' Gillian smiled. 'You see, I want to buy a horse that could win the Grand National.'

Drew appeared to have been rendered speechless. Feeling that somebody had to say something, Jemima worked some saliva into her mouth. 'You said this involved me. I don't really see—'

Gillian took a deep breath. 'I'm not sure that you'll agree, of course. Especially not now that you've told me—er—what you told me. But, you see, Glen must know nothing about me buying the horse. Or owning it. So, I wondered whether you'd be an absolute angel and let me run it in your name?'

CHAPTER TWELVE

Over my dead body, Jemima thought. Categorically, unequivocally, positively, not a chance.

Gillian was looking at her expectantly. 'Jemima?'

'No way. Sorry.'

'Maybe you'll change your mind when you've actually seen a race.'

'I'll never change my mind. And I've told you I don't intend watching any races. I don't want to be involved. Ask someone else.' Jemima tried to keep her tone as neutral as possible. 'Is this why you brought me here tonight?'

'Of course it wasn't. How could you think such a thing? Drew—tell her what she's missing . . .'

Drew, obviously trying to avoid a re-enactment of the battle scene from *Braveheart* spoiling the summer evening, shook his head. 'I'm sure Jemima has her reasons. Let's buy the horse first, shall we? There'll be plenty of time to sort out the minutiae later.'

Jemima looked at him with grateful admiration. Not only gorgeous, but a diplomat to boot. Maddy was a lucky woman.

'And I think it would be better to keep it just between ourselves for now, don't you?' Drew continued. 'The fewer people involved the better, especially if it has to be secret from Glen. You know what the jungle drums are like.'

Wearing a seraphic smile, Gillian nodded dutifully. Really, Jemima thought in irritation, she was in serious danger of turning into a Stepford

Wife.

Drew seemed relieved. 'Look, I've got to get Blue Ruin into the parade ring for the first race. There are bloodstock sales at Newmarket in a couple of weeks so I'll get Tattersalls' catalogues and ring you. We'll both have to fabricate some reason for being away from the village at the same time.'

'And we'll invite Charlie,' Gillian said happily. 'I want Charlie to ride in the National on my horse—so I guess he ought to have a say.'

God, Jemima thought, the whole thing was growing more bizarre by the moment. She almost expected Mike Leigh to come striding through the crowd and yell, 'Cut! It's a wrap!'

'Do you want me to tell Charlie the good news?' Drew had ducked back under the rails.

'Please.' Gillian beamed. 'You're far more discreet than me.'

Understatement of the year, Jemima thought. 'As you've both obviously got millions of things to discuss, I think I'll go back now.'

Drew bit his lip. 'Sorry—we're being rude. Tell Mad we'll be along in a moment.'

Gillian fluttered her fingers in a little wave. 'Didn't I tell you it was exciting, Jemima? I know you've only seen the sordid side of racing until now—'

'Gillian!'

'Oh, yes.' She cast a sideways glance at Drew. 'Sorry. I forgot. Let's talk later? On the journey home?'

Jemima turned away and started to push through the crowds. She could hear Gillian laughing behind her and Drew's answering chuckle. Feeling

168

paranoid, she hoped they weren't laughing at her. No, they'd probably already forgotten her existence. They'd be heavily into fetlocks and hocks, or whatever it was that Vincent used to blame when a horse didn't win, for ages yet.

She forced her way further through the swelling crowd. Neither Drew nor Gillian—and she'd honestly expected more from Gillian with her religious connections—had a clue about their responsibilities. Didn't they realise what they were doing? Some poor horse was going to be bullied into submission and asked to jump mountains while throughout the country people would pile money they could ill afford on to it. And these same people wouldn't care about the horse when it fell and broke its neck. Why should they? All they'd care about was the fact that the rent money had gone down the drain.

She paused and squinted against the sun. The area beneath the trees seemed to be a mass of tents and she headed hopefully towards them. One of them must be Maddy's. She needed a drink. She wanted to go home. She didn't belong here among these hardened racegoers.

'Ouch!' She glared at the man who had just stamped on her canvas boot.

'Christ. Sorry. Didn't see you. It's so crowded.'

She carried on glaring. Her toes hurt. She was cross with Gillian, and she was at a bloody racecourse. She sighed. 'It's okay. I wasn't looking either.'

He smiled as he walked away. He was quite pleasant, she decided. Not a ten-plus, devastating, havoc-making, pulse-racer like Charlie Somerset, or drop-dead gorgeous like Drew, but nice. Still, he was at a race meeting which meant he was a gambler, and therefore strictly off-limits.

She skirted the spaghetti junction of guy ropes round the Peapods marquee and wished she'd leased her bookshop in the middle of an urban sprawl that had no interest in horse-racing whatsoever.

'Hi,' Maddy said as she sat down. 'Did you find Drew? Where's Gillian?'

'They're—er—still talking.' Jemima thought it best not to say anything else. If Glen and Gillian didn't share secrets, then possibly Drew and Maddy didn't either.

There seemed to be even more people gathered around the bar than before, and she felt the usual rush of panic. Grow up, she told herself silently. Don't blush. Don't stutter. You own a bookshop. In less than a month these people will be your customers.

The thought cheered her considerably, so much so that when Maddy waved the wine bottle in her direction she accepted the offer of a refill. 'It was kind of you to ask me to come this evening.'

'Even though you're not keen on racing?' Maddy looked amused.

'This isn't like I'd imagined racing,' Jemima said slowly, careful not to offend her hostess. 'This bit here is really nice. But I'm not going near the course or the bookmakers.'

'Famous last words.'

'No, I mean it.' Jemima twirled her glass.

'I used to think like that. Very much the outsider looking in. And now,' Maddy grinned as she looked round the marquee, 'I'm so steeped in it that I can't imagine any other way of life. You'll probably

170

change your mind when you've been in the village for longer. I think most non-horsy people feel the same way at first. Anyway, you obviously don't want to talk about horses, so tell me about your shop. I can't wait for it to open. I read all the time— well, when Drew and the animals and Poppy and my work allow me to. Are you having an opening party?'

They talked about the bookshop, and Georgia and Rosa, Fran and Lucinda, joined in. They seemed genuinely delighted about the shop opening, and advised her on the books they liked— and those they didn't. The men, like all men at functions the world over, Jemima thought, were still at the bar. In her element at last, she began to relax.

Sadly the relaxation coincided with the multicoloured arrival of Suzy, Luke and Richard prior to the first race, and Jemima found herself almost drowning in a sea of garbled introductions and excited forecasts.

She studied them from behind her spectacles. Suzy was bird-thin and gorgeous, Luke Delaney was simply beautiful, and Richard wasn't, but was very sweet. She'd always believed that jockeys would be snarling and surly. They always looked so skeletal and dour on the television when Vincent was watching Channel Four.

She glanced over at Charlie Somerset. Nothing dour about him. He was welded to Lucinda now, licking trickles of wine from her shoulder, and hadn't even appeared to notice her—not that she was surprised. She'd known a lot of men like Charlie Somerset in Oxford. Truly fabulous-looking men whose vanity would only allow them to

171

date equally physically perfect specimens. Jemima, pretty sure that she fell short on all counts, had never had the confidence to be interested.

Once the jockey trio had trooped off to claim their mounts, Maddy tipped her chair back and blinked into the sunshine. 'Oh, great. Here they are at last. Oh, hell, Drew, what's wrong? Is it Blue Ruin?'

'Yeah, the bloody thing has spread a plate in the parade ring and no one can find the sodding farrier. Who'd be a trainer, eh?'

'Probably ninety per cent of the people here,' Gillian said, still, Jemima noticed, beaming like an idiot as she sat down. 'They think it's all champagne and roses.'

'More like shit and heartache,' Drew said, kissing Maddy briefly. 'Can't stop, sweetheart. You okay?'

'Fine. We'll start dishing up the food after the first race. And don't shout at the horse, Drew. I'm sure he couldn't help it.'

'I never shout at horses, dogs, cats, children—or you.' Drew's eyes crinkled at the corners. 'Don't make me out to be an ogre.'

'Want some help in rounding up the farrier?' Charlie Somerset unpeeled himself from Lucinda, and drifted across from the bar. He kissed Gillian in passing. 'Enjoying yourself?'

Gillian flushed with pleasure and kissed him back. 'Of course. Charlie, have you met Jemima?'

Jemima thought that whatever else they did, the racing fraternity did a hell of a lot of kissing. And it wasn't just luwie air-kissing either, it was the real McCoy.

But Charlie Somerset, who was even more stunning close to, didn't attempt to kiss her. Instead he stretched out his hand. 'I've been avoiding you like the plague, actually. I know you're an Oxford bluestocking and own the bookshop. I think with my IQ being in minus figures and my preference for stockings being black, it rather puts me out of your league. Anyway, it's lovely to meet you.'

Clever, Jemima thought grudgingly. Very clever. She tried to think of something equally witty to say in reply and couldn't. Charlie Somerset—she *had* heard of him. Of course she'd heard of him. 'And you. I know where I've heard of you before. You fell off in the Grand National, didn't you?'

'I did. Thanks for reminding me.'

'Ouch.' Gillian looked at her reprovingly as Charlie ducked beneath the awning in Drew's wake. 'That was a bit unkind.'

'I thought it was pretty cool, to be honest.'

The voice came from behind her. Jemima turned her head.

The man who had trampled on her foot was laughing. 'If I'd known we were in the same party, I'd've helped you hobble back. It was nice to see Charlie put in his place for once. He's used to women swooning at his feet—and all points north.' He plonked himself down beside her. 'You don't look at all like a swooner to me. I'm Matt Garside. And you must be Jemima. I've heard all about you from your father.'

Dear God! Jemima tried to yank her brain into gear. 'Really? When?'

Maddy, however, forestalled any further conversation by clapping her hands, then giggling. 'God, sorry. I do this so often with Poppy. I've started to assume everyone is about a year old! Drink up and we'll go and watch the race. It's bound to be delayed by at least fifteen minutes now—especially if Drew can't find the farrier.'

As everyone scrambled out of the marquee, Jemima remained rooted in her chair. What the hell was she supposed to do now? Be polite and join in? Stick to her principles and remain seated? Gillian, the turncoat, had already gone, her arm round Lucinda Cox's well licked shoulders.

'We'll be along in a moment,' Matt Garside said to Maddy. 'I need a drink first.'

'Don't wait for me,' Jemima said, when he'd returned with two Diet Cokes and a lot of ice. 'I'm not going.'

'I didn't think you would, somehow. Vincent said you weren't keen. That's why I was surprised to see you here.'

'Really?' What else had Vincent made public about her? 'How do you know my dad?'

It wasn't quite as awful as she'd expected. Nowhere near as bad, really. They'd met in the Cat and Fiddle. Become drinking chums. Her father seemed to have given Matt the authorised, sanitised version of the Carlisle story. She had no intention of enlightening him.

There had been one heart-stopping moment when Matt, chuckling, had said that Vincent had claimed to have been trained in gardening at Bisley. Easy mistake to make, Matt had said, but Vincent had insisted that, no, it was no mistake. He had the Royal Horticultural Society certificates to prove it. Some wag in the Snug of the Cat and Fiddle had suggested that he must have been taught to shoot high-velocity seeds into the soil.

Apparently Vincent had got quite uppity at that point, and had said he'd go back to his cottage

174

to get his paperwork if his word was going to be doubted. The whole pub had been in uproar, Matt told her, arguing over Wisley or Bisley. The landlord had prevented it from becoming a full-scale punch-up by producing his *Guinness Book of Knowledge*.

Vincent had said of course he meant Wisley—easy mistake to make—especially after several pints . . .

Jemima didn't know whether to laugh or cry.

'He's a gem, your father.' Matt drizzled more Coke over her glass of ice. 'You must be proud of him.'

'Very,' she said shortly, racking her brains to find another topic. She'd kill Vincent, of course. But not until after she'd killed Gillian.

Matt didn't seem in any hurry to rush off to join the others to watch the race. The delay was still being announced over the Tannoy. Spreading a plate sounded fairly terminal.

'What does that mean? Does it hurt the horse?'

'No more than you chipping a finger-nail, but it's a damn nuisance. It means losing a shoe. At least it was in the parade ring. Sometimes it happens down at the start—that really dogs everyone off. Don't look so confused—it'll all become crystal clear in time.'

Jemima knew that it wouldn't, thankfully. 'It's a whole new language. And I was never any good at those.'

'Do you want to talk about it? Why you don't like racing?'

'Not really.'

'Okay, then.' He leaned back in his chair and crossed his legs. 'Let's find something we can

175

discuss without coming to blows. Politics? Religion? Music? Art? Not food, because I know you work in the Munchy Bar and I'm constantly starving. I know, literature. Tell me about books.'

He was wonderfully easy to talk to. He had none of the hormone-stirring appeal of Charlie, and Jemima, recognising a kindred spirit, relaxed again. They talked at length about the bookshop—he was well read and enthused over a range of authors—and it was only when an enormous cheer shattered the background hum that she remembered where she was.

'Sounds like they might be ready for kick-off at last. Do you want to watch?' Matt asked. 'It might help. I mean, I'm not sure why you don't like racing, but I guess it's pretty boring if you're not involved.'

Oh, God. Which way should she leap this time? She muttered about being an animal lover and hating to see such glorious animals so cruelly treated.

'No cruelty involved,' Matt said, standing up. 'Honestly.'

'But the whips—'

'Whips are part of the tack. They have to be carried. It's in the rules. Racing is an archaic game—nothing much has changed for centuries. You'll notice that most jockeys only use their whips to keep the horse in a straight line—just flicking them alongside in their eye-line. It's for balance. Good jockeys can ride a horse with their hands, their heels, their knees, and their brains. And,' he finished, 'there are dire penalties for those jockeys who abuse the whip.'

'I had no idea. I didn't even know there were rules. I suppose I shouldn't criticise something I

176

know nothing about.' Jemima was floundering. Why couldn't she tell him the truth? He seemed so nice. So understanding. 'Go on then, yes—I'll watch from a distance—but . . . but would it be okay if we didn't go anywhere near any bookmakers?'

'Fine by me.'

They crossed the soft, mossy grass towards the parade ring. Away from the shade of the marquee and the umbrella of trees, the sun still scorched from a flawless sky. The pre-parade ring was now empty and the horses were being led lazily round the larger circular paddock, while their jockeys huddled in a rainbow clump in the middle.

'Wait here while I go and get a couple of racecards,' Matt said as Jemima joined the crowd clustered against the white rails. 'They'll all be cursing Drew to high heaven. They hate delays with the first race. Throws everything out, you see. I won't be long. Don't move.'

As Jemima watched the hypnotic sexy sway of the horses' glossy hindquarters parade in front of her, she was nudged rather unceremoniously aside by a rather portly man in a straw hat and braces who seemed to want her particular spot on the rails. Jemima glared and clung on. The man squirmed in beside her, smelling strongly of beer and sweat. Vincent's cronies had always smelled like that during her childhood, Jemima thought, moving away.

She found a new vantage point between two very young, very pretty girls clutching autograph books. There was a stir in the paddock as Drew's lad led in Blue Ruin, now apparently—at least to Jemima's uneducated eyes—perfectly shod, and a desultory cheer went up. Somewhere a disembodied voice testily declared that the jockeys should mount for the first race, and Suzy hauled herself easily into Blue Ruin's saddle with a wry grin at Drew.

Jemima's neighbours immediately started squealing and she looked at them with some concern.

'It's Luke Delaney,' the youngest one gasped.

Her companion looked as though she was about to burst into tears. 'I can't believe we're breathing the same air!'

They gave matching shuddering sighs and beamed at her in sisterly comradeship. 'He's lush, isn't he?'

'Wouldn't kick him out of bed, would you?'

'Er . . . no, probably not.' Jemima tried not to laugh at the adoration on the teenage faces. She hadn't realised that jockeys had groupies, too.

'You moved.' Matt's voice was accusing. 'I nearly accosted a fat man in braces.'

'He was a bit ripe so I came over here.' She refused the proffered racecard. 'Have you put money on Blue Ruin?'

Matt squeezed himself in between her and the Luke Delaney fan club, who gave him simpering smiles. 'I'm not allowed to gamble.'

Christ! He was another one! A bankrupt! A GamAn member!

'I'm a jockey,' Matt said. 'Jockey's aren't allowed to bet.'

Jemima felt cold suddenly. She should have known.

Matt sensed her recoil. 'Is that a problem?'

The biggest problem in the world. It was as awful as a vegetarian discovering that the love of their life worked in an abattoir. And just when she'd thought she'd found someone . . .

'We're quite civilised,' Matt said, as the horses streamed out on to the track. 'Some of us can even read and write.'

And torture horses and bankrupt the unwary . . .

'Jemima—'

It was hardly a road to Damascus revelation, but Jemima knew that the decision she made now would probably change her life. Her life—her new life—depended on the goodwill of the Milton St John residents. All her life—her old life—she had hated everything that this evening stood for. Forwards or backwards? There wasn't a choice.

She looked steadily at Matt. 'I'll watch the race with you.'

*   *   *

At just after eight o'clock they made their way back to the Milton St John contingent. There had been five races so far. Drew's horses had won two and been placed in the others, so the atmosphere in the tent was euphoric.

Jemima had been reluctantly impressed by the spectacle. Thanks to Matt's information about the whips, she'd watched carefully and discovered that he was right. And the jockeys didn't wear spurs as she'd always believed. And the horses seemed to enjoy themselves. And none of them were limping or bleeding at the end. Of course this was flat racing—they were only doing what came naturally to them—running as a pack. Jumping, she was sure, was far more barbaric.

'It wasn't too bad, was it?' Matt bit into a fat-free prawn. 'You'll be spending all your spare time in the Vicarage tuned to Channel Four and poring over the *Racing Post.*'

'Hardly, but thanks anyway.' Jemima accepted a cold cloudy glass of white wine. 'You've laid several of my ghosts this evening.'

'I'm glad. I was wondering . . . Can I give you a lift home when all this is over?'

Jemima looked across the crowd to where Gillian was hobnobbing with Drew and Charlie Somerset. It was a bit of a Solomon's baby dilemma. Being forced to choose between travelling with Gillian, who would no doubt try to coerce her into giving her name to this secret horse, or a jockey who was, of course, an animal abuser and the scum of the earth.

Put like that, it wasn't so difficult.

'Yes,' she said to Matt. 'That would be lovely.'

CHAPTER THIRTEEN

'Holy hell!' Suzy Beckett's voice echoed along the flagged hall from Peapods' kitchen. 'Bloody men! Why do they have to have sodding selective hearing? They never listen to a whole story, do they?'

'Have you tried talking calmly to him?' Maddy's big-sisterly concern was apparent from her tone. 'Luke's never going to take you seriously if you just yell at him—'

'Luke doesn't take me seriously full stop. He doesn't understand. He can't see why I don't want to stay here for ever. This is it as far as he's concerned. He thinks that because he's made it to the top with Emilio Marquez, and now that I'm a fully-fledged jockey and John Hastings has offered me a retainer, that I should grab the good life here and be grateful!'

'Well, he's got a point . . .'

Suzy's voice had risen sharply. 'No, he damn well hasn't! I don't just want to live in Luke Delaney's shadow—however wonderful it is. I want a career of my own! I've got ambitions—plans—'

'You're still only nineteen, Suze. You've got years yet—'

'Ten at the most! I want to win Classics! I want to be—'

Maddy had interrupted gently. 'Do you still love him?'

'Of course I love him. I've always loved him. But that's not the point, as you well know. Come on, Mad, if you're going to tell me that love can conquer all, then it's a bit pot and black kettle, isn't it?'

Drew, who unseen in the study had been half-listening to the conversation while digging out his car keys and mobile phone, suddenly wished he was somewhere else. Maddy was silent for an unsettlingly long moment. Suzy and Luke's problems were fairly commonplace: their relationship was volatile, and it was well known in the village's racing circles that Suzy wanted to move on, move away, achieve greater things. But if Maddy was going to reveal some inner secret . . .

'So?' Suzy had demanded. 'Have you told Drew yet? You haven't, have you?'

Maddy's answer had been almost inaudible. He'd had to hold his breath—God forgive him—to hear her.

'No. Not yet. How can I? The decree nisi is due any day and he's dead set on getting married as soon as the divorce is absolute . . . I simply can't tell him—'

'Well, you're going to have to soon. He's already making plans. God, we're a right pair, aren't we?'

Should he wait and hear more? Of course that would have been the obvious thing to do: stand there and listen. Find out. But he'd known he wouldn't. He never had. Since childhood he'd tended to look on the half-full glass side of life. If things were bad, he'd always reasoned, he'd know soon enough. No point in panicking too early.

That may well have got him through the angst of his youth, he thought grimly, but he was a big boy now. He'd had to face up to the reality of Peapods going bust. But he couldn't ever face losing Maddy.

Feeling sick, Drew had coughed loudly, dropped his car keys several times and then, whistling cheerfully, had walked into the kitchen.

Maddy and Suzy, nursing coffee cups at the table, had both smiled at him.

He'd stretched his face into the shadow of an answering grin, bending down to kiss Poppy, stroke the cats and pat the dogs. Anything to delay looking into Maddy's eyes. 'I'm just off. I don't know how long I'll be. I'll ring later . . .'

'Take care.' Maddy had kissed him as he straightened up, and Suzy had winked, and he'd wondered if he'd dreamed the whole thing.

Sadly, he knew he hadn't. As he drove away from Peapods, his head felt wrapped in cotton wool, and there was a nasty punching pain just beneath his ribs. Suzy was obviously no longer deliriously happy with Luke—and Maddy . . . Maddy didn't want to marry him.

He had driven away from Milton St John on autopilot, and was scarily on the M4 before he realised it. He'd opened the windows, turned up the volume on the radio, and managed to concentrate for the rest of the journey.

Things had been going really well in the three weeks since the string of successes at Windsor. His chasers were at least being placed—albeit at the smaller meetings—and Kit and Rosa Pedersen had agreed to help him out financially for a further twelve months. Not that it was a complete rescue package, of course. Things would still be very tight. But they'd agreed to pay for the mortgage on Peapods so that all his money could go into running the stables. It wasn't brilliant—but it was a help.

And they'd also agreed, in private, that this should be Peapods' last year as a mixed yard. One side would have to go. It looked, as he'd suspected, as if it would be the jumpers. They simply didn't command the same prize money. Which meant that Charlie, of course, would definitely be out of a job.

Drew sighed heavily. Since Alister's defection, Charlie had been taking on the role of unpaid assistant trainer. He was pretty sure he wouldn't want to do it full-time. Charlie had no plans to retire yet awhile. Charlie still had dreams to chase. Charlie wanted to win the Grand National as much as he did—and now it looked as though this would be their last chance. He'd have to sell off the National Hunt side of the business immediately after next year's Aintree meeting.

Which was why he was tearing across the breadth of England to go to the Newmarket sales when he should be at home facing the crisis in his relationship with Maddy. But then he wasn't supposed to know there was a crisis. And this trip to Tattersalls had been arranged for over a week. Not that he thought Gillian Hutchinson had a clue what she was doing. But if she wanted him to buy her a Grand National horse, then buy her a Grand National horse was what he was going to do.

*   *   *

'Drew!' Gillian's voice brought him back to the present. 'Wake up!'

'Sorry.' He blinked in the sunshine. The bustle of Newmarket's Park Paddocks seemed muted and far away. 'What have we decided?'

Gillian waved her catalogue under his nose. She had travelled from Milton St John in Charlie's Aston Martin and still looked a bit shell-shocked. 'Lots 37, 96 and 102. Well, not all of them, of course. As long as they're as good as they sound in the catalogue. Charlie's gone for a scout round.'

Drew forced another smile. He still had this nagging empty feeling round his heart. As soon as the Tattersalls catalogues had arrived, and he, Charlie and Gillian had holed-up in Charlie's cottage to read them, Gillian had wanted to buy every one of the eight-hundred-odd horses listed. She seemed very hazy as to how much money a horse—plus its upkeep and fees—would cost, and Drew was no nearer finding out how much she intended spending.

She had just waved her hands vaguely and said, 'Whatever it takes . . .'

Drew tried to concentrate on the catalogue again. All three horses that they'd short-listed

184

had good National Hunt credentials, having been placed in previous races, and had excellent three-generation pedigrees. Any one of them could be a superstar. Any one of them could be an expensive failure.

'We should go and have a look at all three in their boxes and then have them walked and trotted before we make a final decision on which one we're bidding for.' His voice surprised him. He sounded normal. Should he ask Gillian or Charlie if Maddy had said anything to them about getting married? No. He'd rather not know. Or would he? 'And if I'm buying it for you, you're going to have to let me know how much we're spending.'

Again, Gillian looked irritatingly vague. 'I suppose I'll just tell you when to stop.'

Brilliant, Drew thought. He was beginning to have serious doubts about all this. If she'd dragged him here with a couple of hundred pounds' pin money that she didn't want Glen to know about, he'd throttle her, so help him.

Gillian hadn't even wanted him to tell Maddy where they were going today. And Glen, for God's sake? What on earth was he going to think when he found that St Saviour's was the proud owner of several thousand pounds' worth of horseflesh? And Bathsheba Cox and Bronwyn Pugh would have a field day! And then there were all the other assorted problems—like colours and ownership and registration—all of which would be impossible if Gillian wished to remain anonymous.

'Did—um—thingy—the girl from the book-shop—did she change her mind about you registering the horse in her name?'

'Goodness, no!' Gillian flapped her hands a bit

more. 'We've had a few very strained days. We're only just back on speaking terms. I suppose I was pretty insensitive to even suggest it.'

'Why?'

Gillian blushed. 'Well, no—I can't tell you. I promised I wouldn't. Although,' she smiled sweetly through the pale wisps of her hair, 'it looks as though she may have changed her mind about disliking *everything* connected with racing.'

Drew, who was beginning to wish that he'd asked Maddy outright what was going on because at least that would have stopped the panic churning in his stomach, said nothing.

Gillian sighed. 'Matt Garside. She went home with him from Windsor, remember?'

'Oh, yeah.'

'Well, he's taken her out twice since!'

Not finding anything either remarkable or interesting in this statement, Drew again remained silent. Sometimes Gillian Hutchinson was too wet for words. Not like Maddy, who could make him feel that everything she said was significant to him. Her gossip was never cruel, she usually made even serious topics sound funny, and it all had some point. Maddy's gossip, Maddy's warmth, Maddy's love, had changed his life. Christ, he'd rather lose Peapods a million times over than lose Maddy. And Poppy—how could he live without Poppy Scarlet?

'And Gillian was practically jigging on the spot, 'Matt's a jockey!'

'Yes. So?' Drew attempted to shake off his inertia. The paddocks were getting crowded. 'He's a nice bloke and Jessica . . . no, Jemima, seemed very pleasant. Good luck to them.'

'But she hates jockeys!' Gillian said. 'She hates

186

racing and gambling and—oh, well, everything.'

'Good,' Drew said, staring into the distance. 'That's lovely.'

The Park Paddocks sales complex reminded him of a very upmarket holiday village on the Costa del Sol or somewhere—not that he'd ever been—but the vast spread of long low whitewashed stables, and the black-and-white half-timbered buildings, and the blue-and-white striped awnings, all had a sort of seaside atmosphere. The sun dazzled from the whiteness, adding to the Mediterranean feel. He almost expected to see waiters with umbrella-laden cocktails and pretty girls in bikinis.

He wished Charlie would hurry up. The place was filling quickly, and they should examine the three horses before the start of the sale. The big fishes were out in force. He recognised several very influential trainers and their well-heeled owners, all milling around, wearing their tweed caps and cavalry twills and hacking jackets like the badge of some exclusive club. Drew, who trained in jeans and a battered leather flying jacket in the winter, and jeans and T-shirt in the summer, knew that in his black cords and denim shirt he looked like an outsider.

Maybe he was. Maybe he should never have left his little pond in Jersey. Horses were being trotted now, showing off for their prospective buyers. If he'd stayed in Jersey, training his few horses for their appearances at Les Landes, shoring up the stables' existence by hiring out hacks to holidaymakers, then he wouldn't be in these dire financial straits. But then, if he'd stayed in Jersey, he would never have met Maddy . . .

Money! Was that it? It was as if an electrical

current had shot from the soles of his feet. Was that why Maddy didn't want to marry him? Because Peapods was only just breaking even? Was she disappointed because he couldn't even afford to give her a clothes allowance each month? Caroline, his almost-ex, had insisted on a clothes allowance even though she'd had her own business. Well, Maddy had her own business, too, and Shadows paid for Vincent and Holly, and dog and cat food, and Poppy's Pampers—

'Crap.'

'I beg your pardon?' Gillian looked up from her catalogue. 'Was that a general observation, or have you spotted a specific?'

Drew, who hadn't realised he had spoken aloud, stared at her in irritation. 'What?'

'You said crap.'

Had he? Bloody hell. 'Sorry. Thinking out loud—Gillian, do you think Maddy wants a dress allowance?'

'I should think Maddy would rather have her navel pierced. Good Lord, Drew. You know Maddy. She's the most unmaterialistic person in the world. She hasn't the slightest interest in money. She still shops in Oxfam because she enjoys getting a bargain. She tells me I'm a real spendthrift every time the Next Directory arrives. What on earth gave you that idea?'

He really didn't know. It was just preferable to any alternative.

'Forget 37 and 102—' Charlie panted to a halt beside them. 'It's got to be 96. Number 37 is far too green—he'll maybe come useful in a couple of seasons but no good for what we want—and 102 has bitten his lad three times while I was there. So

188

96 it is. Bonnie Nuts—awful name, of course, but lovely compact quarters. Sound jumper, I'd stake my life on it. I reckon that's the one. Okay?'

'Bonnie Nuts . . . Lovely . . .' Gillian smiled serenely. 'It sounds like Christmas.'

God Almighty, Drew thought. What the fuck was he doing here?

Several rather expensive-looking women were gazing at Charlie with undisguised lust. One or two of them flickered their Elizabeth Arden eyelashes in Drew's direction. He ignored them. Charlie, of course, didn't.

'Pack it in. You've got enough problems with Tina and Lucinda.'

'And we should be having a look at Bonnie Nuts.' Gillian had got hold of Charlie in an almost proprietary manner and was steering him away from the Jaeger brigade. 'The sale's about to start. Drew, I said—Drew!'

Again, he had to drag himself back. Somewhere, from one of the offices, Gershwin was flooding across the emerald lawns. Maddy loved Gershwin. Maddy was always singing snatches of Gershwin songs—always off-key and usually with the wrong words. At least, she always had been—How long was it since he'd heard Maddy singing? How long since he'd bothered to ask her why she'd stopped? When had he become so wrapped up in the yard that he'd assumed she was as concerned as him, without bothering to ask? In fact, just how long was it since he'd actually asked Maddy anything personal about herself?

That was it! She'd found someone else because he'd become complacent! Selfish bastard that he was! He'd ring her. Tell her to get a baby-sitter in.

189

They'd go out to eat tonight, and hang the expense. It would probably be the Cat and Fiddle so that they could both get drunk and walk home, like they'd used to: arms round each other, stumbling and giggling as a result of copious alcohol and the dubious contents of the Cat and Fiddle's entrées. God, he couldn't wait to ring her! It was going to be all right!

'You go on to the upper sales paddock. Get a look at the horse from close quarters. I'm just going to make a phone call.'

As Gillian dragged Charlie away from the predatory female danger, Drew punched Peapods' number. The answerphone was on. Shit! Where was everyone? He tried the office line. Engaged. Bugger! He dialled the house again and left a message.

Having told Maddy how much he loved her, and to get Holly to baby-sit, and to get herself ready for one of the Chef's Specials at the Cat and Fiddle, and he'd be home as soon as possible, and adding how much he loved her again for good measure, he felt almost euphoric. Stupid sod! How easily he could have blown it!

*   *   *

Bonnie Nuts was no Desert Orchid. However, Drew knew from experience that it was a good rule of thumb to assume that the less visually pleasing a horse, the better its physical ability. Not always, of course. Maybe not this time . . . Good God— what was the matter with him? This horse, this undistinguished chestnut gelding, could be bringing home the bacon at the next Grand National.

He looked more closely. Bonnie Nuts had an intelligent, handsome head, and a muscular neck. He was moving well. Drew homed in on the hind-legs—the most vital part of any jumper. They were powerful, promising supersonic propulsion. The hocks were straight, wide and well balanced, a good indication of nimble and athletic movement.

Beside him Charlie was muttering enthusiastically about the excellent slope from shoulder to elbow, the high withers, the short back. Gillian was cooing over pretty eyes and a sweet little face. Drew really felt he should be at least grabbing the middle ground. There were several other prospective bidders watching Bonnie Nuts as he progressed round the ring.

He nudged Charlie. 'He's well-ribbed.'

'Yeah, and plenty of bone below the knee.'

'Very sound. Fetlocks and pasterns all look A-okay from here. Let's go for it, then?'

'Oh, yes.' Gillian clasped her hands. 'He's such a lovely colour.'

*　　　*　　　*

The auction ring was as spectacular as any theatre. With its sloping tiers of tip-up seats, its discreet spotlighting in the gleaming rafters, and its multicoloured banks of tumbling flowers, it looked very like the new Globe. The wood panelling was rich and golden, the roped-off parade ring sanitised with sawdust, and the air was filled with hardly-suppressed excitement. With a third of the sales for the day already completed, Drew followed Charlie and Gillian into their seats.

'You feel like you should have popcorn and a

191

choc-ice, don't you?' Gillian said, squeezing herself very close to Charlie. 'Ooh look!'

Drew looked. A man with rainbow dreadlocks and a Versace suit, accompanied by what looked like the Blues Brothers, had just wandered in. He'd noticed them in the upper sales paddock. 'I think he's interested in Bonnie Nuts.'

'Don't you know who he is?'

Drew didn't. He shrugged at Gillian. 'Why? Do you?'

'Fizz Flanagan. He's a rapper. The twins adore him. They've got all his CDs.'

'He's into horses,' Charlie said. 'Big time. Jenny Pitman's got most of them.'

There was no time for any more speculation. Bonnie Nuts was led into the ring. Led round, he was unfazed by the lights or the hum of expectancy.

'Number 96, a chestnut gelding by Bonnie Prince out of Goodnight Sweetheart. Excellent record. Sire and dam both winners. Who'll start me at twelve thousand guineas?'

Drew, floundering, knew you didn't go in on the first bid. The auctioneer rapidly reduced his opening gambit to eight thousand. Gillian nodded. Fizz Flanagan's minders nodded again. Drew went in immediately, raising his hand. So did they. The majority of the crowd held their breath.

'At fifteen thousand to you,' the auctioneer nodded at Drew. 'And sixteen. Seventeen—oh, and twenty—'

'Don't let him have it,' Gillian hissed wildly through the wisps of her hair. 'Go straight up to twenty-five.'

Drew did. Charlie coughed. Fizz Flanagan's minders got it up to thirty. Drew was sweating.

'Thirty five—and forty. Are we all done at forty-five thousand? The bid is with you.' The auctioneer turned towards the Blues Brothers.

'Fifty!' Gillian yelled, waving her catalogue. 'Fifty thousand for Bonnie Nuts!'

'Can you afford that?' Drew blinked. He was pretty sure the horse wasn't worth it.

'Double it,' Gillian said smugly.

'Fifty thousand!' The auctioneer roared. The Blues Brothers didn't move.

Charlie looked as though he was going to faint as Fizz Flanagan shook his head, leapt over several rows of seats and headed towards them. The crowd fell apart like the Red Sea.

'Hit him first,' Charlie advised, sliding towards Gillian. 'If that fails, I'll pull his hair.'

Fizz Flanagan, who probably topped six foot five, towered over them. His grin was like a sliced melon. He gathered Gillian against the Versace and kissed her. Drew noticed that she put up very little resistance.

'Good luck with him, darling. I like a lady with balls.'

'Sold to Drew Fitzgerald! Lot number 96. And madam,' the auctioneer leaned forward, 'may I put you straight? The horse is not called Bonnie Nuts. A swift history lesson. Bonnie Prince Charlie— as in the sire—left his sanctuary on Jersey to sail to safety in France under cover of darkness. As he left he said "Goodnight" to the island—as in Goodnight Sweetheart, the dam. With me so far?'

Charlie and Gillian nodded. Drew was laughing. He was way ahead of them.

'The horse is called Bonne Nuit, madam. Good night from the Bonnie Prince.'

'Thank you.' Still pressed comfortably against the Versace, Gillian squinted at Drew. 'What's so funny?'

'My house in Jersey—' Drew thought he was going to cry. This horse was going to be his salvation. 'My parents' farm—it's in Bonne Nuit Bay.'

'Spooky!' Fizz Flanagan whistled. 'Shall we all go and have a drink?'

Agreeing to meet them in the bar, Drew whizzed off to make the arrangements for transporting Bonne Nuit back to Peapods, sign all the necessary documents and hand over Gillian's banker's draft. He couldn't wait to tell Maddy. Everything— absolutely everything—was going to be all right now.

Half an hour later, Bonne Nuit sorted out, Drew found Gillian and Charlie sharing tequila slammers with Fizz Flanagan and the Blues Brothers.

'I'm not going to stop. I want to get home. I've registered myself as the owner until we decide what we're doing. We'll sort out all the arrangements tomorrow, okay?'

Okay, they agreed.

'Of course,' Gillian said happily. 'I suppose, under the circs, we couldn't expect Jemima to let us use her name, could we?'

'Why not?' Not that he really cared. He wanted to get home. He needed to be with Maddy. He wanted to share this with her. He wanted to cuddle her and tell her how unbelievable she was.

'Goodness, Drew! It's obvious. This Grand National showdown is going to be Kath Seaward versus you. Lancing Grange versus Peapods. Dragon Slayer versus Bonnie Nuts. Matt versus

Charlie. Now Jemima's involved with Matt, it's obvious whose side she's going to be on, isn't it?'

*   *   *

Drew drove home as if the hounds of hell were chasing him. He doubted if Charlie could have topped it. It was going to be fantastic now. Bonne Nuit. Bonne Nuit. The words were his mantra. . . .

He screamed the Mercedes over Peapods' cobbles. Practically falling out of the door, he greeted the dogs briefly and belted into the sitting room. Holly looked up from the sofa, shifted the cats from her lap, and flicked off the TV's remote control.

Drew was buzzing. 'Hi. Where's Maddy? Is she getting ready? Did she get my message?'

'Doubtful,' Holly said, uncurling her legs from the cushions and placing the sleeping Poppy in his arms. 'She hasn't been in for ages. She and Fran thought they'd treat themselves to a girls' night out. She said to tell you not to wait up.'

July

CHAPTER FOURTEEN

Jemima Carlisle. Vincent stood on the curve of gravel and looked up at the dark green fascia and the ornate gold lettering. *Jemima Carlisle.* She'd made it.

'Dad! Where have you got to?'

'Just coming. Don't be such a slave-driver!'

Jemima appeared in the doorway. She looked gorgeous, he thought, in a long black skirt and a black vest, with her hair caught up with a clip, and a million watts of happiness shining from her eyes.

'I open tomorrow. I'm hours behind schedule. We've only got this evening and I want everything to be perfect.'

He looked at her. 'Just give me a few more minutes to stand and stare and bathe in reflected glory.'

'Two minutes.' She pulled a face. 'Any more and you're sacked!'

Vincent poked out his tongue and they laughed together. This was all that he'd wanted. Well, nearly all. It was all that he'd wanted for Jemima, then. He watched her skip back into the shop—her shop—and heaved a sigh of contentment.

It was a greyish evening, chilly for mid-July. It didn't matter. The rain had stopped again, and the pink-tinged clouds on the horizon heralded a fine day tomorrow. He'd learned that bit of folklore from Maureen. Not so much the red sky at night part, as the position of the clouds at dusk and the smell of the air from the Downs. If he wasn't careful he'd be emitting sporadic 'ooh-ars' along with the octogenarians in the Cat and Fiddle's Snug Bar.

Vincent walked back into the shop. Whatever Jemima might say—and she was a perfectionist, his daughter—it looked pretty damned good to him. The shelves were lined with books, all the packaging had been dumped in the skips in the yard, publishers' posters adorned the walls, the chairs and tables were set out in the browsers' corner, and there were beanbags for the kiddies. He couldn't see that there was much left to do. Jemima, obviously felt differently.

She dropped the pile of paperwork she was carrying and hugged him. 'Sorry to sound like a nag. You're lovely to offer to help. I know you've been working all day.'

He was delighted that she'd asked him. And work was becoming a pleasure, although he was a bit worried about Maddy. Since the débâcle with the walled garden, he'd studied books, magazines and television programmes. He'd managed to introduce a child-safe waterfall to Maddy's pond, and successfully pruned a few small fruit trees. The sit-on mowing machine was a breeze and satisfied his Formula One fantasies, and he now had commissions for his special brand of low-maintenance Japanese garden from three other trainers in the village.

'What do you want me to do next?'

'The stationery.' She picked up several boxes and deposited them in his arms. 'Could you put it away, please.'

'I thought I had. About half an hour ago.'

'You did. In the storecupboard. It needs to be under the desk.'

'Yes, ma'am!'

He balanced the boxes in a neat stack and carried them across the spotless sisal floor. He hoped Maddy was okay. From years of practice in the bedsit, he had learned to take very little notice of what other people were doing, but he couldn't help being rather concerned about the atmosphere at Peapods. He had toyed with the idea of mentioning it to Jemima, but decided against it. She might get worried that he was about to lose his job—and that would never do. Just so long as Jemima and everyone else thought that his sole income came from Drew Fitzgerald's pocket, then no awkward questions would be asked.

Still, it didn't stop him fretting about Maddy. He'd become very fond of her. She seemed listless these days, and she wasn't quite as chipper with him—or with anyone else as far as he could see— as she had been. And Drew—well, he was almost morose. Which, as Ned said, with the new horse in the yard—and apparently owned by one of the princes from an oil-rich country—was altogether odd.

And Vincent hadn't heard Drew and Maddy laughing for ages. And they didn't sit together in the garden any more and giggle with the baby and the animals. Knowing how painful his own marriage break-up had been, he hoped upon hope that there weren't any problems of that nature.

He had, on the QT, mentioned it to Maureen in the Munchy Bar. He liked Maureen a lot. He thought that her Brian was a bit of a knob to be away on his long-distance lorry-driving lark, leaving her alone all the week. He and Maureen had shared one or two vodka-and-limes in the Cat and Fiddle of an evening, and very enjoyable they'd been, too.

Maureen had definitely no-no'd the idea of any marital problems at Peapods. She would have heard, she'd said, if there was anything wrong in that department. Mark her words, duck, she'd said, Bathsheba and Bronwyn would be straight on the case. Money worries—yes, but they were, according to the grapevine, on the up now. No, Bathsheba and Bronwyn were still fighting their anti-porn campaign and worrying over Lucinda who seemed to be having a lot of sleep-overs with her girlfriends, and still had several A-level exams to take. There was not a whiff of things not being as they should be at Peapods.

It hadn't stopped Vincent worrying, though. Secretly he looked on Maddy as a surrogate daughter, and sometimes wondered if he should ask her if everything was okay. She'd paid him at the end of the month, and thanked him for fixing the gutters, and for the waterfall, and for putting up a new security lighting system in the yard. She hadn't smiled at all.

Vincent had pocketed the money—he'd asked for cash because he said he hadn't got his bank account sorted out yet—and thanked her effusively. Her mouth had smiled then, he'd noticed, but her eyes had remained blank.

As well as being paid by Maddy, he had earned himself a nice little bonus. Not, of course, that the bonus came from gardening, as such. Ned Filkins certainly knew a thing or two, and now that Jemima was walking out with Matt Garside—Vincent had had to pinch himself when she'd told him—the future looked very bright indeed.

'Dad! You're day-dreaming!' Jemima's tone was

mock-severe. 'Where've you put the stationery this time?'

'Cupboard under the desk—as instructed.' Vincent dug his hand into the pocket of his corduroys and pulled out a fistful of notes. 'But this is more important than your invoices and headed notepaper.'

'Nothing's more important than—bloody hell! Where did you get that from?'

'I've been paid. Now,' Vincent licked his forefinger and thumb and began peeling off fivers, 'I owe you for all the time in the bedsit, plus the twenty you loaned me, plus the cost of the magazines, plus a bit extra for being a star and not abandoning me.'

'I can't take all that. I don't want it. I didn't expect—'

'Take it.' Vincent pushed it into her hand. 'Please, Jem. For the first time for ages I can actually do this. Please take it. I'll be very hurt if you don't.'

Jemima smiled, looked at him with those huge eyes behind her glasses, then threw her arms round his neck. 'You're great. Oh, I always knew you'd do it. All you needed was trust and a fresh chance and some time to gain your self-respect.' She leaned away from him. 'I'm so proud of you. And yes, okay. I'll take the money. I'll save it, just in case you ever need—'

'I'll never need again,' Vincent said, feeling slightly uncomfortable. Why did Jemima always manage to find that one tender spot in his conscience? 'I'm getting myself straight now. I thought I might even buy myself a little car.'

'God—I'm impressed.' Jemima had returned

to the book-shelves just inside the door with the banner proclaiming *'New Publications!'*. 'Maddy and Drew must be paying you megabucks.'

Vincent back-pedalled. 'Well, I won't be buying anything straight away. I just meant that I should be able to afford something sooner rather than later, you know.'

Jemima nodded, and fiddled again with the rainbow rows of new books. Whoops, Vincent thought, not very clever of him. He'd promised Ned Filkins that he wouldn't throw his money around.

'Best not draw attention to anything, Vince, mate,' Ned had said. 'Keep the bunce under your mattress and sleep on it, eh?'

In the four weeks since the race meeting at Windsor, when he and Ned had met up in the deserted Cat and Fiddle and then driven into the wilds of Berkshire in Ned's Cortina, Vincent had made more money than he would have believed possible. That first night, his stake had—by necessity—been very small, and Ned had trebled it for him. Since then, the stakes and the earnings had grown.

'Best not get involved with anything in the village yet awhile,' Ned had advised, that first night in the tiniest pub Vincent had ever seen. 'Keep the shit off your doorstep, so to speak. There's a lot of money to be made on the network.'

The network, it appeared, threaded itself through every stable in the downland area. Lads who were underpaid, lads with a grievance, lads who had been sacked from yards, lads who had all manner of pressing financial problems—they were all there with information available for a price.

'Listen and learn,' Ned had said, as they'd sat in

a very dark and grimy corner. 'I knows them and they knows me. You're new. They won't trust you for a bit. We'll just go halvers. Okay?'

Vincent had said okay, and felt dubious. But not for long. There were things he'd heard that night that made his hair stand on end. Good God—how was any honest punter ever expected to make a profit? Was everyone on the fiddle?

Not everyone, unfortunately, Ned had said. If they were it'd have made his game a lot easier. Most yards were dead straight and had watertight security, and the racecourses were red-hot on dope-testing, so any betting coups had to be pretty clever to beat the Nanny State. Vincent, fiddling with his pint, had stated categorically that he had no wish to become involved in anything at all which would lead to injury of either horse or jockey.

Ned had looked at him with disdain. 'What we do don't hurt no one—except in their pocket.' He'd thrown back his Guinness with alacrity. 'Don't you worry about it, Vince, mate. Just get ready to count the lucre.'

And Vincent had. The first few tips he and Ned had shared had been for last races on cards at far-flung meetings. Hot favourites had proved to be luke-warm, and nicely-priced outsiders had romped home. Luck of the draw, Ned had told him, deftly stripping off the outside layer of a roll of banknotes. Nothing iffy about it at all. Information available to anyone with a pair of eyes what could see and a set of ears what worked.

They weren't always successful, of course. But for the first time since Vincent had started gambling in his teens, he was winning far more than he was losing. And the buzz was back. The sheer surge of excitement when he tuned into the racing results, or looked at the evening paper. The adrenalin-rush high that simply couldn't be beaten when he saw his selection at the top of the list.

Ned always placed the bets, and at first he'd assumed they were with one of the local betting shops. Vincent, whose mind could work out odds quicker than a calculator, was always surprised at how much return he'd got for his money. Had Ned, he'd enquired, got special rates at Ladbrokes?

Ned had guffawed loudly at such innocence. The winnings, it transpired, passed down a fairly long chain. From the course and through several pairs of hands. No tax to pay, no one any the wiser. Ned had tapped the side of his nose several times to indicate that there was no more to be said. Vincent, who had a thousand pounds now under his mattress in the Peapods cottage, was delighted to remain dumb.

Small beer, mate, Ned had said. Now we trust each other, we're going to move up into the big time.

'Dad!' Jemima said again. 'Dad? What do you reckon?'

On the corners of the counters she'd just arranged big vases of golden flowers—despite his heavy horticultural reading Vincent couldn't have told you their name for a king's ransom—with trailing dark green leaves. They looked very swish.

Rosemary had always had a good eye for colour, and even when they'd been living without any money, she'd managed to pull all their bits and pieces together to look stylish. Jemima had inherited her flair. He blinked.

'Very nice,' he said gruffly. 'Lovely, Jem. It looks

a million dollars and so do you. That young man of yours has put the sparkle back in your eyes.'

'The shop has done that.'

'Maybe—but he's a nice bloke.'

'Yes,' she grinned, 'I suppose he is. For a jockey.'

It was still a surprise to him that Matt Garside and Jemima were accepted as an item in Milton St John. He hadn't questioned her very closely about how it had happened and, when he'd made some joke about naming the big day, she'd gone rather frosty on him, and said that they were just friends— and that Matt was good company—despite his career status. And, no, she had no intention of going racing, even though the meeting at Windsor had been much nicer than she'd expected.

She would never change her mind about racing— or gambling—and although she had to concede that all the people involved were lovely, she would never become one of them, or take part in the racing scene. Matt, apparently, had told her how much he respected these views, and even admired her for holding them.

Matt, Vincent reckoned, was a pretty clever bugger.

She had gone so far as to explain to him—not that it was necessary, but he'd remembered to listen—that as Matt was a jump jockey, and Kath Seaward was taking a short break in the Isle of Man, which was as far abroad as she ever ventured, then he was at a bit of a loss during the height of the flat season. No doubt, she'd said, when they got back into the swing of things for their jumping or whatever technical term they called it—then she wouldn't see Matt for dust. Until then, it was rather nice to have company; someone to go to the cinema with, and to share a meal, a drink, that sort of thing, as long as he didn't mention horse-racing. Did he understand now?

Vincent had said he understood perfectly. After all, it was more or less what he and Maureen were doing—and he hadn't as much as held her hand.

Still, Ned Filkins had been very enthusiastic about Jemima and Matt—although Vincent had said there was no way on God's earth that he'd involve either of them in anything even slightly unsavoury on the betting front.

'Well, no, of course not, Vince, mate.' Ned had looked quite affronted. 'But she might just let slip a little snippet—you know, something useful that we can turn into hard cash.'

Vincent had laughed. Ned didn't know his daughter. Jemima, he was sure, preferred to think of Matt Garside as a farmer's son helping out in a stables—rather than as the top-flight jump jockey that he really was. If Matt Garside gave her a sure-fire millionaire-making tip, Jemima, even if she recognised it, wouldn't pass it on. And certainly not to him. Why should she? He was a reformed character as far as she was concerned.

'You'll be at the opening?' Jemima checked the books again for the umpteenth time. 'Tomorrow morning? Maddy will let you off, won't she?'

'Course she will. She'll be here herself—well, everyone will who can, love. Maureen's even closing the Munchy Bar for a couple of hours. And apparently old Bronwyn next door is leaving her Bernie in charge of the shop so that she can be here. Don't worry. The whole village is behind you.' He kissed her. 'I'm so proud of you. I only wish your mother could be here tomorrow—'

208

'Don't. I phoned her and told her. She sent me a congratulations card.' Jemima sketched a smile. 'I told her you were here, too, and that I was keeping an eye on you.'

Vincent sighed. She wouldn't care, he knew that. 'She didn't—um—say anything about me?'

Jemima shook her head. 'Sorry, Dad. I tried. I don't blame her, though. Not really. She's made a new life, like we have. She's using her maiden name now. I don't think either of us figure very much any more. Still, she's well and happy—and so are we. We can't ask for any more really, can we?'

Vincent reckoned he could, actually. But it obviously wasn't the best time to say so.

Jemima switched off all the lights and locked the door. For one awful moment he thought she was going to cry, but an entirely different emotion was in her face when he looked at her.

'I'm so bloody happy. I've dreamed about this for so long. Oh, God—what if it's not a success? What if no one comes? What if—?'

He took her hands in his. 'Listen to me. Forget the what ifs. You've done it. You've got your own shop. Never, ever, regret the things you've done. Only ever regret the things you haven't done. And make sure that you have a go at everything you want to. That way there can never be any regrets, can there?'

'Oh, Dad . . .'

Dropping her hands, he turned away. If she cried now he'd cry with her. He knew he would. He took in several deep breaths—if Maureen was right then tomorrow would be a scorcher, the wind was sweet and warm from the hills—and composed himself. 'Um—do you fancy a drink?'

Please, please let her say no. Oh, what a rotten sod he was!

'No, thanks. I'm meeting Matt. We're going into Upton Poges to see some friends of his.'

'Shame.' May God have mercy. 'Some other time then. Give my best to Matt, and I'll see you here bright and early tomorrow.'

'Good night, Dad.' She kissed his cheek. 'And thanks for everything.'

Vincent watched her climb into Floss, tuck her skirt underneath her and drive away round the curve of the High Street. Close call, that one. He shoved his hands in his pockets and headed for the Cat and Fiddle.

Ned was waiting for him, as arranged. His pint was already beside Ned's Guinness on the table. It was almost like being married.

'Been waiting long?' Vincent slid into his seat. 'I stayed longer than I thought at the shop. Jemima wanted everything just right for the morning, naturally. You should see it. It's going to be great. I'm so pleased for—'

'Very nice, I'm sure.' Ned cut him short. He was obviously in no mood for paternal eulogies. His eyes skimmed the bar. 'Now, I want you to listen, Vince, mate. I've got a plan to make us very rich indeed.'

Vincent sipped the froth from his pint and nodded enthusiastically. Ned hadn't let him down so far. And very rich was what he'd always wanted to be. What he deserved to be. What he would have been if he hadn't had such darned bad luck.

'Your daughter still lovey-dovey with Garside, is she? Good. Now, I've got it on really good authority—from my nephew Jace, who got it from a bloke what goes out with one of Drew Fitzgerald's lads' sisters—that that bit of info you gave me about the new horse in Peapods' yard is dead right.'

What bit of info? Vincent screwed up his eyes and concentrated. What had he said to Ned about new horses at Peapods? Ah, right—yeah . . . He'd bragged that he knew the horse that Drew had bought in Newmarket was going to be entered for the National. God help him, he didn't really have a clue. He just hadn't wanted to lose face.

'It's a definite for the National. No—' Ned held up his hand. 'Let me say my piece. I've heard that Fitzgerald has bought it for some big pop singer bloke—'

'I thought it was for a Saudi Arabian prince?'

'Ah, yes, well . . . A bit of a hiccup in the old info system there, I reckons. No, it's definitely some pop bloke. Bloody rich, an' all.'

'Like Elton John?'

'Richer than him!' Ned scoffed. 'Real rich. Anyway, as I was saying, this horse, Bonnie or something he's called, didn't you say? Or that might be the pop singer—our Jace weren't too clear on that point neither . . . Anyway, the horse is definitely going for the National. And Charlie Somerset is going to ride him.'

Vincent studied his pint. He drank some more. He wasn't quite sure how he was supposed to react. He couldn't see an awful lot in this news to get excited about. If it was true, and not just his own rumour being fed back to him, then it was good for Peapods. Drew Fitzgerald could do with a top-notch horse, and young Maddy might cheer up a bit.

'Give me strength.' Ned's eyes bulged. 'You

211

don't get it, do you? This is the one we've been waiting for. The big one. The lottery jackpot, Vince, mate. We've got a ready-made scam sitting right under our noses.'

They had? Vincent, whose gambling exploits had taken in all manner of very complicated bets with various bookmakers, and who had gone as far as bluffing his backers with non-existent stakes, and had once even hedged his bets with a struck-off bookie he'd met in a pub, had never known anyone involved in a real-live scam before.

Was this what he wanted? Well, yes . . . But not, definitely not, if it was going to do any damage to anyone at Peapods, or Jemima.

Ned obviously saw the flicker of doubt. 'Don't sweat, Vince, mate. What I'm saying is that with this Bonnie horse *and* Dragon Slayer in the village *and* both going for the National, we're going to make ourselves a fortune come next April. We've got ourselves nearly nine months to do the groundwork. Nine months' hard labour—and then a life of luxury. What do you say to that, then?'

Vincent nodded. That sounded okay. Ned was going to start placing bets on both horses while their odds were still being quoted at a phenomenal price. 'I reckon we better get started as soon as possible before anyone else catches on.'

'That's what I hoped you'd say.' Ned clapped Vincent's shoulder and stood up. ''nother pint, Vince old son? To celebrate?'

CHAPTER FIFTEEN

Less than thirty minutes to blast-off. Jemima, who hadn't slept, paced the sisal floor, looking at the clock. Surely there was something wrong with the hands? She was convinced that they'd been pointing to 9.33 four hours ago.

A veiled sun, primrose yellow, cast misty shadows through the windows. The shop was cathedral quiet. The books were closely packed in their multicoloured rows, and Jemima ran her fingers along the corrugations of the massed spines, praying that by the time she bolted the door at five there would be satisfying chunks of emptiness on the shelves.

Everything was ready. The bottles of wine—red already corked on the tables with dishes of nibbles from Maureen; white in the fridge along with huge jugs of fruit juice—were waiting with a phalanx of wineglasses courtesy of the Cat and Fiddle. The chairs and tables and beanbags were placed at customer-enticing angles; the walls were gaudy with dozens of posters all proclaiming this year's hottest seller. A pile of dark-green bags with gold lettering—recycled paper, naturally—were stacked in an optimistic pile by the till. The shop was ready. She couldn't do any more. Now it was down to the customers.

Would there be any? What if no one came? Where were they?

She peered through the bottle-glass distortion of the door, holding her breath. God! There was a massive crowd outside! She took off her glasses and peered again. Well, not so much a crowd—more a clump. Her spectacles and the optical illusion of the window had made everyone look like two-and-a-half people. Thank goodness for that. Two-and-a-half Bathsheba Cox's storming through her Adult Fiction section was a pretty scary prospect. Her last-minute decision not to put her stack of Fishnets on display for the opening was, she felt, probably wise. No point in alienating half her clientele on her very first morning in business.

Jemima wiped her hands down her purple skirt. Her opening-day outfit—something she hadn't even thought about until the last minute—was very similar to her long skirt and matching vest of yesterday. It had absolutely nothing to do with the fact that Matt had said last night that she looked lovely, and that her hair, escaping from its clip in silky strands, was amazingly sexy. She'd received these comments with cool acceptance, but inside, she'd glowed with pleasure. She was beginning to become very fond of Matt. They never discussed his job. The friendship would be fine for the summer—she blanked out what might happen in the autumn when he started racing again.

Still, she glanced again at the clock, those sort of things could be worried about in a million years' time. Right now, this was the biggest moment of her life. Five more minutes. She was determined not to jump the gun and yank the doors open early. She was going to be cool and professional if it killed her.

She stood in the middle of the floor. There was a faint crackle from the speakers. Her audio book sessions would start tomorrow; having completely forgotten about providing any background music, she'd loaded the deck with tapes nicked from Levi and Zeke. Some of them were totally unsuitable but, as they ranged from Postman Pat to the anarchic rap of Fizz Flanagan, she was sure there'd be something for everyone. Just like her books.

It was an odd thing, she thought, as the clock's hands clambered towards the top of the hour, to have reached nearly thirty and never possessed anything before. Apart from Floss and her ragbag of clothes, this shop represented the first stability in her life. Most women of her age had mortgages on red-brick security and Ikea furniture and zippy little Golf GTIs which they upgraded every year. She had had nothing. Until now.

Okay. Ten o'clock. She took a deep breath and walked towards the door. This was the most terrifyingly exciting moment of her entire life. Just for a split second she froze on the spot. Would she ever cope? All those people—they'd all be staring at her! She'd be centre stage—when she'd far rather be huddling in the wings.

Then she thought about Vincent, and how proud he'd been last night, and Matt's encouragement, and about the card she'd had from her mother, and the good-luck bunch of flowers from Laura and the ex-Bookworms. She'd also had a home-made card from Levi and Zeke which depicted a lot of aliens on motor bikes, and more normal ones—all with Bronwyn Pugh's distinctive orange price stickers half-scraped off on the back—from most of the villagers. They believed in her. It was time she started believing in herself.

She wrenched the bolts back, turned the key, and opened the door.

It couldn't, as she thought afterwards, have been

described as a stampede—but it was certainly a very satisfying surge. And she needn't have worried about being stared at. No one gave her more than a passing glance, a quick smile, a hasty good morning, before they homed in on the shelves and the refreshments. Reeling slightly, she realised that she had underestimated the enthusiasm generated in a village by any new arrival. It didn't matter whether it was animal, vegetable or mineral; the overwhelming rural curiosity was dying to be satisfied.

Helping Gillian at a couple of Bring and Buys in the back room of the Cat and Fiddle should have prepared her for Milton St John's jumble-sale mentality. Nothing was left uninvestigated. People were two or three deep round everything. She'd planned to stand behind the counter and announce that everyone should help themselves to refreshments and browse at their leisure. They wouldn't have heard her if she'd tried, she thought, biting back a grin. All the glasses were being filled—Milton St John never believed in waiting until the sun was over the yard arm—and the plates piled, as the books were tugged from the shelves.

Levi and Zeke, along with most of their classmates—it was by accident rather than design the first day of the school's summer break—had turned up Fizz Flanagan to disco level and were bouncing up and down on the beanbags with a selection of Barbara Taylor-Bradfords. Poppy Scarlet, dumped by Maddy in the middle of the beanbag mayhem, gurgled on a rusk and bounced along with them.

Vincent hugged her and planted a huge kiss on her cheek. 'All your hard work has paid off, Jem, love. Oh, bugger—I'm going to cry.'

'Don't you dare,' she said severely. 'You go and stop those kids from wrecking the beanbags—and only tell me it's a success when I make my first million.'

'Bloody incredible.' Matt appeared beside her. 'Oh ye of little faith. Where're the biographies? You have got an entire section on Lester Piggott, I take it?'

She punched him happily.

'Told you it would be brilliant, didn't I?' Gillian shouted as she passed, a couple of novels by Norma Curtis tucked under her arm. 'And I'm so glad we're mates again. I'd've hated to miss this.'

Jemima was glad they were mates again, too. The week after Windsor had been difficult, with neither Glen nor the twins knowing why she and Gillian were barely speaking. But gradually, as with most fallings-out, the atmosphere had defrosted, and she and Gillian had once again been able to sit, curled on the floor in the Vicarage flat, and get very squiffy on a couple of bottles of Valpolicella. Most things had been sorted out in a rather weepy alcoholic haze.

There would be absolutely no need, Gillian had assured her, for her to become involved with her racehorse. Drew was going to take care of everything. Ownership, when necessary, would be made public—and hang the consequences. She was very sorry to have upset Jemima; it was just the excitement of the moment.

They'd hugged and opened the second bottle. Vincent had been discussed in passing, and Matt Garside in more depth. The source of Gillian's finances had been hinted at—Jemima had gathered it was something to do with an advance on a novel that Gillian didn't want Glen to know about until the contracts were signed in case he was disappointed—although she may have misunderstood this point—and they'd sworn each other to secrecy about Gillian's new 'baby' who was eating his head off at Peapods, and Jemima's background, and then, still rather weepily, had watched *Steel Magnolias*.

Jemima watched the villagers swarm in and out of the shelves. No one had actually bought anything yet, of course, but there was plenty of time. It was just such a good feeling to stand here and watch them bringing her dreams to reality.

All the villagers were there. Even the ones who had looked askance when she had told them what she planned to do. Most of the trainers, the stable staff, several jockeys, and a whole flush of people from the new estate on the Upton Poges road, had turned up.

The Bath Oliver brigade from the Munchy Bar were mulling over the row of Patrick O'Brians, there was a scramble from the St Hilda's girls for the Elizabeth James and several of the stable lads had a new Bernard Cornwell in their hands.

Jemima stood on tiptoe, trying to see over the heads. Vincent, bless him, having read the riot act to Levi and Zeke, was now acting as tour guide as though the shop had the floor space of the Waterstones in Charing Cross Road. And, if the sea of white Orion cardigans round the Ann Pursers was anything to go by, Bathsheba and Bronwyn must have marshalled the entire massed ranks of the WI.

Jemima blinked back her tears. Oh, sod it. Her

glasses were misting up. She removed them, wiping the lenses on the hem of her purple skirt.

'Excuse me. Do you have a corner for easy-readers? Or the *Beano*?

She blinked again. Even blurred, Charlie Somerset was unmistakable.

The jeans and polo shirt were both black this time but the silky hair falling into his eyes was still the colour of beech leaves, even without her glasses. She shoved them back on again, wishing that she hadn't put her hair up. This was definitely a moment to hide behind it.

'Children's section to the left. We don't do comics.'

'Really?' Charlie grinned. 'You do surprise me.'

Arrogant sod, she thought, watching him push through the crowd, kissing cheeks, smiling, talking to everyone. Lucinda Cox who was dutifully standing beside Bathsheba and studying the coffee-table glossies, she noticed, didn't even look at him. That little affair must have bitten the dust. Still, Gillian said he was dating Linda Evangelista or some other superstar model, so no doubt village girls were a mere dalliance.

She was interrupted in her musings by her first sale.

Bronwyn Pugh, clutching Colin Bateman's latest, was rifling through a Margaret Thatcher handbag. 'Charlie has just told me I should read this,' she found her snap-clasp purse. 'He says his mother loves them. Very much like Catherine Cookson, apparently.'

Oh God. Should she be honest? Should she act as adviser or just take the money and run? Bronwyn, she reasoned, might quite enjoy it. And who was she to act as censor, anyway?

The cash register flashed for the first time. The first green-and-gold Jemima Carlisle bag was tucked away. It was a moment she'd remember for the rest of her life.

After that, the sales were steady. People came and went and Fizz Flanagan blasted noisily from the browsers' corner. All the seats were taken and Vincent rushed backwards and forwards, refilling glasses and plates.

'I'm going back to the Munchy Bar for reinforcements, duck,' Maureen puffed. 'They're eating you out of house and home. I'll make a few sandwiches. Smashing do.'

All those years of working in Bookworms really should have prepared her for the oddness of people's tastes. She had long ago given up her early-bookseller game of matching the title to the customer. She was wrong every time. They were buying books, and that was all that mattered.

'Do you want some help?' Lucinda Cox leaned across the curve of the counter. 'There's quite a queue. I could put things in bags if you like.'

'That would be great. Thanks.'

They halved the queue in no time. Lucinda, looking very demure in a denim skirt and white St Hilda's hockey shirt, was an ace packer. 'I could do this through the summer, if you liked. If you were looking for staff, that is?'

Jemima wasn't. Or at least, she hadn't been. Maybe it would be an idea. 'Wouldn't you find it boring? Wouldn't you rather help out in the Munchy Bar, now that I've left, or something?'

Lucinda shook her head, making the black plait swing from side to side. 'Maud will be back from her hysterectomy next week. Anyway, I love books. I'm going to read English at Southampton—always supposing my grades are good enough.'

Jemima pulled a sympathetic face. She remembered the horror of her own A-levels. There wasn't, however, much chance to discuss this, as a further gratifying queue of customers was forming.

'Won't your mother mind?' Jemima yelled in the next lull. The twins were playing something rather doubtful by the Prodigy at full blast. She leaned across the counter. 'Dad! Sort them out!'

'No,' Lucinda smiled sweetly. 'She thinks it would be a lovely idea. Keep me out of mischief, you know?'

Whether Bathsheba had any idea of what sort of mischief Lucinda had managed to cram into her A-level revision periods remained a mystery. Still, Jemima thought, as Charlie, his arm round Maddy's shoulders, passed them again without glancing at Lucinda, it was all over now. The Prodigy died with an alarming wail.

'Shame,' Bronwyn said. 'I've always liked Mario Lanza.'

Jemima did a few mental calculations. She would need time away from the counter to restock, meet the reps, do the paperwork, go to the bank. She nodded to Lucinda. 'Okay. But I won't be able to pay you very much. And it definitely won't be full-time. Say a couple of mornings and all day Wednesday?'

'Brilliant.' Lucinda tucked the mixed blessings of Muriel Gray and Jane Asher into the same bag for one of the Bath Olivers. 'I'll just go and tell Ma. She'll be ever so pleased.'

Jemima preened herself. Not only was she

running her own shop—but she now had staff. How long would it be before the Jemima Carlisle chain became the subject of take-over headlines in *Publishing News?*

By midday the first flush had faded. The shop still had a dozen or more customers, the shelves had a respectable amount of gaps, and the pile of green-and-gold bags had diminished to a satisfyingly low level. The villagers had been fulsome in their praise, and nearly everyone had purchased something. Jemima felt absolutely shattered.

'Only another five hours to go,' Matt said, sitting on the counter. 'I'll take you out to celebrate tonight. Where do you fancy?'

'I won't be fit for anything except bed.'

'Fantastic. A bit forward of you at this stage in our relationship, I might add, but—'

Jemima groaned. They'd only recently got round to kissing good night. She really wasn't ready . . . Realising that he was laughing at her, she blushed and looked away.

'Cat and Fiddle? Eight o'clock? I'll pick you up.' Matt slid his feet to the floor. 'I've got to go and do some work for the afternoon. We're not all our own bosses, you know.'

She watched him saunter through the door. Like Charlie, he was dressed in jeans and a casual shirt. Unlike Charlie, female heads didn't turn as he passed. She was glad. She was also glad that he hadn't expanded on his afternoon's work. She knew it would be something to do with the Lancing Grange horses, but as long as neither of them said so, it was okay.

'Shall I go and put the kettle on?' Lucinda asked.

'Is there a kitchen or something?'

'Good idea.' Jemima was gasping for a caffeine kick. 'Yes, everything's just through the door beside the loo. Let's have a cuppa while we're a bit quieter. There might be coach-loads this afternoon.'

Bronwyn Pugh had disappeared to make sure Bernie hadn't let armed robbers do away with the Village Stores profits, and Maureen, accompanied by Vincent, had returned to the Munchy Bar. Gillian had dragged the twins back to the Vicarage, and Maddy had rescued Poppy Scarlet and also returned to work. Charlie Somerset had gone without saying goodbye to Lucinda. Most of the people left in the shop were comparative strangers. Only Bathsheba, her legs stretched uninhibitedly in front of her as she relaxed in one of the low chairs, was familiar.

'Kind of you to give Lucinda a little job,' she bellowed across the shop, watching her daughter disappear through the kitchen door, her eyes full of maternal pride. 'Much appreciated. It's a difficult age, isn't it?'

Jemima nodded, not entirely sure whether Bathsheba was referring to Lucinda's hormonal turbulence, her own mid-life crisis, or Jemima's rather late blossoming. She hoped her nod covered all eventualities. 'She's a charming girl. Very bright. Very pretty.' God help her, she wasn't going to add 'just like her mother'—not even for the ring of the cash register.

'Too pretty.' Bathsheba put down her Anita Burgh. 'It's been quite a worry ever since she came back from boarding school. Far too much temptation for an innocent girl in this village. I'll be glad when she goes to university. All those tutors

223

and dons and whatnot to keep an eye on her.'

Jemima flinched. She'd had enough experience of the Oxford cloisters to be pretty sure what sort of eye the tutors would keep on the nubile delights of Lucinda Cox.

'I'm pleased to see that you've set standards,' Bathsheba continued. 'No pornography on the shelves. Very gratifying. Especially with you being in cahoots with Mrs Hutchinson.'

Jemima thanked her lucky stars for the decision on the Fishnets. 'Oh, I don't think you could actually describe Gillian's writing as pornographic. She's had stories in *People's Friend.*'

'That's as maybe,' Bathsheba frowned. 'But she refuses point-blank to join in our campaign to clean up people's reading matter. Says there should be freedom of choice. Pah! Poor Glen must have his hands full with her. The old Reverend Perkins, now, his wife, she knew her place . . .'

Aware that she was about to disgrace herself by laughing, Jemima nodded again and slid out from behind the counter. 'I'll just go and see how Lucinda's doing with the coffee. Would you like a cup?'

'Just so long as it's decaff—and no sugar.'

Chewing her lips and trying to think about serious things like world poverty, Jemima slammed the kitchen door shut and leaned against it. Jesus! Bathsheba was unbelievable! Just wait until she told Gillian!

The kettle, stone cold, sat on the worktop. There was no evidence of mugs, spoons, coffee—Where the hell was Lucinda?

'Lucinda! Skiving already, eh? Not an auspicious start—oh . . .'

'Hi,' Lucinda, wearing underwear that had certainly never seen the light of St Hilda's regulation uniform list, slithered out from the depths of the walk-in larder. 'Sorry. I got a bit sidetracked.'

Jemima tried to close her mouth. It stayed resolutely open.

'My fault.' Charlie Somerset, his hair in his eyes, emerged from the larder, tucking the polo shirt into his jeans. 'You know how it is?'

Jemima, who didn't have a clue, was still speechless. Lucinda, unabashed in lacy bra and knickers, started filling the kettle with water. She grinned over her shoulder at Charlie. 'Oh, don't worry. Jemima's okay. She's cool. She won't breathe a word to Ma.'

CHAPTER SIXTEEN

The horse was definitely going to be a winner. Easing him from a canter, Charlie patted Bonne Nuit's chestnut neck in delight. The bond which had been formed at Newmarket had strengthened during the last few weeks, and had now developed into total understanding and mutual admiration.

Without being too girlie, Charlie reckoned that it was exactly like falling in love. At least on his part. Even if Bonnie hadn't quite got round to wearing his heart on his hock yet, Charlie felt he was certainly in the first flushes of infatuation. Horses, like people, had different personalities. Some you got on with, some you didn't. Some remained aloof, some were so pea-brained or bad-tempered that they shut you out, but not Bonnie. Bonnie—and despite his historic and rather beautiful name, the poor animal was destined to be known affectionately as Bonnie Nuts by everyone in the yard—was sweet-natured, kind, and very bright.

Charlie, who could honestly say that he'd loved almost every horse he'd ridden, had never before felt this rush of affection. Not only was Bonnie his last chance for National glory, he was also his friend. And, boy, did he need a friend at the moment. Having no one else to confide in, Bonne Nuit's chestnut ears had been privy to Somerset secrets that would have turned the racing hacks green with envy.

Just how long had he honestly expected to get away with running Lucinda and Tina in tandem? Lucinda, with her cool acceptance of their affair, knew all about Tina, of course. Tina, on the other hand, was unaware of Lucinda's existence. And Tina, having a couple of days between assignments, was at that moment on her way down to Milton St John to have discussions with Kath Seaward about Dragon Slayer's forthcoming season.

'A rather nice opportunity for you to show me the rural sights, darling,' she'd whispered huskily into the telephone the previous evening. 'And as that will take all of five minutes, we'll have to find something else to do to pass the remainder of the time, won't we?'

Charlie groaned, and Bonne Nuit, sensing his jockey's partial close-down, immediately started to amble. Charlie laughed, leaned forward, and tugged the horse's ears. They were very alike. They'd pull out all the stops when it mattered but had no intention of overexerting themselves: at

226

least, not as far as work was concerned.

Oh, God. What a screw-up! Lucinda and Tina. In the same village. At the same time. Even if he managed to keep them apart, there was bound to be some joker who'd say something.

'Which one, eh, Bonnie? Both—or neither? Nah—not neither. I've given up fags, booze, food, sleep—I've got to have something to keep me sane.'

Bonne Nuit tossed his head and blew loudly down his nostrils. He sounded as disapproving as a crusty old colonel. Charlie laughed. 'Yeah, sure. You like Lucinda. So do I. But you haven't met Tina yet. You really shouldn't pass judgement. Still, if I did have to choose—'

He sighed. Lucinda was so wonderfully uncomplicated. She expected nothing from him at all—except a good time—and as she gave that in return, they were both happy. And now she was working at the bookshop there was even more opportunity of their meeting up without Battleaxe Bathsheba having any idea what was going on. And Jemima—he laughed out loud, making Bonne Nuit spook—once she'd recovered from that first shock of finding them together, seemed to have given the affair her blessing.

In fact, Jemima's attitude intrigued him. She seemed totally uninterested—and had said that as long as they kept their activities to a minimum during Lucinda's working hours, it was no concern of hers. What they did in the kitchen, the storeroom or the shop's yard, during Lucinda's breaks, was none of her business. Jemima, he thought, was exactly what Lucinda had said, pretty cool. For the first time in his life he envied Matt Garside.

Now that Peapods, thanks to Gillian's whim or

windfall or whatever it was, had acquired Bonne Nuit, he no longer needed to envy Matt Dragon Slayer—but he was rather in awe of his shy, intelligent, and witty girlfriend. He had never had anyone like that. Not someone who was a friend as well as a lover. She had a sparky sense of humour and, despite the grungey clothes, she was very attractive. In fact, those long skirts and baggy tops were quite a turn-on. Undressing Jemima would be like getting to the prize in 'pass the parcel'. The glasses magnified her already large eyes, and that glorious shaggy hair framing her face was dead sexy—simply begging to be tousled and tumbled.

Still, remembering her barbed opening remark regarding his ignominious exit from the National, she was not as gentle as she looked. And she always made him feel intellectually inferior. Not that he'd ever admit that to anyone except Bonnie, of course. And Matt was a well-read bugger. They'd have loads in common.

So, where was he? Oh, yeah, Lucinda or Tina? Well, Lucinda certainly had all the plus points. But then again, being seen around with Tina Maloret was bloody good for the ego. He rocked in the saddle, conscious of the fact that he should be working. Bonne Nuit bucked a bit and side-stepped prettily, becoming as adept as his jockey at putting on a show. No, the women in Charlie's life had suited him admirably up to now, giving him laughs and satisfaction in equal measure. But neither Lucinda or Tina could give him what he suspected Matt and Jemima had; the thing that he'd envied most in Maddy and Drew's relationship: a special something, a togetherness, a friendship, something more than merely sex.

Bollocks. Forget women. At least for the moment. He kicked Bonne Nuit into a canter, crouching low, instinctively adjusting his body to the striding rhythm. These early-morning workouts were becoming as soothing as the tack-cleaning. They understood each other so well. And while Bonnie didn't immediately look like a champion—Charlie was the first to admit he had none of Dragon Slayer's broad bands of muscles or fiery, tossing head—he knew from all his years in the saddle that the potential was there.

The canter became a full gallop, with the dust from the tracks puffing up in clouds beneath Bonnie's hooves. For a full five minutes Charlie concentrated on nothing else but the power beneath him, the timing, the awesome realisation that Bonne Nuit knew exactly when he was supposed to change gear. And he jumped magnificently. His lad at the Newmarket sales had said as much, but Charlie had taken it with a pinch of salt. For once, as he and Drew had discovered when they'd first popped Bonne Nuit over the Peapods hurdles, there was no need to add seasoning. It happened to be completely true.

'Time for another breather.' He slowed Bonne Nuit to a collected walk, just in case Drew was watching. 'No need to overdo it. Just keep exploding like that on the hill at Cheltenham and the elbow at Aintree and you and me will be in the money.'

He yawned and stretched, gathering the reins between his hands again, straightening up in the saddle. The sky was streaked with pink, the Downs still shrouded in their dawn mist. There was no noise except for birdsong and the constant

229

whisper of the wind through the coarse grass. Other yards were just bringing their first lots up on to the gallops, but he and Drew had already been there for two hours. Drew's insomnia and sudden feverish desire to work for twenty-six hours a day was beginning to take its toll.

And there was still Bonnie's daily schooling over the jumps in the privacy of Peapods' yard to do before he even thought about his training stint with Drew's flat horses. If Tina was expecting an all-night performance from him he'd have to get some sleep this afternoon. It really would, he decided, be sensible to finish the Tina fling. But he never knew when he might be called upon to replace Matt on Dragon Slayer. And, anyway, there was always the risk that Lucinda would read something heavy, like commitment, into her being the only woman in his life.

And there was no bloody way that he was ready for commitment.

Drew, on Solomon, was belting up and down the short gallop, head down, looking like a manic Paul Revere. He was an excellent jockey but Charlie watched the performance with some concern. These early-morning sorties, away from the prying eyes of the other stables and the scouts, had become a regular occurrence. It was as if Drew had to prove something to himself. He rode like a man possessed. Charlie was pretty sure that Solomon, who was knocking on, would die from exhaustion long before Drew did.

'Time to call it a day.' Drew wheeled round in front of him, motioning towards the ribbon of horses heading for the gallops. 'Especially now Kath's out. I don't want any of the Lancing Grange crew getting wind of Bonnie's ability yet.'

Charlie let Bonne Nuit fall into step beside the sweating Solomon. 'I think they already have. You can't keep secrets in this place.'

'You're not supposed to, I agree.' Drew's tone was bitter. 'Although some people seem to manage it. Gillian, for one, seems to have kept milord here secret from Glen. And Maddy isn't doing too badly either, is she? Or am I the only one in the whole fucking village who doesn't know what's going on?'

And kicking Solomon into a lung-splitting canter, he disappeared towards Milton St John.

*　　　*　　　*

Fifteen minutes later, back in Peapods' yard, Charlie swung himself from Bonne Nuit's saddle and stormed through the mêlée of lads and horses, and into Solomon's box. He was rugged, but not sponged.

'Drew!' Charlie removed the rug and briskly rubbed the flecks of foam from Solomon's quivering body. 'Drew! Where are you?'

'He's giving instructions to the first lot,' Frank, the yard's head lad poked his head round the door. 'Do you want me to do Bonnie?'

'Please. Ta.' Charlie continued ministering to Solomon. Poor bloody horse. What the hell was Drew playing at? Charlie had—briefly—been around trainers who didn't care and only saw their animals as money-making machines. But Drew had never been like that. He loved them, for God's sake!

Once Solomon was warm and dried, calmed and babied, and eating his head off, Charlie bolted

231

his door and stood in the yard. The first lot had vanished into the early morning, already winding their way up on to the gallops. Vincent, who had now added yardman to his various duties, was sweeping up the stray bedding which had wafted from the stables, watched with lazy curiosity by the indolent cats. The dogs were chasing imaginary rats in the food store. The smell of bacon wafted from Peapods' kitchen, and the blackbirds were trilling from the roof of the clock arch. It was all so normal.

'Did Drew go out with the first lot?' Charlie called across to Vincent.

'No. He's in the tack-room. Least, that's where he went—I guess he's still there.'

'Cheers.'

Charlie practically kicked open the tack-room door. Even at this hour it was fustily warm, with the rays of the sun gleaming from the leather. Charlie inhaled the smells; it was even better for relaxation than that lavender-oil rub that one of his ex's had experimented with when she was on an aromatherapy course. Mind you, it wasn't half as much fun . . .

'Drew!'

'Don't shout.' Drew emerged from the saddle room. 'What's up?'

'Solomon. I've seen to him.'

'Jesus!' Drew smacked the palm of his hand against his forehead. 'I'd forgotten—'

Charlie, who was all fired up to yell, took one look at the despair in Drew's eyes. 'He's fine. Warm, dry, fed and watered. Are you going to tell me what's going on? Is it this place? Are you going bust? I thought Kit and Rosa—'

'Maddy.'

Charlie blinked. He loved Maddy. Awful things like terminal illness flashed through his head. He coughed. 'What? Is she ill?'

'Of course she's not ill.' Drew clutched a light-weight racing saddle against his chest as if he wanted to choke the life out of it. 'She's never ill. She's going to leave me.'

Charlie laughed. Afterwards, he realised he was damned lucky that Drew hadn't punched him, but really—it was ludicrous. 'Of course she isn't going to leave you. What the hell gave you that idea?'

'I overheard this conversation . . . She was talking to Suzy . . .' Drew slumped on to the bench, not bothering to clear away the debris. Cups and packets of biscuits, crash hats and gloves all tumbled to the floor.

'Is that all?' Charlie said when Drew had finished. 'That's all you heard? And you haven't asked her?'

Drew shook his head. 'It's not just that. And no, I haven't. I don't want to hear the answer. She's changed. I know she doesn't want to marry me. She's not happy. And don't make some fucking fatuous remark about her being worried over money. I tried that one, but it didn't fit. Maddy has never given a toss about money. What would you do?'

'Ask her,' Charlie said. It seemed relatively easy. Mind you, he'd never felt about any woman the way Drew did about Maddy. Maybe that made things a bit more difficult, but even so . . . And the conversation with Suzy could have been about anything. Women always had such heavily coded communication systems. No man was ever *supposed* to understand what they were talking about.

He picked up a bridle and ran it through his hands. Automatically, he reached for the saddle soap the way he would once have reached for his cigarettes. Poor Drew. Bottling it up for God knows how long, letting the fear fester. He tried to make a joke of it. 'So? What other evidence have you got? You only need to worry when she turns her back on you in bed.'

'She does.'

Holy shit. 'What? Since when?'

'Months. Weeks—oh, I don't sodding know!' Drew stood up as suddenly as he'd sat down. 'I can't even remember the last time I actually saw her naked!'

Charlie blinked again. Drew had never discussed the intimacy of his relationship with Maddy. He loved and respected her far too much.

'I'm going to get a cup of coffee.' Drew kicked at the door and stomped into the yard. 'And apologise to Solomon. I don't want you to breathe a word of this to anyone, okay?'

'You don't think if I had a word with Maddy . . .?'

'No, I bloody don't!'

*   *   *

They'd exercised the third lot together; put Bonnie over half-a-dozen hurdles, and had breakfast in Peapods' kitchen with Vincent and Holly and most of the lads who just happened to drop in. Maddy, with Poppy Scarlet under one arm, had kissed Drew on the forehead in a sort of distracted manner and gone to work. She looked okay, Charlie thought. But she was—well—distant. Maybe he could have a word with Fran or Gillian or one of her other friends. Maybe she'd said something to them.

It was still playing on his mind when he drifted into the bookshop just before lunch-time. There were a handful of customers looking round the shelves, a couple sitting reading at the table while their children romped on the beanbags, and Jemima was serving someone at the counter.

'Lucinda's just popped into the Munchy Bar for sandwiches,' Jemima said across the head of her customer. 'Go through and put the kettle on.'

Charlie did. Jemima treated him as part of the furniture now, and much as he hated to admit it, he actually liked being in the shop. The books had a distinctive smell, and the brightly coloured jackets were fascinating. How on earth did publishers keep coming up with something different? And it was successful—well, so far, at least. The trade, Lucinda said, was steady and Jemima, getting towards the end of her first month, was confident about her figures. Despite his early misgivings, he could now see the appeal of a place like this in Milton St John where, by necessity, most leisure-time was active. Like Jemima, the bookshop was serene . . . Serene—he mulled over the word as he spooned coffee into three mugs. Yeah, it was a good word for her: she seemed to glide, with those long skirts, and her eyes were always calm behind her glasses, and her voice was soft.

The customer had gone when he carried the tray back to the counter. Jemima, who was running a Stanley knife through the tape sealing a box of books, pushed her hair out of her eyes. 'Cheers. You're a star. Were you taking Lucinda out—or did you intend—um—staying in?' She was laughing.

235

'Oh, hell—you know what I mean.'

'We're staying in. Fully clothed.' Charlie grinned back. 'Here, you have your coffee and I'll do that.'

He had almost expected her to refuse the offer, to become all feisty and feminist and insist that she could manage. Instead she smiled, handed him the knife, and sat on the high stool behind the counter, lifting her skirt and curling her legs round beneath her as she watched him. Slicing the tape on the first box, Charlie nearly had his fingers off. Those legs! Wow! Why the hell did she keep them hidden?

Stephen Fry's voice flowed quietly from the audio system and, apart from the occasional turning page, the shop was silent. After the rigours of the morning, Charlie wallowed in the tranquillity. Course, he thought, lifting the first armful of books from their confines, it wouldn't always suit his mood to be this quiet. Some days a blast of Judas Priest would please him far better than the mellifluous Mr Fry—but right now it was perfect.

'Where do these go?'

'Over there.' Jemima leaned from her stool and pointed. No jewellery, he noticed. But scarlet nail varnish. 'Adult Fiction. Just dump them anywhere. I'll sort them later.'

'I can put them away. I do know my alphabet.'

'Really? Okay. Go on then.'

He started pushing Venice de Bono and Star Windsilver and Emmanuelle Synclaire—God! the names these authors dreamed up!—on to the shelves. The books were all the same: shocking pink covers criss-crossed with black—like fishnet—and their titles . . .

'They're porn!'

'No, they're not.' Jemima giggled. 'They're

erotica. Female writers writing for the enjoyment of female readers. Don't be so sexist.'

Charlie was shocked rigid. He couldn't wait to read one. 'Do they sell well?'

Jemima uncurled her fabulous legs from the stool and padded across the shop. 'This is my first consignment. We sold Fishnets in my previous shop in Oxford and they went very well—but we'll have to wait and see.'

Bathsheba Cox and the Ladies' League of Light—or whatever they called themselves—would have a multiple heart attack. Charlie finished unpacking the first box. He picked up the top book from the next. *Spanky Panky* by Bella-Donna Stockings. Fucking hell! 'Can I read this?'

'If you pay for it and then only when you've finished the shelf-stacking.'

Charlie did both. Jemima was just sliding the Fishnet into its green-and-gold bag when Lucinda returned with lunch.

She stared at the bag. 'Is that a present for me?'

'Charlie's suddenly developed a taste for literature,' Jemima said, her eyes innocent behind the spectacles. 'No doubt he'll share it with you later.'

She took a round of tuna salad and returned to the stool. Charlie, drooling with starvation, dragged his eyes from the Munchy Bar's squishy delight and watched as, unself-consciously, she lifted her skirt and curled her legs again. Matt Garside was a lucky bastard.

Lucinda sipped her coffee and ran cool fingers down his cheek. 'I'm off at two. Are you free this afternoon?'

'Sorry, I've got a pressing solo engagement with

my Wallbank-Fox.'

Jemima chuckled in the background. Charlie looked at her in surprise.

Lucinda was frowning from one to the other. 'Come on, then. Give. Who's Hellbent-Fox? Another one of your model friends, I suppose.'

'It's a bed.' Jemima bit into her sandwich. He couldn't watch. 'A very swish bed. It's a very close-run thing between that and a Staples as far as I'm concerned.' She licked mayo from the corner of her mouth and smiled demurely at Charlie. 'I did have a life before I came here, you know.'

Charlie suddenly didn't doubt it. He winked at Lucinda. 'That's it. I'm getting some kip. I've been up on the gallops since before it was light. Even superstuds need their sleep.'

'Which excludes you then.' Lucinda was still miffed.

Sliding his arm around her shoulders he kissed her. He didn't want to upset her. 'You could always come and tuck me in—'

The arrival at the counter of two of the browsers, ladies from the new estate, each carrying a book, interrupted the flow. Jemima, putting down her sandwich, slid from the stool and did the business, closing the till with a satisfying clunk.

'Mind, I'd've probably had two or three more if the prices weren't so high,' the elder of the two said a bit sniffily. 'They're half the price in Tesco.'

Jemima nodded. 'True. But I can't compete with their bulk-buying. And you don't get a sit down and a cup of coffee for free in Tesco, do you? And then there's the travelling . . .'

Slightly mollified, the ladies shuffled out. Smart move on Jemima's part, Charlie reckoned. But they

238

had a point. Most of the stable staff were poorly paid, and their families didn't have much left over for luxuries.

'Maybe you should run a library as well. Sort of . . . I don't know . . . If they buy one book they can borrow another two for—say—fifty pence each for a couple of weeks. Have a special section or something.' He stopped, aware of their stares. 'Oh no, tell me to shut up. I'd hate anyone to tell me how to ride horses.'

'Someone needs to.' Lucinda grinned.

But Jemima wasn't laughing. 'Do you think it would work? Wouldn't I be clashing with the mobile library van?'

'Oh, that disappeared with the council cuts in April.' Lucinda had entwined her arms round Charlie's neck. He kissed the soft underflesh by her elbow. She shivered. 'Ma said it was a good thing. She reckoned the Mills and Boons were becoming salacious.'

Jemima slapped her hands on the counter. 'You know, I think I'll give it a try. Lucinda—your man's a genius!'

'I do know.' Lucinda shivered again as Charlie nibbled her arm.

'I was thinking more on a cerebral level, actually.'

Bloody hell! Charlie made a mental note to check up on cerebral in Holly's dictionary when he got back to Peapods. He flicked at Lucinda's plait. 'I'm always glad to be of service. Look, sweetheart, how about us all going out one night? Into Upton Poges or somewhere? Me and you, and Jemima and Matt?'

'Super.' Lucinda snuggled closer. 'What do you

reckon, Jemima? How about Saturday night?'

Jemima, who seemed to be miles away, looked at Charlie for a second then shook her head at Lucinda. 'Nice idea, but I don't think so. I don't want to become embroiled in the racing scene, you know that. And after all, he's a jockey.'

'So's Matt,' Charlie protested.

Jemima shrugged. 'Not as far as I'm concerned.'

* * *

It had been a long day. Charlie just wanted to sleep. Tina, firing on all cylinders and illegal substances, didn't. Having seen action, the Wallbank-Fox was silent. While Tina frolicked in Floris foam, Charlie sneaked into the sitting room. Jesus. It was gone midnight. He'd been awake for twenty-two hours. No doubt Drew would be thundering on the door again in a minute, ready for the next day. Christ— was it all worth it?

He poured three fingers of whisky. As both he and Tina were on starvation diets, they hadn't eaten. Charlie knocked back the whisky in one go. He knew exactly how many calories it contained. He reckoned Tina had just rid him of four times that amount. He sank into the deep-cushioned sofa, his eyelids drooping.

'Oh, no, you don't.' Tina, almost wrapped in one of his scarlet towels, dripped suds across the wooden floor. Her wet bleached hair was slicked back close to her head and looked black. Her slanting eyes were predatory. She sat astride him. 'There's no way you're going to sleep, sunshine. I haven't seen you for weeks. I haven't had my money's worth yet.'

August

CHAPTER SEVENTEEN

'Congratulations!'

Five glasses were raised in salute: one in acknowledgement. The Vicarage flat, awash with wine bottles of varying degrees of expense, and one of Pol Roger courtesy of Charlie, had its windows open to the warm August night. The Verve symphonised quietly from a corner, hardly able to make themselves heard above the waves of laughter.

Jemima, who couldn't remember the last time she'd had a girls' night in, hung her legs over the arm of the sofa and tried to think where she'd put her spectacles. It didn't really matter. Someone would probably sit on them later. Anyway, even if she could find them they wouldn't be much use, everything would be blurred.

'Another toats—er, toast—' Gillian staggered to her feet, scattering cigarette ash. 'To Lucinda! Again!'

They dutifully raised their glasses. 'Lucinda!'

Three As at A-level was as good as it got, Jemima thought, basking in reflected glory and feeling almost motherly.

Lucinda, who had escaped her parents' planned celebratory dinner at her Aunty Brenda's, was blasé. 'Ta. English and history were a breeze. I was a bit screwed over sociology. I did hardly any revision—thanks to Charlie.'

'You'd have got a triple A with a gold star if it had been biology.' Suzy squinted through her wineglass.

Lucinda squinted back. 'Charlie says I did, actually. Still—here's to freedom!'

Southampton University, Jemima thought as she leaned across the sofa and practically squeezed the dregs from the nearest bottle, probably wasn't everyone's idea of freedom—but it was far enough away from Bathsheba to warrant celebration. She had been surprised at Lucinda's readiness to spend her evening of glory in the flat. She'd been pretty sure that Lucinda would have rather been whooping it up with her schoolfriends or Charlie, but apparently not. St Hilda's successful sixth-formers would be out clubbing on Friday night, Lucinda told them, and Charlie was away until Sunday. He'd got something planned for then.

'I'll bet he has.' Suzy, looking like a fragile porcelain doll despite her spiky white hair and rather bizarre outfit of satin vest, pedal-pushers and boots, rolled her eyes. 'Won't you miss him when you go to university?'

Lucinda looked as though the idea had never occurred to her. 'Dunno. Shouldn't think so. It's not until October. We probably won't be together then, anyway. You know what he's like.'

'Yeah. Bloody incredible.' Suzy sighed happily.

Jemima felt very old suddenly. Lucinda was just eighteen, Suzy only a year older. She probably looked younger than either of them, but between them they knew more and had done more than she'd managed to achieve in her nearly-thirty years.

'I'll miss Jemima, though,' Lucinda said. 'Still I can always come back and work at the shop in the holidays, can't I?'

'Course you can.' Jemima was touched. 'It won't be the same without you.'

Finding her glasses perched on a bottle of Sauvignon looking like a Hitchcock caricature, she at last managed to focus. Well, almost. She beamed happily around at everyone: at Suzy, and Maddy, and Maddy's best friend Fran, and of course Gillian, who had all seemed delighted to accept Jemima's invitation in spite of the differences in age and status.

Lucinda handed her a bottle. 'Can you get the top off this one? Gillian can't find the opener.'

Wrestling with the fastening on the bottle of Lambrusco Rosé with her teeth, Jemima realised with a jolt that in fact they did all have something in common. Bloody horse-racing. All except her. Suzy was a jockey and lived with a jockey; Fran was married to a jockey; Maddy lived with a trainer; Lucinda had Charlie—and Gillian owned a racehorse. While she—

Jesus! She *was* one of them! The realisation made her sit up suddenly, and the pale pink bubbles cascaded over her fingers. She was considered one of the crowd—because she was going out with Matt. But she *wasn't*. Since Windsor, she'd never been near a racecourse, and she took no notice of the strings as they sashayed past her bookshop on the way to the gallops each morning. And she and Matt never discussed anything to do with racing. She would never, ever be one of them.

'You okay?' Maddy was looking at her with some concern. 'Did you say something?'

Had she? 'Oh, yeah. Fine. Really, thanks.'

She sloshed back a quarter of the glass. Would they all be here tonight if it wasn't for her relationship with Matt? Did they all think that, despite her protests, she'd joined the club?

'Can I ask a question?' Gillian waved her hand in the air. Fortunately it wasn't the one with the glass in it. 'Can I ask Lucinda a question that's been bugging me for absolutely ages?'

They all looked at her doubtfully, with the exception of Fran, who was sitting cross-legged on a Buffy the Vampire Slayer beanbag nicked from the twins, and was singing along quietly with the Verve. Lucinda shrugged. 'Not if it's sociology.'

'I want to know,' Gillian sat on the arm of the sofa and spoke very carefully, 'what you think of Tina Maloret. And I want to know how you can bear to share Charlie with her. I think, in your position, I'd be forced to violently remove at least one set of those spiky eyelashes.'

Jemima closed her eyes. It had bothered her, too, although she would never have dared to ask.

'They're real,' Lucinda smiled. 'The eyelashes. And the hair. And definitely the finger-nails—I've seen the scars. And I don't share him, Gillian. We're all free, grown-up, independent people. Anyway, if there's any division of spoils being done, then Tina is sharing him with me. She was there first. I'm the other woman—or one of them. So it's not a problem. See?'

'Not really. I mean, I'm an old married woman and of course I don't—er—fancy Charlie or anything like that,' Gillian paused to glare at Suzy who had screamed with laughter, 'but surely, it must hurt to know that he's—um—well, with someone else?'

Lucinda seemed to find this amusing. 'Nah. Not at all. Maybe it would be different if Charlie and I were in love and committed—but we're not. We're just having fun. Charlie Somerset might be just the

246

most gorgeous man in the world—but he's also monumentally unfaithful. No woman would ever take him seriously. Not unless she wanted to end up getting hurt. Which I don't.'

Christ, Jemima thought, impressed. How cool. Had this girl ever been young? She seemed light-years older than anyone she'd ever met. She peered at Lucinda. Was she telling the truth? It appeared she was. She'd immediately returned to laughing over something with Suzy. Gillian was looking quite pink. Whether from wine or shock or lust for Charlie it was impossible to tell. Jemima somehow couldn't imagine them asking her the same probing and intimate questions about the stoical Matt.

'How's Matt?' Maddy must have read her mind. 'Working hard on Dragon Slayer's prep?'

His what? Jemima blinked.

'She means,' Gillian leaned across and managed to slide gracefully on to the sofa without disturbing either her wine or her cigarette, 'how is he coming along in his preparations for the National?'

Jemima tried to concentrate. It was very difficult as Lucinda and Suzy were now behaving like proper teenagers for once by shrieking loudly and anatomically about Charlie and Tina. 'I've no idea. Why? Is it important?'

'She's hoping you'll drop a few pearls,' Gillian continued, speaking in the careful way of someone who is surrounded by far too many empty wine bottles and knows that there's still a fair bit of evening left. 'You know, you and Matt—pillow talk. Something she can go back and tell Drew. Him and Kath are going to be all-out battlers at Aintree, and any bits of information regarding Dragon Slayer's condition and performance will be gratefully received.'

Jemima's mind was blank. Surely they'd only just had the Grand National? Did it all start again straight away then, like the Eurovision Song Contest or the Olympics?

Maddy shook her head. 'I wasn't fishing, Jemima, really. Don't listen to her. Just because we've got Bonnie in the yard doesn't mean that I'm on a spying mission. I was just being nosy about Matt. I mean, when I first met you, you were so anti-jockeys, and now—'

'I still am. Matt isn't like a jockey—'

The Verve had it to themselves. The flat was silent. Everyone stared at her.

'Well, I mean—we don't actually discuss horses or anything—'

'Old Matt got hidden depths, has he?' Suzy stretched across the floor towards another bottle. 'Too busy demonstrating his stud value to discuss horses, is he? I've always wondered what he was like in bed.'

'I wouldn't know. We don't do that, either.' Christ. Why had she said that? Now they were all looking at her with expectation.

'To be honest, I've never quite figured out what you two *do* do together,' Gillian said. 'I mean, I know he never stays over when he comes here because I watch him leave from our window. And you don't stay at his house. You must have something in common—and as it's obviously not sex or horses, I'm baffled. Is he into train-spotting or stamp-collecting? Come on, Jemima, tell us what you and the mysterious Matthew get up to in your spare time.'

Jemima pulled a face. What exactly did they do? Well, they talked, and went for meals—not all that successfully because Matt only ate naked salad—and they went to the cinema. It was pretty boring, looking at it like that. 'Not a lot, really. He's just a friend.'

'Holy hell.' Suzy sat up, and having lost her glass under the sofa drank straight from the bottle. 'That's a bit unusual in this place. Being friends first. Usually no one makes friends until after they've been to bed.'

'Maddy did with Drew,' Gillian said. 'Didn't you, Mad? And now we'll soon be hearing wedding bells.'

Suzy and Maddy exchanged glances.

Gillian giggled. 'Oooh. Not a rift? I wondered why we hadn't received an invite. I mean, I knew you'd have a civil ceremony so Glen wouldn't be involved, but with the divorce coming through next month, I was sure—'

'There's no rift,' Maddy said, pushing her wayward hair behind her ears. 'We—um—just haven't got round to finalising anything yet.'

Suzy took another swig from the bottle. 'Crap, Mad. Tell them. They're your friends. They'll understand.'

'Shut up!' Maddy hissed. 'Just because you and Luke are washed up and public about it, it doesn't mean—'

'Me and Luke are *not* washed up! We're just having a difference of opinion!' Suzy tried to stand up and couldn't manage it. She sat heavily on the edge of the beanbag, dislodging Fran who didn't seem to notice. 'But you must tell Drew how you feel, Mad. He deserves to know the truth.'

Gillian leaned forward, ears pricked. 'What's going on? Have I missed a major village scandal?'

'If you have, then so has Ma,' Lucinda said. 'And that's unheard of. I haven't had a whiff of this one.'

'That's because there's nothing to get a whiff of,' Maddy said quietly. 'Suzy's exaggerating.'

Suzy's answering 'Bollocks' didn't seem very helpful. Jemima, seeing tears welling in Maddy's eyes, interrupted gaily, 'Anyone like a nibble? The twins made them. They're mostly Marmite.'

Everyone, except Maddy who stumbled away from the sofa muttering about going to the loo, took something dark brown and glutinous from the proffered plate. What a lot of undercurrents, Jemima thought, licking a rather pleasant if unusual combination of Marmite and rosé from her fingers. Everyone, it seemed, with the possible exception of Fran who was totally sloshed, had something they were hiding. Including her.

As if on cue, Fran suddenly started singing again, despite the fact that the Verve had stopped. Jemima picked her way across Suzy and Lucinda and replaced the CD with one of the twins' favourites. Fizz Flanagan started punching his anarchy into the silence.

'Cool! He's the owner of Bonne Nuit,' Suzy shouted above the rapping. 'I can't wait for him to come to Peapods. He's dead lush.'

Jemima shot Gillian an enquiring glance. Gillian shook her head so violently that her teeth rattled. God! Maddy and Drew; Suzy and Luke; Lucinda keeping Charlie secret from Bathsheba; her own dark hidden agenda with Vincent; and now Gillian still refusing to acknowledge ownership of the horse. That the information was kept from Glen, she knew, but she'd certainly expected Gillian to have shared it with her friends. Especially Maddy. Which meant that Drew hadn't told Maddy, either . . .

Hiding behind the pale curtain of her hair, Gillian managed to avoid Jemima's eyes and smiled. 'I've met him, actually. Fizz Flanagan. He's very pleasant.'

'You haven't! Where?' Lucinda was attempting to remove Marmite from her hair and gave it up as a bad job. 'At a gig?'

'Vicar's wives don't do gigs, dork!' Suzy was alert, too. 'Come on, Gillian. Where'd you meet him?'

Get out of that one, thought Jemima, who knew every detail of the Newmarket sale story off by heart. She beamed at Gillian. 'While you're explaining your relationship with Fizz to the girls, I'll just go and see if Maddy's okay. She's been a long time.'

*   *   *

Maddy was sitting on the edge of Jemima's bath looking sick. Jemima perched beside her. 'Do you want a coffee? I probably should have handed round the Marmite soldiers first. It might have mopped up a bit of the booze.'

'No thanks.'

'And there's nothing else I can get for you?' Jemima felt at a bit of a loss. She didn't know Maddy well enough to mention the problems with Drew. And she'd had far too much to drink to risk mentioning her father. 'There's some brandy somewhere.'

'I'm not drinking, thanks. I'm chauffeuring Suzy

251

and Fran.'

Unsure as to whether it was polite to leave a guest perched on the edge of your bath while you returned to the jollity, Jemima stayed put. She didn't mind too much. The bathroom had grown to be one of her joys. Gillian's taste for cream Victoriana decorated with rosebuds and forget-me-nots wouldn't have been her first choice, but it was lovely. And it was streets ahead of the cracked and mismatched porcelain in her previous bathroom.

Maddy took a deep breath. 'Sorry if I've put a dampener on things.'

'You haven't! Honestly! These things happen—'

'They do to me.' Maddy looked at her through a tumbled mass of auburn curls. 'I really wanted this to be perfect. I thought, just for once, that something I did wouldn't end up in a God-awful mess.'

Floundering, Jemima patted her shoulder. 'I'm sure it'll work out. Whatever it is.'

'No, it won't. Drew wants to get married next month.'

'And you don't?'

Maddy shook her head. 'It's all gone wrong—oh, bugger. I wasn't going to cry—'

Jemima yanked off yards of loo roll and pushed it into Maddy's hand. Radiohead seemed to have taken over the sitting room and were singing sadly through the crack in the door. It seemed very suitable.

Oh, sod it, Jemima thought. I'm hardly the best-qualified person to deal with relationship problems. She knew she was going to have to change the subject. There weren't many to choose from. 'Er—my father seems very happy at Peapods. I'm so pleased that he's settled.'

Maddy's snuffled reply was unintelligible. Jemima hoped it was enthusiastic. She tried again. 'You don't mind him moonlighting for the other trainers, then? Apparently he's getting a lot of work.'

Jemima again interpreted the hrummph from beneath Maddy's curls as an affirmative. 'Oh, good. Only he really needs to build his self-esteem.'

Well, didn't they all? Except Lucinda, of course. The entire evening looked like developing into a Vanessa Feltz special.

'Vincent's been wonderful,' Maddy sniffed, screwing up the loo roll and lobbing it neatly into the lavatory pan. 'And not just with the garden. He's done loads of retiling on the stable roofs, and all the electrics, and he's built a sandpit for Poppy. And a swing . . . He made her a swing from one of the apple trees with a little box-seat so that she can't fall out. He says he'll replace it with a proper seat when she's old enough.'

Jemima found it difficult to swallow. Vincent had made a swing like that for her, too. A million years ago, before she'd known about the rows and the tears and the lack of money. There'd been a garden with trees, and a rope swing, and Vincent had pushed her high into the pink-and-white blossom and she'd shouted, 'Higher, Daddy! Higher!' and her mother had been there, laughing . . . She snatched at a handful of loo roll and blew her nose.

'Must be catching.' Maddy sniffed again, then looked at Jemima with swollen eyes. 'You're very kind. I'm so sorry. I keep crying these days.'

Jemima, who hadn't had a good cry for years,

253

nodded in solidarity. 'My mother used to say it was the best thing in the world.'

'Mine said it all the time, too.' Maddy rubbed her eyes. 'She just never said it made you look so bloody ugly afterwards.'

Jemima managed to giggle. Maddy looked as though she might join in. She gave a further sniff. 'Thanks for not asking awkward questions. No wonder Vincent's so proud of you. Still, it's like father like daughter, I suppose. You've both done well since you came to Milton St John. And he's so good with his money, isn't he?'

Jemima, who had been about to suggest that they rejoined the party, was instantly on full-alert at the mention of Vincent and money in the same sentence.

'He puts me to shame,' Maddy said, easing herself from the edge of the bath. 'I mean, we can't afford to pay him very much—and I know he's got his other little jobs—but managing to save enough to buy a car—'

'What car?' Jemima had seen him at least twice in the last week and he hadn't mentioned buying a car. He hadn't mentioned it since the day before her shop opened. 'Is he still thinking of buying one?'

'He's already got it.' Maddy paused in the bathroom doorway. 'A really nifty little thing— oh, don't ask me what it is—I'm the world's worst driver. But he's as pleased as punch with it. Oh, hi, Gillian. Yes, I'm fine. No problems.'

'Goody.' Gillian, still fully equipped with cigarette and glass, was hopping from foot to foot in the hall. 'If you two have finished bonding, do you think I could squeeze in for a wee?'

They left at just after one. Gillian, who had offered to stay and help with the clearing-up, had got as far as the sofa and was nursing the plate with the remainder of the Marmite soldiers. Jemima, knowing that there was no way on earth she was going to tackle glass-washing at this hour, stacked everything into the sink, sloshed on enough Fairy Liquid to disperse an oil slick, ran the tap for thirty seconds, and closed the kitchen door.

There were far more important things to think about than squeaky-clean crystal. She'd have to go and see Vincent in the morning. Where the hell had he got enough money to buy a car? Demolishing every shrubbery in Milton St John under the pretext of being a wow with Japanese garden design, wouldn't buy him a car. And he couldn't get credit. There was no question of a down-payment and easy terms. He'd been gambling. She knew he'd been gambling. She'd throttle him. He'd *promised*.

'All done?' Gillian's eyes were glittering. 'I'm going to have one hell of a hangover tomorrow. It went very well, don't you think?'

Jemima supposed it had. There had been a lot of soul-baring.

'When are you going to tell everyone that you own that horse?'

'Uh?' Gillian blinked under the no-nonsense punch of the question. 'Where did that come from?'

'I was just thinking that we were all keeping secrets tonight. I wondered how long you intended keeping yours.'

'Until I don't have to.' Gillian uncurled herself

from the sofa and handed the Marmite soldiers to Jemima. 'Drew's been a star about the whole thing. We've registered the horse—but until it runs for the first time, I don't want anyone to know. You haven't told anyone, have you?'

'Of course not,' Jemima mumbled, having stuffed a Marmite nibble into her mouth and immediately wishing she hadn't. 'Will Glen be furious when he finds out?'

'Furious? No, of course not. He'll probably just have me excommunicated.'

CHAPTER EIGHTEEN

Kath Seaward pushed her panama—a memento from her holiday on the Isle of Man—up away from the bridge of her nose, and looked enquiringly across her desk at Tina Maloret. 'Surprised to see you down here again so soon. It's only two weeks since you were last in the village. Unless it's because you can't keep away from bloody Somerset, in which case you must be sodding insane. Does this mean we're definitely on for the National?'

'Dead-on definite. Dragon Slayer looks superb.' Tina raised perfectly etched brows across Kath's office towards Matt. 'How's he riding? Jumping well?'

'Out of his skin. As you'll see in a moment when we go up on to the gallops.'

Matt disliked brainstorming sessions, especially impromptu ones like this. They always caught him off guard. Kath, however, insisted on these owner-trainer-jockey discussions; she said it forged a link.

She never went quite so far as to admit to anything quite so girlie as bonding. But more than anything he felt uneasy with Tina. To her, Dragon Slayer wasn't living, breathing, flesh, blood, and muscle, with brains and emotions. To her, he was pure business. And no other owner had the ability to make him feel so amateurish. So inadequate.

He tried to outstare her. It was like trying to outstare a snake. 'He's never been better. Actually, if you want my opinion, I think we should be putting him into an August bank holiday meeting somewhere just to keep him on the boil. We've got a week to get the entries in. Say at Huntingdon—somewhere out of the way.'

He felt, rather than heard, Kath's hiss of breath. She'd told him to keep his mouth shut. But he was the one doing all the work on the horse, wasn't he? He was the one who felt the adrenalin pumping, the muscles tightening. He was the one who knew just how great Dragon Slayer was, how much he was dying to get out there and run for ever.

'I don't think we actually asked for your opinion, did we?' Tina crossed her legs, which despite the heat were encased in sheer shiny stockings, and leaned towards him. 'You stick to your job, sweetie, and let Kath make the decisions.'

Kath, damn her, laughed. 'That's right. Keep the buggers in their place. I wasn't planning on running him until September. I think we'll just up his work-rate a bit until the weather cools off. We'll give him an extra gallop or two to test his stamina and make sure he hasn't gone soft through the summer.'

Matt shrugged. 'Whatever. I just happen to know that Drew has already entered their thing for some early races.'

'And you think I don't know that?' Tina's smile was smug. 'I do sleep with the pilot, darling. It's very handy. A leg in both stirrups, so to speak.'

Matt was about to follow this up, but caught Kath's eye just in time. Charlie bloody Somerset—again. Was that all women ever thought about? What the hell did he have, to make even the hard-nosed Tina look almost kittenish when she mentioned his name?

Sod them, then. This was no place for him. He wanted to be out on the gallops, or with Jemima. Preferably on the gallops. Jemima was so wrapped up in the bookshop that she probably wouldn't have time to listen to him. No, that wasn't fair. Jemima always listened. It was just that she wouldn't want to hear about Dragon Slayer.

The whole affair with Jemima was bloody frustrating. He knew he'd left it far too long. They'd been dating—God! He hadn't even thought in those terms since he'd been a teenager!—for most of the summer. Nearly three months. He should have made a move weeks ago if he was going to. But he liked Jemima—respected her—there was no way he was going to force her into a relationship she didn't want. And Matt was sure that, like most of the women he met, she wouldn't want what he was offering. It was just so bloody unfair. Charlie was tumbling girls into bed faster than Dawn Run did the Cheltenham Hill, and he and Jemima were still merely holding hands.

'We'll bring Dragon Slayer gently up through the hurdles until the Hennessey,' Kath was saying. 'Then give him a bit of a breather up to Christmas. Maybe take him to Windsor or Ascot.

Then, depending on his early showing, I think a possible King George on Boxing Day, definitely Cheltenham, and then on to Aintree. We'll pop him over whatever else comes to hand in between. Sound okay?'

Tina nodded. 'Perfect. And with Matt in the saddle—and despite my Somerset affiliations, I honestly can't see Mr Garside allowing himself to come unstuck: he's far too used to doing exactly what he's told—maybe we'll get somewhere this time.'

Matt said nothing. He never rose to her sarcasm, although her tone always raised a faint frisson—of what? Excitement? Danger? Dragon Slayer deserved the accolade—and so did he. He wouldn't blow the National like Charlie had—but it had nothing to do with what Tina wanted. It had very little to do with his alliance with Kath or Lancing Grange. It had everything to do with his self-esteem.

'Too right.' Kath rearranged the panama and pushed back her chair. 'Much as I hate to slag off your playmate, Tina dear, Charlie Somerset is no fucking use to anyone.'

'Oh, he has his uses.' Tina stood up too. Her dress was short and dead plain. Matt realised it had probably cost a fortune. 'But he won't stand a chance against us. Drew Fitzgerald is going shit-shaped according to the gossip—not Charlie's, let me add—the boy is revoltingly loyal. Apparently he's on the edge of a breakdown because that woman he lives with won't marry him. Silly sod.'

Matt clenched his fists and managed to stay silent. Like everyone else in the village, he had been stunned by the deterioration of Drew and Maddy's relationship.

Tina raked lilac nails through her blonde hair. 'And I'll make sure that Charlie is so knackered that he can't even pull his boots on. This Bonnie animal they've got has come from nowhere— probably a cheapo-buy from the horse-rescue centre—you know how soft they are at Peapods. No, I think we're holding all the aces this year. Especially if Mandy or Maggie or whatever her name is, shows sense and dumps Fitzgerald at the optimum moment.'

Unable to stay in the same room any longer, Matt nodded at both women and stomped out of the office. He practically belted across the yard.

Dragon Slayer rocked his head over his door, drawing back his lips in what Matt always reckoned was a welcoming smile. Matt fed him the routine handful of carrots, pulling his ears. Dragon Slayer responded as he always did by smacking his head lovingly into Matt's shoulder.

'I'm going to win the big one,' he spoke against the hard cheekbone. 'And if I manage to pick up the Hennessey and the King George and the Gold Cup on the way, then fantastic. But whatever it takes, I'm going to do it.'

Dragon Slayer blew down his nostrils in calm acceptance.

'You'd better,' Tina said.

Matt sighed and lifted his head away from Dragon Slayer. He hadn't heard her cross the yard. He didn't want her there.

'I will.'

'Make sure you do.' Tina traced a pattern on the flagstones with the toe of her very expensive shoe. 'Because, if you don't, I can fix it so that you'll never ride anywhere again. Ever. Not even a local point-to-point in your little hick Devon village—which, I understand, is even more archaic than this dump. Foul up on this one, and I'll take the greatest pleasure in organising a smear campaign that will ensure you never ride professionally again. Do I make myself clear?'

'Crystal.'

Matt felt the hair standing up on the back of his neck. Everything about her scared and enticed him. How the hell could straightforward Charlie have got close to a woman like this? She was wasted on him. For a split second he toyed with the idea of enlightening her about Lucinda. But only for a second. Charlie was his mate—and years ago they'd made a blood-brothers pact never to split on one another, whatever the circumstances. Anyway, Lucinda was a nice kid. Let Tina discover it for herself. He just hoped he was around when she did.

Kath, who with the panama and the baggy cream jacket looked exactly like Somerset Maugham, was moving along the boxes towards them, having a few words with each horse in turn. Tina watched her and then narrowed the already slitty eyes. 'We're going to win, Matt, sweetie. It's down to you.'

He knew it was. But he'd win for himself. It was possibly the only chance he'd ever have to prove that he was superior to Charlie. Christ—should he be thinking like that? Weren't they supposed to be all-for-one and one-for-all mates? Rivals, yes—but close friends underneath it all. This was one occasion, Matt knew, when friendship would have to take a back seat. For the rest of the forthcoming National Hunt season it would be him and Dragon Slayer daggers drawn against Charlie and Bonne

261

Nuit.

As if reading his thoughts, Dragon Slayer clamped huge yellow teeth gently into Matt's shoulder and dribbled in encouragement.

'Good God.' Tina backed away. 'How can you let him do that?'

'Easily.' Matt shoved Dragon Slayer aside and unbolted the door of the box. 'It's called mutual admiration. You should try it some time.'

'That's the idea.' Kath reached them. 'Nice to see you getting to know each other. At least you two can relate on a professional basis, without having to reduce it to baser levels like fucking Somerset.'

Tina smiled. 'Matt is just going to demonstrate his equestrian skills. Shall we take my car on to the gallops?'

*   *   *

The gallops were practically deserted. Matt knew this was why Kath had arranged the session for early Saturday afternoon. All the other stables were either taking their breaks or away at race meetings, so there would be no interruptions; and, probably more importantly, no Peapods representatives to watch their progress. Despite her hauteur, he knew that Kath was still stinging from this year's Aintree failure. She wanted to win the Grand National with a fervour which almost matched his own.

Far below him, he could see them, the two women who controlled his destiny. Strange really, he thought, easing Dragon Slayer into the gentlest of canters, that he didn't think of it as three. Jemima didn't figure in this part of his life. No, Kath and Tina dominated his future in a way that

Jemima never would.

Leaning against Tina's car, field-glasses glued to their eyes, they were waiting for him to prove that their faith and investment had been justified.

'Come on, then.' He shifted forward in the saddle. 'Let's show them what you can do.'

Dragon Slayer, impatient for freedom, pawed the ground like a bull, quivered for a second, then rocketed forward. They thundered up the chalky inclines, alone except for the massiveness of the sky.

Like all the downland riders, Matt was well aware that the natural undulations provided the training. Nothing man-made could ever test a horse's stamina more thoroughly than those upward climbs. Dragon Slayer ate up the ground without effort, the bunched muscles making light work of the hills, the hooves simply skimming from the cushioned surface. It was like riding the wind. There was nothing in the world like it.

Exhilarated and excited, Matt displayed the partnership's prowess for a further fifteen minutes, and was drenched in sweat and pleasure when he trotted back down the track.

'Nice.' Kath nodded the panama and patted Dragon Slayer's glistening neck. 'Very nice.'

'It'll do.' Tina seemed almost bored. She ignored Dragon Slayer and looked at Matt. 'The horse looks a lot fitter than you do, sweetie. And I've heard that you're wining and dining that girl from the bookshop. Maybe you should give it a miss. After all, you can see what excesses of the flesh have done for Charlie.'

'Oh, come on,' Kath interrupted. 'You can hardly compare Matt here with Charlie, can you?'

'No.' Tina narrowed her eyes. 'I don't suppose you can.'

* * *

An hour later, showered and still kite-high, Matt walked into the bookshop. The fan on the counter was working overtime, and the door was wide open. Even so it was stiflingly hot. Jemima was busy. The bookshop always did good business on a Saturday afternoon, especially when most of the yards were involved with meetings. A lot of wives and girlfriends—and many of the people from the new estate—took advantage of a couple of free hours to come in and browse, buy the evening's supper from Bronwyn's shop, and then round off the afternoon with a cup of coffee at the Munchy Bar.

'Won't be a sec,' she mouthed at him. 'I've got a rush on.'

He sank down on a corner of one of the sofas. It still galled him that Jemima hadn't asked how the session had gone. She never did, of course. He just wished she would.

She'd done well, he had to admit. The shop was rarely without customers, and Jemima's shy smile and gentle voice, and the time she'd spend just talking to people in that way she had that made it seem like you were the only person on earth who mattered, had helped a great deal. She had been accepted very quickly.

And the shop was happy; there was always something going on. As well as the library system—Matt had laughed at the ludicrous notion when she'd told him, and laughed even more when she'd said it had been Charlie's idea—which was a firm favourite, she'd introduced a bring-and-buy book stall in one corner, and pensioners' discounts, and story readings for the kids, and a sort of parish notice-board where events and items were advertised. Jemima's bookshop was fast becoming a Milton St John focal point.

She had changed dramatically from the gauche, almost angry girl he'd met at Windsor racecourse. Matt really wished he could claim the credit. He shifted on the sofa as three women, all clutching bright pink books, tried to squeeze in with him. Was he jealous of Jemima's success? Yes, probably. He exhaled. He'd spent his whole bloody life being jealous of someone. It seemed ingrained in him to be discontented with his lot and yearn for the bit of life that was just out of reach. At home in Devon, his older brother had excelled at agricultural college and was going to inherit the farm; here in the village, Charlie stole a march on him in every area; and now even Jemima was making more of her career, in a much shorter space of time, than he had.

Still, he stretched his legs out in front of him. Not for much longer. They'd all be eating their words next April when he was led into the winner's enclosure at Aintree. Even Jemima would have to acknowledge that not only was he a jockey, but that he was simply the best, when his triumphant face was seen by millions as he accepted horse-racing's most prestigious award.

The women on the sofa were flicking through their books, nudging each other, pointing out bits and giggling. He glared at them with dislike. They'd burst his bubble.

Jemima, her hair falling across her face, her

glasses perched on the end of her nose, was still busy at the counter. He watched her. She was bloody attractive, even in that long, funny dress. And she was probably wearing boots despite the heat. What else she was wearing was a mystery. She may well be stark naked beneath the flowing folds, but Matt was pretty damn sure he'd never find out.

'Oh, I've got to buy this!' One of the women eased herself to her feet. The others sort of melted into the vacant space like liquid mercury. 'This'll spice up the Saturday-night routine!'

Her friends gave her rather raucous and salacious encouragement. Matt frowned. What the hell were they reading? He squinted sideways at the stack of bright pink book jackets. Who on earth was Bella-Donna Stockings? And the title—*Spanky Panky?* Christ! How long had they been on the shelves? Jemima would be laying herself open to all sorts of trouble if the Parish Biddies got wind of it.

He pushed his way to the counter. 'Those books—the pink ones with the black fishnet on them—they're pretty near the knuckle.'

'That they ain't.' His sofa companion was just tucking her Jemima Carlisle bag away. 'You keep your nose out, Matthew. You're like all men—haven't got a bloody clue what we women wants.'

'And that told you.' Jemima grinned at him. 'They're very popular—especially Bella-Donna Stockings. I have to keep reordering her entire backlist. The most surprising customers seem to love them. I feel very much like Glen must do in the confessional. You wouldn't believe who's bought them.'

'Not Bathsheba Cox or Bronwyn Pugh, I'll bet.'

'Well, no. Fortunately they don't even seem to

266

know that they're on the shelves. Lucinda always spreads herself in front of them every time her ma or Bronwyn come in. I don't suppose it will be long before someone tells them, though.'

Not in Milton St John it wouldn't, Matt thought. He shrugged. 'What do you fancy doing tonight? I wondered if you'd like to come round to mine? We could get some wine and I'll make some pasta, and maybe eat in the garden.'

'It sounds lovely,' Jemima said, 'but I was going to start stocktaking tonight ready for the autumn lists. I probably won't be finished before midnight. Can we do it some other time? Would you mind?'

He shook his head. Did he have a choice?

'Matt!' The imperious voice from the doorway sliced right through the bookshop buzz. 'Matt!'

'Who the hell is that?' Jemima blinked.

Shit. Matt sighed. 'Tina Maloret. Haven't you met?'

'No.' Jemima looked intrigued. 'I've heard all about her, of course. And I've seen her picture everywhere. God, isn't she glamorous?'

Women had some funny ideas about glamour, he thought. He reckoned Jemima, with her shaggy hair and her lovely face, was far prettier than Tina with her skeletal body and hawkish cheekbones. Even though the entire village knew about Tina's relationship with Charlie, and were used to seeing her on her rare visits to Milton St John, everyone in the shop turned and stared as she stalked towards the counter.

Ignoring Jemima and the riveted eyes, Tina put her hand on Matt's shoulder. 'Can I have a word?'

'If we have to. Jemima, I know you and Tina haven't met. Tina, this is—er—my girlfriend,

Jemima Carlisle.'

They looked at each other. Matt was aware of some undercurrent. He couldn't quite fathom it. Their smile of greeting reached neither pair of eyes. 'You wanted to talk to me?'

'Not in here.'

'Oh, if it's horsy talk he's all yours.' Jemima returned to her customers. The other two sofa browsers had decided to buy their pink-and-black books too. 'I'll see you later, Matt. Maybe in the morning?'

'Oh, goodness. Fishnets.' Tina's eyes homed in on the jackets. 'How very advanced! I thought everything in here would be written by Mr Digweed. Charlie's got the new Bella-Donna Stockings at home. Is that where he bought it from? Here?'

'Christ, no.' Matt laughed. 'Charlie only comes in here to—'

'Help with the shelf-stacking,' Jemima slid in neatly, glaring at Matt. She turned to Tina. 'And we actually stock all kinds of books. Not just ones with pictures.'

Matt grinned to himself as he followed Tina's angry shoulders from the shop. Fifteen-love to Jemima.

'Bit of a cocky cow, isn't she?' Tina said, once they were outside. 'You obviously enjoy being dominated. And why the hell does Charlie help her with the shop?' She jutted her chin forward. 'She got the hots for him, has she?'

'Definitely not. Anyway, no doubt you have and can't wait to get at him—so don't let me keep you. What was it you wanted to say? Is it a message from Kath?'

'No, sweetie. It's a message from me. What are you doing later? Of course, if you're seeing little Miss Toffee-Nose in there, I'm afraid you'll have to cancel it. This is far more important. We have things to discuss.'

'We don't. And I don't want to have to spend more time with you than is absolutely necessary. Or are you and Charlie into threesomes?'

Tina laughed. 'Enticing though the prospect is, I'm afraid that Charlie is apparently having dinner at Peapods tonight. Some sort of rescue mission on the Fitzgerald romance to which I was not invited. So, I'm kicking my heels until bedtime. Which is why I thought we should spend some time talking about Dragon Slayer's training schedule.'

No way. Matt thought that probably half the men in the country would kill to be in his position at this moment. 'It's really nice of you to ask, but—'

'Before you turn me down flat,' Tina linked her arm through his, 'just let me remind you that it is the owner of the horse who selects the jockey. And you do want to ride Dragon Slayer in the National, don't you, sweetie?'

CHAPTER NINETEEN

Some August bank holiday this was turning out to be. Wet, windy, and with no recreation being offered locally other than the Scouts' and Guides' Jamboree on the football field. Vincent, having decided that he'd rather be struck down by bubonic plague than have to guess the weight of the cake or the number of beans in a jar, had chosen to seek solace away from the village. He splashed his car through the puddles along the High Street in the wake of a dozen others on a similar mission. Only the fact that Maureen, looking like a queen in turquoise lurex, was sitting beside him, could raise his spirits.

Jemima had been very angry about the purchase of the car. So had Ned Filkins. Jemima, of course, had demanded to know where he'd got the money; Ned knew only too well. He hoped that he'd managed to placate them both without resorting to too many lies. Well, it *had* been the absolute truth when he'd assured Jemima that he hadn't set foot inside a betting shop since arriving in Milton St John. And it had been very nearly the truth when he'd told Ned how much the Smalls and the James-Jordans were each paying him to introduce Oriental splendour to their gardens. Vincent still felt that he'd left an unfortunate element of doubt in both their minds.

And because of that, he thought as he peered through the slash of the windscreen wipers, here he was on bank holiday Monday, with Milton St John horses running right across the country— from Cartmel to Newton Abbot—and him warned off by both Jemima and Ned from setting foot on a racecourse.

'I'm well tuned in to the grapevine,' Jemima had said, frowning at him. 'And even though I'll be out of the village for the day, I'll know if you've been gambling. So don't try anything behind my back. You've done so well so far. I'm really proud of you . . . Promise me you won't go racing, Dad, please.'

Vincent had promised. It had been very difficult—especially as Drew had asked him if

270

he'd like to accompany the Peapods contingent to Fontwell to see Bonnie Nuts pop over a few anonymous hurdles. He'd mentioned the proposed outing to Ned. Surely, if they were going to be gambling heavily for the next few months on Bonnie and Dragon Slayer, it would be as well for one of them to test the water, so to speak.

Ned had been adamant. 'Steer clear, Vince, mate. I don't want you seen nowhere near any horses. It's far too soon. I don't want no one getting a whiff of what we're up to. Right?'

Right, Vincent had agreed; actually he'd agreed quite easily because so far he hadn't got a clue what they *were* up to. As far as he could fathom, nothing much had happened. Certainly he'd parted with five hundred pounds as a stake to illustrate his allegiance. Ned had assured him that this would be returned a hundredfold eventually, but he needed to grease a few palms. Vincent was all for that.

Even so, as this was one of his very few days off, the urge to have a flutter with some of the money which was lying heavily under his mattress, was extremely strong. He'd have liked to have a real slammer on Bonnie Nuts. Show a bit of solidarity. For some reason, Kath Seaward wasn't running Dragon Slayer anywhere—which meant his preparation was probably that bit forward.

And that was another thing: Lancing Grange didn't have any runners today, and Matt hadn't been listed as riding for anyone else in the morning papers—but he wasn't spending the day with Jemima. Jemima, going out with the Hutchinsons *en famille,* had told him that Matt wasn't joining them because he was working. But if Matt Garside, Vincent gripped the steering wheel with paternal

271

ferocity, was playing fast and loose with Jemima's affections, he'd bloody kill him.

'Sure you don't mind doing this?' Maureen turned from the passenger seat. 'If you'd rather be spending your holiday Monday with Jemima, just say.'

'God, no. I mean, Jemima's going out with Gillian and the Vicar and the twins to a fair or something, which really isn't my scene.' Vincent knew that it wouldn't be polite to say that, given the choice, he'd far rather be at Fontwell Park with Drew and Charlie and Bonnie Nuts. 'This will make a nice change.'

'For me too, duck.' Maureen snuggled happily down in the passenger seat.

Brian, Mr Maureen, was spending his bank holiday driving his forty-foot articulated lorry somewhere in Spain. Vincent reckoned Brian was more of a prat than ever to be passing up the opportunity of three days in Maureen's voluptuous company.

Mind, he thought, following the line of cars through the village and glancing at the rows of soggy tarpaulins across the football field, anywhere was preferable to being in Milton St John. Poor little Maddy obviously didn't have a choice, having been co-opted into serving the Jamboree teas. He'd watched her shoving Poppy Scarlet's buggy across the damp ruts with the other young mums, her head down beneath the sagging bunting. There had been no improvement in the atmosphere at Peapods.

Having inveigled his way into the position of acting yardman, he'd hoped that not only would he be able to filch information for Ned on Bonnie's progress, but that he'd also have an opportunity to help Maddy. It hadn't worked out that way. Everyone was very tight-lipped. Drew was stalking about looking like he had double neuralgia, and Maddy seemed to have aged ten years. At least, Vincent thought, being ever the optimist, they were still together. But for how much longer?

'Got anywhere in mind?' Maureen burrowed into a bag of toffees and handed one to him. 'Better be indoors, I reckons. This bloody weather won't let up for a couple of days yet.'

Vincent didn't doubt it. Maureen's meteorological talents were deadly accurate.

He shifted the toffee into his cheek. 'I thought we could have a spot of late lunch somewhere. Make a change for you not to have to do the cooking. Then maybe we could catch the early house at the cinema in Wantage, and be out in time for the last knockings at the Cat and Fiddle.'

'Magic, duck. A real lovely day.' Maureen's eyes sparkled almost as much as the rest of her. 'I'm right glad that you moved into the village.'

Vincent was pretty pleased himself, too.

He drove away from Milton St John, through Lambourn, and hit the network of tiny single-track roads that criss-crossed the Downs. With the rain sweeping across the misted hilltops it was as if they were the only people alive. Sitting next to Maureen, warmly cocooned against the downpour, Vincent reckoned that if he couldn't be at Fontwell, this was as near as damn it a pretty good substitute.

'I don't reckon I've ever been out this way.' Maureen narrowed her eyes and squinted at the rather daunting tunnel of dark and dripping evergreens. 'And I've lived round here all me life. Do you know where you're going? Or is this a magical mystery tour?'

'A bit of both.' Vincent swerved the car into a tiny car park. 'No, you wait there. I'll open the door for you. Can't have that smashing frock getting soaked, can we?'

They scurried into the pub, Vincent's jacket protecting Maureen's rigid beehive from the worst of the Berkshire elements. In daylight the pub's interior didn't look anywhere near so poky as it had on the occasional evenings when he and Ned had been there. In fact, in daylight it actually looked quite quaint. Not surprisingly, they had the microscopic bar to themselves.

'Get yourself settled.' Vincent steered Maureen towards the table tucked out of sight in the curve of the window. 'Vodka-and-lime okay?'

'Lovely.' Maureen reached out a pudgy and heavily ringed hand to touch Vincent's arm. 'This is a real treat. I'm dead happy.'

So was he, Vincent discovered with some surprise, as he covered the bar in three strides. This was the happiest he'd been since Rosemary had left him. All he needed now was for Ned's money-making scheme to pay off, and life would be simply perfect.

The landlord folded away his *Sun*, unpeeled himself from a stool and negotiated a large dog, a pile of crates and three mammoth jars of pickled onions. He peered at Vincent. 'Not a nice day for it, chum. Come far? Ah—haven't I seen you in here before?'

'No. I've never been this way,' Vincent lied confidently. 'You're a bit off the beaten track for passing trade, aren't you?'

'Ah, you could say. You sure you haven't been

here—?'

'Positive. Are you doing food?'

The landlord jerked a thumb towards a blackboard. 'All fresh. Our Winnie can rustle up any of them. Whatever takes your fancy. A bit of a River Caff foodie follower is our Winnie.'

Encouraged, Vincent skimmed the menu, ordered two vodka-and-limes, and returned to Maureen. 'Pie and chips, sausage and chips, egg and chips, bacon and chips, egg, bacon, sausage and chips . . .'

'Home from home, like,' Maureen said comfortably. 'I'll go for the pie, duck, and double chips and bread and butter.'

'We'll make that two, then.' Vincent nodded in admiration. He liked a woman who knew her mind. 'And another vodka to wash it down?'

Our Winnie may have got a bit confused about which caff on which river, but she could rustle up double pie and chips in record time.

'Bloody marvellous.' Maureen wiped up the remainder of her brown sauce with her last slice of bread. 'That's the stuff to give the troops, eh, duck? Let me get the drinks this time. You going to risk another vodka?'

Vincent wasn't. He'd been without wheels for long enough; he wasn't going to let a breathalyser take them away. 'Better make mine a half of lemon-and-lime.'

He settled back in his chair and watched pleasurably as Maureen made her way to the bar. She was a fine figure of a woman. The turquoise lurex clung to the ample curves and stopped an appreciative distance above the shapely knees. Pity about Mr Maureen, really. If the adenoidal Brian—

275

Vincent had seen the wedding photographs—wasn't on the scene, he might just think about making this more of a permanent arrangement. With the rain still trickling against the steamy windows, and the fragrance of our Winnie's culinary efforts floating on the fug, it was wonderfully soporific.

A car rattled through the damp gravel of the car park and scrunched to a halt. Vincent took little notice. Probably someone else hoping to escape the joys of a wet bank holiday. No one came through the door. A second car eased to a halt. Still no one came in. Vincent didn't think about it much. Might be a courting couple on a bit of a cloak-and-dagger mission. Married, like as not, and not to each other. The thought of clandestine lovers on this dreary day warmed his heart.

'There we are.' Maureen placed the drinks on the table and wriggled her bulk with intriguing rustles into her chair. 'I've just seen something kind of funny.'

'Ah?' Vincent gulped at his lemon-and-lime. Our Winnie's lunch had left a bit of an afterburn. 'And what's that then?'

'When I was waiting for my change. You can see right through to the back kitchen—and I couldn't believe my eyes.' She leaned across the table, her cleavage sparkling with bits of stray lurex. 'Matt Garside and Ned Filkins came in through the back door.'

God almighty! Vincent choked on his lemonade. Surely not? Ned would have told him if things were moving in that direction—wouldn't he? 'Are you quite sure? I mean, it's pretty dark in here and—'

'I know what I saw.' Maureen's beehive nodded in righteous indignation. 'And they're odd

276

bedfellows, aren't they? I mean, what with Ned getting booted out of Lancing Grange—and Matt still being Kath Seaward's blue-eyed boy. They're not usually bosom buddies. Oh, I knows they have a pint or two sometimes in the Cat and Fiddle, but that's only if Matt can't avoid it. And why isn't Matt with your Jemima today, then?'

Vincent thought he could hazard a pretty good guess. How wrong had he got this? He had assumed that all they were doing was spreading early bets on Bonnie and Dragon Slayer, but it appeared they weren't. He swallowed the rest of his drink. And Matt had told Jemima he was working. Pretty damn lucrative work if he was taking backhanders from Ned for information on Dragon Slayer. And probably from him too? Is that where his five hundred quid had gone? Tucked away in Matt Garside's pocket?

The implications were horrendous. He'd have sworn on Rosemary's life that Matt Garside was as straight as a die. Charlie Somerset, now he looked like a right rogue, but Matt? No way. And he was going out with Jemima. Vincent closed his eyes. How much did Jemima know? One thing was for definite—he wanted to get Maureen as far away as possible before either Ned or Matt saw them.

'Come on.' He stood up quickly, making the listless landlord jump. 'I don't know about you, but I don't want to be spending the best part of my day off with the likes of Ned Filkins.'

'Me neither.' Maureen gathered herself together. 'But I thought you and Ned were mates. Don't you want to ask him what he's doing? I mean, it's all a bit James Bond, isn't it?'

Shepherding Maureen back out into the car

277

park with very little of the earlier gallantry, Vincent muttered about Ned probably canvassing Matt about getting a reference for a new job or something similar.

'Get away,' Maureen puffed as she fastened her seat belt. 'They wouldn't need to come out to the back of beyond for that. They could be doing that in Milton St John. And no one within a peacock's shout of the village would give bloody Ned Filkins the time of day, let alone a job. And why wasn't they in the bar? Why was they sneaking around the back? And why—good God!'

The car rocketed forward, the G-force leaving Maureen pinned back against her seat.

'Sorry.' Vincent looked sheepish. 'A bit heavy on the old pedal there. All right?'

The beehive nodded dubiously. Vincent, praying that neither Matt nor Ned had recognised his car, switched on Melody radio and hoped a swirl of Al Martino would seduce Maureen's mind away from Ned Filkins. As it happened she had a very pretty voice, and he was tapping his accompaniment to 'Spanish Eyes' on the steering wheel long before they'd left the avenue of sinister evergreens.

He'd have to see Ned at the earliest opportunity, of course. If the game had shifted up a gear he wanted to know about it. But what exactly was Matt doing? He hardly needed to sell information to Ned, did he? Surely Matt was loaded. And he was dead loyal to Kath Seaward; everyone in the village knew just how much Lancing Grange wanted to win the National.

'Excuse me, duck,' Maureen's voice broke in rather weakly over the top of 'Mona Lisa', 'but do you know you're doing nearly a hundred?'

278

Good God. Vincent immediately took his foot from the accelerator and tried not to flinch as the hedgerows whistled past with vertigo-making speed. It took some moments to reach a respectable forty-five, by which time Maureen and Al were duetting to 'I Left My Heart in San Francisco'. Maureen seemed to get to the high notes a tad sooner.

Okay, then . . . Maybe it was Charlie that Matt was selling information about. Him and Charlie were mates, after all. That must be it. Ned had recruited Matt to be in on their scam, too. Not to give information about his own horse—but to suss out the opposition.

This deduction pleased Vincent. It might not be exactly honest, but at least it was more acceptable than the alternative. He'd hate to think that Jemima was going out with a cheat.

'Fancy a cup of tea and an iced fancy in Wantage before we do the pictures?' He felt quite jaunty now. 'I reckon we could squeeze a snack in, don't you?'

'Absolutely, duck.' Maureen leaned forward and applied a slash of orange lipstick in the vanity mirror. A lot of it missed. 'My stomach's fair rumbling.'

*   *   *

It wasn't until they were halfway through the latest Bruce Willis, snuggled in the cosy warmth of the cinema and sharing a bucket of popcorn—sugared not salted—that Vincent felt suddenly deflated. With his arm resting along the back of Maureen's seat, the beehive lolling a bit scratchily but companionably against his cheek, and Bruce just in the act of blowing up Los Angeles in glorious Technicolor, he should have been on top of the world. And he had been. It was only when he thought back to Ned and Matt and the poky pub that he realised his Charlie Somerset theory wouldn't hold water.

'Bugger.'

''s okay.' Maureen snuggled a bit closer. 'The kiddie gets saved in the end.'

'Oh, right. Good.' Vincent squeezed a fistful of lurex.

He stared at the violence unfolding before him, and knew that if Matt was giving Ned information about Charlie, or Bonnie Nuts, or Peapods generally, then it could have been done quite openly in the Cat and Fiddle. They were, as Maureen had said, often seen together in there. No one would make anything of it. There was no reason at all for them to be sneaking about in the middle of nowhere unless they were meeting someone else—which would mean Matt Garside was definitely on the take.

Vincent sighed heavily. Maureen eased the lurex even closer. 'You old softie. Don't get so worried. Here, have some more popcorn.'

*   *   *

But it had been enough to take the shine off the evening. Well, almost. Sitting in the cinema's flickering darkness, Vincent had done a bit of quick self-analysis. Prying into the deepest recesses of his moral standards, he came to the conclusion that the only sticking point in Matt and Ned being together

280

was Jemima.

He mulled this over during the tear-jerking bit where Bruce was rescuing the kiddie—and its very attractive mother who appeared to have had all her clothes ripped to pieces in a rather designer way—from the post-nuclear holocaust. The kiddie's mother, who was extremely grateful, hadn't even chipped her nail varnish. Anyway, thinking through the whole thing, it was just Jemima's connection that he was worried about. If Jemima hadn't been walking out with Matt Garside, then having one of the country's top jump jockeys on your side in a bit of a betting coup, could only be to the good. Vincent sighed again. Now he'd developed a bloody conscience, for God's sake. And it was all Jemima's fault.

*   *   *

By the time he and Maureen got back to the Cat and Fiddle and had secured the only vacant table— the one by the juke-box, always the least popular— Vincent had decided that there was no way he was going to mention anything to Jemima. He'd speak to Ned first. There still might be some reasonable and absolutely innocent explanation.

'Sorry?' He looked up at Maureen who was hovering by the table clutching her purse. 'Oh, yes, thanks. I'll go for a vodka—or two. I can always leave the car in the car park and walk back to Peapods, can't I?'

Maureen smiled coquettishly. 'You could. Or, on the other hand, the pub's car park is right handy for the Munchy Bar. Even less of a distance to walk . . .'

Vincent watched Maureen power her way

281

glitteringly towards the bar with his mouth open. Was that what he thought it was? Had he just been propositioned? He grinned in delight. Bugger Mr Maureen with his adenoids and his forty-foot lorry.

'I don't know what you're smirking about—' A strident voice crashed in on his fantasy. 'But this will wipe the smile from your face.'

Bathsheba Cox loomed over the table waving one of the green- and-gold bookshop bags beneath his nose. Behind her, Lucinda pulling agonised faces and shaking her head, was mouthing at him.

'You've lost me straight away,' Vincent said. He liked Lucinda. Nice kid. The old woman was a battle-axe, though. 'Anyway, the bookshop is nothing to do with me. If you want a refund you'll have to wait until Jemima opens up in the morning.'

'Jemima? Jezebel!'

'Here, hold up.' Vincent was instantly on the defensive. 'What the devil are you talking about?'

'This!' Bathsheba shook the bag open, allowing a bright pink- and-black book to tumble on to the table. 'This filth! I found this in my daughter's bedroom! My little Lucinda is being corrupted by your daughter's pornography!'

Spanky Panky by Bella-Donna Stockings. Christ. Vincent blinked. It probably wasn't the best moment to say that he doubted if the book— however raunchy—could teach Lucinda anything that Charlie Somerset hadn't. 'I don't know anything about any books. And I'm damned sure that Jemima wouldn't stock anything iffy. Why don't you ask her?'

'I've tried. Believe me.' Bathsheba was turning a sort of mottled purple. 'The Vicarage is empty. I'm quite prepared to wait outside all night if necessary.

The Vicar must be told what sort of harpy he's harbouring! And that—that—den of vice must be closed down.'

'Don't be so bloody stupid.' Vincent was defensive. 'Jemima's a proper bookseller. Trained. With certificates. She wouldn't stock no under-the-counter stuff. Look, I think you might have got the wrong end of the stick, my love.'

'Don't you "my love" me! I know exactly which end of the stick I'm holding, Mr Carlisle. And, should you see your daughter before I do, I'd appreciate it if you'd tell her that I'll not rest until her shop is closed. Milton St John is a pillar of moral rectitude. We will not be desecrated by outsiders!'

'Stone me.' Maureen eased herself and two double vodkas between Bathsheba and Lucinda. 'What's going on here then?'

Vincent, aided and abetted by Bathsheba, filled Maureen in on the salient points.

Maureen picked up the book from the table and laughed so much that the lurex sparkled off in all directions. 'This isn't pornography, you silly woman. This is Fishnets. I've got 'em all—and darn good reads they are, too. My mum loves them an' she's well into her eighties.'

'Does Jemima stock them, then?' Vincent was a bit at sea here. 'I can't say I've noticed them.'

'Well, they're hardly your thing, duck, are they?' Maureen sat down accompanied by that tempting rustle of silk underwear. 'Of course she stocks them. And,' she glared at Bathsheba, 'they sells like my hot lardys. You'll have a battle royal on your hands if you try and ban them.'

'If that's what it takes.' Bathsheba's lips quivered.

'I shall be calling my ladies together first thing. Come on, Lucinda, let's go and start making plans.'

Hell's teeth, Vincent thought, watching as Bathsheba shepherded the still-silent Lucinda through the Cat and Fiddle's throng. And just when things were going so well for Jemima and the bookshop, too. Poor kid—not only was her boyfriend not all he seemed, but now she'd got the Ladies' League of Light up in arms, too. She'd need a bit of parental support from her old dad now, and no mistake. The thought pleased him. It was far too long since he'd been able to help Jemima.

'Sad old cow. She won't do nothing.' Maureen, knocked back her vodka. Her eyes twinkled. 'I've got a copy of that book back home. So drink up duck, I think you could do with a bit of a reading lesson—if you catch my drift.'

Vincent caught it. No double vodka had ever been consumed faster. He couldn't remember a better August bank holiday. With his arm round Maureen's cushioned shoulders, he walked jauntily out of the Cat and Fiddle.

Outside, Maureen gave a shuddering sigh. 'Oh, shit and corruption!'

'What? What's up?'

'That.' Maureen's sigh was like a dozen deflated air balloons. 'Look! Bloody look!'

Vincent looked. Brian's, Mr Maureen's, forty-foot articulated lorry was just pulling to a halt outside the Munchy Bar.

CHAPTER TWENTY

Drew didn't want to open the door. So far the day had been good. Well, as good as a wet bank holiday Monday could be. And certainly better than most of his days recently. At least Bonne Nuit's trip to Fontwell had been successful. How the rest of the evening would go was anyone's guess.

He stood in the no-man's-land room between the kitchen garden path and the flight of uneven stone steps leading to Peapods' back door. He'd always thought of it as an outhouse, but Maddy had insisted that he had delusions of grandeur and that it was simply an overgrown porch. In the two years that they'd been together it had acquired a personality of its own, becoming filled with odd bits of riding gear, Wellington boots, old coats, dogs' leads, things that might come in handy if they ever remembered what they were for, and the larger of Poppy's toys. In the six months that his wife—no, ex-wife, now—Caroline, had been in charge of the house, the room had been cold, clutter-free, and empty. Just like his life.

Maddy had changed everything for him and Peapods. And now she was going to take it all away. He was sure she was. Despite all his efforts since the Newmarket sales, the barrier was still there. He'd tried talking to her, asking her what he'd done, telling her how he felt, but she kept saying there was nothing wrong. Maddy, who he knew better than he knew himself, was telling him there was nothing wrong! He had even resorted, on Charlie's advice, to wining and dining and sending flowers. She'd been pleased but it hadn't melted the pain in her eyes.

He took a deep breath and pushed the door. It wouldn't budge. Locked? He jiggled the handle. Definitely locked. Still, Maddy quite often put the catch on if she was alone. Drew knew she still hadn't got quite used to living in the echoing vastness of Peapods. It didn't necessarily have sinister connotations. Should he knock? On his own door? Get real. Maybe he should just trail round to the front of the house and let himself in the main door. Or through the office, or the conservatory. It wasn't *that* unusual to find the back door locked, after all.

Bending down, he peered through the keyhole. He could see into the kitchen. The key wasn't there. Maddy must have locked it from the outside. He felt along the dusty ledge above the lintel and found the key. Maybe she'd taken the dogs out for their last run. If Poppy didn't want to sleep, Maddy would take her out in her buggy with the dogs trotting alongside. That was bound to be what had happened. She'd probably left him a note.

He opened the door. He had to talk to Maddy tonight. Cards on the table. It couldn't be put off any longer. They'd shilly-shallied round it for long enough. If she was going to leave him he had to know. The decree absolute was through—at least it had been posted in both the court in Jersey and in Newbury. Caroline had telephoned happily to relay the news even before his solicitor did, and to say that the vital piece of paper would probably arrive in about two weeks' time and could she be invited to the wedding? He'd assumed she'd been joking. He hadn't been sure. He wasn't sure about anything

286

any more.

The kitchen was as chaotic as usual. He loved what Maddy had done to this room. She was everywhere. All her cooking paraphernalia jostled for space with books and magazines, more of Poppy's toys, and things that got put down on the way through to somewhere else and stayed put. He and Maddy had always gravitated there at the end of each day. It was lovely on winter nights to come in from the yard, sit in front of the fire, ease off his boots, eat one of Maddy's dream meals and talk to her above the background hum of the radio. Or on summer evenings, when the windows were thrown open to the scents of the garden and the air was soft, they'd sit at the table in the dusk and drink wine and eat cold new potatoes in mayonnaise and laugh about getting fat together.

Would they ever do anything together again?

Tonight the kitchen was empty apart from the animals. There was no note. The dogs scrabbled across the flagstones to greet him, the cats stretched out in front of the switched-off boiler, looked up, yawned, and slept again. There was the remains of beans on toast on the table, and half a cup of cold coffee.

'Maddy!'

Silence.

'Mad! Maddy?'

Drew exhaled. Peapods was totally silent. There was no sound of the television in the sitting room, or Poppy's laughter from upstairs. There was no sound of anything except the ticking of the clock echoing in the hall. Maddy might have gone to bed, of course, exhausted by her stint in the refreshment tent at the Jamboree, but somehow he doubted it.

The house had a hollow feel, an air of emptiness, as if there had been no one there for quite some time.

Throwing open doors, calling, Drew covered every room. Maddy and Poppy Scarlet had gone. Trying not to panic, not to allow the horrendous thoughts to bubble to the surface, he thundered back through the house. She must be somewhere. He flicked the answerphone in the hall. A string of messages from friends and owners—but not the voice he wanted to hear. Maybe she'd phoned through to the office. Maybe she was in there. Poppy liked playing with the computer. He almost laughed—she certainly didn't take after him.

There was nobody in the office. Outside in the yard he could hear the lads piling out of the hostel on their way to the Cat and Fiddle. They were joking and swearing. It all sounded so normal.

Maddy might have gone to Fran's after the Jamboree; she might have gone to see Suzy. She might have gone to any of the dozens of other friends she had in the village. But, if she had, why hadn't she left him a note? Should he ring round and ask them? If he did, would they guess why? Did they all *know* why, for God's sake?

Making sure the dogs were secure in the kitchen, he crashed out into the yard. The rain misted through the twilight. Vincent's cottage was in darkness. So was Charlie's. They were Maddy's other bolt-holes. He'd hoped against hope that she might be there. He rubbed his eyes. He couldn't bear to lose her. He couldn't live without her. God! How many times had he heard other men moan similar words in maudlin drunkenness? How many times had he felt some pity for their plight, but not truly understood? But then, they hadn't been losing

288

Maddy, had they?

He crossed the cobbles and unlocked Bonne Nuit's box. In the dark-red glow of the stable Bonnie regarded Drew with calm and intelligent eyes. He patted the chestnut neck. 'Sorry to disturb you. I need someone to talk to.'

Bonne Nuit pushed his head against Drew's arm. Today he'd believed that this horse would be his salvation—but what was the point of Peapods surviving without Maddy?

Merely hours earlier he and Charlie had congratulated each other on their buy, and wondered if Gillian had had the advantage of spiritual guidance. Bonne Nuit had finished in third place behind two experienced jumpers and, as they'd hoped, had drawn no interest from the punters whatsoever. Plenty of time now, they'd said, to organise his training schedule and build him up into a potential National horse. There would be ample opportunities over the next couple of months to try him out at various meetings and develop his stamina and fitness. And if everything went to plan, the Hennessey at Newbury in November would be his first big race.

Charlie had reported that Bonnie knew exactly what had been needed today, had kept plenty in reserve, and thoroughly enjoyed his trip. They'd grinned at each other, almost convinced that they might just have pulled off the miracle. The coup that every trainer dreams of: a horse from nowhere that has big-time ability. And not only was he a star on the course, Bonne Nuit had a dream of a temperament. He'd travelled back calmly in the horse box, eaten well, and settled easily.

Drew tugged the velvety ears. 'Where's she

gone? What am I supposed to do? Hang around like a wimp? Or am I going to make a king-sized prat of myself and rampage round the village like Othello in overdrive?'

Bonnie snuffled his contempt. Drew wasn't sure which part of the sentence he'd disagreed with. Probably both.

'Okay, then. Half a pint of whisky and the telly until she comes home?'

This seemed more acceptable. Bonnie head-butted Drew's arm. He rubbed the horse's long bony nose. 'But what if she doesn't come home? What if she never comes home again?'

It was unbearable. Drew hadn't felt this aching desolation since his parents had died. The pain of knowing he'd never see them again. He couldn't bear it.

Blinking, he bolted Bonne Nuit's box, gave the other horses a cursory glance and dragged himself back to the house.

He turned on the television and poured half a tumbler of whisky. Neither offered any comfort. The cats, seeking warmth, crept in and curled by the empty hearth. They stared at him over their shoulders, as if blaming him for the lack of crackling flames. The dogs, more forgiving, all flopped on the sofas.

Another half-tumbler of whisky from the decanter. It wasn't Glenfiddich. He couldn't touch Maddy's Glenfiddich. What a selfish bastard he was. All he'd worried about was Peapods' survival, about winning the Grand National, about being a top trainer. He'd always assumed that Maddy would be there to share it with him. It was because of Maddy that he'd got this far. Without her there was nowhere to go.

The dogs pricked their ears above the irritating roar of the television. Drew was instantly on his feet. He was already smiling. They hadn't barked. Their tails were thumping as the sitting-room door opened.

'Mad! Where the hell have you been? Oh —'

Charlie shrugged. 'Wrong size, wrong colouring, wrong sex—otherwise pretty close. And much as I like you, I really wouldn't want to share your bed.'

Drew slumped down on to the sofa again as the dogs wagged round Charlie. 'I thought that—'

'I was Maddy.' Charlie helped himself to a small whisky and a lot of slimline ginger ale. 'Yeah, I gathered. Where is she, then?'

'I have no fucking idea.'

'Jesus.' Charlie lolled into a fireside chair. 'Don't scream at me. I came for a bit of comfort and advice—not a bollocking.'

'Comfort and advice are in short supply.' Drew drained his glass. 'She's gone.'

'Gone where? No—no, sorry. I mean, she can't have gone. This is Maddy we're talking about. Maddy wouldn't have gone anywhere—you and Maddy are like sausages and mustard. Steak and chips? No, well, Morecambe and Wise—er— perhaps not. Still, you get my drift.'

'Shut up, Charlie.'

Charlie sank back into his chair. 'Have you had another row?'

'A row would be a step forward. No, she just wasn't here when I got back. Not a sign of her or Poppy. Shit, Charlie—what's happened to us?'

Charlie shook his head. 'I don't know. I've tried to talk to her. She seems the same to me—'

'No, she doesn't. That's bullshit and you know it. Everything started to go wrong when I told her about the divorce coming through. As soon as she knew I'd be free to marry her she changed.'

'Don't marry her then.' Charlie swirled his diluted whisky. 'Just carry on as you are. I know I'd run a mile if I thought my freedom was about to be curtailed. Maybe she's just scared of the actual ceremony. Have you tried asking her?'

'Of course I've tried bloody asking her!' Drew roared, making the cats flinch. 'What do you think I've been doing for the last three months! All she says is there's nothing wrong and she doesn't want to talk about it—oh, and why are we rushing into it when we're okay as we are?'

'There you are, then. Tell her you don't want to get married—'

'But I do! I've wanted Maddy to be my wife from the first moment I saw her! I want Poppy Scarlet to have proper parents, I want everyone to know how I feel about Maddy—I want the whole world to know—'

'That's an awful lot of "I wants",' Charlie interrupted. 'I didn't actually catch any "Maddy wants" in there—'

'Fuck off! Don't sit there and lecture me! You can't hold down a relationship for more than five fucking minutes!'

Charlie laughed. 'Very true. Which is one of the reasons I came to drown my sorrows with you. I was going to drag you to the pub and bend your ear a bit—but it's obviously not a good time.'

'No, it isn't. But go on, anyway. The trivia of your love life just might take my mind off my own problems.'

He hadn't meant to sound so bitchy, Charlie had always been a good mate, but he really didn't want to hear about the acrobatic Tina, or Lucinda, or whoever else was currently topping Charlie's seduction list. His ears strained towards the telephone and the door.

'Lucinda had left a message for me on the answerphone when I got back from Fontwell.'

Big bloody deal, Drew thought. Charlie's answerphone was always being used up by women. He constantly missed spare rides because trainers couldn't get through. If that was all he'd come over to moan about—

'Her ma, the mighty Bathsheba, found a book I'd given her in her bedroom—'

Jesus! So what?

'And it was still in Jemima's bookshop bag, and Bathsheba is now on the rampage. She wants the shop closed down. And she's told Lucinda she's not to work there any more. And she tried to get Lucinda to tell her who'd given her the book, and Lucinda being a little star said she'd borrowed it from Maddy—'

Was there any point in this? Drew tried to work out any relevant implications. Lucinda was going to study English at university, wasn't she? Surely the discovery of a book in her bedroom was likely to make *News at Ten?*

'—which would explain away the inscription, of course. But it does mean that Bathsheba may start asking you some questions. And—'

Why the hell would Bathsheba Cox want to close the bookshop because Charlie had written in a book he'd bought there, and—'What bloody inscription?'

'I sort of wrote something appropriate . . .'

'What?'

Charlie had the grace to stare at the carpet. 'You wouldn't really want to know—but I didn't sign it, so I wondered if Bathsheba asks you, if you would be a real pal and say that you'd written it and given it to Maddy . . .'

'Not a bloody chance. I warned you early on about messing with Lucinda. She's a lovely kid—and, while she may well have her head screwed on and got you sussed, Bathsheba definitely won't see it that way. You may have some very heavy parental questions to answer regarding your activities over the last few months. I've got enough problems—I don't need yours as well.' He slumped back into the cushions. 'Oh, shit. You know I don't mean it. Go on then. Tell me about it.'

Charlie did. Drew reached for a further whisky and wished he hadn't asked. Still, it would be nice to see Bathsheba go ballistic when he told her he'd written in the book—just what exactly was cliterature anyway?—for Maddy. He'd have to tell Mad, first, of course. They'd share the joke and then—

'Bollocks.' How could he share it with Maddy? The despair kicked in again.

The shrill of the telephone made him jump. Zapping the still laughing television into silence, Drew grabbed the phone. 'Yes?'

'Hi, Drew. It's Fran.'

Shit. Shit. Shit. 'Oh, hello—um—Mad's not here just at the moment—'

'I know. That's why I'm ringing.'

The carpet dipped and swayed. His palms were damp. 'Oh, is she with you?'

294

'No, but Poppy is. I've got her for the night. I'm really sorry. I was supposed to ring and tell you ages ago.'

Christ Almighty! Maddy had gone! She'd left him and Poppy—'Tell me what?'

'Oh, that Suzy and Luke had a real bust-up when they came back from Epsom. Actually, Richard said they were snarling at each other even in the parade ring—'

Oh, God. Cut to the bloody chase. 'Sorry, Fran—I'm not following you. Is Poppy okay? Where's Mad?'

'Poppy's fine. Sharing Jack's bed and sleeping like an angel. What? Oh, yeah. Well, Suze phoned Maddy in hysterics. And Maddy thought it would be better if Poppy stayed here while she went to do her big-sister act, and it all happened dead quick. And she asked me to let you know, only Jack's got colic and wouldn't go to sleep straight away, and I've only just remembered that I hadn't—'

'Where's Maddy?'

'At the cottage with Suzy. But—'

Drew hurled down the receiver and grinned at Charlie. 'Finish the whisky. Watch the adult channel. Eat whatever you can find in the kitchen—and there are some fags in the visitors' box. Enjoy yourself—and tell Bathsheba whatever you like. I'm going to sort out my life.'

*　　　*　　　*

Not even stopping to grab his flying jacket, Drew tore out into the darkening drizzle. Slithering on the cobbles, his jeans and denim shirt were soaked before he'd reached Peapods' gate. A huge

295

articulated lorry, snaking its way along the High Street in the direction of the Cat and Fiddle, halted his progress.

'Hurry up,' he muttered, recognising Maureen's Brian in the cab. 'For God's sake, hurry up.'

Hardly waiting for the tail-lights to pass, he dashed across the road and up the cottage's overgrown path. He'd have to go to the front door; only the new and unwary visitor would be reckless enough to attempt to circumnavigate the debris accumulated by the back door. In daylight it was treacherous; after dark it could prove fatal.

He squatted down and rattled the letter-box. In the two years since Maddy had vacated the cottage, neither Suzy nor Luke had fixed the doorbell or the knocker. God—it brought back memories. All his early wonderful times with Maddy had been spent here. How bloody cruelly ironic it would be if this was where it was going to end.

He rattled the letter-box again.

'Hang on,' Maddy's voice echoed cheerfully from the other side, 'I've just got to kick the rug away—although why you haven't got your key—ah! There!'

The door flew open. Maddy, just pushing her hair back from her eyes, and smiling, had never looked more beautiful. She blinked at him. 'Oh—I thought you were Luke. There's nothing wrong with Poppy, is there? Has Fran phoned? Sorry I wasn't in—but this has been like Goths and Vandals. Oh—you're soaked. Come in—how did Bonnie do? Did he win? I tried to check the results but you know what the Jamboree committee are like—'

'Mad, I love you.'

She kicked the door shut. 'I know. I love you, too. Is that what you came to tell me?'

'Yes.' He reached out and touched her cheek. 'Well, no. I thought you'd left me.'

Maddy giggled. 'Which means Fran, silly cow, forgot the phone call? Don't be daft, Drew. If I was going to leave you I'd take the animals and the Glenfiddich.'

Drew swallowed. He hurt from loving her. 'Naturally—how stupid of me . . . So, what's going on here? Is Suzy in bed?'

'Suzy has buggered off to somewhere called Fernydown. I haven't got a clue where it is—anyway, she's apparently gone to plight her troth to some woman called Naomi Briskett-hyphen-Something, who has promised to turn her into the next Pat Eddery.'

Drew laughed. Funny—he'd thought he'd never laugh again. 'Naomi Birkett-Spence. Yeah—she's even more scary than Kath Seaward. So, Suze is going to jack in John Hastings, Luke, Milton St John—and tilt at the Fernydown windmill next season, is she?'

It didn't surprise him. The Fernydown horses were all selected for their Classic capabilities. The Birkett-Spence team specialised in turning out prospective champion jockeys. Failure wasn't even a contemplation. Great for Suzy—bloody tough on Luke.

'And Luke?'

'Is staying the night at Emilio's. He's absolutely broken-up, poor love. I was just going to hang on a bit to see if he came back. I thought he'd need a shoulder—'

He pulled her to him. She didn't wriggle away. He kissed her. 'So, while we've got the place to ourselves, can we talk?'

297

'Like we used to?' Maddy ducked under his arm and walked into the kitchen. 'Over Glenfiddich and Mars bars and Gershwin?' She rattled water into the kettle. 'Not a hope. This place is now filled with Evian water, crispbread and Nirvana. How about coffee?'

'Great.' Drew sat at the table. The kitchen was a tip. It didn't matter. He still loved it here. 'Mad—do you want to get married?'

She didn't answer. He splayed his fingers on the table and stared at them. He couldn't look at her. 'Okay. Different question. Do you want to marry me?'

She stopped spooning Nescafé into the mugs. 'Not now.'

He closed his eyes. His heart was thumping. 'Does that mean you might at some time?'

He could hear her sloshing water on to the granules, adding milk. She handed him a mug and sat down opposite him.

'When you married Caroline—what was it like? No—I'm serious. Tell me. Was it the cream of Jersey society, and all top hats, and Caroline in a designer gown?'

'Sort of. But it isn't—'

'And did you think she looked stunning? Ravishing? The most beautiful woman in the world?'

'No—yes—oh, fuck it, Mad—I don't know!'

'You're a bad liar.' She snaked her arms round his neck for a second, then pulled them away and stood up. 'Drew, look at me. What do you see? Not tall, willowy, fabulous Caroline—but short, fat me. Right?'

He wanted to laugh. 'Mad, you're truly gorgeous.

I wanted you the minute I saw you. I fell in love with you straight away. I can't bloody live without you. I want you to be my wife—my partner, my friend, my lover—not some bloody trophy! I want you!'

She bit her lip. She had tears in her eyes. 'And I want to marry you more than anything else in the world. I always have. It's been my dream for two-and-a-half years. I want to walk down the aisle, or the register office corridor—in something elegant. I want to look beautiful for you. I want to make you so proud. I don't want to be second-best—'

For God's sake! He reached for her but she side-stepped his hands. 'No, Drew. Listen. I knew when the divorce would be through. I'd planned to diet, to exercise—to be perfect for September. And it's all gone wrong.'

'Mad, darling. I don't care if you wear what you've got on now. I love you in leggings and a T-shirt. I love you in bloody anything. I just want you to marry me. How bloody shallow do you think I am?'

'Look!' Angrily, she peeled the baggy T-shirt over her head and tugged off the leggings. Standing in the middle of the kitchen floor in her bra and knickers she turned in a small circle. 'Now do you understand why I can't bloody marry you in September? Look at me!'

Confused, he shook his head. She was voluptuous, cuddly, exquisite. He wanted her fiercely. She was totally gorgeous. 'You look wonderful.'

'Drew!' Her sigh could have rattled the windows. She cradled the mound of her stomach. 'Look! I'm five months pregnant.'

Sodding hell! He leapt to his feet, knocking over the chair in his delight as he grabbed her. 'Oh, my God. Mad, that's incredible. When? How? I mean, why the fuck didn't you tell me?'

'Don't swear,' she muttered against his chest. 'Because the timing was all wrong. When I found out, it was just when we thought Peapods was going under—and then the divorce was going through, and I knew we could get married in September—and it was all bloody wrong!'

How could this be wrong? How could anything so utterly joyous be wrong? His eyes were misted with tears again. He kissed her. 'You should have told me. I can't understand—'

'Because I wanted our wedding to be perfect. You've given me everything. I wanted this to be right for you. I didn't want to waddle down the aisle in something massive, or eat my wedding cake on a maternity ward, or—'

'Idiot.' He smiled into her hair. 'When's he due?'

Maddy moved away from him, and wrinkled her nose. 'Spooky. I'm sure it's a boy, too. Oh—and that's another piece of perfect timing, actually. It's—um—Christmas Eve.'

'Bugger,' he pulled a face. 'I hope you'll have time to stuff the turkey before you go.'

'The chestnuts are already in the freezer, actually. I've even peeled the sprouts.'

He hugged her again, almost speechless with happiness. 'So we can get married at any time before that—and don't—' he grinned at her '—start talking crap about wearing skin-tight dresses and looking like a stick, okay? I shall be the proudest, luckiest man in the whole damn world.'

She smiled—the old Maddy again—with happiness. 'You really don't mind?'

'Mind! Mind?' He picked her up and swung her round. 'Maddy Beckett—just give me an opportunity to show you how much I mind!'

Grinning hugely, he kicked open the kitchen door and carried her across the hall towards the bedroom.

CHAPTER TWENTY-ONE

Opening the shop on Tuesday, Jemima had a strange sense of unease. It had dogged her since the previous evening. Silly really, she thought, as she propped the door wide, allowing the gloriously warm sun to break on either side of Brian's articulated lorry in the lay by, and stream across the sisal floor. Everything was going so well. There was no logical reason to feel like this.

Several strings of horses were making their way up the bridlepaths on to the Downs. The morning was fresh, and had that tantalising smell of clean air and warm earth after rain. The hills were diamond dewy from yesterday's downpour and, shrouded in an expectant heat haze, heralded a scorching day. Jemima reckoned that Pluvius must have a real grudge against bank holidays. The small shiver which suddenly edged along her backbone had nothing at all to do with the vagaries of the weather. Whatever it was had bothered her all night, making her restless; and when she had slept, her dreams had been violent and troubled.

It may well have been accelerated by her day

out with the Hutchinsons, of course. She'd spent more time getting soaked to the skin on Bradley-Percival's white-knuckle rides with the twins the previous day than in the whole of the rest of her life. And she'd lost count of the number of toffee apples and candy-flosses she'd eaten. And Gillian and Glen, delighted at how well their day had gone, had insisted she stayed downstairs to join in the Vicarage supper which had been very grown-up and included port, some excellent Cheddar, and a helping of WI pickled onions.

But it hadn't been a physical churning that had disturbed her sleep—rather a faint niggle of foreboding. She had expected Matt to ring during the evening to check that she was back. When he hadn't, she'd telephoned him twice, and both times got the answerphone. And Matt had been behaving differently for the last couple of weeks, but she put that down to the fact that the jumping season was about to begin, which would obviously test the strength of their relationship. Not that she worried unduly about her future with Matt. She wasn't really sure she'd got one.

She had managed to talk to her father before she went to bed. Vincent had been surprisingly grouchy, and, for him, rather unforthcoming about his bank holiday. He'd sworn that he hadn't been near a racecourse or a bookmaker, and she was almost sure that she believed him. He had muttered something about not trusting people, and some villagers not being what they seemed. It had all sounded a bit Ides of March, but when she'd questioned him, he'd become vague and suggested that she kept out of Bathsheba's way for a bit.

Maybe, she thought as she straightened shelves

and put the float in the till and topped up the pile of green-and-gold bags, all these things combined were enough to give anyone nightmares.

Five past nine. Lucinda was late. She was usually there before Jemima these days, jigging from foot to foot, spilling over with stories. Jemima had been looking forward to hearing the next exciting Charlie Somerset episode as they shared their first cup of coffee. She was really, really going to miss Lucinda when she went off to university.

'Morning, duck.' Maureen poked her head round the door. The blonde beehive had been dismanded and now looked like a rather precarious bleached sweep's brush. 'A word to the wise. Can't stop. Our Brian came home unannounced. I'm all behind meself. Just watch Bathsheba. She was in the pub last night having a bit of a rant about them Fishnets. Forewarned is forearmed, if you get my drift.'

Jemima did. Vincent must have been in the Cat and Fiddle last night too, then. Fascinating. She was still saying thank-you as the rather tousled Maureen disappeared. It was a bit of a bugger. Still, she'd had a pretty long stay of execution. Was that what the premonition had been about? Bathsheba and the Parish Biddies being up in arms about a small percentage of her stock? No, course not. Bound to be a storm in a teacup. Let them have their say—after all, there was nothing they could do about it, was there?

*   *   *

Business was slow. Ten o'clock and she'd only had two customers, neither of whom had bought

303

anything. She wasn't surprised. She knew from the Bookworms years that the day after a bank holiday was never a good time to find people willing to part with money.

Slotting *The Wind in the Willows* into the audio system, Jemima rested her elbows on the counter and listened. The story never failed to charm her. It was one of the first ones she remembered Rosemary reading to her. She had always thought Vincent was very much like Mr Toad. Maybe one day she'd read it to her own children. She would have to get a move on. She closed her eyes as the story unfolded.

These mythical children, who had become rather blurred in her imagination and were probably about fifty years out of date as they rather resembled the Ovaltineys, were sitting with glowing faces and rapt attention at her feet as she read to them. The vision dissolved. They weren't real. She wasn't even sure she liked them.

Levi and Zeke were amusing; Poppy Scarlet was gorgeous; and Fran's three children were street-wise, noisy and a bit scary. She didn't really know any other children, and certainly had no maternal feelings towards those she did. No children then. Maybe no permanent man ... Maybe she'd become a sort of elderly bohemian slapper, still entertaining gentlemen callers and wearing copious strands of jet beads when she was into her eighties. By which time, of course, the Jemima Carlisle chain would be established world-wide ...

'Jemima!'

'Uh?' She opened her eyes and blinked. The sun glancing from the windows cast prisms on her glasses. Someone was outlined in the doorway.

'Jemima! Guess what?' Gillian floated into the shop. 'I just had to tell you—Oh, no Lucinda this morning? Did she have a heavy bank holiday?'

'I've no idea. If she's not here in half an hour I'll have to ring her. What?'

'It's so exciting!' Gillian sank on to the sofa in a cloud of swirling lilac cotton. 'Drew's been to see Glen. He's still there. We're going to have a wedding.'

'Maddy and Drew?'

'Of course Maddy and Drew.' Gillian frowned. 'For goodness' sake try and keep up. Oh, and Bonnie Nuts ran ever so well yesterday. Charlie was brilliant on him. Drew says I've even got a bit of prize money for coming third. Anyway, what I came to tell you was apparently Mad's pregnant again—and Drew was telling Glen that a fortune-teller told her ages ago that she'd have three children and they want to get the wedding over before this one arrives and—'

Jemima smiled with happy self-indulgence. She was so glad that Maddy and Drew had sorted out their differences. She still wasn't sure why Maddy hadn't wanted to get married, but at least one Milton St John relationship seemed to be back on an even keel. 'Are you sure you should be telling me this? Isn't it a bit indiscreet?'

'Good Lord! I haven't even got to the best bit.' Gillian looked affronted. 'Drew is asking Glen to approach the Bishop for dispensation to get married in St Saviour's. Wouldn't that be lovely? It might be a bit tricky—with him being divorced and everything—but it's worth a try. Glen's all for second marriages taking place in church. He says God's greatest gift is forgiveness. Luckily . . .'

Jemima laughed. She knew that Gillian hadn't confessed about Bonne Nuit yet.

Still chattering about everyone having to get something new to wear and speculating on the venue for the reception, Gillian drifted out of the shop again to impart the happy news to Maureen and the Munchy Bar's clientele. The grapevine was flourishing nicely this morning, Jemima thought, as she explained the library system to a clutch of elderly ladies. It certainly wouldn't give Maddy and Drew any chance to make their own announcement. Everyone in Berkshire would know by lunchtime.

Half past ten. Lucinda was never unreliable. She'd have to ring her. It occurred to her as she punched out the number that when Lucinda went to Southampton she'd have to find a replacement. She had come to rely on her so much, and certainly couldn't run the shop single-handed. Still, she thought, as the Coxes' telephone continued to ring, that was a happy problem really. She'd never expected to be so successful.

No one answered. She put down the receiver and wondered whether the entire Cox clan had gone out for the day. Somehow she couldn't imagine it. Maybe Lucinda had spent last night with Charlie—the mythical school-chum sleep-over again—and Bathsheba was probably crusading round the estate drumming up support for her latest cause.

'Jemima!'

'Christ, Gillian. You've already told me, remember? Maybe you're supposed to be in Bronwyn's telling her?'

'She already knows. She's in the Munchy Bar huddled with Bathsheba and that rather poisonous

306

Petunia Hobday. They kept trying to beckon me over but I ignored them. No, listen, this is something else.'

Jemima listened. Suzy and Luke had split up. It all sounded fairly acrimonious. Suzy would be leaving the village after Christmas. Luke had moved in with his trainer, Emilio Marquez. Shame, Jemima thought, and wondered irrelevantly if the news might at least cheer up the members of the Luke Delaney fan club.

'You didn't think to ask Bathsheba about Lucinda's whereabouts, I suppose?'

'Of course not. Do you think I'm totally tactless? The lucky child is probably still curled beneath Charlie's feather and duckdown. Oh, damn. It's the hit squad. Is there time for me to get out the back way?'

There wasn't. Bathsheba, Bronwyn, and Petunia stood in the shop's entrance, blocking out the sun. The elderly ladies round the library shelves moved closer together. Gillian slid behind the counter beside Jemima.

'I think you owe us an explanation,' Bathsheba boomed. 'I understand that you have been peddling pornography.'

Fighting the desire to laugh, Jemima feigned innocence. 'Not as far as I'm aware. Was there something unpleasant in your last Elizabeth Elgin?'

There was a collective intake of breath, a mass quivering of chins. Bathsheba held Bella-Donna Stockings aloft. 'This—this is dissolute licentiousness!'

'And I think you'll find that's a tautology, actually,' Jemima said smugly as Gillian disappeared beneath the counter.

'I don't care what fancy name you give it, my girl. Filth is filth. And we wish it to be known,' Bathsheba sucked in her breath, 'that the Ladies' League of Light will fight a non-stop battle until the shelves are divested of this rubbish. Either that—or your shop closes down. Understood?'

'Yes, thank you.' Jemima was still afraid that she was going to giggle. 'Um—I suppose this wouldn't have anything to do with Lucinda not appearing for work, would it?'

'Lucinda is staying out of harm's way with a schoolfriend. I'll make sure she never sets foot in this den of iniquity again. Pure as the driven snow, is Lucinda. I will not have her innocence corrupted in this shop.'

Petunia Hobday blanched a little. Bronwyn looked slightly uncomfortable. Still, Jemima thought grudgingly, give them their due, whatever they knew they obviously weren't about to snitch. Maybe she'd underestimated Charlie Somerset's appeal to the female population of Milton St John. The library ladies took the opportunity to file out silently.

Gillian, on her hands and knees, was heading towards the kitchen. Unfortunately, Bathsheba spotted her. 'Mrs Hutchinson! A word if you please!'

Gillian looked up from the sisal and smiled as she scrambled to her feet. 'Sorry—I'd—er—dropped a contact lens.'

'Didn't know you wore glasses, Gillian, dear.' Bronwyn Pugh looked concerned. 'Well, no, I suppose you don't—not if you wear contacts. Have you tried disposables? My Natalie says—'

'Bronwyn!' Bathsheba reined in her henchman.

'Now, Mrs Hutchinson, you will no doubt be joining us on this anti-pornography crusade? Vicar has already been informed. We're holding a meeting in the back room of the Cat and Fiddle on Friday evening. I shall go home now and plug into the computer and post notices. We can rely on your support this time, I take it?'

'Oh, absolutely.' Gillian flashed apologetic glances towards Jemima. 'I had absolutely no idea—'

Bathsheba cut in. 'Me neither, Mrs Hutchinson. Me neither. I'm very, very disappointed. I would probably have remained as unenlightened as yourself if I hadn't found this in Lucinda's bedroom—borrowed from young Maddy Beckett apparently—but definitely purchased from this shop.'

Jemima coughed.

'And what Drew Fitzgerald has written in it is almost worse than the book itself—'

'Really?' Gillian had already reached out a hand. 'May I?'

'No, you mayn't! I shall be taking this up to Peapods forthwith. I will expect some sort of apology from the pair of them for the corruption of a child. And not only will I be canvassing locally—I intend to write to the publishers and demand an explanation.' She turned to Bronwyn and Petunia. 'Come, ladies! There's work to be done.'

Exit the three witches: stage left, Jemima thought, as they stomped out on their air-cushioned soles. She glared at Gillian. 'Thanks for your support, pal.'

'Oh, I know. I'm sorry. Silly old besoms.' Gillian was even paler than usual. 'They can be so vindictive. It's hell sometimes not knowing which bloody side I'm supposed to be on. But Glen won't like this, Jemima. I'm sure he won't. As Mrs Vicar, I'll have to at least pay lip-service. It's not personal. You do understand?'

Jemima supposed she did. Gillian was in a difficult position. It would be interesting to see just who was on her side if battle lines were drawn.

*   *   *

By the end of the afternoon, Jemima had had enough. Lucinda hadn't appeared, and the jungle drums had reached the new estate, causing a rush on Fishnets. The elderly ladies who had been interested in the library when Bathsheba appeared, returned with reinforcements, obviously hoping to catch a replay. Also, because the children hadn't yet gone back to school for the autumn term, the shop had been filled with young mums and bored toddlers and one of the beanbags had burst. Having swept up the last of the polystyrene beads, Jemima cashed up, switched the sign on the door to 'Closed', and promised herself an early night.

She ought to see Vincent, she knew, and she supposed she should ring Matt again. What the hell—they could both wait another day. Lucinda worried her more. She hoped that Bathsheba hadn't shackled her in her room. She'd ring her later. Maybe even pop round if Bathsheba went out. And then she ought to speak to Glen about Fishnets—he was her landlord, after all. She didn't want to risk homelessness again . . .

Mr Maureen's lorry was still occupying most of the lay-by. The sun was now glinting from the other side, illuminating some graffiti on the trailer that would make even the most ardent erotica-reader blush. Jemima lifted her face to the afternoon rays and hoped that the hoo-ha over the books would die a death. While accepting that no publicity was truly bad, she would have preferred not to have to fight this particular battle. Especially not now, when things were picking up nicely.

There was only a slight breeze, and it wafted the warm dust around the High Street in little swirling clouds. The chestnut trees gave welcome shade as she walked slowly towards the Vicarage. In a couple of days it would be September, and before long the leaves would turn to fire and fall. They'd been in tiny unfurling clusters when she'd arrived in Milton St John. The spring and summer had passed quickly. So many things had changed.

Oh, sod it. She stopped walking. Bathsheba Cox was standing four-square in St Saviour's shrubbery with Glen, gesticulating towards the bookshop. She really didn't want to face her again. Not yet. And certainly not with Glen. Hating public confrontations, she looked for an escape route. She was tired and sticky. She wanted a shower and some sleep. She didn't want to spend the next half-hour or so wandering round the village until the coast was clear.

A clump of leaves suddenly swirled past her ear. An eddy of small twigs rapidly followed. Jemima looked up into the massive spread of the chestnut tree. Could it be squirrels? Oxford hadn't prepared her for wildlife appreciation. There was a further flurry of leaves, a creak of branches, and a hissed expletive. Pretty street-wise squirrels, then. Intrigued, Jemima moved closer to the trunk and

311

peered upwards. A pair of feet encased in grubby white trainers and attached to faded denim legs were just visible.

The rest of Charlie Somerset leaned down and grinned.

'What the hell are you doing?' She cricked her neck back further. 'Is Lucinda up there with you?' It seemed the only rational explanation. Surely there had been some historical figure who had sought sanctuary in a tree? Jemima rather vaguely remembered that that had been an oak. And that the person in question had been royalty escaping executioners. Not much difference, really.

Charlie put a finger to his lips and shook his head. Jemima frowned. This was all a bit too Famous Five for her.

'Yes, I'm sure I saw her leaving the shop, Vicar!' Bathsheba's voice carried along the street. 'No, I'm determined. I'll wait here until she arrives. Or failing that, I'll go and find her. We need to thrash this out.'

Charlie leaned down a bit further. 'Climb up here. There are some low branches round the side. She won't see you.'

Not on her life! Jemima couldn't remember when she'd last climbed a tree. And Charlie Somerset was the last person on earth she'd want to take refuge with.

'I'll just walk along towards the shop,' Bathsheba was saying to a rather bemused-looking Glen. 'She won't escape me.'

Oh, shit. Grabbing her skirt in one hand, Jemima caught the lowest branch and hauled herself from the ground. The trunk was rough and crumbly and most of it seemed to stick to her. Inelegantly, she reached for the next branch and found she could go no higher. She was standing on her skirt, for God's sake. Irritably, she dragged at it, and almost fell. She negotiated two more branches. It had taken for ever and she was still only three feet from the ground.

'Give us your hand,' Charlie hissed from somewhere above her. 'The old bag's on her way.'

Mauled by Charlie or savaged by Bathsheba? What a choice! She let go of the branch she was holding and swayed alarmingly.

'Give me your hand!' Charlie's hiss was nearer now. 'Jemima!'

His grip was strong—probably from all those years of beating horses, she thought—and he yanked her unceremoniously up the trunk.

'Ouch.' Every bit of exposed flesh made sandpaper contact with the bark. 'Let bloody go. I can manage.'

He let go, and she was surprised to find that she could. She dragged herself upwards again until she was level with Charlie. The ground seemed an awful long way below. Her glasses were skew-whiff and her hair had fallen across her face. Scrambling awkwardly, she sat astride the branch, her back to the trunk, and shook.

'Okay?' He was laughing. 'Not very fit, are you?'

Bastard. She couldn't speak. She had to be doo-lally. Normal, sensible Jemima Carlisle from Oxford would have calmly confronted Bathsheba Cox and defused the situation. True, she would probably have blushed and stuttered a bit, but she would have remained on the ground to do it. What was it about Milton St John that made the sanest of people behave like fools?

She rested her head against the trunk. She rather liked it. It felt secure. She still didn't dare look down.

'She's heading this way,' Charlie whispered. 'Don't even breathe. She's got radar.'

Jemima didn't doubt it. Growing a little more used to the motion of the branches, she allowed herself to peer through the waving greenery. Bathsheba, oddly truncated, was immediately below her, staring towards the bookshop. Smothering an insane urge to giggle, Jemima felt young and giddy and a bit wicked. She hadn't felt like this for— well—she'd probably never felt like this before.

'You're mad,' she hissed at Charlie who was relaxing on an opposite branch. 'Do you do this much?'

'Only when I'm escaping from Lucinda's moralistic ma,' he stage-whispered. 'Or angry husbands. Don't panic. I'm not loopy.'

She raised her eyebrows. 'No, course not. I mean this is quite a normal thing to be doing. I do it all the time—bloody hell!' Her grip relaxed a bit and a shower of leaves tumbled downwards like confetti.

'Christ.' Charlie leaned over precariously. 'Have we been spotted?'

Jemima held her breath, and squinted downwards. Bathsheba was now staring straight up into the tree. She pressed herself closer to the trunk and prayed. If she'd almost lost her grip on the branch, she had certainly lost her grip on reality. What other rational explanation could there be for sitting up a tree with the biggest lady-killer since Casanova?

After what seemed like three hours, Bathsheba stopped staring and trundled away towards the bookshop, disappearing behind Brian's lorry. Jemima, who hoped that she'd read the graffiti, exhaled at the same moment as Charlie.

'So, does Bathsheba know about you and Lucinda, then? Is that why you're up here? And where is Lucinda, anyway?'

'No, no, and at the cottage. She tried ringing you last night to warn you, but your phone was engaged. I was on my way to see you to impart the news, and then I saw Mrs C, and well, I had a bit of a guilt trip—even though she doesn't know anything—and I sort of shinned up here until the coast was clear. I gather I was a bit late doing my Ghent to Aix bit?'

'Just a bit.' Jemima was impressed by the literary allusion. Maybe Lucinda's A-level revision time hadn't been completely wasted. 'So? What now?'

Charlie shrugged. 'You could scramble down and risk being spotted, or you could stay here and talk to me until she's gone.'

'Not much of a choice.'

'Sod you, then.' He stuck out his tongue and drew his knees up to his chin. 'I can't say you'd be my first pick as a companion, either.'

She grinned. It was probably true. Maybe if she'd had thigh- high PVC and fluffy eyelashes and a minus IQ she'd have been acceptable. Maybe if Charlie hadn't been a jockey and immoral and totally gorgeous it would have been different. They had nothing in common.

She leaned back against the trunk, enjoying the breeze through the leaves that sounded like crashing surf, the creak of the branches like wind in rigging, and the dip-and-sway motion. It was exactly like being on a ship. The pressures of the day were forgotten, the faint premonition of doom was receding. Pushing her glasses up her nose, she looked at Charlie. Maybe he wasn't quite so mad after all. This was better than any other relaxation therapy she'd ever tried.

Bathsheba's voice, carrying now from the other direction, dispersed the euphoria. Both she and Charlie peered downwards.

'Old bag's giving up,' Charlie reported. 'She's yelling something at Bronwyn—oh, and heading off towards home. Give her a couple of minutes to get round the corner and you'll be okay.'

'Thanks.' She sighed. 'Do you think she'll really make things difficult for me?'

'I don't think she'll close the shop. But she can be dead persuasive. She'll probably hire flying pickets or something. Still, you're tough—and clever. You'll be more than a match for her. It's a shame about Lucinda, though.'

It was. Lucinda had been invaluable in the shop and had become a good friend. Jemima realised she would probably miss the friendship more. 'That's rich coming from you.'

'Lucinda and I know exactly where we stand—or rather, don't . . .'

'And Tina?'

'Is unaware of the situation and not really part of this conversation. Unless, of course, you want to trade under-the-sheets gossip about Matt. In which case,' Charlie's eyes gleamed, 'I'd be all ears.'

'God, no. I've never been a believer in kiss and tell.' Which was, on reflection, just as well, she thought, as there was very little kissing to tell anything about. 'Unlike some in this village, I think my private life should stay just that.'

'Bugger,' Charlie said good-naturedly. 'Matt

won't say anything about you, either. Boring sod. I suppose you want to go home now, do you?'

'Yes, please.' Tentatively straightening her legs, Jemima slid towards the edge of the branch. She peered downwards. The ground looked a very long way away. Getting down was going to be a darn sight harder than getting up had been.

'Do you want any help?'

Jemima shook her head. 'I can manage, thank you. Ooops!'

Charlie hauled her back. 'Head first is not the best option. What sort of childhood did you have? Didn't anyone teach you how to climb trees?'

'Unlike some, I wasn't privileged enough to have a nanny, a minder, a valet, a butler, a resident fitness instructor and tree-climbing tutor—'

Charlie laughed at her. 'Put your left foot here. Hold on with your right hand. There . . . See? Easy. And I didn't have those things, either. I had a wheelchair-bound father, an over-protective mother, no brothers and sisters, and acres of space. I learned self-sufficiency at an early age. No—not that branch—the next one.' He sat back and looked at her. 'You'd probably find it easier if you tucked your skirt into your knickers.'

She slithered down the remaining three feet of trunk, grazing her hands. Much of the tree still seemed to be attached to her hair. Charlie swung effortlessly between the branches and dropped easily beside her.

He was quite some athlete, she thought reluctantly. And okay, really. 'Thanks.'

'No sweat. I'll ask Lucinda to ring you, shall I?'

She nodded. 'We'll have to try and work something out. Now all I've got to do is explain

317

things to Glen before Bathsheba's meeting on Friday.'

'Good luck.' Charlie managed to squeeze his hands into the pockets of the skin-tight jeans. He started to walk away, then stopped. 'Oh, and give my love to Gillian.'

September

CHAPTER TWENTY-TWO

Matt had absolutely no intention of seeing Tina Maloret again. With Kath at the Lancing Grange brainstorming sessions, or in a crowd of thousands at the racecourse, it might be okay. But he didn't want to be on his own with her. He'd never trusted her—and now he knew he couldn't trust himself, either.

Still, right now he had other things on his mind. It was the last race at Worcester on a golden afternoon; the first Friday in September. Dragon Slayer was hot favourite. Five to two on at the last show. Kath Seaward had chosen different tactics from Drew for the season's inaugural airing of her potential champion. Not for Lancing Grange the obscurity of an unannounced outing at Fontwell. Dragon Slayer was far too well known for that. Kath Seaward planned to do it in style.

Concentrate, Matt told himself as he and Dragon Slayer made their way to the start. Concentrate on this race. Worry about everything else later. Dragon Slayer, preening, prancing, putting on a show for the public, obviously couldn't wait. Matt would have liked to wait for ever.

He wished he could tell someone. Confess all. Make a clean breast of it. But he couldn't. And Ned Filkins knew he couldn't. Ned knew all about his weakness. Ned was blackmailing him with the secret. But Ned didn't want cash for his pay-off; he just wanted Dragon Slayer to lose. And money *had* changed hands. He'd actually taken money from Ned. Blood money. Thirty pieces of silver.

Whatever. Doing so had sealed his fate.

He hadn't received the huge wads of notes that Vincent seemed to hand over to Ned on a regular basis: that went to the snouts who snuffled for information. But just once, during the summer, when Matt had been desperate—and greedy—Ned had loaned him money. Ned knew how much he needed money. And Ned, with his bloody scumbag contacts, knew where Matt's money went. Knew exactly when it was time for his next fix.

When Ned had offered him five hundred pounds it had been like handing out lifebelts to the *Titanic*'s orchestra. He'd grabbed it with both hands.

And he'd been suckered from that moment.

Reluctantly, Dragon Slayer slowed his canter as they approached the start. Twelve horses, twelve jockeys, all of whom he knew well. Not Charlie today, though. Thank God, not Charlie. He didn't want to face Charlie, with his good-natured grin and his bloody serendipity attitude to life. Charlie Somerset had it all—and would probably have even more. Birth—that's what did it, Matt knew. You were dealt a hand at birth. It simply wasn't fair that Charlie Somerset had got all the aces, while he was left with the jokers.

The circling horses were familiar; so, too, the routines of girth-tightening and checking the stirrup leathers. The usual banter, ribaldry, slanderous remarks. All the same. But he wasn't.

The starter had snapped out the roll-call, and finding everyone present, was calling them into line. Matt tried to swing Dragon Slayer round to face the front. This was the first part. He had to remember to draw no attention to himself. Be casual. So, no lining up on the inside. As far away from the public as possible. The invasive eye of the course camera was another matter. Still, he kicked Dragon Slayer gently, urging him towards the outer rail, so far—dead simple. No problems. Most jockeys preferred the inner at Worcester. No one was going to fight him for his starting position. He glanced round him and exhaled. None of the other jockeys seemed remotely interested in him.

Maybe, he thought, it wouldn't be too difficult. He had never worried too much about having a conscience. He had never needed to. He'd always played everything straight on the course. No one had ever tested his morality before. Now it was being pulled in all directions at once.

One of the rank outsiders was side-stepping and twirling like a liberty pony beside him as Matt held on to his position. Everyone was watching the side-show. Christ! Were they now wondering why he hadn't joined the jostle for the grandstand side of the track? Hell—he was already becoming paranoid. Get a grip!

The starter was barking sarcastically at the unfortunate jockey and his prancing horse at the starting gate. All eyes still seemed to be on him. Matt turned his head away, fiddling with his stirrups, and felt sick.

Then there was Jemima . . . Poor Jemima, who was probably at this moment facing the wrath of the massed ranks of the Parish Biddies without him being there to back her. He had promised he'd get back to Milton St John as soon as he could. He'd told her not to worry about Bathsheba's meeting; that he'd lived in the village for long enough to know that these protests would soon be swept aside in favour of some further outrage.

He'd had to show her some support, hadn't he? Especially now. He knew how concerned Jemima was about the damage Bathsheba Cox could cause to her livelihood. Jemima, on the other hand, was blissfully unaware of the damage he was probably about to cause to his own.

Dragon Slayer, as always tuned-in to his jockey, read the dilemma in Matt's mind and executed a neat circle, wedging his rump against the tape.

'Garside! Turn around! Round! Face the front jockeys!' The starter looked like he was about to have apoplexy.

Matt yanked at Dragon Slayer's head with uncharacteristic force. The horse, unused to this handling, gave a jolt of surprise and resentment but turned round. The few hardy racegoers who always clustered at the start, jeered derisively at Matt's cavalier treatment. The remaining eleven horses, spooked by the eruption of noise, all shimmied out of line again. The starter and his assistant gave synchronised groans.

Matt shortened Dragon Slayer's reins and kicked him gently towards the elasticated webbing stretched across the course. Calm down. It was okay. They were facing the right way, they weren't looking at him, and he'd still got the outside rails all to himself.

It was all too much to think about. Ned Filkins . . . He was sure, whatever Ned said, that bloody Maureen had seen them together at that pub on bank holiday Monday. She must have told Vincent she'd seen them—he'd blinked in disbelief at Vincent's car in the car park—and Vincent was Jemima's father, for God's sake. Would he have told Jemima that, on the day he was supposed to have been working, Matt had been spotted skulking in the backwoods with Ned Filkins?

'About sodding time!' The starter decided to go for it. He raised his flag.

The fear mounted. It wasn't fair. It wasn't bloody fair!

The tape sprang away and the twelve contenders catapulted forward. Worcester was a fairly flat and untaxing steeplechase course. Kath had chosen to send Dragon Slayer there for his first race of the season to test the muscles after the summer rest. Matt knew he'd win easily—everyone at Lancing Grange knew he'd win easily.

It was up to him to make sure he didn't.

Delighted at being back on a racecourse, Dragon Slayer was trying to leap away, to jump the hurdles he could have practically stepped over. Matt held him in check, his mind throbbing with possibilities. Maybe in the days of frequent racing skulduggery that the retired stable lads still cackled about, pulling a horse had been a simple matter. Then there had been fewer stewards, and no SIS, no invasive cameras, no video footage. Losing this race on Dragon Slayer was surely going to be a great deal more difficult than winning it.

Eighteen fences. Two circuits. They were halfway round for the first time now, Dragon Slayer soaring across the brushwood, eating up the ground with huge strides, head and shoulders ahead of the rest of the undistinguished pack. He was infinitely superior, far more talented, than the rest of the contenders. Oh, Christ. His reputation would slide even further down the scale. Matt Garside—couldn't win if you gave him a two-day start. He could hear it now . . .

No point in doing anything right now, Matt thought, head down. Dragon Slayer was scrubbing easily along between fences, rocketing over the hurdles as they appeared, still a length ahead of the rest of the field. It could easily have been twenty. Several of the other horses were crashing through the fences and landing badly, but there had been no fallers.

Even if a fall, a peck, a stumble may have looked more authentic in front of the stands, Matt knew he couldn't do it. Dragon Slayer merited better than that. Intelligent and sensitive, he'd hate the humiliation as much as his jockey.

They were up and over the fence which would be the last next time round. The landing was inch-perfect. The grandstand crowd roared their approval. If he was going to get away with it, it would have to be on the back straight. The open ditch. Could he pull it off there? Most of Worcester's casualties were at that particular obstacle; it would have to be there or nowhere. Three more fences, then, he thought as they swept round the top turn, three more fences and he and Dragon Slayer would be out of the race.

Safely over the next. Two more to go. Short-term pain for long-term gain—wasn't that what he'd been told?

Over the next as well. He was jumping so well. Too well. Feet to spare. Next one . . . Next one . . . It made sense. It wasn't cheating. It wasn't—It was securing the future. Three more strides. Two. Screw it—now.

Dragon Slayer, in mid-flight, felt the reins tighten as Matt asked him for an extra stride. Matt, instantly aware of the shock shooting through the

326

bunched muscles, tried to put things right. It was too late. Dragon Slayer knew the instructions were directly at odds with his instinct. That one second of confusion was all that was needed. Easy. So easy. Too bloody easy in fact.

Wrong-footed, Dragon Slayer splashed his hind-legs into the water on landing, stumbled, scrabbled frantically, then jerked himself upright. Half the field had passed them. The groan from the stands was audible. Dragon Slayer, brave and honest, was immediately into his stride again, thundering forward, trying his hardest, wanting to catch up. He wanted to win. He didn't know that he couldn't.

Matt exhaled angrily. He couldn't do this again. Not for the rest of the season. Whatever the cost. He was willing to break Dragon Slayer's heart—but he wasn't going to break his spirit.

They caught most of the contenders on the run-in and finished sixth.

*   *   *

The home-going punters had almost disappeared by the time he emerged from the changing room. Slinging his holdall over one shoulder, he made his way across the paper-strewn pathway and into the car park. Kath was waiting for him.

'Get in.' She was wearing the trench coat, with the panama on the back of her head. 'Don't talk to me now. Just get in.'

Matt scrambled into the passenger seat. Guilt engulfed him in red-hot waves. She must know. Lighting a cigarette, steering with one hand, Kath had the BMW roaring away from the course in minutes. Matt wished he'd driven himself—even began to think longingly of being a passenger in Charlie's Aston Martin.

'I was wrong,' she said, settling at eighty on the A38. 'I should have listened to you. We should have had Dragon Slayer out earlier. Should have followed Drew's example and gone to Fontwell. It's something we're going to have to watch. He always used to spook at open ditches. My mistake. I'd forgotten. Not too disappointed, are you?'

'No—no . . . Are you?'

'Fucking pissed off at the time, but it happens. He recovered well. He'd still got the beating of them. He should have won, of course. But at least this time I can't blame the jockey.'

Kath edged up a gear and overtook a convoy of coaches. Everyone on the back seats waved. Matt looked down into the footwell just in case they'd gambled everything on Dragon Slayer and recognised him.

Zigzagging back into the left lane, oblivious to the horn-blowing and light-flashing around her, Kath shrugged. 'Do you remember what he was like in the first couple of years we had him? Real bastard at the water. I thought he'd got over that. Still, it was a good exercise. So, apart from the balls-up, how did he feel?'

'Excellent.' Matt tried to sound normal. He'd got away with it. If he could fool Kath he could fool anyone, surely? 'I mean, really good. He'll win next time out, no problem.'

Kath turned her head and gave him one of her rare smiles. 'Yes, he will.'

Shit. He stretched his mouth into an answering grin. Now he wasn't sure. Did Kath suspect anything? Ever since he'd dismounted, he'd expected the stewards to haul him in. A well-beaten odds-on favourite—especially one of Dragon Slayer's stature—always aroused suspicions. He'd listened to the changing-room chatter without hearing a word. Each time the door had opened he'd expected someone to call his name.

But they hadn't. Everyone had seen Dragon Slayer shy away from the ditch. His fellow jockeys had been sympathetic and mickey-taking in equal measure. They all knew it happened. It had happened to all of them at some time. No one doubted that Dragon Slayer's stumble was anything other than an early-season *faux pas.*

*   *   *

After a further hair-raising hour, Kath screeched the BMW to a halt outside his house. 'See you for work tomorrow morning,' she said as he hauled the holdall from the back seat. 'I won't take you back to the yard. I don't think you'll be too popular. The lads will have put their wages on Dragon Slayer today. They'll blame you for buggering up their spending money.' She revved the engine and leaned from the window. 'It'll probably cost you a few pints tonight.'

It was going to cost him a hell of a lot more than that, Matt thought sadly.

Kath revved even harder, then, as the car jerked forward, she leaned from the window again. 'Oh, Matt! One thing you might give a bit of thought to. If Dragon Slayer hated the ditch so much, why did he jump it like a stag on the first circuit?'

Shit. Shit. Shit. With a sick churning in his

stomach, Matt unlocked his front door and dropped the holdall in the hall. He should have known he couldn't fool Kath. Oh, God.

He stumbled across the cluttered living room towards the drinks tray on the sideboard. The light on the answerphone was flashing. He played both the messages as he shed his suit jacket and tie and poured a huge gin and slimline tonic.

Jemima, reminding him of the meeting—and asking him to meet her in the Cat and Fiddle if he got back in time. No mention of the race—but of course, there wouldn't be, would there? And Ned, sarcastically congratulating him on a blinding result, and suggesting that they met up for a pint and a chat pretty damn quick.

Christ. He poured a second gin and wiped the messages.

*   *   *

The Cat and Fiddle was bulging at the seams. The Ladies' League of Light meeting was obviously over, and the protagonists had spilled into the lounge bar. Matt veered away from the perms, sandals and cardigans all bobbing round the Vicar, and headed for the Spit and Sawdust. Several morose lads from Lancing Grange were clustered round the juke-box sharing a lemonade shandy. Matt, backing up, gave them a wide berth as he made his way to the Snug.

It was like walking into hell. Not only was Jemima sitting at a table with Maureen and Gillian, but Vincent and Ned were pressed chummily together on one of the benches, and Charlie Somerset was chatting to Kath. Dear God.

They all turned to look at him at the same time.

330

He swept a smile round the room and made for the bar. It was going to take ages to get served. The longer the better as far as he was concerned, even though he was gagging for a top-up of gin.

'I'll get yours.' Charlie elbowed his way in beside him. 'I'm buying another for Ms Seaward and the girls. You can get the next round. Bad luck about today. Still, shit happens. Go and talk to Jemima, I'm sure she needs your support.'

Trying to organise his scattered wits, Matt blinked. 'I didn't know you and Kath were on speaking terms again. When did that happen?'

'What?' Charlie caught the barman's eye and rattled off his order. 'Oh, yeah. Well, a crowded bar makes for strange stablemates. We're not sitting together by choice. She still reckons I'm the pits—don't worry. Your job's safe. Look, Matt, don't misunderstand me, but I reckon you ought to sort out your priorities.'

Sweating with guilt, Matt found himself jostled by several villagers. He jerked away from them irritably. They laughed, making ribald comments about his failure to win. Frowning, he turned his back. 'Which priorities?'

'If you need to ask, then you've got a major problem.' Charlie collected the glasses together. 'Jemima, of course. Stop screwing about me and Kath ripping each other to shreds, and ask Jemima how the meeting went.'

'I did intend to.'

Charlie balanced his collection of gin, beer and assorted wines. 'Well, don't sodding intend—bloody do it.'

Matt did. Easing himself between Maureen's purple satin and Gillian's muted silk, he leaned

331

across the table and kissed Jemima's forehead. He'd aimed for her cheek and hoped he might get her mouth. It was all too squashed to be accurate.

'How did it go? Bathsheba's meeting?'

'Well, as I was excluded—and Gillian swapped sides—I was in the middle of finding out.'

'I've been debriefed,' Gillian smiled radiantly across the table at Charlie. 'And I wish you'd all stop frowning at me. I didn't have a choice. I was strictly Mrs Vicar tonight. With Glen chairing the meeting, what else was I supposed to do?'

Matt didn't really care. He tried to reach for Jemima's hand and couldn't make it. 'So? You're still trading then? Bathsheba hasn't slapped on an embargo?'

'Damn well better not try, duck.' Maureen was displaying her usual generous amount of cleavage. 'No, the silly old bag is having a general public meeting at the end of the month. Village hall will have reopened then, see. She reckons she'll get a full house.'

Jemima appeared to drag her eyes away from Ned and Vincent. 'Tonight was highly undemocratic—all antis barred. Apparently she's stirring everyone up, ordering them not to set foot inside the shop if they want to protect the good name of the sisterhood—that sort of thing. I don't know how it will affect sales . . .'

'Not at all,' Gillian and Maureen said together.

Matt shrugged. 'It could have been worse, then.' It could have been a million times worse. Jemima was only being bothered by maybes. His life was being pulled apart by definites.

She still looked unhappy. He wanted to tell her to smile and not worry but the words weren't there.

He wanted to tell her that she was beautiful—because she was. He wished that three months ago he hadn't been such a gentleman when she'd been shy and unsure of herself, and he hadn't wanted to take advantage of her vulnerability. Now he knew that he'd left it too late to develop their friendship into anything else. Or had he? He wished they could be alone together to find out. More than anything he wanted to invite Jemima back to his house and sit quietly in the dark and be comforted.

She was sipping her wine, looking distracted. Her eyes weren't on him. They had slipped back to Vincent and Ned in the corner. He wished she'd speak to him about racing.

'Matt—' Kath Seaward had left Charlie and was leaning over their table on her way out of the pub. 'After first lot, come to breakfast tomorrow. There are things I want to discuss. Okay?'

Panic prickled up from his toes. Calm down. 'Okay. Er—anything in particular?'

'Yes.' She swept her glance round the rest of the Snug. 'I've picked up one or two bits of gossip tonight that seem to throw some light on what happened today. I'd like to know what you think. 'Night.'

Christ. Exhausted as he was, there was no chance of sleeping tonight now. He'd toss and turn and the horrors would multiply in the dark, dead hours. He felt like a hunted animal.

Charlie had vanished through to the Spit and Sawdust. Ned and Vincent were draining the last dregs from their glasses. Gillian and Maureen were giggling together. Jemima, still opposite him, looked troubled. He thought about moving the chairs round so that they could at least be side by side. He couldn't be bothered. He didn't want to hear about the bloody bookshop. God, he thought, what a lot of fuss over nothing. Getting panicky over a lot of silly old blue-rinsed bags who objected to a couple of novels. She ought to try walking in his shoes. She ought to try having an entire race of demons riding on her shoulders.

'Any more room for a little one?' Vincent beamed round the table. The beam faltered slightly when it reached Matt. 'Shift up, Jem, love, and make a space for your dad.'

'You park your bum here.' Maureen patted the half-inch of her chair that was visible on either side of the purple satin. 'Jemima can snuggle up a bit to young Matthew. They both looks like they've lost a quid and found a tanner.'

There was a lot of clattering as the seating was rearranged. Jemima looked as though she'd rather be anywhere than snuggled up to him, Matt thought. What was the point in carrying on like this? They were getting nowhere. And if Vincent had joined the group, did that mean Ned was following? And did he really want to be sharing a table with Maureen and Vincent—both of whom could surely blow his cover?

He stood up. 'Actually, I'm pretty knackered. I think I'll call it a day.'

He wanted Jemima to come with him, but he couldn't ask her in front of her father. And she'd probably say no anyway.

'Perfect timing.' Ned Filkins clapped him on the shoulder. 'I'll walk along with you, Matt, me lad. We're going in the same direction, aren't we?'

Fuck it. Matt swallowed. 'Yeah, I guess we are.' He leaned across Maureen and kissed Jemima haphazardly on the top of her head. 'I'll ring you tomorrow. Okay?'

She nodded and sort of blew him a kiss in return.

Outside, the night had closed in. The lights spilled out across the car park and the Cat and Fiddle's clientele were still coming and going. Ned, whose head didn't quite reach Matt's shoulder, looked like a malevolent goblin in the gloom.

'Not quite what we had in mind, Matt, now was it?' His eyes swivelled in all directions. 'Very artistic, I must admit. And lucrative. The lads and me cleaned up on betting against Dragon Slayer— but we don't want to overdo it. We thought you'd get a place. We don't want him fucking up every race and Mizz Seaward deciding that he's past his sell-by and despatching him to the knackers, now do we?'

Matt shook his head.

Ned continued to bob alongside. 'You'd better win for the next couple of outings—or run your best. We still want to be on song for the Hennessey. The ole cow was asking questions in there tonight.'

'I think she's going to be asking me the same questions in the morning.'

'And you've got your answers off pat, haven't you? Stick to what we agreed. No bullshit—the ole cow's too clever by half. Don't want to arouse no suspicions now, do we? Me and the lads'll be in touch. Okay?'

Matt said nothing. There was nothing to say. If only it were that simple. If only it were Ned and a fistful of bent stable lads determined to make a killing. Christ! He could handle that.

Ned punched him playfully on the arm. 'Don't look so down, boy. Just do what you're told and

335

you'll be laughing along with the rest of us come Aintree, won't you?'

CHAPTER TWENTY-THREE

Really, Jemima thought, closing her account-books, Bathsheba's boycott had made no difference. If anything, September's sales were slightly up. Fishnets were still very much in demand, and she'd ordered all the new tides. Mind you, after the meeting in the village hall it might be a different story. She'd heard a rumour that Bronwyn Pugh, using the same tactics, had defeated a millionaire alliance which had wanted to turn Milton St John into the next golfer's paradise.

In the quiet of the empty shop, she whizzed through the spreadsheets on the computer, made sure the columns tallied with her handwritten figures, and printed them out. Next stop the accountants in Upton Poges to drop off the paperwork, followed by depositing the takings in the bank, then possibly a veggie kebab take-out from Leon's Turkish Delight in Upton Poges High Street, and an evening of doing nothing very much. There would be absolutely no point in making the meal for two and inviting Matt. He was still existing on lettuce leaves and self-pity, and seemed to spend all his free time in the sauna.

Hurling the briefcase on to Floss's back seat, she reversed away from the lay-by. Bronwyn, collecting in the litter bins from outside the Village Stores, kept her head down. Maureen, sluicing down the pavement in front of the Munchy Bar, waved vigorously. That just about summed it up, Jemima thought, easing off the clutch as she turned Peapods' corner; either for or against. There were going to be no half-measures.

The journey into Upton Poges usually took her about fifteen minutes. At this time of day, in the middle of all the home-going traffic, it would take possibly twice as long. It didn't matter. She had nothing to rush for. To be honest, the lack of life outside the bookshop was beginning to bother her. In Oxford, she'd had various consecutive relationships, and plenty of manless gaps, neither of which had been a problem. She'd always been in control of her love life. This something-and-nothing affair with Matt was beginning to appear pretty pointless. She was sure he felt he same way. Perhaps one of them should be brave enough to say goodbye.

Maybe if she discussed his job with him it would give them some common ground—but because she refused to ask about his race-riding, he ignored everything that happened during her working day, too. It made conversation a bit stilted. And it honestly wasn't just because he was a jockey, she told herself above the hum of TVFM, although that didn't help. No, Matt, she was sure, could have been employed in any profession and there would still be no vital spark.

She enjoyed his company, and liked him . . . That was it, she thought, trying not to plough Floss into a clump of fitness-freak office workers who were cycling home wearing crash helmets with their sober suits, she *liked* Matt. She'd liked him from the moment they'd met—and nothing had changed. She sometimes wished that he wouldn't be

337

so damned respectful and—well—nice. If only he'd rush into her flat one evening, throatily declare uncontrollable lust and, brooking no arguments, tumble her into bed. She giggled at the unlikely image. But at least then she wouldn't feel quite so bloody *sisterly* towards him.

Everyone else in Milton St John seemed to be firmly into a steamy and satisfying relationship of one sort or another. Except Suzy, of course, but then she'd probably had enough steam in her two years with Luke to last her a lifetime. All the current gossip centred on Maddy and Drew's forthcoming wedding. Whether it was because Gillian still had a bit of pull with the Bishop or not was unclear, but dispensation had been granted for them to be married in St Saviour's. The ceremony had been arranged, rather imaginatively, Jemima thought, for November the fifth, when Maddy would sail down the aisle—or was it up?—at exactly seven-and-a-half months' pregnant.

Couldn't they have arranged it more quickly? Jemima had enquired of Gillian.

Gillian had looked askance at such innocence, and explained that this was the only way the nuptials could be slotted into Bonne Nuit's training schedule. It would also give everyone three weeks in which to recover before the Hennessey. The Hennessey Gold Cup at Newbury was apparently one of the big dates on the racing calendar: Gillian had explained it all to her in words of one syllable. Bonne Nuit would be making his first bid for the major spoils. Charlie would be riding Bonnie, Gillian had said, and Matt would be on Dragon Slayer. Surely he'd told her? Jemima said he might have done. It would be the first time the two horses

338

had been pitted against each other. It would be a great day out.

So it might be, Jemima thought as she indicated towards Upton Poges, but it wouldn't involve her. She'd asked Gillian if Bonne Nuit's ownership would be public knowledge by this time, and Gillian had got quite agitated and said no, she didn't think so. It wasn't important. Bonne Nuit's anonymous training fees were serving their dual purpose. They were making a satisfactory dent in the Hutchinsons' bank account and shoring up the Peapods survival bid. Jemima still didn't quite understand what was going on.

But then, she didn't understand a lot of what was going on in Milton St John if she was honest. The village was like a river-gliding swan—two-thirds visible, calm and serene—and the remainder hidden and churning turbulently at an altogether different pace.

At least Lucinda was settled, she thought with almost motherly satisfaction, as she negotiated the congestion in Upton Poges High Street. After Bathsheba's initial outburst, and that rather surreal incident with Charlie in the chestnut tree, she'd managed via Vincent to get a message to Lucinda at Charlie's cottage. The KGB could learn a lot from Milton St John, she reckoned. They'd met in a suitably cloak-and-dagger way on one of the downland bridle-paths, and decided for the sake of peace that Lucinda shouldn't return to work in the bookshop.

'But I want to work there! I wasn't running away from you. I've never run away! I'll work until I go to university as planned,' Lucinda had insisted, the plait swinging angrily from side to side. 'My ma is not going to dictate to me! Oh go on, Jemima please!'

Jemima had had to be quite firm, and point out that a banshee-wailing Bathsheba stalking through Romantic Fiction every five minutes trying to reclaim her daughter would bankrupt the bookshop even more easily than the bulk-buying operations of the conglomerate chains.

Eventually Lucinda had capitulated, deciding to accept an invitation to spend the remainder of the time before she decamped for Southampton at a schoolfriend's parents' apartment in Spain.

'Real chum, this time?' Jemima had enquired. 'Not another Somerset euphemism?'

'Sadly, not.' Lucinda had scuffed at the dusty ground with the toe of her Buffalo trainer. 'Rebecca Maxwell-Dunmore. Sod all like Charlie. But—' she'd brightened and grinned at Jemima, 'she's got a really ace older brother.'

They'd parted friends. Jemima missed her—and so, she suspected, did Charlie who occasionally drifted into the bookshop for a chat, but never bought anything. Neither of them mentioned the chestnut tree. Sometimes Jemima wondered if she'd dreamed it. Who, apart from the skeletal Tina Maloret, was occupying Lucinda's place in Charlie's Wallbank-Fox, she had no idea; but her place in the bookshop had been taken by Tracy, a rather frighteningly efficient young mum from the new estate.

She parked Floss behind the Masonic Hall, shed herself of the least interesting but vital parts of the bookshop's operation at their various destinations, and decided against the take-away. Instead, she fought her way through Salisbury's, and emerged triumphant with a couple of bottles of Chardonnay and the makings of a blue cheese pasta salad. Deciding that this sounded extremely virtuous, she also lobbed a chocolate fudge gateau into the basket and promised herself she wouldn't eat it all in one go with a spoon. She would invite Gillian to supper—and possibly the twins, she decided, hurling in pizzas. Glen was heavily involved in organising the Michaelmas and Harvest Home church festivals which would mean she could legitimately exclude him.

Her relationship with Glen since the League of Light meeting had become rather strained. Poor man. She liked and admired him and certainly didn't want to make his conflict of interests any worse. Feeling guilty about her part in the latest village uproar, she'd even gone to church on the previous Sunday.

Apart from weddings and funerals and the odd inebriated Midnight Mass during her Oxford Christmases, organised worship had been lacking in Jemima's routine. Sitting between Gillian and the twins—whose usual sacrilegious spikes of hair had been flattened for the morning service—she had gazed alternately at the glorious centuries-old architecture of St Saviour's and Bathsheba Cox and the Parish Biddies who were packed into the front pews, staring at Glen in slavish adoration. She had enjoyed the hymn-singing, and recognised the prayers from childhood. She hadn't felt any spiritual uplift as far as she could tell, but maybe it had earned her some Brownie points.

Leaving Upton Poges and hitting the traffic going the other way this time, the return journey to Milton St John was equally slow. It still didn't matter. Jemima deposited her shopping in the kitchen, opened all the windows to the last knockings of the beautiful evening, and went in search of Gillian.

She found her crouched over the word processor in the summer-house, a cigarette smouldering in the ashtray, and an empty wineglass beside it. Having issued her invitation, which Gillian accepted with almost indecent haste when she mentioned the chocolate fudge gateau, she also invited the twins. Levi and Zeke were out at a birthday party—the burger and video type, Gillian explained quickly—just in case Jemima should think the boys had gone soft, and Glen was involved with his festival organising and choir practice, so she'd be along in an hour or so if that was okay.

The hour or so gave Jemima enough time to knock up the pasta salad, chill the wine, defrost the cake, have a shower, and rinse through her underwear. Deciding against trailing down the three flights of stairs to the Vicarage washing-line, she draped the scanty bits of lace over the radiators. She'd have to remember to switch them on later. A rather gory detective film on the television added an interesting background to this scene of domesticity. If she wasn't careful she'd be knitting for the Bring and Buy next.

A faint rap on the door interrupted an exciting development in the film; the detective had just got his kit off and was romping—far beyond the call of duty—very enthusiastically with a buxom policewoman. Squinting, her eyes still on the screen, Jemima walked across the room and opened the door.

'Oh!' Glen looked embarrassed. 'I thought

Gillian said she was coming to supper. Have I got it wrong?'

Jemima fumbled in her pocket for her glasses. 'No—er—are you joining us?' Would the pasta salad stretch? The gateau certainly wouldn't.

'Sadly, not.' Glen edged past her and seemed transfixed by the television. 'I just wondered if I could have a word about Bathsheba's next meeting?'

'Yes, of course.' She slid across the room and quickly zapped off the humping detective. It was far too late to hide her underwear. 'Is there a problem?'

Glen collapsed on to the sofa. 'It's all one huge problem, to be honest. But I really didn't want you to think that because I'm sitting on the platform with the ladies, that their views are necessarily mine. I'm not in favour of pornography, of course—but Gillian assures me that these—um—Fishnets aren't in the least salacious. The last thing I want is to cause you any professional hardship.' He sighed. 'This has really put both Gillian and myself in an awkward situation.'

Jemima knew. She was touched that Glen had made this effort. She thought she ought to make one of her own. 'I had intended to be at the village hall to fight my corner. Would you like me to boycott the meeting? Would that make it easier for you?'

'Heavens, no. You have every right to defend yourself.' He spread his hands in a helpless gesture. 'I sometimes get very frazzled by the outer limits of being a clergyman. I'd fondly believed at theological college that it would be all services and soul-saving. Maybe a little ministering to the sick

343

and giving comfort. I had absolutely no idea that I'd have to be an ombudsman and arbiter—as well as judge, jury, and executioner.'

'I do understand, really. And I promise, whatever happens at the meeting, I won't blame either you or Gillian for not being on my side.'

Glen looked relieved. 'I also think that your friendship with Gillian has helped to stoke the fires. I'm well aware that Bathsheba has never considered Gillian to be the most suitable Vicar's wife, despite her attention to parish duties. I've tried suggesting that she dresses a little more conventionally—and maybe isn't quite so open about smoking and drinking—but then, that's what makes her Gillian. I love her very much, you know.'

Jemima was getting misty-eyed. 'And that probably gets up a few noses, too. I mean, Bathsheba and Bronwyn and Co.—they're all fixated on you. You're a good-looking man who is gentle and kind—and in a position of power. It's heady stuff. I have a feeling that Fishnets may be just the tip of the iceberg. It's probably got far more to do with them fancying you rotten, and finding any old excuse to have you press your gaiters next to their support stockings in the village hall.'

'You'll make me blush,' Glen said, smoothing his hair.

God, Jemima thought, no wonder he caused ructions beneath the polyester bosoms. He was far too devastating to be let loose on all those middle-aged ladies with confused hormones.

'So, that's it really.' He stood up. 'I'm sure Gillian will echo my words to you. I just needed you to know that I'm not personally insulted by anything you sell—but that in my position—'

'Have you read any Fishnets?'

'What? No, of course not. They're not my sort of thing—and I get very little time—'

'Don't you think you should? You'd have a rounded opinion then, wouldn't you? Oh, I'm not doing a marketing campaign on you—you don't have to buy them. Borrow them from someone. Gillian's probably got all of them.'

Glen paused on his way to the door. 'Oh, I think you're wrong there. Gillian favours more romantic fiction. Haven't you read any of her short stories?'

Jemima had. They were pure hearts and flowers and happy endings. It hadn't stopped the cupboard in the summerhouse being stocked with raunch. So, that was another thing Glen didn't know about. She wasn't sure which would shock him more: the fact that Gillian was a closet erotica fan, or that she owned a racehorse which was tipped to win the Grand National.

'Anyway,' Glen was smiling again, looking even more like Richard Gere, 'I'll let you get on with your preparations. And tell Gillian not to hurry back downstairs. I'll put the boys to bed.' He held out his hand. 'I just wanted to have all this out in the open, you understand? I think I'm fairly liberal and I try to be tolerant, but if there's one thing I can't stand, it's subterfuge. Good night.'

Bloody hell, Jemima thought as she closed the door. Chicanery could be Milton St John's middle name.

*　　　*　　　*

They'd eaten most of the pasta salad and had hacked the gateau down the middle and heaped

345

half each on two plates.

'Yum.' Gillian washed down the last remains with a mouthful of Chardonnay. 'Totally blissful. Thank you so much. So? Was I second choice for this evening? Did Matt turn you down? If so, then he's a sad case.'

Jemima pushed the cake plates to one side and topped up the glasses. 'Matt didn't get invited. He wouldn't have eaten anything anyway. He's living on nervous energy and fizzy water.'

'One of the drawbacks of dating a jockey. Still, if he'd eaten all this lovely food he'd have been able to work it off later, wouldn't he? Wouldn't he? Jemima!' Gillian's mouth dropped open. 'You mean you still haven't—haven't—'

'No, we still haven't. And we're never likely to. And I don't want to talk about it. And I don't want to talk about him being a jockey, either. So, please change the subject.'

It proved pretty difficult. Most of the village gossip seemed to revolve around horses or sex. They managed to cover Luke and Suzy's estrangement; Maddy and Drew's wedding— Charlie Somerset as best man, of course, with Fran, Georgia, Rosa and Suzy as bridesmaids— and possibly Fran's daughter Chloë, and Lucinda if she wanted to be, and Poppy Scarlet if they could get her to toddle down the aisle; and then went on to Charlie and Tina's rather behind-closed-doors affair; and the forthcoming Hennessey Gold Cup.

'In which your Bonnie Nuts will be aiming for glory, no doubt?' Jemima stretched out on the sofa, relegating Gillian to the edge. 'And, as no one apart from Drew, me and Charlie knows its true ownership, you'll have to stuff a hanky in your

346

mouth if it does well—and, of course, not swan around in the winner's box—'

'Enclosure,' Gillian corrected, 'and stop sounding so bloody smug. I've kept your secret about your father, haven't I? I don't expect you not to keep mine. Actually—' she wriggled further back into her scant allocation of cushions, 'I think Vincent has rather taken a shine to Maureen. How do you feel about having the Munchy Bar as a step-mum?'

'Maureen's married,' Jemima said. 'I think she and Dad are just good friends.'

'No one in Milton St John is just good friends—except you and Matt, of course. Goodness, don't you ever get—well, you know—urges?'

'Of course I get urges. Just not with Matt.'

Gillian reached for the remainder of the wine. 'Really? Then who—?'

Jemima suddenly remembered a bottle of Beaujolais tucked away in the larder and struggled to her feet. 'Don't change the subject. You do know that according to the grapevine, your Bonnie Nuts is owned by Fizz Flanagan, the entire Saudi royal family, Sharon Stone and Prince Philip? Quite a consortium.'

'They'd make a stir in the paddock at Aintree, granted.' Gillian raised her voice as Jemima headed for the kitchen. 'And I'll divulge all when the time is right.'

Jemima returned with the bottle. 'Which will be when?'

'Not yet. There will have to be a bit of heart-to-hearting between Glen and myself before I go public.' She sighed. 'It's all got into such a terrible tangle, to be honest.'

Jemima had guessed as much. She had long since given up trying to work out why Gillian needed to lose her money. The high earners like drugs, armed robbery, or prostitution seemed hardly likely, and there really didn't seem to be any other way—especially not in Milton St John—to make a killing. Unless, of course, it was blackmail. There would be tons of scope for that.

Glen had apologised to her on several occasions for the exorbitant rent she was allegedly paying on the Vicarage flat. If it hadn't been for Gillian knowing about Vincent's peccadilloes, she might well have told him that in fact she parted with less than a quarter of that amount.

Jemima poured Beaujolais into both glasses. It went cloudy. It would probably give them tannin poisoning. 'Are you running a betting ring? Is that where your income is from? Or have you won the lottery? I suppose the church frowns on gambling almost as much as I do. Is that your hidden vice?'

'I wish.' Gillian swigged back half the contents of her glass and lit a cigarette. 'Oh, bugger—Jemima, haven't you got any idea? I wish I could tell you. I wish I could tell bloody someone. Can you imagine being a vicar's wife and having this sort of secret on your shoulders?'

Jemima couldn't. Her imagination stretched wildly—but she couldn't think of anything other than the blackmail bit—and Gillian was always so damned indiscreet. Was it a lover? A very wealthy lover who paid for Gillian's services? Nah. Not possible. Glen and Gillian were dopey about each other. So what else could be so appallingly awful for a vicar's wife?

Of course! A crisis of faith! Gillian could no

348

longer sustain her belief in the ideals of the Church of England—and had joined some sort of religious splinter group. That would be pretty drastic—but would it necessarily generate an unhealthily high income? Not really. Not unless Gillian had set herself up as one of these new preachy women who appeared on cable telly and asked people to shower them with cash 'to strengthen their allegiance to the new church'.

That had to be it! Gillian had gone cult. It would certainly explain why she didn't want Glen to discover the source of her income. Such discovery would spell certain disaster.

Jemima exhaled loudly. 'I think I understand . . . I think I *might* have guessed. And if I'm right—then, has Bathsheba got wind of it, too?'

Gillian turned pale and took another frantic swig. 'I think she may have an inkling, yes. Oh, it's such a relief—I'm so glad that you *know* at last. But you do understand now why Glen mustn't find out?'

'Absolutely.' Jemima nodded fervently and wished she hadn't. The mixture of Chardonnay and Beaujolais made her head spin. 'But isn't there anyone sort of holy you could discuss it with? What about your matey Bishop?'

'God.' Gillian blinked. 'Lovely as Derek is, I don't think he'd be at all the right sort of person to confide in. Anyway, he'd be honour-bound to tell Glen.'

'Would he? Don't they have a code of practice in the Church of England, then? I'd have thought it would come under the same sort of umbrella as the sanctity of the confessional.' She would really have to avoid mixing her drinks. She'd be tuning in to *Songs of Praise* before she knew it.

Gillian looked uncomfortable. 'I don't think so. I think an issue of this—um—nature would come outside that. The clergy are a bit of a closed shop.'

'Are they? Well, of course I don't have your inside knowledge, but if it were me, then in your position I'd try to discuss it with someone higher up. Someone a bit—well—closer to God, I suppose. Look, I don't blame you. With all these wars, and so much cruelty, and world starvation—it must make even the strongest Christian doubt sometimes.'

Gillian put her empty glass on the coffee table and stubbed out her cigarette on the cake plates. 'Jemima, sweetie, what exactly do you think my secret is?'

'Well, a sort of crisis of faith? A shift in beliefs? A sideways move towards the happy-clappies?'

'Christ.' Gillian pushed the pale hair behind her ears. 'I thought you said you *knew.*'

'Not knew, exactly. More, guessed. Why? Isn't that it?'

'No, it bloody well isn't.' Gillian bent down and hauled her handbag on to her lap. She rifled through the accumulated junk, and eventually extracted a few sheets of scrumpled paper which she shoved into Jemima's hands. 'Go on. Read it. I can't keep it to myself any longer. When you've read it you can tell whoever you like. It might come as a relief.'

Jemima straightened her glasses, her eyes skimming over the double-spaced pages. She thought her mouth might have dropped open but she wasn't sure. Maybe the mixture of wines had been more potent than she'd thought. She turned back to the first page and started reading again, this time more carefully. It didn't change the words.

They were still the same.

Feeling completely stunned, she let the papers fall into her lap. She stared at Gillian in disbelief. 'Good God! This is totally pornographic!'

'Erotic,' Gillian corrected wearily. 'Still, at least now you know where the money comes from, don't you?'

Jemima nodded weakly. She did. Gillian Hutchinson, Mrs Vicar, sat in the summerhouse and wrote porn. Gillian Hutchinson was Bella-Donna Stockings.

CHAPTER TWENTY-FOUR

Wearing her most businesslike outfit of long skirt and patchwork jacket, Jemima sat at the back of the village hall and wished Gillian hadn't told her. It was going to be difficult not to laugh.

Bathsheba and Bronwyn were already on the stage, flanked by Petunia Hobday and two or three camp followers. Glen was doling out kind words and probably causing menopausal mayhem. It was, however, reassuring that the hall was far from full.

Jemima also wished that Gillian hadn't chosen to wear the gold-and-green floaty frock with the matching long silk scarf wound carelessly round her throat. She looked far too beautiful. If Bathsheba even had an inkling about the dual identity, she'd surely go in for the kill.

After Gillian had made her confession, and they'd abandoned the wine for a stiff slug of whisky, and Jemima's head had stopped spinning, they had decamped to the summerhouse. Gillian had switched on the word processor, scrolling through the files, then sat back and left it to Jemima.

They were all there. Six Bella-Donna Stockings novels in their entirety. Starting with *Boys and Girls Come Out to Play*—and ending with *Spanky Panky*. Jemima still didn't know whether she was shocked rigid or stunned with admiration.

Gillian had taken over the controls again. 'This is the current one, *Bonds that Bind*—mind you, that's just a working tide, it'll probably be something else. And then, there's a rough synopsis here for the next one.' She'd pushed back her chair with a sigh and lit a cigarette. The blue smoke had curled idly through the still air. 'I've thought long and hard about this—well, you have to with Fishnets—no, sorry, bad-taste joke—and I can't see any other way than to carry on.'

'Without telling Glen?'

'I can't tell Glen. How the hell could I tell Glen? He thinks that it's the women's mags that keep me in Monsoon and our bank balance in the black. He's so *proud* of me. And, whether he's supposed to or not, he enjoys not being broke. And I'm contracted to another three-book deal. Even with the money I've spent on Bonnie Nuts and your mythical rent, if I gave up now he'd be in for a hell of a financial jolt—'

Jemima had scrutinised the screen over Gillian's shoulder. 'He'd get more of a jolt if he read that!'

'You're shocked, aren't you?'

'Of course I'm shocked. But not as in "Disgusted of Tunbridge Wells". I'm just amazed that you've got away with it for as long as you have. I'd only just got my head round you being a vicar's wife and looking like a *Vogue* cover-girl. To find that you write porn as well—'

'Erotica,' Gillian had corrected quickly. 'And I've always believed one should fully utilise one's God-given gifts.'

'Oh, come on. You can't get out of it like that. God gave you the writing talent, I'll agree, but he didn't make you write por—er—erotica.'

'God isn't blatant.' Gillian had looked quite affronted at this naivety. 'I discovered my gift quite by chance. I had to do a more juicy piece for one of my regular magazines and found I could write racy stories really easily. My editor suggested I should contact Fishnets for their guidelines—and I've never looked back. As far as I'm concerned, God gave me this opportunity, and it's made life easier for Glen and the boys—as well as harmlessly entertaining for the people who read my books. And if Bathsheba thinks that I'm a scarlet woman, then she should remember Jesus and Mary Magdalene.'

'I don't think that was the same thing at all, was it? Anyway, your books are—well—where on earth do you get your ideas from?'

'A vivid imagination and a happy sex life,' Gillian purred. 'After all, Agatha Christie spent a lifetime writing whodunnits—but she never actually murdered anyone, did she?'

'No—but—'

'And you know as well as I do that Fishnets don't degrade women. And I never go outside the teachings of the Church. I always have single heroines who are driven by love as well as lust—and they always get married in the end.'

In the face of this equanimity, Jemima had felt that there was absolutely nothing left to say.

The village hall was rumbling with anticipation. It was getting late. Most people had given up *Coronation Street* and the Cat and Fiddle to be there. They were eager to get started.

Matt had promised to pop in, but Jemima doubted that he would. Tina Maloret had arrived in the village that morning and had been closeted at Lancing Grange for discussions on Dragon Slayer's suitability for the Hennessey, or so Gillian had said. Matt, naturally, hadn't talked about it with her. She knew though that he'd had an unsuccessful week, with defeats at Hereford and Plumpton. There had been a group of Kath's stable lads in the shop the previous day muttering over not being able to afford the latest Stephen King, bemoaning the fact that their gambles had once again gone down the pan, and saying that bloody Matt Garside had lost his nerve.

Jemima had tried not to listen. She had so many problems of her own, and she felt totally unequipped to deal with Matt's.

Vincent, accompanied by Maureen, had promised moral support, and they were sliding noisily into the seats on one side of Jemima. The chairs on the other side remained empty. It seemed that no one else was prepared to risk Bathsheba's wrath by being seen to consort with the enemy.

'No Matt?' Vincent asked, after making sure that Maureen was comfy. 'I thought he'd be here to hold your hand.'

Jemima shook her head. Vincent's tone was a bit caustic, she reckoned. Didn't he like Matt? Funny, she'd never asked him really. No—he's discussing tactics with Kath.'

'Not at this time of night he isn't, duck.' Maureen frowned. 'Kath's an early-to-bed early-to-rise girl. Everyone knows that. She wouldn't be discussing anything with anyone after eight o'clock at night.'

Jemima pulled a face. Maybe she'd got it wrong. She'd have to ask him later. She leaned towards Vincent. 'Pity he's not here, though. You men look slightly outnumbered.'

Bernie Pugh and Ted Cox had been press-ganged in and were sitting in the front row looking like they were at a vasectomy clinic. Apart from them, the congregation—if that wasn't too flippant a description—was predominantly female. Maddy, who was now obviously pregnant and looking absolutely stunning; Suzy, back in the village just for the evening which was really sweet of her, Jemima thought; and Fran, she knew, were firmly on her side. Kath Seaward, Kimberley Small and Diana James-Jordan had also, rather surprisingly, promised their high-powered backing. Otherwise, she thought, staring at the faces, it was difficult to sort out the pros from the antis. She had a feeling that if they knew the true identity of Bella-Donna Stockings someone would have had to send out for riot police and tear gas.

Glen was calling the meeting to order. She avoided meeting Gillian's eyes. Screaming with laughter now wouldn't do either of them any good at all.

'Ladies!' Glen rapped smartly on the shabby table as he scanned the gathering. 'Oh, and yes—gentlemen. Let's have some silence and a short prayer for God's guidance.'

355

Heads bowed and mouths worked fervently.

'We all know why this meeting has been called.' Glen's tan was set off to perfection by the sweatshirt. 'And, while I agree wholeheartedly with your dislike of pornography, I hope that we can keep a sense of proportion this evening. We live in a democracy and, as such, should be willing to be tolerant of the requirements of others as long as they remain within the law.'

This alone was enough to have Bathsheba on her feet. As she trumpeted her opening volley, the door opened. Jemima turned her head and almost laughed. Charlie Somerset had just sidled in.

'I thought I should be here,' he whispered, clattering along the row and sitting next to her. 'After all, if Bathsheba hadn't found that book I gave to Lucinda, none of this would have happened.'

'It probably would,' Jemima whispered back. 'Eventually. Anyway, everyone thinks that book belonged to Maddy and Drew, don't they?'

'Yeah, luckily.' Charlie smiled along the row at Vincent and Maureen. He leaned back in his chair. 'Where's Matt?'

Jemima shrugged. 'Not sure. Still doing something horsy, I would imagine.'

'He should be here chucking in his support.'

Jemima said nothing. She didn't support Matt in his work. Why on earth should she expect any support from him?

The debate appeared to be gathering momentum. Bathsheba was doing much of the talking. It all seemed to revolve around filth and the vilification of women. There was a short outpouring on the hard work of the foremothers of Milton St

356

John who had apparently fought tooth and nail to prevent the corruption of future generations. Gillian, on the stage, spotted Charlie and waved. He waved back.

'Anyway,' Jemima said, 'I would have thought you'd have been otherwise engaged this evening. With Tina being in the village.'

'She isn't.'

'She is. Gillian said. She's at Lancing Grange discussing things.'

Charlie didn't look riveted by this piece of news. Strange, she thought, that he didn't appear to know.

Bathsheba was now waving a Fishnet above her head. 'This is the filth I found in my child's bedroom!'

Charlie groaned.

And,' Bathsheba continued, 'this is what I intend to weed out! Kill the root and destroy the plant! Bella-Donna Stockings writes vulgarity in its basest form! She, and her cohorts, must—and will—be stopped!'

There was a ripple of applause as Bathsheba sat down. Jemima, who was still pretty sure she was going to laugh, didn't dare to look at Gillian.

Glen was on his feet again. 'We've all heard both sides of the argument—and I'm afraid we're no further forward. I can't see that there is anything we can do to stop these particular books being published, or to prevent people who wish to read them doing so. I suggest that we now pray for the matter to be reconciled and—'

'Excuse me!' Charlie grinned towards the stage. All heads turned. Jemima shrank down in her seat. 'Can I just make a comment?'

357

Gillian, who had been looking depressed, perked up suddenly. Glen nodded. 'Yes, of course. I wasn't sure that there was a lot of point throwing the meeting open to the floor. I thought all of you had made your views known. However—yes, Charlie— if you've anything illuminating to add, then we'd be glad to hear it.'

Charlie stood up. His thighs in tight denim were on Jemima's eye-level. She tried not to look at them.

'I thought that I should put in a word for Jemima.'

Everyone was staring at her now. She fixed a rictus smile and gave a sort of nervous-tic nod of the head.

Charlie carried on happily. 'Well, it doesn't seem fair that a minority want to put her out of business. The bookshop has become a real focal point of the village—there's something for everyone. And that's how it should be. Freedom of choice. I don't think these Fishnet books can harm anyone,' he glanced down at Jemima, 'not that I've read them, of course. Anyone who knows me will realise that I never got further than *Janet and John* Book Two. I just wanted to say that I've been told by people who have, that they're all about women being in control of their own lives. Which is,' he turned the beam to Bathsheba, 'exactly what you're arguing for, I believe, Mrs Cox?'

Gillian led the clapping, which was much louder than Bathsheba had received, as Charlie sat down. Maureen and Vincent leaned across Jemima to congratulate him. Jemima stared into her lap.

'Okay?' he whispered. 'I thought I ought to say it. I've felt so guilty.'

358

'Thanks—but I wouldn't have thought guilt bothered you too much.'

'It doesn't usually.' Charlie looked a bit perplexed.

Bathsheba had lumbered to her feet. 'I don't want to put Jemima out of business! I don't see why I should be painted as the villain of this piece! All I want is for her to stop selling corruptive material. And if she doesn't, then—' still clutching *Spanky Panky* she held a rather pudgy arm aloft, 'to that end I intend to hold a candlelit vigil outside the bookshop! I shall expect every decent woman in this village to support me—including Mrs Hutchinson.'

Gillian nearly tumbled off her chair. Jemima chewed the inside of her mouth to stop the giggle escaping. Glen was nodding. 'Of course. I'm sure my wife will be delighted to lend her support in any tangible way. The least we can do—although I'm not sure that a vigil as such will make any difference—'

'That's as maybe.' Bathsheba resumed her seat with a crash, 'but it will be a display of purity against sleaze. It may not stop the books being sold—but it will make a point for all *respectable* women! I will be posting notices later regarding the date.'

The meeting came to an untidy conclusion at that point. Desperate to get outside and have a good laugh, Jemima belted towards the door. Watching Gillian join in the candlelit vigil to protest about her own books was going to be absolutely wonderful.

It was raining. The light from the village hall spilled in gleaming puddles. The people following her were pushing up umbrellas and turning up collars.

'Coming for a drink, Jem, love?' Vincent asked. 'That wasn't as bad as it could have been, was it? Silly old bat—who'll want to take part in her vigil anyway?'

'Not many,' Charlie said, joining them and shrugging into his leather jacket. 'I'll have to give Lucinda a ring and tell her how it went.'

Jemima had received a postcard from Lucinda in Spain a couple of days earlier. It had mostly been concerned with how Rebecca Maxwell-Dunmore's older brother was shaping up. Maybe, she thought, Lucinda had written this because Bronwyn Pugh read all the unsealed mail that passed through the Village Stores and this was what she wanted Bathsheba to know. Jemima hoped so. She realised suddenly that she didn't want Charlie to be hurt.

'I won't have that drink, thanks, Dad,' she said quickly. 'I'm sure Maureen will be ample company—and I've got a lot of paperwork to get through. I hadn't realised that it would be so busy. We're getting all the Christmas books in now. I might even have to ask Tracy to work full-time until the new year.'

'Whatever, love. Just don't work too hard.' Vincent kissed her cheek, and linking his arm through Maureen's, headed pubwards. He stopped. 'And you can tell me to mind my own business, of course, but when you see Matt I think you should give him a bit of a bollocking. He should have been here tonight.'

The other villagers also seemed to be making a bee-line for the Cat and Fiddle. Charlie grinned at her. It was a nice grin. Lopsided. And his teeth were crooked. 'Pity you're so busy. I was going to suggest the pub, too. I wanted to ask you something.'

'Can't you ask me out here?'

'It's wet and you'll probably say no.'

'That sounds promising.' She dodged to one side as Bathsheba, Bronwyn and Petunia waddled from the hall, all tying rain-mates beneath their chins. They looked as if they were going to form a three-pronged attack. Oh, God. Why was it always like this? Charlie or the Parish Biddies? She shrugged. 'Okay. Cat and Fiddle it is. But just one drink.'

*   *   *

Avoiding Vincent and Maureen and all other interested parties in the Snug, they settled for the Spit and Sawdust. Jemima had to wipe her glasses on the hem of her skirt while Charlie was at the bar. They always steamed up on wet nights. He carried two glasses of dry white wine carefully to the table, and it annoyed her that she noticed that he was a million times more attractive than any other man in the pub.

'Go on, then.' She sipped the wine. 'Ask.'

'It's to do with Drew and Maddy's wedding.'

She blinked. She'd imagined a million things, but not that. 'It's still on, isn't it? There hasn't been another hitch?'

'God, no.' Charlie pulled a face at his wine. 'They're embarrassingly ecstatic. No, it was more to do with a wedding present.' 'They said they didn't want anything—need anything. Gillian said there wasn't a list. I think we're just going to buy them a vat of Glenfiddich.'

'They'd love that. And no, there isn't a present

list as such. And this is not strictly a present. Shit.' He put the wineglass down on the table. 'Look, I've discussed this with Suzy and Fran and Georgia—them being closely involved, and they said I should ask you—'

'Do you want to buy them a book as a wedding gift?' She was a bit doubtful. It hardly seemed appropriate.

Charlie shook his head. 'We wondered if you'd do a turn?'

A what? 'I'm not an entertainer—'

Charlie had the grace to look embarrassed. 'Gillian said that you took your clothes off and leapt out of cakes.'

Jesus Christ! She'd kill her! She'd emblazon 'Gillian Hutchinson is Bella-Donna Stockings—True!' on every bloody wall in the village! Indiscreet cow!

'I almost leapt, almost dressed, out of one cake. A long time ago. I'll never do it again.'

Charlie looked crestfallen. 'Are you sure?'

'Absolutely positive. It was one of the worst moments of my life. Sorry, no, I won't. And Gillian shouldn't have told you.'

'Probably not—but I wish I'd been there.'

Jemima clutched at her wineglass and took a huge mouthful. She'd suddenly come over all hot. 'You'll have to think of something else.'

'I can't—Oh, you mean for Drew and Maddy? Oh yeah, I have.' Charlie gave up on his wine. 'But it won't be half so exciting. You leaping out of a mock-up cake would have added tons of Pizzazz.'

'I'm sorry to disappoint you.'

'You don't.'

She laughed and finished her drink. 'I'll have to

go. I honestly do have a lot of work to get through. If I'd known tonight's meeting was going to be such a damp squib I wouldn't have even come—' She stood up. 'Thanks for your contribution, though. I'm glad someone's on my side.'

Charlie stood up too. 'Most people are. Your shop has added a lot to the village.'

'And my kitchen and my erstwhile assistant even more?'

'Dunno about erstwhile.' Charlie grinned. 'If it means dead sexy, then yeah.'

She laughed again—then stopped. 'Bugger.'

'What?' Charlie followed her eyes. 'Oh, yeah. Double bugger.'

Matt and Tina Maloret had just walked into the pub. Vincent and Maureen must have got it wrong, Jemima thought. They must have been talking tactics. They looked as though they still were.

'I'm going out the back way through the kitchen,' Charlie said. 'I really can't cope with bondage and torture this evening. See ya.'

She watched him go. Was he joking? She couldn't imagine for the life of her why Tina Maloret would even contemplate hurting him. Still, maybe he enjoyed it. What did she know?

'Jemima!' Matt's smile was plastic. 'I wasn't expecting to see you in here. The meeting over, then?'

'Obviously.' She was annoyed that he hadn't asked how it went, and knew that she shouldn't be. It must be how he felt every day when he'd been hurtling over hurdles and she never even mentioned it.

Tina, turning heads in sprayed-on leather jeans, a transparent shirt, and a fur jacket—Jemima hoped it wasn't real—frowned. 'Were you with Charlie just now? I thought I saw him.'

Jemima shook her head. Matt's laugh came as an either-end-of-the-mantelpiece pair with the plastic smile. 'Hardly. Jemima doesn't like jockeys, remember?'

'Who does?' Tina nudged him.

It was quite a familiar nudge, Jemima thought. Was this developing into another of those Milton St John-type Shakespearean: romantic tangles? Did she care? Would Charlie? Coming up with two maybes and a don't know, she shrugged. 'I was just leaving. I've got tons of orders to catch up on. I still haven't got used to dealing with reps yet—and I'm not very good at saying no. I'll probably have enough books to stock Hatchards.'

Neither Matt nor Tina seemed to find this in the least interesting. She picked up her patchwork jacket. It was still damp.

'I'll—er—run you home,' Matt said. 'Tina and I had finished talking business. And I'm sure she's dying to find Charlie.'

There was a lot of eye-meeting going on between them. Tina nodded. 'I hope I come as a pleasant surprise. He doesn't even know I'm in the village. 'Bye then, you two. Be good.'

Her laugh followed them out into the car park.

There was no need at all to run her home, Jemima said. They could walk it in two minutes. Matt said they'd get wet and to get in, so she did. They parked outside the back door of the Vicarage.

'Do you want to come up to the flat?' She knew it sounded as though bubonic plague would be more pleasant. She couldn't help it. She was completely knackered. 'For a coffee or something?'

'There isn't a "something" on offer though, is there?' Matt's face looked very pale beneath the Vicarage's security lighting.

There wasn't. They both knew it. Feeling very tired, and fazed by the hours of paperwork ahead of her, Jemima touched his cheek. 'Maybe another night?'

Matt grabbed her hand, holding it trapped against his face. His eyes were almost sad as he bent to kiss her. 'Yeah. Maybe.'

The kiss became suddenly more intense. Jemima started to kiss him back, and immediately realised it wasn't right. She began to push him away. 'Sorry—Matt—no, I can't—'

'Won't.' His voice was bitter as he fumbled with the buttons on the patchwork jacket. Being damp, they gave litde purchase. 'Why not? Am I that repulsive?'

'No—of course not.' The buttons had given way. 'But not like this—not now.'

'Now or never.' Matt lunged at her again. 'Come on, Jemima. Stop playing at being the Virgin Queen—or aren't I good enough?'

He was hurting her. She wasn't afraid. Just angry. 'Matt—you're great. We just can't—I can't—'

'You can. Oh, you can.' He had managed to get himself anchored in the gap between the seats. Most of his weight was pinning her down. His free hand was scrabbling at her skirt, trying to yank it past her knees. 'See—it's not that bad.'

'Bloody pack it in!'

Oddly she was far more concerned about the outside light illuminating the sordid scene to the entire Hutchinson family, than she was about Matt violating her body. She'd had enough experience of gropers in Oxford to know she could handle him.

'There! Is that nice?'

It wasn't. She wriggled towards the passenger door, turning her head away from his probing mouth. 'It's damned uncomfortable. Look, stop playing silly sods and come indoors. At least we'll be comfortable in there.'

He turned her face towards him again. 'And you'll let me stay the night, will you? Even though I'm a jockey?'

'It's got stuff-all to do with you being a jockey.'

Hallelujah! She'd managed to find the door-catch. Fiddling with it, the door suddenly sprang open and they both tumbled sideways. The Vicarage drive was wet and pebbly. *From Here to Eternity* it wasn't.

Jemima scrambled to her feet and ran towards the house. Matt, panting slightly, followed her. Where was her bloody key? Why could she never find it? Ah! She shoved the key into the lock.

'Well?' Matt, looking dishevelled, stumbled on the doorstep. 'Am I coming in?'

She knew she should say no. She didn't want to sleep with him. If she slept with him, it would move things in a direction she really didn't want to go. On the other hand, if she said no, she'd feel like a complete cow. Maybe she could make him the offered coffee, and they could sit and listen to some music, talk. It might calm him down. She almost laughed. She'd actually *wanted* him to behave like this, hadn't she?

'If you promise not to leap on me again. If we can just sort a few things out. I'm not a lump of meat, Matt. Nor am I some sixteen-year-old who enjoys a quick grope and fumble. Yes, okay—but

366

only if—oh, God!'

She stopped and looked at him. He was crying.

October

CHAPTER TWENTY-FIVE

Handing over five thousand pounds in cash to anyone would be a bit risky, Vincent felt. Handing it over to Ned Filkins in the windswept darkness of the Downs was downright insanity.

'That's it, Vince, mate.' Ned flicked through the collection of fifty-pound notes. 'Your pension. Your security for your old age—or not-that-much-older age, come to mention it. Only another five months to go, then think of the bonuses you'll pick up in April. Better 'n any bloody Tessys or Peppas.'

'And it's guaranteed? Safe?'

Ned tapped the side of his nose. 'Safe as the Bank of England. Have I ever let you down?'

Vincent had to admit that he hadn't. The stakes may have got increasingly high, but the returns had grown to reflect them. He'd got no complaints. Well, not about the money. But as gambling went, it was a bit boring, if he was to tell the truth. Half the fun of betting was making your selection, piling on the dosh, and then sweating through the race, living or dying on the result.

Gambling on horses was all about being there at the race meeting, sharing the excitement, soaking up the atmosphere. The smug feeling you got watching the real mugs waving their tenners at the bookies, knowing that they'd made the wrong choice—and that your horse would be romping home to glory ahead of theirs. Watching their faces as they ripped up their betting slips while you queued at the pay-out bag for yet another wad of crumpled notes.

With the selective memory of all addicted gamblers, Vincent only ever remembered the winners.

This handing over of cash with no idea how it was being spent, and then being clinically paid the winnings days later, took the edge off the fun. Still, he couldn't complain about the income his outlay generated. The stash under the mattress made it difficult to sleep at night.

'Couldn't we have done this in the pub?' Vincent queried as they picked their way unsteadily down the bridle track in the pitch dark. Milton St John, emblazoned by a thousand pinpricks of light, curled far below them. 'Do we really have to be this furtive all the time?'

'Fewer people who knows, the better.' Ned's voice was whisked away over his shoulder on the reed-whistle of the wind. 'But now you've brought it up, I've got a little surprise for you. No—leave your car here. It's well hidden. We'll take mine. I think it's time you got involved with the big boys.'

Vincent, climbing into Ned's leatherette seat, had dire feelings of foreboding. The big boys didn't sound like the collection of grouchy stable lads he'd already met. They didn't sound much like jockeys on the take either. They sounded scarily like the huge men with fur collars and padded shoulders with whom he'd had dealings in the past. He never wanted to become involved with them again.

Wasn't he getting a bit out of his depth here? He shook himself No—it'd be all right. Course it would. If Ned was to be believed, then this scam would bring in far more than he could have hoped to have earned in a lifetime's hard work. There would have to be some risks. It wouldn't be half so exciting without them, would it?

Ned didn't turn the engine on, and freewheeling, they bumped down the bridle track in darkness. Ned had left the car's headlights switched off, too. It felt a bit like plunging down a lift-shaft—not knowing when you were going to hit the bottom. There were still dozens of things Vincent wasn't too clear about, and Matt Garside was top of the list. Ned had got very cagey when he'd mentioned him.

'No sweat, Vince, old chum. Don't even think about old Matt He's a good 'un.'

Was he? Vincent sincerely hoped so. He still wasn't sure how Jemima felt about the lad. They'd been seeing each other for some time now, so she must feel *something* for God's sake. He'd swing for anyone who hurt Jemima, so help him.

Ned had become a touch more brittle when Vincent had mentioned that he and Maureen had spotted Matt hobnobbing with Ned on bank holiday Monday.

'Ah—right. Yeah . . . Bit of unfinished business. Lancing Grange business, if you get my drift. Mizz Seaward, the ole cow, hadn't paid me everything I was owed. Matt was sorting it out for me. What? No, nothing to do with our bit of business, Vince, mate. Nothing at all.'

Vincent hadn't believed a word of it.

They'd reached the web of single-track roads now, and Ned switched on the headlights. Dipped. Tunnel vision. They didn't show anything other than the dank October hedgerows and a sweeping arc of blackness where the night sky dissolved into the downland horizon.

Ned's car didn't have the luxury of a heater and Vincent pulled his padded jacket more closely

373

around him. And now there was this other thing with Matt. It had bothered him a great deal. Maybe if he'd spent more time with Jemima they'd have had the free-and-easy father-daughter relationship you saw on the telly. As it was, despite loving her to distraction, he was a little in awe of her. She'd grown up without him. She was a woman, for heaven's sake. She could sleep with whom she liked.

Vincent winced. He closed his mind to that side of Jemima's life. It was just that he was sure—dead sure—that Jemima wasn't in love with Matt. And that seemed to cheapen it somehow.

He hadn't believed it at first when Maureen had told him. She'd got it second-hand from Gillian Hutchinson. Matt's car had been parked outside the Vicarage *all night* after Bathsheba's meeting! First time ever! And Matt had slunk away, bug-eyed, the next morning. Obviously hadn't slept a wink, Gillian had told Maureen. And Jemima had been over half an hour late opening up the bookshop.

Bout time an' all,' Maureen had said to him. 'Not natural. Lovely young girl like Jemima. Maybe we'll have two weddings to look forward to, now, eh, duck?'

Vincent doubted it. Drew and Maddy's wedding preparations were all-invasive at Peapods. But it was great to hear Maddy singing again, and to hear the shared laughter. Pregnant! That was what the trouble had been! Silly figgit! Why, in his day very few people got married until the lass was three months gone—and these days no one bothered at all. He couldn't understand the fuss.

No, the Peapods wedding would be the talk

of the village for months to come. He couldn't somehow see Matt and Jemima treading the same path. And, to be honest, he couldn't swear that he'd seen Jem and Matt together much since the village hall meeting. If Matt had spent the night with her, then there hadn't been a repeat performance— or maybe they'd just been discreet. Not that she'd said anything—but then she wouldn't, would she? Jemima still carefully guarded her privacy—she'd be mortified to think that he'd joined in the village speculation. And he could hardly *ask* her, could he? It wouldn't be proper.

'Okay, Vince?' Ned broke into his train of thought. 'You're very quiet. Don't fret, me old mate. Your money's quite safe. And after tonight, if all goes according to plan, I think you might plan a little excursion to the races. Just to watch our investment grow, so to speak. You've been very patient. And loyal. I likes to reward me mates. Especially the loyal ones. Loyalty counts for a lot in this game.'

Vincent perked up. He hadn't set foot on racing's hallowed grounds for months. Even Jemima believed him now and didn't ever quiz him about gambling or racecourse visits. He'd ask her to come with him. Just to prove that he could be trusted. She might even enjoy it. Especially now she and Matt were—well, um—together. It still seemed incredible to Vincent that his daughter could have a close relationship with a jockey and pretend that he worked in a biscuit factory or whatever it was she did. There'd be women out there simply gagging to walk in her shoes.

Still, things might improve now. Jemima appeared to have settled into Milton St John's horsy environment really well. Yes, he'd ask her to come racing. And then they could take Maureen with them as a threesome and that might stop the tittle-tattles too.

Ned was thundering the car at a steady fifty across what appeared to be a field. Total blackness swooshed past the windows. Vincent clung gamely to his seat belt. Maureen hadn't repeated the August Monday stop-over offer. Not that there'd been an awful lot of opportunity. Her Brian had given up his transcontinental trucking for a while and was on short hauls.

'You never know, duck,' she'd said with a sigh, 'when he'll be home these days. More's the pity.'

Maureen, together with Drew and Maddy, had transformed his existence, he thought. Maddy had given him a job which he'd been frankly crap at, and had been so patient with him while he learned; and they'd given him the cottage which was as snug a home as any man could wish for, and Drew had extended his duties to take in all the yard work. He'd even shown him how to muck out and feed and groom the horses for when they were short-staffed.

Vincent, who had lost entire fortunes on horses' noses, had never been within touching distance of them before. At first the horses had frightened him—he'd had no idea they were so huge and powerful—but gradually they'd built up some mutual trust. Now he'd go into the boxes to rake out the soiled straw and move half a ton of animal with no more than a sharp and friendly slap on the rump.

And Maureen . . . Well, Maureen had simply made him forget about Rosemary for days—and nights—on end. He could pay her no greater compliment.

'Here we are,' Ned said, slamming on the brakes, and sounding rather relieved. 'You all right, Vince? The suspension's not what it was.'

Vincent muttered that he was fine, just fine, and scrambled out into the night. He gazed around him with disappointment. They were outside the back-of-beyond pub. He thought Ned was taking this clandestine stuff a bit too far. Few people even found their way here by road—he was pretty sure there had been no need to take the cross-country route to shake off any followers.

'Will—er—the big boys be waiting for us inside?'

'Dunno.' Ned panted as he fitted a Heath-Robinson type immobiliser from his steering wheel to the accelerator.

Vincent thought this was right over the top. Ned's clapped-out Fiesta was hardly the sort of car any self-respecting joy-rider would be seen dead in.

Eventually they shuffled inside. The pub was empty. The laconic barman was sitting on his stool still reading the *Sun*. Our Winnie's culinary delights had been wiped from the blackboard.

'A pint of Guinness, please, landlord.' Ned approached the bar with an immense stage wink. 'And a vodka-and-lime for my friend.'

'Bitter,' Vincent said quickly. 'A pint of bitter.'

Ned raised weaselly eyebrows. 'Oooh, pardon me! I understood it was always vodka-and-lime these days.'

Vodka-and-limes were associated with Maureen. He couldn't possibly sully the memories.

They sat in morose silence in the window-seat. Vincent flexed his fingers in anticipation; Ned smacked his lips noisily; the landlord crackled the pages of the *Sun;* the clock ticked and the dog snored.

The door flew open. 'Sorry I'm late.' Matt Garside poked his head into the bar. 'Have you been waiting long?'

Vincent was sure his mouth was gaping as he tried to smile. Aware that he looked like the village idiot, he stopped. Ned had got to his feet and was ushering Matt towards a free chair.

'Good evening,' Vincent said as Ned returned to the bar for Matt's Diet Coke and their refills. It seemed stupidly formal but he was very out of kilter here. Was Matt racing's Mr Big, then? Or had he just popped in for a drink? He'd have to be very careful. 'Nasty night.'

'No frost, though,' Matt said, not meeting his eyes. 'Should be okay for racing tomorrow.'

Vincent trawled round for something else to say. 'Er—Jemima not with you, then?'

'No.'

Vincent exhaled. For the first time he wished Ned would come and join them and take up the slack. Matt dissected a beer mat. The dog rolled over, stretched, and slept again.

'Riding tomorrow, are you?'

'Yeah, at Towcester.'

Vincent swallowed the last dregs of his bitter. This man might one day be his son-in-law. It was not an auspicious start to family outings. Thankfully, Ned arrived back then, carrying three glasses. The atmosphere chilled a bit further.

'Right.' Ned settled himself between them. 'Now, let's get down to business.'

Afterwards, Vincent thought, there were a lot

of things he should have said. As Jemima's father there were a lot of things he should have done, God help him. He could—and should—have walked out straight away. As soon as he knew. But, oh, it was so sweet. So easy. And almost infallible.

The money-making scam Ned had so far been pulling was simply that. A tax-free way to raise the stake necessary for the next phase. The big boys, it appeared, were nothing more than a figment of Ned's imagination. Just to add a bit of spice. This, like all clever and illegal schemes, involved very few people.

Just the three of them, it transpired. Vincent, pretty hazy as to why he'd been included in the triumvirate, tentatively enquired. If, as he suspected, Matt had been using his relationship with Jemima to claw him in, then he was going to the police or the Jockey Club or both, so help him.

Matt assured him that meeting Jemima at Windsor, seeing Jemima since, had absolutely no connection. This—um—suggestion had come up later. Much later. He looked pretty uneasy about it, to be honest, Vincent thought. He wasn't sure he trusted him.

Ned wiped the Guinness froth from his upper lip and explained the principles to Vincent. It had been a gift from the gods, Milton St John having two horses going for the same crown. Two excellent Grand National prospects: Drew Fitzgerald and Kath Seaward, both desperate to win—if for entirely different reasons. Of course, as with all scams, there were other horses to be considered in the equation, but Ned had done his homework. Yeah, sure, there would be an element of risk, but what was speculation without a risk, eh? Wasn't it what those stock-market laddies did all the time, eh?

Vincent was confused. 'But why involve me? Why not keep it all for yourself?'

'Peapods,' Ned said simply. 'I still had me contacts at Lancing Grange. I needed an ear at Peapods. Bloody Drew Fitzgerald's lads sodding adore him. They wouldn't even tell you the colour of his bloody socks. I was looking to have a foot in each camp, so to speak. You arrived at just the right time, Vince, mate, what with the job going there and everything. And you were broke. And it's all worked out nicely, hasn't it?'

Jesus! It had, of course. Vincent closed his eyes. He'd been giving away Peapods' trade secrets for months! And increasing Ned's stake money. Christ. This was bigger than anything he'd ever dabbled in before.

Matt didn't look at either of them while the plan was explained. His knuckles on the Coke glass were white, Vincent noticed. There was a muscle twitching in his cheek.

Simply—oh, so simply—what was going to happen was that Dragon Slayer, who was already ante-post favourite, would lose the Hennessey Gold Cup next month. Bonnie Nuts, if everyone was to be believed, could win it. Ned would be putting little each-way bets on Bonnie all round the country so as not to sod up the odds. No one would suspect.

They'd clean up nicely. This procedure would then be repeated elsewhere—hopefully culminating at the Kempton Christmas meeting and the Cheltenham Festival. Bonnie would finish higher than Dragon Slayer whenever they were pitched against each other. Dragon Slayer, it would then

380

be assumed, had gone off the boil—and should start somewhere around thirty threes or lower for the National. Bonnie Nuts would hopefully be favourite. They would then play their ace card. Every single penny of their by-then considerable winnings on Dragon Slayer for the National.

Kath Seaward might suspect but she couldn't prove anything—Matt would see to that. He'd keep assuring her that the horse would come right in time. The same with the owner—Matt, Vincent noticed, actually winced when Ned mentioned Tina Maloret—and, of course, Matt would be as perplexed as anyone over the lack of form. The stewards could do what they liked—they'd not find any evidence of drugs or tampering . . .

Matt had proved that he could pull a horse with the best of them—and the racing press had been full of Kath's comments regarding Dragon Slayer's dislike of open ditches. Then, when Dragon Slayer won the National, everything would be all right.

Vincent let all this whizz round in his head. A million questions begged to be asked.

He looked at Matt. 'But what if Bonnie Nuts really is better? What if he beats you in the National?'

'He won't,' Ned cut in. 'Matt will see to that. Charlie Somerset will be unseated somewhere along the way.'

Vincent swallowed. He'd have to warn them at Peapods. He'd have to tell Jemima. He liked Charlie—

'Of course, you won't be saying a word.' Ned fished into his pocket and waved some papers under Vincent's nose. 'My contacts have been very busy researching your background, Vince, mate. Undischarged bankrupt. Umpteen County Court judgments. A suspended prison sentence for defrauding your own company. Repossessions. And a list of debt collectors who'd kill to know your current address.'

It was like an upper-cut to the windpipe. The fragile happiness he'd built up would be wiped out. He'd lose it all: Jemima's love and respect, Maureen's company, and everything he'd found at Peapods . . . Shit, shit, shit.

Matt looked at him with understanding. 'If it's any consolation, I got suckered the same way.'

'It fucking isn't.' Vincent was bitingly angry. There was no way out. Nowhere to go—except along with it. 'And does Jemima know anything?'

Matt shook his head and shredded another beer mat.

Ned was nodding happily. 'Don't look so stressed, Vince, mate. Matt has agreed to come along with us because he wants to win the National. He wants to win the National so much that it bloody hurts. He's been in Somerset's shadow for years. The ole cow, Mizz Seaward, will have what she wants in the end, Peapods will have picked up all the major spoils along the way until the National—and we'll have won the fucking lottery. Where the hell is the problem in that?'

Vincent wasn't sure. All he wanted to do was to get as far away from Ned and Matt as possible. But he still had the roller-coaster ride back to the village in Ned's car. He couldn't even walk it, could he? It was miles across open downland.

Somehow that seemed preferable than spending another minute in this company.

He stood up. 'Thanks for an entertaining

evening, gentlemen. No, no, don't get up. I can find my own way out.'

*   *   *

Two hours later, frozen, drenched to the skin, his legs ripped to shreds by brambles, and more frightened than he'd ever been in his life, Vincent stumbled on to Milton St John's High Street.

The walk through the shrill darkness had at least given him time to think. He wouldn't say anything. He knew he wouldn't—couldn't. But he'd warn Jemima away from Matt Garside. He had to do that. And maybe he'd mention something at Peapods. Maybe drop a few little hints . . . And maybe, just maybe, Bonnie Nuts would win on merit anyway, so it wouldn't be illegal, would it? And as for Matt unseating Charlie in the National—well, that was too Dick Francis for words! No one would be able to get away with that. Not these days. They even had cameras attached to the jockey's crash hats these days, didn't they?

He rounded the Peapods bend. Most of Milton St John was in darkness, the villagers asleep and dreaming carefree dreams. Ned bloody Filkins would come unstuck somewhere along the way, he was sure of it. Vincent swallowed. His mouth tasted bitter. He wondered fleetingly just what indiscretion Matt had committed to get caught up in all this. Sure, he believed the bit about him wanting to win the National. He understood that. But there had to be something else, surely, to make him risk his entire career? Poor sod, Vincent thought: poor, poor sod.

The Munchy Bar flat was in darkness. Brian's

lorry wasn't in the lay-by. Vincent, imagining Maureen curled asleep, alone, sighed. He needed some comfort tonight. Needed to be held in someone's arms and reassured. Needed to be cuddled and told that everything would be all right.

He plodded on past. It probably would never be all right again.

CHAPTER TWENTY-SIX

There was only a week to go until Drew and Maddy's wedding. The village was in uproar. It was like the Queen's Jubilee and the Millennium celebrations all rolled into one.

Jemima, idly stirring a cup of coffee in the Munchy Bar, was preoccupied with more mundane matters.

'Want to get it off your chest, duck?' Maureen eased herself into the seat opposite her. 'A problem shared and all that?'

It was the Douwe Egberts period of the day. Maureen, having satisfied the needs of the genteel clientele, was raring for a gossip. Jemima continued stirring. 'I'm okay, thanks. Really.'

'That you're not! You can't fool me. It must be something real bad to bring you in here for your coffee break, with you having your own little kitchen and that. Not that you're not a sight for sore eyes and welcome, of course. Would you like a doughnut to go with that? Cheer you up a bit?'

Jemima shook her head. She wanted to tell Maureen, nicely, to go away and leave her alone— but wasn't that the very reason she'd come into the

Munchy Bar in the first place? To be with other people. She hadn't wanted to sit on her own in the bookshop's tiny kitchen, nursing a mug of instant, and thinking. She'd done far too much of that in recent weeks.

'Tracy looking after the shop, is she?'

Jemima nodded. Tracy had been a real boon, but there wasn't the camaraderie she'd shared with Lucinda. Tracy ran a family of six with military precision and had previously worked the night-shift in a petrol station on the A34; a small bookshop offered few problems. And Bathsheba's fatwa had had no effect on sales. The Christmas stocks were already reducing nicely—she had even reordered the more popular titles, and the new displays especially for the festive season were stacked in the stockroom. The bookshop was surviving nicely. Jemima clinked her spoon round her cup again and wished that she was too.

'Not long till the wedding, eh? You'll be going to the church and the do, will you?' Maureen wiped invisible crumbs from the table with the edge of her pinny. 'Nice for you, living on the spot so to speak. Exciting. Young Matt taking you?'

Jemima took a deep breath. The coffee already had a skin on it. It made her feel sick. 'Yes, I think we're going together.'

'Good. Good. Your dad and me thought we'd go along together, too. With my Brian being in Scarborough all next week, like. Makes sense. No point in us both being alone.'

'No, I suppose not.'

'Spoken to your dad lately, duck? I thought he'd seemed a bit off-colour. Peaky.'

Jemima hadn't noticed. But then she hadn't

385

noticed much recently.

Maureen heaved a sigh. 'And Lucinda's coming back from college for the wedding, isn't she?'

'Yes. She's being a bridesmaid.'

'That'll be nice. Especially with Charlie being best man. They'll be able to dance together after, without ole Bathsheba's forked tongue making mischief, won't they?'

Jemima supposed so. She hadn't really thought about it. Maybe Charlie had asked Tina Maloret to the wedding. Maybe Lucinda would turn up with Rebecca Maxwell-Dunmore's older brother, or some new man from the university. She honestly didn't care.

'Funny colour for bridesmaids, if you ask me. Dark green. Damn unlucky colour for a wedding. Whose idea was that, then?'

'I think it's Maddy's favourite. And Drew's dad was Irish. I don't think they consider it unlucky.'

'A nice pink would have been more proper. Or blue. Or—'

Jemima stopped listening. If only that was all she had to worry about; the colour of Maddy's bridesmaids' dresses. The last four weeks had been truly awful—and they shouldn't have been. They should have been fun. It was all Matt's bloody fault that she felt like this. If it hadn't been for him, then she could have joined in with the rest of the village in the excited run-up to the wedding. She and Gillian could have giggled together over Bella-Donna Stockings, and planned their strategy for tonight's League of Light vigil, and laughed about the complete irony of the situation.

As it was, although they'd had a few quiet sniggers together at Bathsheba's expense, and

386

off-handedly discussed hats or not for the wedding, Jemima's heart hadn't been in it. She felt as though all the troubles she thought she'd left behind in her other life, had returned with a vengeance. She felt bloody *guilty*.

All those years of worrying about money, and her parents, and whether they were going to be allowed to stay in the house, and if there'd be more rows, and if someone even more sinister than the last caller was going to hammer on the door at midnight, had come flooding back.

Peering out of her childhood bedroom window early in the morning, praying that the postman would pass them by, and hating him when he didn't. Stuffing her fingers in her ears when her mother opened the letters and cried. It could have been yesterday.

Watching burly men with clipboards carry away the things that had been familiar to her for as long as she could remember and hurl them into the back of a van. Knowing she'd never see any of them again. Crying herself to sleep.

Listening, hunched under the bedclothes, to her mother shouting and her father saying over and over again that it would be all right. He'd got a plan. They'd be rich one day. The memories had come back to haunt her.

Being there when her mother had said she'd had enough. She was leaving. Leaving Vincent, leaving her. And then she'd known it was her fault. She had done something to drive her mother away. Even though Rosemary had hung on, the threat was always there. The guilt had destroyed her carefree teenage years.

It had taken years to rebuild her confidence. As

she got older she'd realised of course that it hadn't been her fault; that she had no reason to torment herself with guilt. Bookworms and Oxford had been like a false skin, useful while the scars healed. But the full recovery had taken place in Milton St John. And now bloody Matt Garside had reopened the wounds.

'You're fretting about tonight, I'll be bound.' Maureen's beehive quivered with indignation. 'Well, you've got no need. A lot of daft old besoms holding a silent vigil with bloody candles! Pah! Anyway, look at the weather. That'll douse a few flames.'

It was a typical grey October day. There had been no gentle decline into autumn. September had been golden, warm and mellow; October had roared in with biting winds and leaden skies. Listlessly, Jemima wiped a spy-hole in the steam on the Munchy Bar's window. The chestnut trees were practically denuded now, their amber and russet leaves clinging to the verges in damp decay, their branches bare and skeletal against the scudding clouds. She'd already seen three seasons in Milton St John. Would she still be around to see the fourth?

'Are you coming tonight?'

'Try and stop me,' Maureen said stoutly. 'We'll all be there for you, don't you fret. Me and the girls have got a little surprise planned for Bathsheba and Co.' She hauled at her bra strap. The cleavage, still on display despite the drop in temperature, wobbled. 'Wonder what Charlie's dreamed up for the wedding reception. He hasn't said anything to you, has he?'

Jemima shook her head. Charlie had been

badgering everyone for the last couple of weeks to make a donation for the communal present. Diana and Gareth James-Jordan had provided a marquee in one of their fields. It had been decided, via the stable grapevine, that in the absence of a wedding-present list and the knowledge that Peapods was not exactly flush, Milton St John would get together and provide Drew and Maddy with the reception in place of a gift. Rumour had it that some cheques had been staggeringly large. Levi and Zeke assured her that they *knew* Charlie had engaged Fizz Flanagan and the Spice Girls for the entertainment.

'Won't be fireworks, that's one thing,' Maureen said. 'Even with it being Bonfire Night. Can't have fireworks near the horses, see. Still, knowing Charlie it'll be bloody good. I can't wait, can you, duck?'

It seemed a very long time ago that Charlie had asked her to jump out of the cake. They'd laughed together, hadn't they? She'd joked with him, hadn't she? It had been merely moments after that, that Matt had spoiled everything.

A flurry of dripping mackintoshes and shaken umbrellas shattered the Munchy Bar's serenity. Maureen sighed and stood up. 'No peace for the wicked, duck.'

No, Jemima thought as she pushed her coffee away, there certainly wasn't.

*　　　*　　　*

The night of Bathsheba's meeting had been appalling. Having decided to invite Matt into the Vicarage to talk, turning and seeing him in tears had terrified her. What had she done to him?

389

'Oh, God.' She'd ushered him inside. 'Matt, don't—' He'd followed her upstairs to the flat. She'd switched on lights, wriggled out of the ethnic patchwork jacket, looked at him helplessly, and done what everyone does in a similar situation. She'd rushed into the kitchen and put the kettle on.

Matt had been sitting on the edge of the sofa when she'd returned. The flat was a mess. There were too many empty wine bottles on the window-sill and two half-finished cups of coffee on the table. Her washing was, as ever, draped on the radiators. If she'd planned on him being there she would have tidied up. As it was, she doubted if he noticed.

She'd sat beside him, not knowing whether to touch him or not. The tears were still in his eyes. She'd reached for his hand. 'It doesn't matter. Look, I'm sorry. It just wasn't right. Not like that—'

He'd looked at her. 'You don't want me.'

Oh, God. Did she? Well, no, not in that way. But now was definitely not the right time to say so. 'That's a stupid thing to say—'

'Is it? About right for me, then. Stupid. Bloody, fucking stupid.' He drummed his bunched fingers against his lips, hiding the tell-tale quiver.

'Matt—stop it. Just talk to me.'

'Talk! That's all we ever do!'

They did. She enjoyed it. 'Yes, well, that's what mates do, isn't it? Talk. Share things—'

'We don't share anything!' He had glared at her. His eyes were glittering with a mixture of tears and anger. 'You don't know anything about me!'

Not fair. Okay, so she didn't know about his life as a jockey—but he'd always understood that was part of the deal. That was how they'd started

390

the relationship—it wasn't as if she'd changed her views.

'What's happened?'

'Nothing. Everything. Shit—what do you care?'

But she did care. She hated to see him so unhappy. 'Can I do anything to make it better?'

He'd laughed then.

'Matt, please—'

'Please,' he'd mimicked. 'Please. No fucking thank-you is what you mean, isn't it?'

She'd stood up and walked to the window. The shrubbery was dark, the Downs darker. This was ridiculous. She had absolutely no idea what was wrong with him. Surely it couldn't be over that fumbling in the car? Christ, they were adults! Most people had grown out of that sort of behaviour by puberty.

'Jemima—'

She had turned round. He'd slumped forward, his head in his hands. 'Jemima, I'm so sorry . . .'

She'd gone to him again, sat beside him, cuddled him. He'd buried his face in her shoulder. She'd thought, inconsequentially, that the kettle must have boiled ages ago. It didn't matter. Probably tea was the last thing on his mind.

'Tell me, Matt. Please.'

He'd said nothing. She'd stroked his hair. Of course, he didn't eat properly, and race-riding was so strenuous, it must put a strain on him. Especially as he was striving to stay unnaturally thin. And she knew, from the gossip, that he'd hit a bad patch. Oh, shit, she should have shared it with him. This was her fault . . .

'Don't say sorry.' She'd taken his face between her hands. 'I've been so wrapped up in the shop and

Dad and Gillian and Bathsheba and everything—
I've been selfish. Whatever it is, we can sort it out.
Nothing's ever that bad.'

'This is.' He'd looked at her again. 'This is as bad
as it gets.'

She had kissed him. It seemed all she could do to
make amends. His lips had remained unresponsive.
She'd kissed him again. Stupid. She'd known it was
stupid. She'd always been intelligent—but she'd
never been bright.

This time he'd kissed her back. And his hands
had clutched at her. And this time she didn't push
him away.

'I'm a jockey,' he'd muttered. 'I'm a bloody
jockey.'

'That's all right,' someone had said in her voice.
'I've never slept with a jockey before.'

And then they'd gone into her bedroom.

And if everything else that had preceded it
had been awful, then what followed was simply
horrendous.

Matt couldn't make love to her . . .

Jemima waved across the headscarves to
Maureen and slunk back to the bookshop. They
hadn't mentioned it since. They had hardly seen
each other. She didn't know which one of them was
more embarrassed. She had never felt so rejected,
so inadequate—so absolutely awful. He'd wanted
her—and then when she'd taken her clothes off, he
hadn't. Didn't. Couldn't. Whatever. It had to be her
fault. She must be totally repulsive.

They had got dressed again, not speaking, and
Matt had slept on the sofa. She hadn't slept at all.

*   *   *

392

'Hiya.' Tracy peered over an armful of books. 'Just had a delivery. Backlists most of them. I've put one of each out on the shelves and I'll put these in the stockroom. Okay?'

'Fine.'

The shop was quiet. A spectral voice was echoing from the speakers, reading the opening chapters of *The Bogwater Witches*.

'My little 'uns love this.' Tracy emerged from the stock cupboard. 'And it's Hallowe'en in a few days, innit? Makes you wonder where the time goes. Soon be Christmas. Oh, while you was in the Munchy Bar, some geezer came in and left some stuff for the notice-board. It's on the desk. I said you'd put it up if there was space. Okay?'

'Fine. Yes, great. Thanks.'

There was always stuff for the notice-board. It had been another well-received idea. People came in to read about jumble sales and parties and to pin postcards in the 'Wanted' and 'For Sale' sections. As often as not they stayed on and bought a book.

Tracy was tidying things up. Gathering herself together ready for the trek across the road to collect four of her children from school and the remaining two from her mum's to go home for lunch.

'I'll get my Bobby to baby-sit tonight,' she said cheerfully, 'so I can come back and give ole Bathsheba what for. See ya later.'

'Yeah. Okay. Thanks.'

The shop was empty now. Jemima listened half-heartedly to the Bogwater story. She didn't want to eat anything and Tracy had tidied everything away. She'd even dusted the shelves and straightened the refurbished beanbags. She was redundant. Unwanted. Un-bloody-desirable . . .

The door rattled open.

'Brilliant. An empty shop and a beautiful woman.' Charlie grinned at her. 'How long have I got?'

She shrugged. A few weeks earlier, she might have been brave enough to say 'As long as it takes' or 'It depends what's on offer' and they'd have laughed. Now she felt she would never be flippant about sex again.

'I thought you were at Cheltenham.' She knew Matt was. He'd told her. Last week some time, she thought.

'The October meeting finished yesterday.' Charlie sat on the edge of her desk. 'I've got a ride for Drew in the last at Stratford this afternoon. Matt's picking me up—still, I suppose you know that. We should have left ages ago. I just wanted to say good luck for tonight.'

'Thanks.'

'I'll probably be back, but it depends on Matt's driving. He's slightly more careful than I am. I wish I'd said I'd take the Aston Martin now. Are you still worried?'

About what? Tonight? Not any more. She tried to smile. 'Not really. I think it'll be quite funny— with the candles, I mean. A bit like a Barry Manilow concert without Barry Manilow.'

'Sounds good to me.'

Charlie rifled through the papers on the desk, completely at ease. Still, why shouldn't he be? He'd spent long enough here with Lucinda, hadn't he? And he'd long accepted her as a friend, treating her with the same happy nonchalance as he did Matt

394

or Drew—and no wonder. She must be about as attractive to men as a warthog with halitosis.

However, despite having sworn never to look at another man as long as she lived, it was impossible not to look at Charlie. Gillian was right. He was just so beautiful. Matt, she knew, always wore a suit to go to the racecourse. Charlie, in his faded jeans and black sweatshirt and worn leather jacket, looked totally fantastic. Still, he was serially unfaithful, and arrogant, and a jockey, and, being able to bed the most beautiful women in the world, he was hardly going to look at someone who induced instant impotence, was he?

'What's this?' He swung a vibrantly coloured A4 sheet between his fingers. 'You're not going to put this up, are you?'

'I expect so. Later. It's probably about some Am Dram thing at Upton Poges or the toddlers' group party or something.'

'It's FARTS.'

'It's *what?*'

'FARTS,' Charlie grinned. 'Unfortunate name. I've never worked out whether it was intentional or not. Fighters Against Racecourse Torture or something. They screwed up the start to this year's National, don't you remember? Oh, no—you probably don't. I keep forgetting you're anti-racing. They're animal rights activists, you know.'

'In that case I'll definitely put it on the board.'

He shook his head. 'A word of advice. Don't. Or at least not until after tonight. You'll alienate most of your support if you do.'

She skimmed over the poster. It showed a horrific picture of a fox being torn to shreds by a pack of hounds, and invited everyone who abhorred blood sports to attend the first meet of the Fernydown Hunt at the end of November to make their protest.

'Do you mean people round here support fox-hunting? How can they? I haven't seen any hunting since I arrived and—'

'The season doesn't start until the first of November. It finishes at the end of March. You've missed it so far.' Charlie swung his feet to the floor. 'Look, however you feel about it, there are a lot of country people in favour. I just don't think it would be very clever to show your colours tonight.'

She blinked. Who, of the people she'd grown to know and like, were animal torturers? This was awful. 'You mean—the trainers—and the jockeys—all *hunt!*'

'Not all, no. But some do. A lot. And a good many of the villagers who have nothing to do with the stables. It's part of the country way of life. They don't see it the way townies do.' He shrugged. 'Milton St John was practically deserted last year when they had those Countryside Campaign marches to Downing Street.'

'But it's barbaric!'

'Everyone has different opinions. For what it's worth, I'd suggest you upset one group of people at a time. Concentrate on the outraged morals of the blue-rinse brigade for the time being. Leave the hunters and fishers and shooters till later.'

Jemima was furiously angry. 'No bloody way! Give me that poster now. It's going up right this minute! Charlie!'

He held the piece of paper above his head. Irritatingly, because he was taller than her, she couldn't reach it. She stood on tiptoe and reached

396

for it.

It's for your own good.' He was laughing as he side-stepped her grabbing hands, folding the poster inside his jacket. 'No, I'll keep it safe until later. I promise you can have it back tomorrow. There now, look—you've lost your glasses.'

'Sod it. I keep meaning to get them tightened. Where are they. She peered at him. As before, being fuzzy didn't even slightly dim his beauty.

'On the desk. It's okay, they're not broken. Here.' Charlie pushed them back on, lifting her hair to hook them behind her ears. 'Better?'

She blinked at him. He was inches away from her. She could smell the warmth of his skin and the spice of his cologne. 'Thanks.'

'You're welcome.' He rested his hands on her shoulders. 'So? The FARTS poster stays in my safe-keeping for now, okay? Unless, of course, you want to do a body search?'

'Take it from me, she doesn't,' Matt's voice rang from the doorway. 'And get a fucking move on, Charlie. We're going to be late.'

CHAPTER TWENTY-SEVEN

Unsure of what exactly to expect, Jemima had returned to the shop at seven and was sitting in the semi-darkness of the security lamps. The rain had stopped and the wind had died away. Maybe, she thought, as the Ladies' League of Light began to mass their troops on the pavement, despite Gillian's protestations, God wasn't too keen on erotica either. He'd certainly given them a perfect night for

397

it.

Gillian had popped her head round the flat door as she was leaving, looking very demure in a knee-length skirt and a shortie raincoat, and with her long pale hair in a bun. 'Suitable, do you think?'

'Way over the top,' Jemima had said. 'They're all going to know something's up.'

'Glen thought I looked nice.'

'I bet the boys didn't.'

'They said I looked like Olive Oyl.' Gillian had sighed. 'You've got to promise not to look at me tonight. We've got to get through this without laughing.'

*   *   *

No problem, Jemima thought morosely, cupping her chin on her hands. She'd had a little laugh with Charlie that afternoon. And perhaps Matt would be more cheerful tonight, always assuming that he bothered to turn up at all. She'd tuned in, by accident, to the racing from Stratford on 5 Live: Matt on Rainy Monday had beaten Charlie on Sebastian's Bat by a short head.

Because the shop had been empty and the sound system switched off, she had only turned on the radio for company. She had never listened before, or watched televised races, or even eavesdropped on the reruns in the Cat and Fiddle—but despite everything, she had been holding her breath for the final furlong.

She'd had no idea it would be so exciting— hearing the commentator's frenzied tones calling out Matt and Charlie's names when she actually *knew* them. It made her feel quite superior, sharing their reflected glory. It hadn't really occurred to her that Matt and Charlie were household names, and with her knowing them intimately . . . Well, no, not intimately, as such. Not a good choice of words under the circumstances. And the strange thing was that she'd wanted Charlie to win.

Maybe that wasn't so strange. She and Charlie didn't share a humiliating secret. Still, hopefully the win meant that Matt's lean spell was coming to an end. With any luck, he'd stop looking like a kicked puppy. One day, they might even be able to cope with the embarrassment.

It was always going to be there. She knew she had handled it badly. She should have reassured him at the time; should have turned it into something they could share—upsetting, but no big deal. If only they could have cuddled and talked and defused the situation. But they hadn't—and she couldn't because it was her fault that Matt found her unattractive—and now it had spiralled out of control . . .

Hearing a flurry of activity, she looked out of the window. Bathsheba had arrived. Illuminated by the orange glow of the street lamps, a woolly hat pulled well down over her ears, she was busily handing out placards and candles. Jemima sighed. There were loads of them—people, not candles. Although there seemed to be plenty of those too, virgin white tapers in little lantern holders. Left over, Gillian had told her, from the Milton St John pilgrimage to Kensington Palace. And it wasn't simply Bathsheba Bronwyn and Petunia and a handful of the WI, as she'd imagined—but also a cross-section of the villagers. Even some men. Not many of them were her regular customers as far as she could see. She'd have to draw up a blacklist.

And where, oh where, were her supporters? Had they all decided to stay at home with the telly? Surely Maureen would be there—and . . . She shrugged. Who else could she expect? Tracy had said she'd come but maybe her Bobby hadn't been able to look after the children. Did it really matter to the citizens of Milton St John whether she carried on in business or not? They all had their own survival to consider—would they be the slightest bit interested in hers?

She brightened. Glen and Gillian had arrived, accompanied, due to all their regular baby-sitters being on the protest, by a rather unhappy-looking Levi and Zeke. Her heart plummeted. Of course, even they weren't on her side tonight, were they?

'Jemima!' a voice called through the back door's letter-box. 'Jem, love! Are you in there?'

Smiling, she hurried through the gloom, tripping over the hem of her skirt, stumbling against the shelving. She should have known Vincent wouldn't let her down. She tugged open the door. 'Why didn't you come to the front?'

'With those old bats out there? Not on your life.' Vincent looked around. 'Why are the lights off? Not—um—entertaining, are you?'

She laughed. Almost. Twice in one day might be a bit much. 'I didn't want anyone to see me. I felt a bit isolated. They're all antis out there. Actually, it seems like a waste of time. I mean, if only Bathsheba and Co. turn up, then it's going to be a bit like preaching to the converted, isn't it?'

Vincent headed for the front of the shop and peered through the window. 'Well, they've managed to light their candles without setting fire

400

to their mittens, so I suppose that's a plus. But I see what you mean about it being a bit one-sided. Matt not supporting you, then?'

She was glad the lights were low. She didn't want Vincent to notice that she was blushing. 'He was racing at Stratford this afternoon. I—um—think he'll try and get back in time.'

Getting serious, is it?' Vincent still had his back to her. 'You and him?'

No. Well, not any different. Actually, probably not as much. I mean, we don't see much of each other now that the jumping season is under way. He's really busy.'

Vincent said nothing for a moment. He didn't move. 'Good.'

'I thought you liked Matt.'

'I did. That is, I do. I just thought—well, that maybe—with you not liking jockeys and racing and things, that it might have, well—fizzled out by now.'

Oh God, it had fizzled out! 'I suppose I've mellowed a bit. The jockeys I've met have been really nice, and everyone in the village is great, and they all seem to adore their horses. And even you've given up gambling, which is brilliant. But no, even so, Matt s not destined to become your son-in-law, if that's what you mean.'

She could have sworn that Vincent muttered 'Thank God'. 'Mind you, there's probably going to be a bit of back-pedalling. Did you know that everyone in this village hunts foxes?'

'Who told you that?'

'Charlie. There's an anti-blood-sports poster somewhere—' Oh no, there wasn't. It was in Charlie's jacket. 'Or rather, there will be. They're holding a saboteurs' rally at Fernydown at the end

401

of November. I'm going.'

Vincent raised his eyebrows. 'I think you should be careful, Jem. You could alienate a lot of people.'

She glared at him. Charlie had said the same thing. Bloody men. 'I don't care. I care about animals and I won't condone cruelty. I can't just stand by and let it happen. Not here on the doorstep.'

'Maybe not, love, and I admire your principles. I'm against it myself, you know that. Me and your mum, we always brought you up to love and respect animals. But this village, and your business, depends on a lot of people involved in National Hunt racing, doesn't it?'

'Yes, but I don't see—' The penny dropped with a huge clunk. It was something that Charlie had omitted to mention. 'God! It's connected, isn't it? Hunting animals and National Hunt racing? That's why it's called . . . and it takes place at the same time of year and . . . you mean, that's what they *do* with their horses when they're not actually racing them? Charge across the countryside killing animals? People like Drew and Charlie and—'

'Some of them hunt, I'm sure.' Vincent looked uncomfortable. 'But then again, lots probably don't. I just think you should find out whose toes you'll be stamping on.'

It would be a damn sight more than toes, she thought crossly. How on earth could these people profess to love their horses—and have loads of dogs and cats spilling about their yards—and then go out and actually enjoy seeing a small, terrified animal pulled to pieces? She had never heard anything so bloody hypocritical in her life.

A squeal of brakes halted her next flood of

invective.

'Reinforcements.' Vincent squinted through the door again. He sounded quite relieved. 'Not sure whether they're theirs or ours. A van and an estate car. Anyone you know?'

Still seething at the duplicity of the racing fraternity, Jemima looked over his shoulder at the vehicles pulling into the lay-by. She didn't recognise them. Obviously anti-erotica supporters by the way Bathsheba had stopped waving her 'Purity for the Pure' banner and was peering inside the car.

'Not mine. Theirs, then. Again. Anyway, what about your faithful fan club tonight? Where's Maureen? I thought she'd be along to support me.'

Vincent looked a bit shifty. 'Well, you know how it is. After a long day at work and everything . . .'

Jemima sighed. It had happened all her life. People promised things—and then simply didn't deliver.

Christ! The lay-by was lit suddenly by arc lights, the curve of shops illuminated like a Blackpool hotel. Vincent, giving the glow no more than a cursory glance, was grinning.

'What's going on, Dad?'

He shrugged. 'Probably the Ladies' League of Light spontaneously combusting.'

'Oh, my God! It's the telly!' Well, maybe the BBC hadn't considered it came within their social parameters, but Meridian and Central obviously had. 'And Thames Valley Radio have sent an outside broadcast! Dad—look!'

Vincent looked. 'Ah, yes. Bill Rennells. Old honey-voice. Your mum used to have a hell of crush on him when he was on Radio Two. I wonder who could have tipped them off?'

Jemima pulled open the door. If the local media were going to zoom in on the meeting, there was no way that she was going to let Bathsheba hog the limelight.

She needn't have worried. Just as Bill Rennells was setting the scene for his listeners, and Anne Dawson was doing the same for the viewers, the Munchy Bar's double doors crashed open. Jemima blinked. The cameras zoomed in. Levi and Zeke giggled. It was the only sound. Everyone else had stopped talking. Most of them looked as if they'd stopped breathing.

Led by Maureen, they trooped out on to the lay-by: Suzy, Fran, Georgia, Maddy, Diana James-Jordan, Kimberley Small, Tracy, Holly, Kath Seaward and about thirty other women. They outnumbered the League of Light by a mile.

Like the Parish Biddies, they were carrying placards; like them, they carried candles, only theirs were scarlet. Unlike the Parish Biddies they were wearing a wild mixture of basques, teddies and suspenders. Their faces were caked in outrageous make-up, with huge pouting lips and kohled-on eyelashes. To a man they were wearing fishnet stockings.

Jemima didn't know whether to laugh or cry so she did a bit of both. 'Oh, my God! They're amazing! They must be absolutely frozen! And no one breathed a word to me!'

'Maureen's idea, love.' Vincent beamed proudly. 'She went to see Upton Poges's Am Dram version of *The Rocky Horror Show* last year and thought it'd be just the ticket. Young Georgia belongs to the group and was very helpful with loaning the costumes. Maureen's been burning the midnight oil all week letting out seams and organising the make-up. Look a picture, don't they?'

They did. Sort of Brueghel meets Beryl Cook.

Maddy, bless her, being so very pregnant, had toned down her costume a bit—otherwise they'd left nothing to the imagination. Jemima's eyes filled with tears again. Oh, they were wonderful! And they were doing this for her! Nothing had ever touched her quite so much.

Parading up and down on their six-inch heels, PVC thigh boots gleaming in the arc lights, giving Girl Power salutes, they were stupendous. Their placards pledged support for erotica, for freedom of choice, for Fishnets, for women's literature, for Jemima Carlisle. The media, ignoring the woolly bonnets and brogues, zoomed in with relish.

'Fucking hell!' Charlie's voice rang through the awed silence. 'I've just walked into my wildest fantasy!'

She turned and grinned at him. Matt, standing just behind him, was slack-jawed.

Gillian, who up to that point had been feebly waving a 'Ban Bella-Donna Stockings!' poster at knee-level and looking sheepish, cast a frantic look at Charlie then slunk up beside Jemima, trying to free her hair from its bun. 'Bugger. You didn't say that he'd be here. Look at me! Frump of the year.'

'Serves you right for not having the guts to come out.' Jemima, on top of the world, poked out her tongue. 'Just think, you could have paraded in your Ann Summers' best solely for his benefit.'

'I don't have any Ann Sum— Oh, right. Metaphorically. Yes, I could, couldn't I? Oh, sod it.'

The noise and the lights had dragged everyone

out of the Cat and Fiddle and the neighbouring cottages. The road was teeming with grinning villagers, clapping their hands and catcalling as the Rocky Horror chorus formed a circle round the anti-erotica faction, and marched with majorette precision. Maureen had obviously drilled them within an inch of their lives. Not one pointy toe was out of step, not one goosefleshed bosom drooped. It was awe-inspiring.

The media obviously thought so. Bill Rennells had joined in.

I thought you'd be out there with them,' Charlie said to her, beginning to regain the power of speech. 'Seeing as how you're a professional. You must even have the right costume.'

I don't. I told you—that was ages ago—' She wanted to giggle, and probably would have done if she hadn't caught Matt's eye.

'Oh. congratulations on your win.'

What? How did you know?'

'I listened. I obviously picked the right time to tune in. Well done.'

Matt looked embarrassed. 'Oh, yeah. Thanks. What did he mean about you being a professional?'

Charlie winked. 'God, don't you two share any secrets? Jemima used to be a lap-dancer.'

'I bloody didn't! I worked for a party company—I had to dress like Marilyn Monroe and jump out of a cake—once.'

Charlie nodded appreciatively. 'Not surprising—you've got incredible legs.'

Both she and Matt stared at him. 'How the hell do you know?'

Charlie grinned, raised his eyebrows, and wandered off to join the Rocky Horrors who were now executing a sort of Tiller Girl high-kicking routine across the lay-by. Carefully wrapping his leather jacket round Maddy's shoulders—she'd obviously been excused this part of the plan—he wriggled himself between Georgia and Suzy and kicked along with them.

'Prat,' Matt said, but with no malice. He didn't look at her. 'I'm glad you listened to the race this afternoon. Maybe things will be—well, okay?'

With the racing or their relationship? 'Maybe.' She wasn't counting on either.

'How come Charlie has seen your legs?'

God—how did she know? It might have been when they were tree-climbing. She couldn't tell Matt that, could she? 'I'm sure he hasn't.'

'But you told him about being a lap-dancer.'

'I was never a bloody lap-dancer! I wore a scanty costume and jumped—or rather, didn't—out of a birthday cake. That's all.'

'That's not all though, is it?' Matt's eyes were desolate. 'You still told him. You didn't tell me.'

'Gillian told him.' God, this was irritating. 'Matt, it's not important right now. Right now, this is the biggest thing that's ever happened to me. At last I know where I stand in this village.'

Matt shrugged. 'Lucky you. I wish to hell I did. You haven't told anyone, have you?'

About what? Petra's Parties? Why should she? Oh, God! He meant about the non-seduction. 'No, of course I haven't. What do you take me for?'

'I'm not sure. I'm beginning to think I've never really known you. Still, that's nothing new. I don't even think I know myself any more. I'm going to get a drink. I'll be in the pub later—if you're interested.'

'Problems?' Maddy, snuggling under Charlie's jacket, asked as Matt walked away.

'Nothing that can't be put right. Anyway, thanks for doing all this for me—especially—' she cast a glance at Maddy's bump, 'when you've got so many other things on your mind.'

Maddy hugged her. 'Don't be daft. We're your friends—it's what friends do, isn't it? I told you when we first met, you sort of get sucked into this village.'

They watched the high jinks for a moment in silence. Vincent, she noticed, was gazing soppily at Maureen. Matt, en route to the Cat and Fiddle, gave him a very wide berth. They must have had words. Poor Matt. She felt a rush of pity. She'd got all the friends in the world—and he seemed to have so few at the moment. She'd go into the pub just as soon as this was over and talk to him. He'd been kind to her, and they'd been close once—maybe they *could* salvage something.

'Are you getting nervous about the wedding?' She looked at Maddy. 'I mean—after what you said at the party—I'm so pleased that everything has worked out.'

'It's worked out wonderfully.' Maddy's eyes sparkled behind the grotesque grease paint. 'I was just being stupid. I've never been happier, and I can't wait for next week. I love Drew so much. I should have been honest with him right from the start. It's always best to be honest, isn't it?'

Jemima nodded. It was.

'Ladies—and gentlemen!' Glen had decided that enough was enough and had grabbed a Meridian microphone. 'I think we ought to call this a day before half my parishioners,' he cast a wary glance at the Rocky Horrors, 'die of hypothermia! I feel that we in Milton St John have ably demonstrated that freedom of expression is alive and well. We are a small community—but a democratic one. God has given us the power to make decisions, right or wrong. I suggest that we now call a truce, and pray for unity—and deliverance from evil.'

Nicely put, Jemima thought, as the League of Light and the Rocky Horrors stopped glowering at each other and bowed their heads. Glen was a bit of a diplomat on the quiet. The ambivalence of his words obviously hadn't been lost on Gillian, either. Just as the prayers came to an end, she lifted her head and winked at Jemima.

'We will not be vanquished!' Bathsheba roared, albeit halfheartedly. 'We will fight on!'

Bronwyn Pugh and Petunia Hobday looked as though they probably wouldn't. Jemima was pretty sure that Fishnets would remain on the shelves for quite a while longer. Some people would buy them, others wouldn't. It was how it should be. Bathsheba might never set foot in the shop again, but that was her choice. One problem solved—three million to go.

The media were packing up, happily assured of several invaluable snippets to fill the next week's schedules. The Rocky Horrors, followed by Charlie and Vincent, skittered noisily back into the Munchy Bar. Jemima hugged them all as they passed.

Having retrieved his jacket from Maddy, Charlie paused in Maureen's doorway, fished in the pocket and held out the poster. 'Here. There's no point in me tearing it up, is there? You're a woman. You'll do exactly what you want, won't you?'

'Of course. Um—did Matt talk about me this

afternoon?' Perhaps he'd sought out Charlie's advice on how to seduce the unseduceable.

'Not really.' Charlie grinned. 'Funny, that. If I were in his shoes I'd talk about you all the time. All he talked about was horses, and more horses. Especially Dragon Slayer not being on form, and how he hoped he'd come good for the Hennessey. Oh, and he seemed quite interested in Tina Maloret, too. Being Dragon Slayer's owner, I expect. I know they don't get on too well. What?'

He looked into the neon-brightness of the Munchy Bar. Suzy was gesticulating wildly. He shrugged. 'I think she's after my body. See you later.'

Jemima pushed the poster into her pocket. She'd have to iron it before putting it up on the notice-board. The curve outside the shops was empty now. It had taken a very short space of time to clear the decks. Everyone had melted away to resume their normal lives. Another small chapter in village history had been written. The High Street was quiet again; it could all have been a dream.

Locking the door of the bookshop, she wandered towards the Cat and Fiddle.

Paying for a white wine, she looked around for Matt. She hoped he wouldn't be in laddish conversation with his racing cronies. Not tonight. She wanted to talk to him while she was still on a triumphant high. She felt able to tackle anything tonight.

She couldn't see him.

'Matt in?' She leaned across the bar towards the landlord. 'Or has he been and gone?'

'In the Snug, love. Quieter in there.'

She took a deep breath and manoeuvred her

way through the tables. Not, of course, that she intended to invite him back to the flat for an action replay of the disaster or anything. She held her wine away from a tumble of stable lads jostling by the fruit machine. It was about time they put the whole thing into perspective. But then, if he really found her so totally unattractive, why didn't they call it a day? At least then she'd know where she stood.

Matt, it appeared, didn't stand anywhere. He was sitting in the furthest corner of the Snug, looking happier than she'd seen him for weeks. He wasn't alone. Tina Maloret, wearing unfashionably baggy jeans, a man's shirt, and looking so sexy that the pheromones were practically visible, was leaning across the table towards him.

Whoops! Jemima started to walk backwards. Tina always made her feel stones overweight and so dreary. Anyway, if they were having a business meeting, she was going to make herself scarce. She had just reached the doorway when they saw her.

'Hi, Jemima.' Matt's greeting was over-loud, and didn't quite match the expression in his eyes. 'Come and join us.'

She could hardly say she wasn't stopping—not while she was carrying a full wineglass. Hoping that they'd think she was just coming in rather than leaving backwards, she smiled her way back across the Snug.

'Tina has just arrived in the village for Maddy and Drew's wedding.' Matt sounded as though he was reading a script. 'It was a complete surprise to find her in here.'

'That's nice. Er—Charlie's in the Munchy Bar. I'm sure he'll be along later ...'

The news didn't seem to delight Matt. Tina was

more philosophical. 'I doubt it. He has no idea I'm here. This'll be the second time I've caught him on the hop. He, didn't seem overjoyed to see me last time either. I suppose I should give him prior notice.'

Jemima sat between them feeling suddenly as welcome as a wasp at a picnic. 'So he wasn't expecting you this evening, then?'

'He wasn't even expecting me for the wedding.' Tina sipped at something very black in a tiny glass. 'He didn't ask me. If I didn't have such a trusting nature, I'd be pretty convinced that he was going to be taking someone else.'

Jemima gulped at the wine. Now she'd have to ring Lucinda before she arrived to be a bridesmaid. She ought to tip Charlie off too. He was just as likely to come swanning into the pub at any moment with Suzy Beckett. God! There were still so many undercurrents.

'But you've had an invitation?' What did she care? The woman was a nightmare. She was itching to get Matt on his own and sort out where they stood while she still felt buoyant.

'To the wedding?' Tina stretched out a languid hand across the table towards Matt, then widened her eyes at Jemima. 'Oh, yes. Matt was such a sweetie. He invited me to come along with you two so that I wouldn't feel such a spare part. You don't mind, do you?'

November

CHAPTER TWENTY-EIGHT

'Damn. Shit. Damn.' Drew wrenched at the cravat. 'Bloody thing! I look like a teddy bear with a bloody bow round its neck!'

'You'd do a lot better if your hands weren't shaking.' Charlie grinned up from his perch on the edge of the bed. 'Do you want me to fix it?'

'No I sodding don't. I'll do it if it kills me. Anyway, you've got your own to do.'

'Not for ages yet.' Charlie glanced at his watch. 'There're still two hours before we're due at the church. You'll be ready far too early.'

'And you won't be ready at all if you don't get a move on.' Drew glared through the mirror at Charlie's reflection. 'Aren't you going to get dressed?'

'Can't see the point, really. Lucinda and Tina will probably rip my clothes off as soon as I walk into St Saviour's. Might as well save them a bit of trouble.'

Drew glared some more and gave up with the cravat. He had never felt so nervous. This was worse than race-riding. This was far worse than jumping over hurdles at sixty miles an hour. It was worse than breaking a bad-tempered yearling. It was even worse than using the bloody computer.

He'd fondly imagined that by getting married at four o'clock in the afternoon, the whole day would be calm. Leisurely even. He'd pictured a relaxed family breakfast—probably with Buck's Fizz, then a walk with the dogs, and maybe even a snooze after lunch. Then he and Maddy would get ready in the friendly chaos of their bedroom, and Poppy Scarlet

415

would be impeccably behaved and look a picture in her frock. It would be completely serene and unhurried.

He hadn't expected Armageddon.

Of course, there were still the stables to do—the horses didn't know it was his wedding day, even though he'd told them often enough, especially Solomon—and then Maddy's mum and dad and her Auntie Barbara and Uncle Gordon and both sets of grandparents had arrived; and Kit and Rosa Pedersen had come over a day early from Jersey, and now Peapods was filled with Fran and her daughter Chloë, and Rosa Pedersen, and Suzy, and Georgia and Lucinda all belting around in sticky-out petticoats and heated rollers.

And to cap it all, Caroline, his ex-wife, had swanned up, cool as anything, in a hired limo two hours ago with Peter bloody Knightley—who was Maddy's ex-boyfriend and Caroline's current business partner!

Charlie, thank God, had offered the sanctuary of his cottage.

'More people.' Charlie peered through the window across the cobbled yard. 'Looks like a family of eight in a Ford Capri.'

Christ! Uncle Philip and Aunt Aisling and the County Mayo brigade. He'd asked them to go straight to the church.

Charlie, still only wearing purple silk boxer shorts, headed for the sitting room. 'I think we could do with a bit of Dutch courage. Not too early for a whisky, is it?'

'About three hours too late. Make it a treble.'

'And have you slur your vows? Not a chance. I take my best man duties seriously. A single with

416

loads of water—and be grateful.'

Drew sank down on the edge of Charlie's Wallbank-Fox. He hadn't expected to be nervous. He hadn't been nervous when he'd married Caroline—or had he? He couldn't really remember. He had vague recollections of sitting in his parents' Jersey farmhouse at Bonne Nuit, looking out over Cheval Roc with the sea hurling itself into the sky, and Kit Pedersen, who was his best man, telling him he was far, far too young. And his mother in tears of happiness because he was marrying Caroline whom she adored, and his father complaining about having to wear a suit. He could remember nothing of the ceremony. There'd been a ride away from the church in a horse-drawn carriage and a sunshine reception on Caroline's parents' lawn where everyone wore extremely expensive clothes and drank champagne and was very polite to each other. He remembered the unreality of it. The feeling that something vital was missing and not knowing what it was . . .

'Thanks.' He took the whisky from Charlie and downed it in one. His hand still shook. 'Any chance of a refill?'

'None whatsoever.' Charlie wandered back to the window. 'Who do you know with a Land-Rover?'

'Half of Berkshire.'

'That sounds about right. There are twenty-seven people on the back seat, and two dogs. And a small horse—no, my mistake. *Three* dogs. Oh—and she's pretty! Who's she?'

Drew staggered from the bed and peered over Charlie's shoulder. A stream of women in hats was disappearing beneath the clock arch. 'Good God! Stephanie Le Mesurier! We were at school

417

together. And the rest of the Jersey contingent. Maddy must have gone through my address book. And keep your hands off Stephanie—she's married to a St Ouen's lifeguard. They sharpen their teeth on granite.'

'Christ,' Charlie grinned. 'I've already got enough problems with the women in my life. Who the hell invited Tina anyway?'

'Didn't you?'

'Course not. Not with Lucinda being a bridesmaid. I was looking forward to the reunion. She thinks it's damned funny—I don't.' He gestured towards the Wallbank-Fox. 'You're lucky that's still standing. It's about the only thing that is. Tina's bloody wild.'

Drew perched more gingerly on the bed this time. Not because he didn't want to crease the trousers of his morning suit, but in case it collapsed. 'In between the shagathon sessions, did she mention anything to you about Dragon Slayer?'

'Just a bit.' Charlie pulled a face. 'That's why she's down here again. She and Kath are dead certain that he'll win the Hennessey now. I gather after the Worcester disaster they cross-questioned Matt and have aimed to put things right. They've been doing a lot of schooling over ditches, and apparently he's over his spooking. Matt reckons he's come right, too. Mind you, they don't know how forward Bonnie is, do they?'

They didn't. Drew allowed himself a smug smile. Both Bonne Nuit and Dragon Slayer had had three outings now, separately, of course; there were going to be no head-to-heads until the Hennessey. Bonne Nuit had improved each time. Dragon Slayer, after that amateurish mistake at Worcester, had won two

418

races in recent days and was currently ante-post favourite. Bonnie's odds were still in double figures, but both horses had started to show in forecasts for next year's Cheltenham and Aintree meetings.

He crossed his fingers. It might just work. Not that he'd be keeping the National Hunt side of the yard going, even if Bonnie did win. Kit and Rosa and the accountants had made it plain that he couldn't afford loss-makers—but it would bump his prestige up no end for the next flat season, and bring in enough money for him to continue. If Bonne Nuit won the National, Peapods would be safe. Both he and Charlie knew that nothing less than a win would do.

He'd explained the situation to Gillian, who had smiled vaguely and said that as long as Bonnie Nuts won the National and prevented Drew from going bankrupt, then God would have worked another miracle, wouldn't he? Drew still thought it was a miracle that no one in the village had yet discovered that Gillian was Bonne Nuit's owner. Gillian had shrugged and said that she might tell Glen—after Bonnie had won the race—but until then it was to remain their secret. Anyway, the village was convinced that Fizz Flanagan was the proud possessor, and who was she to destroy illusions? As to Bonnie's future—well, he was such a sweet little thing—if he won the National then she thought he deserved to retire in comfort. She'd pay Drew stabling fees and visit him.

Drew had pointed out that if he won the National then she would have more money than ever to explain away to Glen. This seemed to have thrown her for a bit—but not for long. She'd kissed his cheek and said she was having great fun, and if there was any money left over he was to share it between charities of his choice.

Charlie had been philosophical about losing his job. He'd said he might even retire and write racing thrillers. Drew, who knew Charlie hated writing anything longer than a cheque, had blessed him for his equanimity. There was always the possibility, of course depending on the National win, that he'd be able to offer Charlie a full-time job as his assistant flat trainer. Which he might just accept if he won at Aintree. If Bonnie didn't pull it off, then Drew was under no illusions that Charlie was more than likely to decamp to Lambourn and have another shot at it. He couldn't blame him.

Then, of course, next year he'd be looking for a new flat jockey. Perry Mitchell, who had ridden for him ever since he'd come to Milton St John, was going back to Hong Kong while he could. The Chinese take-over hadn't yet affected Happy Valley and he knew that Perry wanted to ride his last races there. Maybe he'd ask Suzy—always supposing that she and Naomi Birkett-Spence didn't hit it off.

Still, that was all in the future. He grinned and picked up the cravat again. At least he had a future. Thanks to Maddy, today was going to be the happiest of his life. He wasn't going to let anything spoil it.

*   *   *

It was half past three. The afternoon sun was sliding behind the Hills, but the sky was still as blue as a spring morning. It had been a glorious day. Reasonably warm for November, with no wind disturbing the piles of jewel-bright leaves along

420

the High Street. Drew, sitting beside Charlie in the front pew of St Saviour's, took deep steadying breaths.

The church was decorated in the flames and golds and ambers of autumn. A thousand cream candles flickered gently in the draught from the rafters as the last rays of the sun illuminated the glorious colours of the stained-glass window. Petunia Hobday on the organ was playing a quiet version of 'Rhapsody in Blue', and every single pew was crammed with friends and relations, and some people who Drew'd considered neither but who had turned out for his big day. No, he smiled to himself—*their* big day. His and Maddy's. The day that had been destined to happen ever since Diana and Gareth James-Jordan's drinks party.'

He turned his head, acknowledging the smiles. Everyone was there. All the trainers, the stable staff, the villagers, and hordes of people from Upton Poges and Tiptoe: all looking happy and wearing their best. He hadn't realised that he and Mad were quite so popular. It would have been perfect if his parents had been alive for this. He swallowed. He was sure they were around, somewhere, giving their love and approval.

Caroline in black and yellow was sitting with Peter Knightley and the Pughs. She'd always got on well with Bronwyn and Bernie. She'd kissed his cheek and wished him luck and said she knew he'd be really happy now—just as she was. And there was Luke Delaney, bravely carrying out his usher duties with Rory Faulkner and Kit Pedersen, and trying to look cheerful. Drew sighed. It was going to be difficult for him today. Being here with Suzy. Poor Luke—he sympathised deeply.

421

Charlie nudged him. 'Matt's struck the jackpot, eh?'

Matt, flanked by Tina Maloret in a man's suit, with the jacket unbuttoned just far enough to let everyone know she was only wearing skin beneath it, and Jemima in a long, clinging wool dress the colour of beech leaves, slid into a pew halfway down the aisle.

'He looks pretty miserable, considering.' Charlie continued to stare. 'God, he doesn't know how lucky he is. She's so beautiful.'

'No doubt you'll be able to tell her so all night,' Drew said, wiping his palms on his dark grey trousers. 'She'll be wrecking the bed with you, won't she?'

'Jemima? Christ—I should be so lucky!'

Drew grinned. Charlie had always enjoyed a challenge. He felt Jemima Carlisle was one lady who would always stay just out of his reach. 'Aren't Lucinda and the stalking clothes-horse enough for you, then?'

'More than enough.' Charlie sighed heavily, still scanning the congregation. 'But Jemima's something else. She's sort of like Maddy—you know, my friend. When I think about her, I fancy her like mad—then when we're together she's so bloody controlled, and I wonder what I see in her. Then she giggles, or lets the guard drop, and I know. Of course, she's far too bright for her own good—and she thinks I'm a complete bastard. But we seem to get on well, despite that. It's quite confusing, really.'

Christ, Drew thought, how lucky he was to have Maddy's uncomplicated love. He tried to look stern. The fact that he was shaking spoiled

422

the effect. 'And she's Matt's girlfriend and you're supposed to be calming my nerves. And stop winking at Gillian. I'm still expecting someone ecclesiastical to come belting down the aisle and tell me we can't go ahead with this. Don't rock the boat. Oh, bloody hell—'

Petunia Hobday had ceased the Gershwin and urged the organ into a wheeze of Wagner. The church rose to its feet. Drew could hardly stagger to his. His knees shook.

'Up!' Charlie commanded, with a steadying hand beneath his elbow. 'You've won the Pardubice. This should be a piece of cake.'

Drew stood. Glen, leading the choir, glided by. Levi and Zeke, angelic in their surplices, were piping in enchanting twin falsettos. He turned his head.

Maddy, looking ravishing in a floaty gown of scarlet and crimson, her curls matching the colours of the autumn leaves, and carrying the simplest bouquet of cream roses and ivy over her bump, smiled at him as she came down the aisle. God! He was the luckiest man in the world. She was so, so beautiful. He hurt from loving her so much.

She stood beside him, beaming now. He wanted to kiss her. Her father grinned across at him. Poppy Scarlet, in her miniature dark green bridesmaid's dress, scrambled between them and sat on the chancel steps with a much-chewed Womble.

Glen moved forward, his eyes full of warmth. 'Dearly beloved . . .'

*   *   *

The photographs seemed to take for ever. Doubtful

423

if they'd even come out because the November dusk had swept in from the Downs during the final hymn, Drew's face ached from grinning inanely for hours. And he still wanted to kiss Maddy. Properly. Not the self-conscious peck in the church, or all these posed smooches for the camera. She was snuggled up against him, entwining her fingers with his in the folds of the exquisite dress, every so often lifting her left hand and gazing at the narrow gold band in wonderment.

He had wondered if Maddy would think it a cheapskate gesture to suggest that he gave her his mother's wedding ring, but she'd been unbelievably touched. His parents had been the happiest couple he'd ever known. Until now, of course. He'd felt it would be fitting to pass on the love. Maddy had burst into tears and said she thought it was the most romantic thing she'd heard.

'Just one more!' the photographer shouted. 'Before we lose the light! Friends and family! Everyone in this one!'

There was a mad surge of morning suits and elaborate hats.

'I love you.' Maddy curled towards him as the cast of millions jostled into place among the yew trees. 'I can't believe I was stupid enough not to want to do this—for whatever reason.'

'Neither can I.' Placing a hand on the swell of her stomach he bent his head and kissed her. 'No one could look more lovely. And I love you too, Maddy Beckett. God, no—Maddy Fitzgerald. At last.'

'Maddy Fitzgerald,' she savoured the words. 'If only you knew how long I've wanted to be able to say that. Madeleine Jane Fitzgerald. Doesn't it sound posh? It's going to take a lot of getting used to . . .'

*　　*　　*

At last the photographs were over, and Charlie, Rory, Kit and Luke were shepherding everyone towards the transport. A series of open-topped buses—the same ones that Milton St John used for their Derby Day outings—had been purloined for the short journey to the marquee at the James-Jordans'.

'We won't be able to see a thing,' Maddy's mum, in a purple two-piece with a strip of matching fabric round her shiny straw hat, said as they puffed up the stairs of the leading bus. 'It's practically pitch dark.'

'Part of the treat, Mrs B,' Charlie winked at her. 'All will be revealed.'

Maddy hoisted Poppy on to her lap at the front, squinting downwards, watching everyone else clamber aboard. She squeezed Drew's arm. 'This is the best day of my entire life.'

'And mine.'

The buses with their eclectic cargo, trundled off along the High Street. All rivalries seemed to have been set aside: the League of Light were cheek by jowl with the Rocky Horrors, Kath Seaward, a mass of roses attached to the panama, was laughing loudly with John Hastings, Vincent and Maureen were chatting with Bronwyn and Bernie Pugh, Caroline and Peter bloody Knightley were exchanging business cards with Maddy's Uncle Gordon, and Matt and Tina Maloret were squashed on to the same seat. So where, Drew wondered, was Jemima?

He laughed. Charlie had placed her next to Lucinda and was leaning over both of them from the seat behind. Ten out of ten, Somerset, he thought as they left the village, but I'll lay evens that you don't get any further.

The blackness was interspersed with small orange glows and rocked by staccato explosions, and every so often an occasional rocket starburst its way across the sky. The buses cheered and whooped. Maddy held Poppy up to watch. November the fifth was being commemorated across the country in the time-honoured fashion. For Drew the day would never be the same again.

'Ladies and gentlemen,' Charlie's voice crackled rather dramatically through a microphone as the buses slowed to a crawl, 'before we reach the reception, there are a few things I'd like to say.'

Loud booing drowned him out. Charlie held up his hands. 'It's not a speech. They'll come later. I know you're all dying for a drink, so I promise to keep it brief. I just need to explain the next part of the celebrations—'

Drew looked at Maddy. 'Any ideas?'

'Not a clue. He's played this one very close to his chest. You know Charlie—it could be anything.'

'That's what I'm afraid of.'

'You lot on the first bus are privileged. At least you'll have some idea of what to expect. The ones in the cheap seats—' Charlie jerked his thumb towards the following convoy, 'will be left completely in the dark. Which, actually, is fairly appropriate . . .'

Drew put his arms around Maddy. He loved the feel of her warmth beneath his fingers. She snuggled her head on to his shoulder. He kissed her again, and grinned in the semi-darkness as Charlie perched on the edge of Jemima's seat. It was interesting to notice, Drew thought, that she didn't move away from him. Maybe he should lengthen the odds . . .

'When we get to the marquee—so kindly organised by Diana and Gareth—' Charlie paused for a cheer, 'you'll probably think that we've forgotten to provide any power. Don't be alarmed by the blackout. Once inside, you'll discover why . . . And then,' he indicated towards Maddy and Drew, 'everything else is our wedding present to you both. From Milton St John. Between you, you've made more friends than is decently acceptable. Everyone loves you so much it's quite sickening. Anyway—you're having a fabulous wedding day—and I have no doubt the rest of your life together will be totally blissful! No one deserves it more.'

The bus erupted in cheers as he sat down—again, Drew noticed, extremely close to Jemima.

'Ah,' Maddy sighed, slipping her hand inside Drew's jacket and stroking his chest. 'He'll have me in tears in a moment. Isn't this all too much to take in? Oh, God—I wish we could go to bed right now.'

'Trollop.' Drew kissed her. 'Christ, so do I.'

The buses rolled on to the James-Jordans' largest pasture. As Charlie had said, there was nothing but darkness. Intrigued, Drew pulled Maddy closer. 'God Almighty—what has he concocted?'

She giggled. 'Well, at least it's not going to be *This is Your Life.* We haven't got any fears of our past skeletons coming rattling out of the cupboard, have we?' She jerked her head towards the back of the bus where Caroline and Peter sat side by side. 'We've brought them with us.'

427

Charlie was on his feet and flirting like mad. 'If you'll all follow me—mind the steps, Mrs B—that's the idea. No, it'll be fine. Kit and Rory and Luke will make sure you get into the marquee without any problems. Would you like me to help you with the steps, Jemima? No—okay. I'm sure Gillian would . . .'

Eventually, with much laughing and the occasional shriek as someone stumbled, they were all inside. The marquee, as far as Drew could tell, was about the size of a circus big top. Charlie and the ushers were moving between the guests, handing out filled champagne flutes.

'Everyone got a drink?' His voice echoed through the dim darkness. 'Then let's have the first toast. To Maddy and Drew! Happy wedding day!'

Immediately the salute was echoed by hundreds of voices, then there was the sulphur scent of cordite and the marquee was ablaze with millions of bright white stars. The cries of delight spiralled. Drew shook his head in amazement. The ranks of waiting staff had simultaneously lit sparklers along the top table—it seemed like thousands of them— and they fizzed and crackled, leaving rainbow trails in the blackness.

'Sparklers and champagne. Brilliant. Absolutely bloody brilliant.' He looked down at Maddy. Her eyes were as wide as Poppy's—her smile even wider.

'Okay, more conventional lighting.' Charlie was in his element as the sparklers died away and the chandeliers glowed into life. 'So that you can all find your seats. No, it's okay, Bronwyn—there's a seating plan to your left.'

The marquee's tables were dressed in the same

autumnal colours as the church, and as everyone clattered noisily into their places, Charlie lifted Poppy from Maddy's arms. 'Gillian will take care of her for a moment. There's one more thing that I want you two to see first. The other part of your wedding present from the village. The entertainment.'

The grapevine rumours about Fizz Flanagan began a resurgence. Drew hoped they weren't true. He wasn't sure his Aunt Aisling would be able to cope with the dreadlocks and the anarchy.

Holding Maddy's hand he followed Charlie to the far end of the marquee, and ducked outside. The night was still and black. Like iced velvet.

'We didn't know what to get you,' Charlie grinned. 'And we wanted your wedding to be remembered as one of the all-time Milton St John greats, so—' Placing his fingers in his mouth he let out a piercing whistle. 'We really hope you'll like it.' Then, kissing Maddy thoroughly and shaking Drew's hand, he darted back into the marquee.

Nothing happened for a moment, and then lights started appearing all over the field. Dimly at first, gradually gathering brilliance, illuminating—what? Drew strained his eyes against the darkness. Was that a—? No! And—

'Jesus!' He turned to Maddy in total delight. 'It's a bloody funfair! And—oh, Mad—look!'

The rides and side-shows were ablaze now— and in the centre of them all was a huge and magnificent set of galloping horses, their colours accentuated by gold-leaf, a thousand light bulbs picking out the gaudy perfection.

Slowly it started to revolve, the empty horses galloping just for them. Drew read the curlicued inscription as the massive machine turned—The Bradley-Morland Memory Lane Fair.

Perfect. Absolutely perfect. It couldn't—simply couldn't—get any better.

And then the organ in the middle of the gallopers split the silence and played 'The Wedding of the Painted Dolls'.

CHAPTER TWENTY-NINE

Considering that he hadn't sat on a horse or been to bed with anyone, Charlie reckoned that this had been one of the best days of his life. The reception was still firing on all cylinders, the Memory Lane Fair was going down a storm, and he was sharing the marquee with some of the most gorgeous women in the world.

The muted organ music from the gallopers floated through the tent-flaps in sporadic bursts as the guests poured to and from the fairground, hardly denting the disco's output. The dance floor was still packed, and the more elderly contingent had taken refuge in a far corner and set up an unofficial crèche for the flagging children.

It had been a triumph. For once, something he'd planned had actually worked. Charlie was aware that he was not a great planner. It had always seemed an awful waste of energy before; the best things just seemed to happen somehow, without too much input from him. But this, from its inception, had been pure perfection. Could it work equally as well with other areas of his life? He might, he decided, give organisation a whirl. But then again—

maybe not. He had always been a great believer in 'If it ain't broke, don't fix it'.

Drew and Maddy, who had spent hours riding delightedly on the gallopers and the ghost train and the big wheel, were now jiving in the middle of the floor. Charlie wondered exactly how much more energy it was safe for Maddy to expend. It would he a real bugger if they had to spend their wedding night in the maternity ward of the Royal Berks.

'Hi.' Lucinda, who had been dancing pneumatically with one of Drew's stable lads, flopped down beside him. 'Are we allowed to talk publicly now? You've been avoiding me all day.'

'I haven't. Honest.' Charlie took her hand. She was still very brown from the month in Spain. He had a feeling her tan would be all over. 'It's been a real responsibility, this best man business. I didn't realise that there were so many warring factions to placate, or rituals to observe. Anyway, us being seen together depends on what you've told your ma.' He jerked his head in the direction of the kiddies' corner where Bathsheba was holding court. 'Are we allowed to talk at all? Have we even met? I've been various school chums for so long, I've forgotten just what she knows.'

'Don't be sarcastic. She knows nothing at all,' Lucinda said happily. 'And suspects even less. Have you missed me, then?'

'Not at all. How's college?'

'Ace.'

'And how was Spain?'

'Even acer, ta.' She hitched up her dark green taffeta frock. 'You should see my tan.'

'I'd planned to,' Charlie sighed. 'But with Tina here, it could be difficult.'

431

'Get real!' The plait, dressed for the occasion with amber ribbons, swung from side to side. 'Difficult and you don't go together. We've always managed before.'

He must be getting old—or maybe it was just the effect of witnessing Drew and Maddy's profound commitment. Somehow this creeping about being devious and juggling women was losing its appeal. It would be so nice to know, like Drew, that he had everything he wanted in just one woman. A woman who, equally and miraculously, found everything she was looking for in him. Christ! Now he was getting really worried! Only a few weeks earlier that sort of thing would have been a complete anathema.

He tightened his fingers round Lucinda's hand. 'Come and dance. We can talk on the dance floor— and even your ma won't object to you dancing with best man. It's part of the bridesmaids' duties.'

The music had slowed. Vincent had apparently requested a smoochy number, and he and Maureen were executing a neat military two-step to the strains of Matt Munro.

'Total grot,' Lucinda grumbled, nestling anyway in his arms. 'Are you going to win the Hennessey?'

'Doubt it. Matt should. But Jenny Pitman and Martin Pipe are up for it too—among countless others. Why?'

'I was going to gamble my student loan.'

They weren't really dancing, just cuddling to the music. She was lovely. Young, fresh, vibrant. And completely happy with the no-strings relationship. What the hell was the matter with him? This was every man's dream.

'Do you want to go outside?'

'Christ, Charlie! I thought boys stopped saying that when they left the youth club!'

'Sorry.'

She giggled. 'Yeah, I'd love to. I just adore fairs, don't you?'

'I wasn't asking you to—oh, hell.'

Charlie shook his head, watching as Lucinda, her skirts bunched halfway up her tanned thighs, galloped towards the exit. Was she winding him up? And where was Tina anyway? Would she be watching his every move? Somehow he doubted it. They'd spent very little time together all week, Tina disappearing to closet herself at Lancing Grange with Kath and Dragon Slayer, only returning at night to test the Wallbank-Fox to its limits. And today Tina seemed quite happy being with Matt and Jemima.

'No sweat, sweetie,' she'd purred in his ear during the wedding photographs. 'You're public property today. I'll slap an exclusion zone round you tonight.'

Matt, disliking her as he did, must be finding her company a bit of a drag, Charlie reckoned. Especially when he could be giving all his attention to Jemima. What Jemima felt about the set-up was anyone's guess. She was so bloody enigmatic that she made Greta Garbo look like Lily Savage.

He grinned to himself. Anathema and enigmatic—all in the same hour! It must be an early male menopause. He'd have to ask Diana James-Jordan for her advice on HRT.

*   *   *

Outside, the night was misty, the hanging smoke

433

from a thousand Berkshire bonfires lying low across the Downs. The scent of spent fireworks kindled childhood memories. It wasn't even cold. The marquee was fully equipped with heaters, but even this late at night, they hadn't been needed. Milton St John in full swing could probably outdo the national grid.

Charlie really wanted a cigarette. It had been months now, but the craving was still there. He didn't even have any tack to hand to allay the urge. He exhaled. He'd been really good today—eating everything without sauces, passing on the gooey puddings, and sticking to only the occasional glass of wine. Three weeks to the Hennessey—and despite his casual disclaimer to Lucinda, he was going to win it if he could.

The Memory Lane Fair blazed and blared across the field. The lights were luminescent, and all the rides were full, with crowds still waiting their turn. The organ was playing something stirring—a march of some sort—and Gareth James-Jordan and Barty Small were conducting with wildly exaggerated arm movements. He couldn't see Lucinda.

He could, however, hear vaguely orgasmic groaning.

Sod it. Someone was getting very passionate merely feet away. Probably in the shadows of the marquee's miles of canvas. Not wanting to hang around—he'd never found voyeurism in the least enticing—he started to move quietly, hardly daring to breathe in case he interrupted the proceedings. Stupid really. There were dozens of people around. And judging by the growing ecstatic cries, the entire band of the Household Cavalry wouldn't disturb them. Lucky bastards. Feeling very turned-on, he looked again for Lucinda.

The breathing was quicker; the groans even more exultant. Then one quiet but joyous panting cry. One word. One name. *Matt.*

Charlie stopped dead. He felt sick. No matter that he had seduced half the village in the open air, he'd thought Jemima was above that sort of thing. It didn't go at all with the image he'd built of her. Stupid bastard that he was. And she'd been with Matt for ages—no doubt they did this sort of thing all the time—He'd never thought about it. Never wanted to.

He turned his back on the fair and ducked into the marquee. He wanted a drink. Quickly. Barging through the dancers, he headed for the bar. Of course, it could have been some other Matt, couldn't it? There must have been dozens of Matthews on the guest-list. This ray of hope didn't last long. Having drawn up the seating plan, he knew there hadn't been.

Gillian, carrying two glasses of wine, and looking gloriously ethereal, nearly cannoned into him. They both said sorry at the same time. She smiled vaguely. 'You've organised this so well. It's been lovely, hasn't it? I love weddings.'

'Yeah, so do I.' For a moment he was almost compelled to tell Gillian. Only for a moment. Gillian was the biggest gossip in the world— and anyway, what was he going to say? Matt and Jemima are bonking each other stupid outside? And what can I do about it because I'm suddenly insanely jealous? Just the sort of opening gambit you should use with a vicar's wife. And Gillian would probably say, So what? Or, How lovely.

He tried smiling at her instead. 'I've been

435

neglecting my duties. Drew says the best man must dance with every beautiful woman at the reception. Can I book you now?'

'Yes, please. Actually, I always think it's a shame that we can't have those little programmes the women had at balls years ago, where the men actually bagged a dance at the beginning of the evening and wrote their name down against it. So civilised, don't you think?'

'Yeah. Brilliant idea.' Christ—beautiful she may be, but definitely a psalm short of a psalter. 'Gillian, could you do me an immense favour? Could I have a cigarette?'

The manoeuvre was slightly tricky owing to the wineglasses, but eventually they managed it, and Gillian waggled the drinks at him as she drifted away. Charlie inhaled deeply, immediately giddy from the unaccustomed nicotine rush. God, what on earth was wrong with him? Maybe he'd feel better when he'd had a drink.

Having managed to get served with a double whisky, he looked found for a quiet corner. Some hope. His original seat had been taken by Caroline who seemed to be holding some sort of sales conference with Maddy's mum and dad. And now that Matt Munro had been ousted by Fat Les, everyone over the age of twenty had left the dance floor.

'If I was a gambler—which of course I'm not—I'd bet you a tenner it'll be the Birdy Song next.'

He blinked. The cigarette had made him feel sick. The slug of whisky hadn't helped. Jemima, standing beside him laughing, shocked him rigid. He looked over her shoulder, almost expecting to see Matt rearranging his clothing. Hell—but she was cool. She looked totally unruffled. It hadn't taken her very long to shrug off the afterglow, had it?

'Er—yes. Probably. That or Agadoo. Um—Matt—er—not with you?'

'I haven't seen him for ages. I got buttonholed by one of Drew's Irish aunties. We've been raving about Maeve Binchy for hours.'

'Hours?'

'Well, the last half hour at least. And before that I was with Dad and Maureen, who,' she laughed again, 'were pretending not to be holding hands. Matt probably got tired of waiting for me. Why? Are you looking for him? Shall I tell him you want to talk to him?'

Charlie shook his head. He really felt dizzy now. 'No. No—it'll keep.'

Holy shit! What sort of callous bastard was he? His immediate reaction wasn't sympathy for Jemima because she was being cheated on, but absolute relief. So who was outside with Matt, then? He couldn't swear that he'd recognised the voice, but, to be honest, there hadn't been that much to go on. Women, in his experience, all sounded roughly the same at that point.

Could it have been Lucinda? Not a chance. Even if Lucinda had the hots for Matt, there simply wouldn't have been enough time. Tina? God, no! He knew only too well that Tina never sounded throatily ecstatic. She was too busy inflicting damage. And there had been no accompaniment of ripping flesh. Suzy Beckett? Possibly. She and Luke Delaney had been skirting each other all evening, pretending indifference, flirting like mad with everyone else. It could well be Suzy, especially if she'd had a lot to drink.

Jemima was still looking happy. 'Bronwyn Pugh, radiating sherry fumes, has just told me on the QT that she bears me no grudges about stocking pornography. Isn't that nice? Oh, and I really must congratulate you on organising all this. It's totally brilliant. I've had a wonderful time.'

'Thanks—um—do you want to sit down?'

Jemima shook her head. The shaggy layers of her hair gleamed beneath the chandeliers. The long autumny dress moulded itself to her. Matt Garside, Charlie decided, was completely mad. God, please don't let her say she wanted to go round the fair. He couldn't bear it. Matt could just be going in to bat for the second innings. He really didn't want Jemima to find out. Not that way.

He gulped the remains of the whisky. 'How about a dance?'

To his surprise she smiled. 'Okay.'

'Even if it's the Birdy Song?'

'One of my favourites.'

It wasn't. The Upton Poges DJ, mindful of his eclectic audience, had headed for a selection of the New Wave Romantics. Charlie felt quite nostalgic. Dancing with Jemima wasn't easy. Oh, she wasn't one of those stiff, windmilling women, far from it. Her movements were fluid and assured. It was just that she swayed tantalisingly close in front of him without touching. His instinctive reaction was to slide his hands on to her hips and pull her towards him. It was the way he'd danced for the last fifteen years. But he couldn't. Not with Jemima. Bloody strange. Still, maybe they'd move on to that stage later. They were going to have plenty of time.

438

Charlie was determined that Jemima wasn't going to leave the dance floor until Matt and Suzy were safely—and separately—back in the marquee.

They didn't talk. He didn't need to. He was captivated by her. This was awful. He'd never, ever nicked anyone else's woman. Well—that wasn't strictly true; but they'd always been willing participants, bored with their current partners, happy to have a fling. Charlie felt he was almost providing a service to disillusioned relationships. Everyone always seemed to be happy enough afterwards.

But this was different. He would like to be able to ask Jemima out. Publicly. But even if she agreed, which of course she wouldn't, he couldn't. Because she was Matt's girlfriend. Matt and Charlie had made a pact years before that they would never, under any circumstances, get involved with the same woman at the same time. It was a code of honour. Blokeish? Yeah, maybe. But it had worked really well. Neither of them would dream of reneging on the agreement.

'It all sounds very bizarre, sweetie,' Tina had said when he'd told her about it some weeks earlier. They'd been discussing Matt and Dragon Slayer and Matt and him, and friendships generally. She'd eased herself off the Wallbank-Fox and rolled a spliff. 'Very *Four Musketeers*. So, there's absolutely no point in you yearning for that rather dreary girl in the bookshop, is there? Not if Matt has his brand on her.' She'd laughed when he'd said he had no interest in Jemima, and raked her nails down his back. 'I must say, I really adore these rural customs.'

Charlie was under no illusion that Matt having

439

a quickie with Suzy Beckett was anything other than just that. A mutual arrangement between consenting and like-minded adults. Nothing serious on Matt's part at all. Christ knows why he'd want to, of course, but Jemima, hopefully, would never know.

The music changed. Jemima seemed more than happy to continue dancing. She really was good. She had natural rhythm. She was bloody damn sexy. And lovely. And funny. And tough. And intelligent—and—hang on—if it hadn't been him thinking about Jemima, it would be beginning to sound like a severe case of falling in love. Lust, Charlie cheerfully recognised; love was a virtual stranger.

'Charlie!' Lucinda pushed in between them, then grinned. 'Ooh, sorry, Jemima. Didn't mean to interrupt—mind, it could be rescuing you from a fate worse than death. You two don't exactly see eye to eye, do you?'

'We've managed to disagree about most things so far,' Jemima grinned, still dancing. 'I was merely keeping him warm for you.'

Lucinda was dancing with them now. Charlie prayed that Jemima would stay. He had a quick scan round the marquee for Matt. The bastard was still nowhere to be seen. He looked across at Lucinda. 'Where did you get to?'

'The fair. I've had tons of free rides on the ghost train.' She laughed without inhibition. 'There was this absolutely lush bloke running it—he looked just like Rudy Yarrow! You know, out of the Australian soap on Channel Five? AD suntan and floppy hair. You'd have loved him, Jemima. Anyway, he kept jumping on the back of my car in the darkest scariest bits and she shrugged at Charlie, 'we got on really well and I'm sorry I've been such a long time.'

The plait, he noticed, had been unravelled. Someone had kissed all her lipstick off.

'Your ma will have a fit if she finds out,' Jemima said. 'I'm sure she's already got you lined up for some clean-cut graduate.'

'Speaking of which,' Charlie winced as Bathsheba powered her way across the sprung pretend-parquet, making it bounce, 'I have a feeling we're just about to find out.'

'Keep dancing,' Jemima hissed. 'Maybe she won't notice that Lucinda's all mussed-up.'

'Lucinda!' The roar drowned Duran Duran. 'I do not want you consorting with these people!'

Few around them took any notice. It was far too late in a heavy-drinking day for most of the guests to be fazed by anything. Charlie stared down at the floor—not from cowardice, but because he was sure that if he looked at Bathsheba he'd laugh. Which could be fatal. His own feet were inches from Lucinda's green satin sandals and Jemima's brown suede ankle boots. They were all moving in the same way.

'Charlie!' Bathsheba's roar was even more scary than his housemaster's had been. 'I've been keeping an eye on Lucinda all day. I know she's over eighteen, and thus officially out of my parental control—but I'm afraid I simply cannot condone this sort of behaviour.'

Which behaviour? Lucinda dancing with him and a cast of thousands—or being snogged senseless by some guy she'd met five minutes earlier on the ghost train? It was hardly fair . . . 'Sorry, Mrs C. I'm not sure that I get your drift.'

441

'You have an appalling reputation; your current girlfriend dared to attend church wearing no underwear—and this young lady,' she flicked her head towards Jemima, 'sees nothing wrong in the sale of pornographic literature. I'm sorry, but I really cannot agree that you're fit company for any healthy and pure young gel.'

Which pure young—? Oh, Lucinda. He wanted to laugh. He caught Jemima's eye. She already was. Her shoulders were shaking as she studied the chandeliers.

'Excuse me.' Gillian's voice cut in. 'Can we have that dance now, please, Charlie? Only the boys have gone to sleep on Bronwyn, and Glen thinks we should be making tracks and—oh, hello, Bathsheba. Were you waiting to dance with Charlie, too?'

'I certainly was not! And you should think twice, about it, Mrs Hutchinson. You've salvaged your reputation in this village by backing our anti-smut campaign. But publicly colluding with the main protagonists won't do it any good, will it?'

Gillian looked as though she'd lost the plot somewhere around the word 'salvaged'. She smiled sweetly. 'Won't it? What a pity. Goodness—are you all queuing up to dance with Charlie? Not that I'm surprised, of course—'

Lucinda and Jemima managed a synchronised head-shaking. Charlie shrugged. 'Bathsheba was just suggesting that I wasn't suitable company for Lucinda.'

'Goodness!' Gillian's laugh tinkled off the twinkling glass droplets high in the canvas stratosphere. 'Little bit late for that, isn't it? You and she have been an item for simply *ages*, haven't you?

442

It was like hearing the Queen swear. Nobody quite believed it—The silence was immense.

Gillian, obviously registering her *faux pas* a second too late, immediately made matters worse. 'Well, I don't mean an item as such. Of course, you and Tina have been together as well, and Lucinda has just been a sort of chum for you in your free moments, hasn't she?'

'What sort of chum?' The four words made Bathsheba's chins tremble. 'Lucinda?'

'Charlie used to chat to her when he came into the bookshop,' Jemima said quickly. 'That's all, isn't it?'

Charlie grinned, praying that a boyish smile and a quick display of the crooked teeth would dispel any maternal fears. 'God, yes. Nothing more. Absolutely not.'

'Crap.' Lucinda picked the remaining amber ribbons from the tendrils of her plait. 'Charlie's given extra-curricular studies and cramming a whole new meaning.' She smiled sweetly at Bathsheba. 'We've been at it ever since I came back from St Hilda's.'

Bathsheba caught the inference with both hands. 'You mean—he—deflowered you?'

Jemima gave a snort of laughter which turned into a sneeze. Gillian kindly handed her a Kleenex.

'Of course he didn't deflower me—I lost my virginity at Dominic Birkett-Spence's fifteenth birthday party bloody years ago.'

Bathsheba's cry of anguish was almost swamped by Gillian's cry of delight. 'Oh, super! He's such a nice boy! I know his parents. Lovely family.'

Lucinda swung the crimped hair angrily away from her face and glared at her mother. 'So, before

443

you go hurling accusations of sleaze at nice people like Charlie and Jemima, why don't you look on your own doorstep?'

'Back yard,' Charlie said. 'Or maybe it is doorstep . . .'

Bathsheba hasn't got anything as common as a back yard.' Gillian's brow was furrowed. 'She's got a nice little patio. Did you mean patio, Lucinda?'

'I think we all got the gist.' Jemima stepped in bravely and grabbed Gillian's arm. 'I think perhaps Glen's right and you should be heading home. It's been a long day . . .'

Bathsheba looked old and defeated. She had sort of sagged. Charlie felt sorry for her. It must be hell having kids and loving them and wanting to protect them from people like him. He pulled a sympathetic face at Lucinda. It had been nice while it lasted.

'See you at Christmas,' she said brightly, kissing him on the cheek. 'I'll be home for the hols—unless the Maxwell-Dunmores invite me to go ski-ing. I hope you win the Hennessey. I'll watch you on the telly and tell everyone at college that you're absolutely bloody marvellous—at everything.'

It was small comfort. Jemima had disappeared with Gillian, and now Lucinda was escorting Bathsheba away to the cloakroom. Which left him what? Tina. Every man at the wedding had been lusting openly after Tina. They'd probably all want to go the full twelve rounds in the Wallbank-Fox. As far as he was concerned, they were welcome to try.

She was sitting alone, twirling a champagne flute, smoking something dubious, and swinging her Patrick Cox'd foot in time with Little Jimmy

444

Osmond. It was a relief to notice, as he crossed the marquee towards her, that Drew and Maddy were sitting down too, Poppy Scarlet fast asleep between them, as they toasted each other in Bollinger.

He was suddenly fiercely jealous. It was what *he* wanted. Well, not the Poppy and bump bit—that was out of the question—but the rest. He wanted to share his life with someone, not just his bed.

'Hi.' Tina pushed blonde hair away from smoky eyes. 'Had a nice time?'

'Great. You?'

'Surprisingly, yes. I thought it would be very quaint, but actually there are some really cool people here. Did you know that Diana and Gareth are going to keep the marquee erected and hold a rave at New Year?'

'No, I bloody didn't.' It would cause ructions in the village. Still, it might keep Bathsheba occupied—which wouldn't be a bad thing. He stared at the spliff. 'Sure you're not hallucinating? You didn't get that off Jace, did you?'

'Sweetie, you know I never touch the cheap end of the market. It's true. I was talking to Diana in the cloakroom. She says there's still a lot of money to be made from raves. Well, as I said to her, there probably is out here in the sticks. There's not a decent club for miles—and, let's face it, in this village they still consider putting cheese and pineapple together very avant-garde.'

Charlie laughed. She was always funny when she was stoned. 'Do you want to go home?'

'If home equates with bed, yeah. If home equates with pints of whisky and Aerosmith at killing level, no.'

'No whisky. No Aerosmith. Give me five

minutes. I just want to say goodbye to Matt. Have you seen him recently?'

'Not for ages. He was going round the fairground last I heard. He's probably still attempting to win a coconut.'

He walked out of the marquee again. The Memory Lane Fair was still packed. The gallopers revolved in golden glory, the organ playing raucously. Whoever Bradley-Morland were, they were obviously in for an all-night session. He was close to the roundabout now. Perhaps Bradley and Morland were the couple cuddling in the middle, oblivious to everything. She was extremely pretty. Christ! Was the entire world in love tonight?

He wasn't sure what he was going to say to Matt—even if he found him—but it was important to him to say *something*. Matt had covered for him on countless occasions, so it wasn't exactly a moral issue. It did occur to him briefly that if it had been someone other than Jemima who was involved, he probably wouldn't feel so concerned. Jemima was different—sort of vulnerable—she simply didn't deserve to be hurt.

It was colder now. The last of the bonfire smoke had dispersed, revealing a clear black sky studded with stars. The swell of people pressed all round him, laughing, shouting greetings.

Seen Matt?' he asked each of them. None had.

Sod it. He'd give up and go home. Maybe Tina would be gentle with him.

It was the furtive whispering that caught his attention. The shouts and yells and loudness were everywhere. Hearing someone speaking urgently and quietly in the darkness made him stop and listen.

446

Ned Filkins! For Christ's sake! What the hell was he doing here? He hadn't been on the guest-list.

'. . . just a final word, mate. We don't want nothing dramatic, understand? A couple more wins'll go down a treat—and then the little mishap at Newbury. Okay?'

'Okay.'

Charlie's skin crawled.

'And we'll be watching you, me and Vince, so no funny business. Not unless of course you want everyone to know what we know. Understood?'

'Yeah.'

'Good, lad. You'll be paid well, son, have no fears. And it'll all be for the best, won't it? Now you run back in to your young lady—we wouldn't want her getting any ideas now, would we?'

'Bastard.'

'Takes one to know one, mate. Takes one to know one.'

Two sets of footsteps swished through the grass in opposite directions. Both of them hidden in the darkness. Charlie wiped his hand across his mouth and exhaled. Bloody sodding hell! Matt—taking backhanders from Ned—for what? Something at Newbury? Not the Hennessey—dear God. Surely not? And Vincent was involved. Jemima's father . . .

Charlie groaned. What the hell should he do? Confront Matt? He'd deny it. Tell Kath? She wouldn't believe it. He must warn Jemima. But he couldn't, could he? How the hell could he tell Jemima that the two people she trusted and loved most in her life were cheating—and Matt doubly so?

Shit! She'd hate him for telling her. She'd hate him even more for *knowing*.

447

CHAPTER THIRTY

It was cold. The wind swept across Newbury racecourse on a steel-grey day, blowing discarded betting slips around snugly muffled ankles like cut-price confetti.

Matt sat in the changing room and wondered whether, if he killed himself, anyone would care. He might as well be dead. He was risking losing everything he'd ever wanted. There were no guarantees that he'd gain anything at all out of this; his reputation would be shot whatever happened. Being dead and out of it seemed like a good idea. Getting there, though, appeared to have its disadvantages. Matt reckoned you had to be pretty brave to commit suicide. And he wasn't.

'Cheer up—it may never happen.' Liam Jenkins, half-dressed, slapped him on the shoulder. It hurt. Every part of his body hurt.

Matt grimaced. He'd heard the same words all day. He really should try to look a touch more cheerful. He was riding the bloody favourite in the Hennessey in—what?—just under an hour's time. Almost an hour in which to decide. Such a simple choice. Should he go along with Ned and Vincent and throw the race in Bonne Nuit's favour, even if Dragon Slayer was miles ahead, or not?

Win or lose, the stakes were high in both deals. All he had to do to stop Ned telling Jemima—and, infinitely worse, Charlie and the rest of the world—about his habit, was to chuck away the Hennessey. Oh—and probably the Cheltenham Gold Cup. Sod all, really. Then Dragon Slayer would be out the back door in the betting come the National—and they'd all clean up. Once he'd knocked Charlie out of the frame at Aintree, of course. Nothing to it.

He laughed bitterly. What the hell. If he won or lost he would be finished in Milton St John, finished in racing; he wouldn't even be able to crawl home to the Devon farm and find solace in Jennifer's arms. That was part of Ned's squeeze on him too.

Matt was under no illusions that his parents and his home-based girlfriend would be informed in graphic detail about his nocturnal habits long before he'd even left the Berkshire borders.

The changing room was charged with high energy. The Hennessey was steeplechasing's greatest early-season test. Win this one and you were up there in the highest echelons: your previously unfancied horse ranking alongside the all time greats like Sea Pigeon or See You Then or Red Rum, and hotly tipped for Cheltenham and Aintree. The Hennessey had thrown up stars like Arkle and Mill House. It was everyone's ambition to be the next Scudamore, Francome or Dunwoody.

Matt wiped his hands across his face. They all wanted it so badly. So did he. Oh, God—so did he. It seemed like years ago, that race at Fakenham at the end of last season, when Dragon Slayer had gone like the wind and he knew they could win the National. Then he'd been sure he'd kill to win at Aintree. Now, he might just have to.

So soon after that, it had all crashed around his ears. Jemima—poor girl—had appeared in his life at precisely the wrong moment. He tried not to think too much about Jemima. Of course, the easiest and most sensible thing would be to finish

449

with her. That would be one less lever for Ned to exert. She'd have no reason to be surprised, would she? Christ, he'd been about as amorous as a castrated tomcat for months and then, and then— Matt swallowed. He still felt bloody awful about that night. Jemima hadn't deserved it. And he'd let her think it was her fault. Let her go on thinking it.

Then he'd tried being casual and off-hand and hoped she'd call it a day. But she hadn't. She'd insisted that they talked it over like grown-ups. They were friends, she said. She wanted to stay friends. No need to worry. They liked each other . . . Matt groaned. That was half the trouble, of course. He did like Jemima. He enjoyed being with her. He needed her. She made him feel normal. Decent.

Anyway, at the moment Jemima had a fox-hunting bee in her bonnet. That was another thing he admired about her: she didn't dwell on problems or minor irritations. Not like he did. She faced them, dealt with them, and got them out of the way. She'd worked out all her problems with racing, then the Parish Biddies, then the débâcle of their sex life. Each one had been coped with calmly, sorted, not allowed to interfere too much. She was always in control. Unlike him.

At the moment, her outrage about bloody fox-hunting had taken precedence over everything else. She'd had saboteur posters up in the shop all month, even though he'd told her to take them down. Before long she'd be laying aniseed trails and blowing false halloos with the rest of the great unwashed. He had decided it was probably not the best time to inform her that he spent a good part of his winter months riding to hounds.

450

Still, her current anti-blood sports campaign had its advantages. At least it took her mind off his lack of sexual prowess. He sighed heavily and wished, in that area at least, that Jemima had been different.

And, of course, it had been just after meeting Jemima at Windsor that Ned had discovered the reasons for Matt's trips to London. Sod's law. At the very moment when he had something to bloody lose. Like with poor Vincent, Ned had left nothing to chance. He had evidence. Hard photographic evidence.

Then Tina—Jesus! He'd walked straight into that one, too. Tina Maloret—who he would shortly be greeting with a professional doff of the cap—Charlie's girlfriend. Tina Maloret—the scalding memories of her last visit to Milton St John would stay with him for ever.

And Charlie, bloody philanderer that he was, had this damn stupid public-school code of honour. Screw around all you liked, but you didn't—on pain of death—cheat on a mate, cheat on your trainer, or cheat on a horse.

Matt was doing all three.

Christ!' Philip Franklin stopped in front of him. 'You been passed fit to ride?'

'Uh?'

'You're knocked about a bit. You taken a tumble?'

'Oh—yeah. Not from Dragon Slayer. One of Kath's babies. Schooling, you know? Nothing serious. Looks worse than it is.'

'Must have been a pearler. And straight into a bramble patch by the looks of it. Done it myself. Hurts like shit, doesn't it? You'll know about it later.'

'Probably.' Matt fastened the stock round his throat and pulled Tina's colours over his head.

Charlie was sitting on the bench at the far end, joking with Liam and Philip, ignoring him. He'd practically ignored him ever since Drew and Maddy's wedding. Matt couldn't think why. There was no reason. Unless he *knew*. Christ—what could he know? Which part? There were so many things now that kept him awake at night. Still, surely if Charlie had discovered something, he'd have let rip by now? He was never one to let a boil fester.

'All okay?' His valet looked concerned. 'All the tack and that?'

'Yeah. Fine.'

'You looked worried.'

'Nerves.'

The valet nodded sympathetically and shouldered his way through the noisy crowd to find his next charge. Matt stood up. He didn't want to hang around in here, listening to the bragging, the bravado, the jokes. With Tina's black-and-white jersey hanging loose outside his breeches, he headed for the weighing-room door.

The air was still ice cold. The track was riding fast after weeks of fine weather and keen downland winds. Since Newbury's renovation, the weighing room faced the parade ring and the winner's enclosure. The crowds were packed three deep as the horses were led from the pre-parade ring to plod round, manes and tails tangling sideways in the breeze.

Dragon Slayer wasn't out yet. Nor was Bonne Nuit. There was no sign of Kath or Tina. He could see Jemima though, standing close to the rails with the Milton St John contingent. It was her first trip to a racecourse since Windsor. He knew how deeply she'd agonised about being there. He wished she wasn't.

She looked lovely. The long conker-brown coat and matching velvet hat pulled low over her eyes made her look tall and elegant. The hat probably belonged to Gillian who seemed to have a whole wardrobe full of hippie gear. She was next to Jemima, in a black cloak with the hood up, pointing out something in the racecard, and on the other side was Maureen in a scarlet PVC trench coat and—oh shit—Vincent.

Was Vincent here to report back to Ned? Probably. Who cared? Matt knew what he had to do. He simply wasn't sure if he had the guts to do it.

There was a sudden stir in the paddock; a whole entourage of people seemed to be pushing their way through to the front. Several stewards in sheepskins and trilbys were clearing a path. Royalty? Matt squinted. Well, hardly—not unless the Royals were now into multicoloured dreadlocks and split-melon grins.

Fizz Flanagan was accompanied by a phalanx of minders. Matt nodded ruefully. So he did own Bonne Nuit, after all. Charlie would say nothing to confirm or deny the horse's ownership despite the speculation in the village. And Bonnie was always entered under Drew's name. Still, a lot of owners chose to remain anonymous for various reasons, although Matt could see no reason why the flamboyant Fizz should want to keep it quiet. He had loads of horses spread through various yards. Maybe Bonne Nuit was a tax fiddle. Matt would have welcomed something as minor as cheating the Inland Revenue. He could handle that.

Nearly time. Dragon Slayer's lad was just leading him into the parade ring. Matt took one fond look at the huge black horse, felt sick, and retraced his steps to the weighing room.

Charlie, who was still stripped to the waist and was just coming to the end of a very blue joke, had neat rows of scratches along the width of both shoulders. Matt wanted to kill him.

*   *   *

Okay?' Kath was back in her winter racing outfit of ground-brushing coat and beret. She gave him a leg up into the saddle.

'You know what to do with him. Let him settle. If he wants to front-run don't stop him, although I'd prefer it if he did the first circuit covered up. See how he goes at the water. Get in on middle ground if he feels spooky. Let him find his own pace. We know he's got the stamina for the final four—so if you've got into trouble early on you should be able to get out of it. Right?'

'Right.' Matt gathered the reins between his fingers. He was pretty sure Kath suspected something. She was giving him options. And she hadn't used one swear word. Not even a mild curse. Christ—he was becoming completely paranoid.

Charlie was in the saddle, too, wearing the shocking pink and black colours that Fizz Flanagan had opted for. It had to be some sort of fiddle, Matt thought, because all the other Flanagan horses ran in Fizz's dazzling green and yellow of Jamaica. Looking relaxed on Bonne Nuit, Charlie was grinning at Drew, joking with Gillian, and—good Lord—Jemima. What the hell was Jemima doing in

454

the paddock? Gillian, too, come to think of it? And why did Charlie—even before the biggest race—always seem like he didn't have a damn care in the world?

Tina wasn't about, thank God. He still felt guilty when Tina and Jemima were together, and he certainly didn't want to watch her with Charlie. All the other owners and trainers were clustered round their horses, tightening girths, giving last-minute instructions to the jockeys, while the television cameras swooped and zoomed and the armchair experts crowded on to the rails and gave their loudly voiced opinions.

Jemima seemed to be talking first to Drew, then to Gillian, and then started to walk towards him. He tried to smile at her. The wind froze it into a manic grin.

'Is it okay?' She tilted her head back to look up at him in the saddle, keeping a safe distance from Dragon Slayer. 'Can I wish you luck? Or am I supposed to say break a leg like in the theatre?'

'I'd rather you didn't. I'm surprised you're here—in the paddock I mean.'

'Drew invited me. He thought I might enjoy the race better if I understood it all. Dad's hopping mad. He's always wanted to be allowed in this bit, apparently.' She rubbed her gloved hands together. 'It's freezing. Don't you feel the cold?'

Matt shook his head. Bugger Vincent. He suddenly wanted to kiss her. She looked fresh and clean and sweet and wholesome and—oh, sod it. He leaned down and touched her cheek, pleased that she didn't pull away immediately. 'Have you watched the other races?'

She shook her head. 'Gillian did—with Dad and

455

Maureen. I stayed in the bar. I'm going to watch this one, though. There's a first time for everything, I suppose, and I can always take my glasses off if I don't like it. Oh, hello, Tina.'

Matt straightened in the saddle. He wondered if Tina had seen him touch Jemima's cheek. He hoped not. 'Where've you been?'

'Bloody photographers.' Tina, dressed from head to toe by Joseph Ribkoff, was totally stunning. Jemima, Matt thought, however lovely, looked like a small brown sparrow beside her. 'They wanted to do a social diary piece with Fizz Flanagan, for God's sake.'

Ignoring Jemima, she turned and waved to Charlie. He raised his whip in salute and she giggled. Matt felt another surge of jealousy. Jemima held up crossed gloved fingers at him and moved back towards Gillian.

'I thought she hated racing.' Tina ran her fingers round the top of his riding boot. 'Why the hell is she in the paddock?'

Matt shuddered as the fingers travelled higher. 'Drew's idea of aversion therapy.'

The nails dug into his thigh. 'Sad little bunch, really. The bookseller, the Vicar's wife, the would-be Buddhist trainer, and the playboy jockey. Could turn it into a French art film.'

'You're a bitch.' He spoke the words quietly. Sensuously. The nails dug deeper. 'And we're supposed to be discussing tactics.'

Tina opened the saucer eyes to dinner plates. 'Oh, we are, sweetie. We are.'

With all the jockeys in the saddle, the horses were moving now. Tina, side by side with Kath, had turned into the Perfect Owner, wishing him luck,

456

smiling sweetly. He wanted to win for her. Fucking hell—what a mess!

He plodded in line to the course, then, as the lad let go of Dragon Slayer's reins, kicked off and rode on the wind. The ground was perfect—as it always was at Newbury—the turf luxuriant with just enough bounce to ensure steady galloping progress. God, this horse was brilliant. Perfection. He wouldn't lose on him today. He knew he wouldn't. Let Ned do his worst; today belonged to Dragon Slayer. And to Tina.

He pulled up just past the grandstand, wheeled the horse round and trotted him back up the course for the pre-race parade. Vincent could go back to Milton St John and tell Ned whatever he liked. Dragon Slayer was favourite to win this race—and that was exactly what he intended to do.

*   *   *

The first circuit had been disastrous. Five fallers. Dragon Slayer had avoided the mêlée and had tons in hand. Matt knew he couldn't blow this one now even if he wanted to. Dragon Slayer was determined to win. The crowd had one voice, screaming encouragement each time he came to a fence.

Charlie on Bonne Nuit was scrubbing along beside him, falling a bit behind at the take-offs, but making up ground between the fences. They were on the back straight, leading the depleted field with five fences left to jump. Several of the fancied horses had fallen in the earlier catastrophe. Matt was pleased that there had been no fatalities. It was all part of the game, of course, but bloody upsetting when it happened. Charlie, he knew, cried when horses were killed. Matt never had. He put it down to being brought up on a farm. Life and death both had lesser value somehow when the animals you played with disappeared to market and slaughter on a regular basis.

'It'll have to be at the next.' Charlie was upsides him now. 'The cross fence before the home turn. You won't get away with it in the straight.'

If it hadn't been so serious it would have been funny. Like that ongoing gossiping jockey sketch in *The Harry Enfield Show* that everyone in Milton St John found so screamingly amusing.

'Piss off.'

There was a crashing, turf-shaking thud behind them as something didn't make the final fence. Matt winced and glanced over his shoulder. Philip Franklin was sprawled on the ground. His horse, untangling itself from the dangling reins, was struggling to its feet.

Charlie, sitting easily on the smoothly moving Bonnie, leaned slightly towards him. 'I know what you're up to. I haven't got a clue why—but you're going to chuck this for fucking Ned Filkins, aren't you?'

It was like a punch in the groin. Matt, his mouth already dry, and every muscle aching, sucked more air into his painful lungs and kicked Dragon Slayer forward. Charlie was having none of it. It could have been a two-horse race. The crowd thought it was. He could hear the grandstand erupting.

'Why do you need to take fucking backhanders to throw this away?'

'I'm not taking backhanders!' The words hissed out, hurting.

'I heard you, you shit. At the wedding. I fucking

458

heard you.'

Matt closed his eyes. Dragon Slayer, getting no instructions, was doing what he did best. Racing to win. The cross fence was hurtling towards them. So was Philip Franklin's loose horse.

Delighted to be free, as dangerous as an unguided missile, it cannoned between Dragon Slayer and Bonne Nuit. Charlie managed to snatch Bonnie away from danger just in time. Matt was not so lucky.

Dragon Slayer, rising instinctively to meet the tricky fence just before the turn, put on the brakes to avoid the collision. Matt heard the yells from the grandstand, heard Charlie's shout of warning, then heard nothing else as he was catapulted from the saddle.

December

CHAPTER THIRTY-ONE

Parking Floss beneath the bare branches of a twisted oak tree, Jemima stepped into the desolation of downland December. The steel of the sky threatened sleet at least, and the wind rustled through the dead grass with a mournful Greek chorus whisper. Three weeks before Christmas, and 'In the Bleak Midwinter' could have been written as Fernydown's theme song.

The grim weather didn't seem to have affected the hunt, though. They were there in strength outside the Pickled Newt Farmhouse Eaterie—which Jemima could have sworn had, until recently, been called The Plough or something equally bucolic—drinking stirrup cups. Dozens of foot followers were milling around in Barbours and checked caps, while the Master of Hounds and whippers-in sat ramrod straight on their horses, their scarlet coats a vivid insult.

Jemima took a deep breath. It was the first time she'd seen the hunt in all its glory, apart from on television or tablemats or the faded prints in the Cat and Fiddle, of course. As a spectacle, a rural tradition, it was pretty awe-inspiring. If only they could stay like that, a tableau frozen in time: the horses tossing arrogant heads, the cheeks of the participants made ruddy by a combination of mulled wine and chilled air, and the hounds, tails wagging, noses snuffling, running in skewbald circles. But within moments they'd be off, charging across the fields, braying, view-hallooing, yelling with excitement as they terrified yet another small animal to death.

Jemima squinted through her glasses. There were the James-Jordans—looking like something out of Pat Smythe—and Kath Seaward—and several of the other faces peering from beneath the gleaming black caps were also familiar. She was pretty sure she'd seen most of them in the Cat and Fiddle at some point. The bastards! She'd never ever speak to any of them again. Drew wasn't there as far as she could see—nor Charlie. Thank God.

A British Field Sports lady was eyeing her speculatively, sensing a newcomer, so shoving her hands deeper into the pockets of her reefer jacket, Jemima crossed the road towards a mass of parked cars. Far better to be considered an ignorant townie observer, she decided, than to be mistaken for a camp follower—or, worse still, have the woman in her deerstalker attempt to sign her up for a life of mass slaughter.

Of course, she could have stood her corner and argued the toss, but she was hoping that she would manage to get away with being there today without any confrontation. She certainly didn't want the Milton St John hunting contingent to recognise her and start shouting cheery greetings.

Nearly everyone in the village, seeing the poster in the bookshop, had warned her about becoming involved. Even Gillian and Glen, who were obviously anti-hunt, had explained the wisdom of turning the occasional blind eye. Jemima had considered this pretty unchristian and had said so.

When she'd crossed the road and reached the rows of four-wheel-drives, muddied Land-Rovers and gleaming saloons bearing this year's registration plates which plainly belonged to the hunt supporters, she glanced back across her shoulder. The deerstalker had given up on her, and was homing in on further prey. Relieved, Jemima slipped between a clutch of ancient hatchbacks and rusty vans bearing multitudes of animal rights stickers. These clearly belonged to the other side. She felt more at home here and wished she'd parked Floss nearer.

The more sinister-looking members of the other side, all wearing Fighters Against Racing Torture insignia, were gathered a short distance from the main branch of the saboteurs, blowing on their bare hands, stamping their DMs. The paid-up animal righters, all very studenty and Green-looking, were ignoring them, as though they disliked the body-pierced and dreadlocked crew almost as much as they did the hunt servants. Again, slightly apart from the real anarchists, were a group of the respectable middle-aged middle class, better muffled against the cold than either of the other two groups, but looking no less dedicated to the cause.

The man who had left the poster in the bookshop, and who had called in twice since to see if it was still there, was nowhere to be seen. On the second visit he'd confided in her that his name was Reynard—not his real name, of course, but the one he'd adopted in solidarity with the cause. He had not only had his ears and nose liberally pierced, but also his tongue, which had fascinated Jemima considerably.

'You want to keep neutral,' Tracy had said cheerfully, humping armfuls of Super Gifts for Christmas' across from the stock-room. 'And he's a right weirdo. Some of them protesters is worse

465

than the huntsmen. More violent. More nasty. You managed to beat Bathsheba Cox and her crew—why don't you just leave it at that?'

But Jemima couldn't. Wouldn't. Anyway, she wasn't particularly worried by Reynard's absence at Fernydown. It was rather a relief. He would probably be as persistent as the deerstalker in canvassing potential members. She didn't want to join any of the groups. She felt fairly confident of making her own protest without the need to resort to violence.

It had been a very strange week.

Matt had been released from hospital the day after the Hennessey. Slight concussion and a dislocated shoulder, along with massive bruising, would put him out of action for some tune. Strangely, Jemima thought, Vincent had reacted extremely badly to this news. Maybe she'd misjudged him. Maybe he really did like Matt. She'd been touched by her father's concern and his apparent need to know every detail of Matt's progress.

To this end, Jemima had called at Matt's house most days, staying to chat and make tea. Matt had seemed grateful, but hadn't wanted to talk much. She wasn't surprised. She was just glad that they were friends again, the embarrassment of the non-seduction night a fading memory now.

Dragon Slayer, however, had fared far better than his jockey: once Matt had been dumped, he'd gone on riderless and beaten Bonne Nuit to the winning post by a short head.

Bonne Nuit actually winning the Hennessey had passed her by in a sort of blur. Gillian, who had one minute been weeping noisily about Matt, was

466

suddenly whooping joyously and had belted off to the winner's enclosure to congratulate Charlie.

The whole thing had become farcical after that. Drew had to remind Gillian that, firstly, she was not supposed to be in the winner's enclosure if she wanted to remain anonymous and, secondly, that as a vicar's wife she should refrain from chewing Charlie's face off. Tina had been strangely distracted, seeming more concerned about Matt's accident than Charlie's victory. Vincent and Maureen were practically doing cartwheels, but stopped when Jemima had said, rather frostily, that she hoped her father hadn't put any money on Bonne Nuit.

'Course not, duck,' Maureen had said quickly. 'We're just dead pleased for Charlie and Drew. That's all.'

Then Jemima had asked Drew where Matt was likely to be and had been directed to the medical centre. By the time she arrived he was being loaded into an ambulance. Tina, surrounded by a posse of paparazzi, was giving some sort of press statement. She'd raised an eyebrow as Jemima panted to a halt.

'It's all right. We don't both need to go with him.'

'No, we don't,' Jemima had said, pushing her way through the viewfinders and scrambling into the ambulance. Matt, still in his breeches and jersey, was blinking dazedly and stared straight through her.

'He'll be fine,' the paramedic said. 'Tough as old boots. Bit confused at the moment, I'd say, and bruised to buggery. Still, we'll whip him off to X-ray just to be on the safe side. Are you coming with him?'

467

'There's no need.' Tina had lifted her world-famous legs on to the top step. 'He's my responsibility. He was riding my horse.'

Recognising her, the paramedics ignored Jemima completely and started on further intricate explanations of the treatment he'd need. Jemima found herself bundled out of the ambulance with all the ceremony of someone putting out the weekly refuse sack.

'Mustn't crowd the patient,' they'd said, slamming the doors. 'Ring the hospital later for a progress report.'

Feeling completely out of sync, she'd drifted back to the winner's enclosure, because she had no idea what else to do. Charlie and Drew were being interviewed by Channel 4 Racing, and somehow Fizz Flanagan was in there too, looking bewildered.

'They think he owns the horse,' Gillian had said. 'I couldn't really say anything, could I? How's Matt?'

'They've taken him to hospital. Tina's gone with him.'

'Nice of her. Poor boy. That was quite a tumble.' She turned to Jemima and hugged her. 'Wasn't that just the most amazing thing you've ever seen?'

'Not really. I thought he was dead.'

'Not Matt, silly. They all fall at some time or another. No—I meant Charlie's win. Goodness! I couldn't believe it. I thought I'd just burst with excitement.'

And that, Jemima thought as she walked across Fernydown Common to take up a stance somewhere between the Greens and the woolly hats, was where the really peculiar part had kicked in. She had actually found it the most tremendous

468

experience of her life. The whole race, except the pile-up when so many horses went down and she'd felt sick, was completely thrilling. She hadn't removed her glasses as she had honestly thought she would. She had been riveted to every heart-thumping minute.

When the first horse fell she'd held her breath, stuffing her fingers into her mouth as others were caught up in the catastrophe and the crashing, slithering mass of legs gathered in momentum and size like an equine snowball. She'd prayed as the huge glossy bodies thumped to a turf-shuddering halt, and then prayed again as they'd scrambled unsteadily to their feet. True, the first prayers had been for the horses. But the second had been for Charlie and Matt.

As soon as she'd realised that both the black-and-white and vivid pink colours were still standing, or rather galloping, she had heaved a massive sigh of relief. She hadn't expected the surge of pride, watching Charlie and Matt as they raced neck and neck, athletic bodies crouched low in the saddle, leaning forward, pushing their muscles to breaking point. She hadn't expected to share the excitement of each forging step, each carefully calculated leap, each perfect landing. She hadn't expected the intensity of feeling—or the rush of lust.

She would rather have had her wisdom teeth extracted without anaesthetic than confess how turned on she'd been. Thankfully Matt's fall had acted like a cold shower. Thinking about it later, it had bothered her considerably that she, who hated everything to do with horse-racing, had found the whole thing so damned sexually arousing. Mulling it over late that night she'd come to the conclusion that she was simply getting old and sad and had been celibate for far too long . . . If she wasn't careful she'd be resorting to Maureen's libido kick-start of Fishnets and Cliff Richard videos.

The hunt was stirring. Jemima ducked her head. There would be plenty of time for Diana and Gareth and Kath to recognise her later, she decided. It was simply not good marketing policy to hurl herself across the Common and punch three of her best-spending customers. Right now she needed to get her bearings and control the mounting anger.

Horses were being turned round and reined in, and the hounds gathered together. The protesters immediately stopped chatting and raised their banners aloft. Jemima slid behind a large lady in a tweed mac and wondered what she was actually supposed to do. So far there had been no chanting or shouting as she had imagined there would be, just this sort of silent stand-off.

Suddenly things changed. The Greens, led by a stout girl with a mousy perm, hurled themselves across the Common towards the Pickled Newt's car park and stood in a defiant line across the gravelled track. The woolly-hat-and-mitten brigade dodged round them and tore off in the direction of the distant fields.

She tapped the lady in the mackintosh who had been shielding her, on the shoulder. 'What are they doing?'

'Aniseed trail,' she puffed, fumbling through various cavernous pockets. 'I've got mine all mixed up with my bloody hankie. Ah! Come along!'

'I haven't got any aniseed. I didn't bring sweets . . .'

'Good God!' The mackintosh had Jemima firmly

by the elbow and had struck up a smart jog. 'It's for the hounds. To throw them off the scent. You must be very new. Come along with me. I'll show you the ropes.'

The hunt were pretty angry by now, Jemima noticed, as they tried to edge their horses past the Greens without trampling on any of them. Bridles and bits jangled, and the MFH was brandishing his fist at the girl with the perm who was standing foursquare in his path, and turning almost as pink as his jacket. The Milton St John contingent glared fiercely at the delay as the hounds whirled themselves into balls of brindled excitement.

A distant horn echoed eerily across the dead winter fields, hanging like a mourning wail on the air. The hounds were instantly alert, then, ignoring the whipper-in, started to lope away in the direction of the noise.

'Millie and Frank,' the mackintosh said proudly. 'Well into their seventies. Been saboteurs for years. Frank can throw a whole pack off the scent better than anyone I know.'

The hunt were trying to recall the hounds, control their horses and get past the Greens at the same time. Jemima, who would have loved to watch, found herself dragged unceremoniously through a five-bar gate.

'Stand here,' the mackintosh commanded. 'And throw anything that comes to hand if the sods get through.'

Throw? Anything? 'But it might hurt the horses.'

The mackintosh looked pityingly at her. 'Grass. Twigs. Clods of earth. And not at the horses—at the bloody riders once they start moving. Anything to irritate them and slow their progress. Aim at their chests—we don't want any hospital cases just yet. You must have played cricket as a gel, surely?'

Jemima hadn't, but didn't feel it was the best time to admit it. The mention of hospitals, albeit in the future, was a little unnerving, too.

All around her the anti-hunting strategy was unfolding. The Greens had obviously delayed the start for as long as possible and were now involved in jeering and banner-waving. Those who didn't have banners made do with their fists, while the woolly hats misled the hounds and stirred up general confusion. Reynard's chums, as far as she could tell, did very little except stand and glower in a sinister fashion.

The hunt's foot followers were exchanging verbal blows with the Greens. As the horses were prancing prettily, and the hounds still yelping in the direction of Frank and Millie's hunting horn, nothing had happened yet.

'Gives the fox a chance to escape,' the mackintosh said. 'It's about all we can do really. That and let everyone know what our feelings are. We don't do violence but—' she nodded her headscarf towards the body-pierced brigade, 'they might.'

'And you don't approve?' Jemima, who was absolutely freezing, felt that as long as the violence was directed towards the hunt members and none of the horses or hounds got hurt, it probably wouldn't matter too much.

'No point in sinking to their level. It gets you nowhere with the press and that. Television has to be neutral, see. They can't afford to upset anyone, so for every shot of the fox being ripped to shreds they always show one of the hunt sitting blamelessly on their horses looking put-upon while the hoi-polloi run riot. And then there's letter-bombs and stuff like that. We don't want anything to do with that.'

Jemima didn't either. For the first time she began to question the wisdom of allowing Reynard to put up his poster. Maybe she should have contacted one of the more legally run groups. Had her collusion now marked her down as a potential terrorist as well as a purveyor of pornography in the village? It certainly wasn't an auspicious start to her first year in business.

'Now!' The mackintosh stooped down and tore at a handful of dried grass. 'They're getting through! Throw something! Now!'

Jemima, very doubtful about this tactic, wavered. The first phalanx of the hunt, having outmanoeuvred the Greens' road-block, was trotting towards the gate. The mackintosh hurled her tussock of grass with deadly accuracy. It hit Gareth James-Jordan neatly in the middle of his chest.

'Oh, I say!' He squinted down his long nose, then spotted Jemima. 'Oh, hello, there. Nice to see you again. Lovely day for it.'

'Years of bloody inbreeding,' the mackintosh snorted. 'I'm sure he doesn't know where he is half the time. Nice man really. Probably thinks he's out for a ride. Not her though!'

The next clump of grass bounced off Kath Seaward's shoulder. Jemima turned her head away quickly.

'Fucking antis!' Kath yelled as she trotted smartly through the gate. 'Should have been drowned at fucking birth!'

'You didn't throw,' the mackintosh said. 'You're not entering into the spirit at all.'

Half the hunt and most of the foot followers had got past the Greens and through the gate. Ignoring the banner-waving and the shouts, they streamed behind the hounds across the grey-baked furrows.

Why couldn't they just enjoy doing that, Jemima wondered, and not have to kill anything at the end of it?

Bugger!' The mackintosh was suddenly agitated. 'That looks like trouble.'

To Jemima it looked very much like Reynard. Wearing a sort of dung-coloured blanket and a Rasta hat, with his straggly beard splaying in the wind, Reynard had appeared from nowhere and was gesticulating wildly. The anarchists, obviously fired by the presence of their leader, had taken over where the Greens had failed. In a mass of ill-fitting jumpers and camouflage gear, they hurled themselves into the gateway, prostrating themselves across the path. The dozen or so riders behind Kath and the James-Jordans yanked their horses to a halt.

'Get down!' Reynard grabbed at Jemima's reefer jacket. 'Form a human shield and then kick out at the bastards!'

'Don't!' The mackintosh tugged at Jemima's other sleeve. 'They'll trample all over you! And you stop that! Stop!'

The body-pierced brigade had no intention of taking any notice. Those who weren't already on the ground were lashing out at anything in sight with a selection of broken-off branches, boots, and fists. Jemima, half on her knees next to Reynard, heard the wail of sirens.

'Fucking filth!' Reynard hissed through bad teeth and the tongue stud. 'Wasting pounds of taxpayers' money! Always on the side of the aristos! Bastards!'

The whole thing had turned very nasty. Jemima, shaking off Reynard's grubby grasp, scrambled to her feet and straightened her glasses. The mackintosh was nowhere to be seen. The Barbours were exchanging blows with the anarchists and the remaining members of the hunt had dismounted and joined in. The siren wail grew louder and the first police car bounced across the Common.

'Jemima!'

'Sod off!' Wanting to get as far away from Reynard as possible, she scrambled over the prone protesters. She had absolutely no intention of being arrested for public disorder. She wanted to save the fox, that was all. This violence, as far as she could see, was going to achieve nothing except a criminal record to go with her other misdemeanours.

'Jemima!'

It couldn't be Reynard—he didn't know her name. Ducking through the worst of the brawl, her heart almost stopping at the sight of three police cars disgorging their occupants, she squinted through the heaving mass.

Wearing a leather jacket and dark glasses, Charlie was beckoning to her from the Aston Martin. 'Come over here! Quick!'

Not on her life! He was on the other side. True, he wasn't in hunting pink—but he was a follower. And not even a foot follower. He was no doubt going to watch the kill in comfort. Against violence she may be, but she wasn't going to swap sides at the first sign of trouble.

'Jemima!' He leaned even further from the

window. 'You're doing no good here. Come on!'

She shook her head. The fighting was becoming more intense. There were bodies sprawled across the dead brown grass and on the Pickled Newt's gravelled forecourt. 'No wonder you were so against me putting up the poster! You're one of *them!'*

'I'm not one of anybody—and unless you want to get arrested or killed or both, just get into the bloody car.'

Reynard, having escaped from the punch-up in the gateway, was bearing down on her. Taking one look at the baseball bat which Reynard was trying to push into her hand, she leapt for the Aston Martin.

'Get in and hang on,' Charlie yelled, revving up and bouncing across the Common before she'd even closed the door.

Concertina'd in the passenger seat, her glasses digging into her forehead, she tried to maintain some dignity. It wasn't easy. Pinballing between the Aston Martin's well-worn leather seat and its roof she was pretty sure her bruises would soon rival Matt's. Eventually she managed to sit facing the right way round and untuck her boots from the hem of her skirt.

Once her spectacles were back in position, she glared across at Charlie. 'I can't believe you did that.'

'Did what?'

'Kidnapped me.'

As they were bouncing across the rutted field at 90, Charlie didn't look at her when he answered, 'I didn't bloody kidnap you. I rescued you from Trev Perkiss.'

'Who the hell is that?' Jemima's teeth clattered together with each juddering jolt.

'Your anti-hunting mate. Lives in a council house with his mum on the Tiptoe road. Reynard I believe he calls himself on these sorties. He's Colossus for the bypass punch-ups—Colossus of Roads—I don't think spelling was ever one of Trev's strong points. Oh, and he's also been known as Atlas on anti-nuke campaigns and he was Bes for his poll-tax rioting. Never one to keep all his gods in one basket is Trev.'

Jemima exhaled. 'He's a professional rabble-rouser?'

'He's a professional prat,' Charlie said kindly, swooping off the ruts and into a meadow surrounded by hawthorn bushes. 'Now hang on again and don't shout.'

She had no intention of shouting. The hunt were bearing down on them from the opposite direction: hounds and horses streamed up, over, and under gates, a vivid slash of colour against the bleak backdrop. A real view-halloo echoed through the rapidly closing afternoon.

'I can't believe you're doing this. Coming to watch the kill. You unprincipled bastard.'

Charlie grinned. 'I'm a jockey. I ride horses. We all hunt—remember?'

She itched to slap him. She would never speak to him again.

The MFH and Gareth practically dead-heated to a halt beside the Aston Martin.

'Over that way.' Charlie pointed in the direction they'd just come. 'Two fields. You should have the brush in no time.'

'Great. Good show. We thought he'd got away.'

They touched their caps and galloped off. The rest of the hunt followed in a frenzy of excitement.

'I hate you.' Jemima's eyes were filled with tears. 'I bloody hate you.'

'Part of the country scene, sweetheart.' Charlie started the car again. 'You chose to live here. Anyway, I always enjoy being in at the death.'

As the Aston Martin rocketed across the fields in the direction from which the hunt had come and the baying of hounds and the thunder-echo of hooves grew ever fainter, Jemima wondered if she could kill Charlie now and still survive.

'Okay.' The car almost stood on its nose. 'You can get out now. But quietly.'

She blinked. 'But they've gone the other way.'

'Have they?' Charlie unbuckled himself from the seat belt and scrambled from the car, opening her door. 'Now I wonder why?'

An elderly couple, wearing matching beige anoraks, emerged from the undergrowth picking hips and haws from their hair.

Charlie grinned. 'All okay?'

They exchanged conspiratorial smiles. 'Mr Fox has gone to ground safely. Back to the bosom of his family. He'll live a while longer yet. Your bit all right?'

'Piece of piss. Swallowed it like the brain-cell sharers they are. Gone belting back towards Fernydown following Enid's aniseed trail.' Charlie slid his arm casually round Jemima's shoulders. 'This is Jemima. She might be joining us. Jemima, meet Frank and Millie—leading lights in the local League Against Cruel Sports.'

Completely dumbfounded, Jemima could only shake her head. 'But—but—you said . . .'

'I lied. This isn't something I want made public knowledge for obvious reasons. I love animals. I detest cruelty. My grandfather was killed in a hunting accident—and I could never quite shake off the idea that he maybe deserved it.'

Frank and Millie looked slightly askance at this. Jemima sensed that the flippancy hid far deeper emotions.

'So you're not one of the huntin', shootin', fishin' brigade as everyone in the village thinks you are? But I—I thought that everyone involved in racing was involved in blood sports.'

'Not by a long way. You'd be surprised how many antis lurk beneath the surface. Anyway, my idea of sport is to give the contenders equal chances. When someone hands the fox a hunter-chaser, and gives him servants and hounds to boot, it might even things up a bit.' Charlie let his hand drop and grinned. 'I hope my secret's safe with you?'

God—how many more of Milton St John's secrets was she going to be asked to keep?

Who knows?' She smiled at him, wondering irrationally if she could yank his hand back up to her neck and kiss him. 'You'll just have to wait and see, won't you?'

CHAPTER THIRTY-TWO

'So then what happened?' Gillian wedged one of her many carrier bags beneath her chin while shoving the others under her arm, and attempted to light a cigarette. 'After he'd rescued you from the clutches of the Red Brigade?'

Jemima side-stepped the mass of last-minute Christmas shoppers in Upton Poges High Street. 'Nothing much. And although I don't want to sound really preachy, didn't your mother ever tell you it was slutty to smoke in the street?'

'Frequently. But as I'm giving up on New Year's Eve, I'm stockpiling on nicotine, so stop nagging.' Gillian inhaled deeply and came to a halt outside the doorway of Dorothy Perkins, much to the irritation of a scrum of women who were attempting to get in and buy a little black number for the Christmas festivities. 'Anyway, don't change the subject—what happened with Charlie?'

'Nothing, honestly.'

'Why was he there anyway? I didn't think he hunted locally. Well, not foxes, anyway.'

'He doesn't—well, he wasn't, not then, anyway. He'd just—um—come to have a look at the horses, I think.'

'What on earth for? He must have seen Diana and Gareth's hunters a thousand times.' Gillian paused to admire a slinky silver trouser suit in the window. 'It's more likely that he was there to lust over the women in their breeches. Still, I suppose it was lucky for you that he turned up at all. I warned you about getting involved with the liberationists, didn't I? Do you think silver would suit me?'

'Yes you did, and yes it would.'

Gillian frowned. 'I'm not so sure . . . I'll have to think about it. Oh, go on anyway. Tell me the rest. What happened when he got you into the Aston Martin?'

Jemima was beginning to wish she'd never mentioned the Fernydown escapade to Gillian at all. She'd been rattling on about it for ages.

And there really wasn't an awful lot more to tell. She had no intention of breaking her promise. If Charlie wanted her to keep his animal rights activities secret, then she was more than happy to do so. He had given her the address of the League Against Cruel Sports and she'd already sent off her application.

Reynard and several of his cronies had been arrested, and the MFH had been cautioned for public disorder after he'd kicked one of the woolly-hat crew. Charlie had certainly edged up several hundred per cent in her estimation, but because of her promise to him she could hardly wax lyrical, could she? Still, she'd have to tell Gillian something otherwise they wouldn't ever get past Dotty P's.

'Well, he pointed out the pitfalls of becoming involved with terrorists, and kindly drove me back to where I'd parked Floss, by which time the hunt were returning really miffed because they hadn't seen a single fox all day, and then we went home.'

'And?'

'And nothing. I came back to the Vicarage and he went back, no doubt, to Tina's rather bony embrace.'

Gillian sighed. 'Bloody hell. And he didn't try to seduce you at all? Didn't you ask him in?'

'Hardly. We were in convoy. We flashed lights and waved goodbye at the Peapods corner. Nothing more exciting than that. So—how many more presents have you got to get?'

Gillian stubbed out her cigarette with the toe of her Bally boot and consulted a list that looked about as long as the Gettysburg Address. Jemima, well wrapped against the frosty air, gazed at her reflection in the shop window. Brown hair, long brown coat, brown gloves, brown boots. Still, the vivid orange knitted scarf wound several times round her throat added a bit of colour. Not enough colour to make Charlie blink twice though, if that was the way Gillian's mind was working. And it obviously was.

She could hardly tell Gillian that her one sexual adventure in Milton St John had been so disastrous that there was no way she was going to risk being humiliated a second time. If Matt had found her so bloody unappealing, then Charlie's reaction—with his track record and pick 'n' mix selection of gorgeous women—would be a million times worse.

Gillian was still checking the list. '. . . and I've got gloves for my mother-in-law, and slippers for Glen's dad—my parents are easy—anything alcoholic—and the boys were sorted weeks ago—so I'm practically done. What about you?'

'Just got to get something pretty for Maureen. She and Dad are becoming quite an item. God knows what her husband makes of it. I've bought everything else.'

'You would have—you're so infuriatingly organised. I bet yours are all wrapped and labelled, too. I suppose you can just go and raid your shelves and buy your presents and up your profits at the same time. I'm sure that comes under the seven deadly sins.'

'People in glass houses, Gillian, remember? When exactly are you going to confess about your misdemeanours?'

'Which ones?'

'Bella-Donna Stockings and owning Bonne Nuit? Surely you'll have to tell Glen soon.'

'Glen's only just forgiven me for blurting out about Charlie and Lucinda at the wedding reception. I'm not sure that he could take any more revelations—specially not at Christmas. Maybe I should add confessions to my New Year resolutions.'

Jemima laughed. 'Yeah, and I can just see the headlines in the *Upton Poges Echo:* "Fishnets Fund Floozy's Filly".'

'Totally inaccurate.' Gillian smiled sweetly. 'I'm not a floozy and Bonnie Nuts is a boy. Now, tell me, what have you got for Matt?'

The strings of multicoloured lights rocked backwards and forwards across the High Street. 'God Rest Ye Merry Gentlemen' blared from the doorway of Computers R Us. Jemima continued to stare at the red and green and black and silver party outfits in Dorothy Perkins' window. Matt? Well, Matt was going home to Devon for Christmas in the hope that all his injuries would have healed in time for the January Grand National preparations. He hadn't mentioned Jemima going with him. He hadn't mentioned Christmas presents.

'A book, actually. And not from my shop, before you ask.'

She'd bought him a first edition collection of James Pollard racing prints, feeling that it would serve on all counts. It would prove that she was no longer totally against what he did for a living, while on the other hand it was impersonal enough to be given by a friend.

Gillian wrinkled her nose. 'Not very original. I thought you'd buy him massage oils or something really sexy.'

Jemima wanted to laugh. Sexy and Matt were

still poles apart. He obviously had no interest in her physically. If she'd had a brother they'd probably have the same sort of relationship which she and Matt enjoyed. She hoped that this break in Devon would signify the end of any pretence. They were friends—and nothing more. Thanks to the Hennessey fall they hadn't even been out together for weeks.

'Come on then.' Gillian grabbed her arm. 'Let's go and see what dear Dorothy has to offer in outsize lurid nighties. Something purple and see-through should suit Maureen nicely—not to mention your father.'

*   *   *

Two hours later, surrounded by carrier bags in the warmth of the Vicarage kitchen, Jemima drained her teacup and refused a refill. No, really. I want to finish my present-wrapping. And I'd better call in at the shop and check that Tracy is coping okay. And I've got to take Matt his present before he leaves for Devon tonight, and drop in at Peapods with Poppy Scarlet's stuff—just in case Maddy and Drew spend Christmas at the hospital. And I've still got to go and see Dad. We haven't sorted out who's going where for Christmas Day yet.'

You know you're more than welcome to come to us.' Gillian pulled a loop of tinsel from the depths of the bag and inspected it beneath the overhead fluorescent light. 'Honestly, every year I promise myself that I'll go Conran in Christmas decor. I swear I'll have the Vicarage themed in two colours, or tartan, or minimalism, or whatever is top-of-the-range trendy. And every year I get caught up in the

484

sparkly-tinsel-and-rainbow-bauble syndrome. Still, Leviticus and Ezekiel love it. So? Will you? You and Vincent come to us for Christmas Day?'

Jemima pushed thoughts of past Christmases to the back of her mind. The excitement when Rosemary and Vincent brought down the familiar cardboard boxes from the attic, the unwrapping of the glass balls, the snowmen, the tiny Santa Claus— and the Christmas-tree fairy which had belonged to her mother when she was a child. All familiar, all part of the magic. All long, long ago . . .

'It's really kind of you to invite us, but I think Dad and I would be better alone together. It's such a long time since we had Christmas in the same place. I'm looking forward to it.'

Gillian nodded with understanding. 'Well, we'll be here—in between services, of course—if you fancy a change. Naturally, Christmas is Glen's busy time—almost as bad as Easter. He gets absolutely frazzled, physically and spiritually, poor lamb. It's not just the celebration of The Birth and everything—he often has to mediate in dozens of domestic disputes over the holiday period. People in Milton St John don't seem to be able to spend more than forty-eight hours together without brawling.'

Jemima could quite believe it. She had a feeling, as she climbed the stairs to her flat, that the festive season in Milton St John would be unlike anything she'd ever experienced.

The whole village was already buzzing about the King George at Kempton Park on Boxing Day— when Dragon Slayer and Bonne Nuit would again be pitted against each other—and Kath Seaward had been spouting in the pub about giving the ride to a monkey after the way both Charlie and Matt had each handled her horse.

Then, Maddy's baby was due at any minute, and Bathsheba, Petunia and Bronwyn had temporarily halted their tirade against Fishnets and were currendy up in arms about the proposed rave—now known officially as the New Year Nuke—which was going ahead in the James-Jordans' marquee.

Lucinda, who was spending Christmas in Klosters with the Maxwell-Dunmore family, had sworn to be home for the New Year. She'd phoned Jemima and said she wouldn't miss Milton St John's first ever rave not even for the promise of a long lie-in with Ronan Keating. Tina, it was rumoured, was holidaying in the Virgin Islands— which everyone thought highly inappropriate—but at least it would leave Charlie with fewer options. And Matt, of course, would be in Devon—which would leave Jemima with no options at all.

*   *   *

With light spilling out of its leaded paned windows, the bookshop looked very Dickensian in the afternoon darkness. It was humming nicely. There was still a stream of customers seeking stocking fillers, and the holly and ivy decorations made it appear even more cosy and comfortable. The sofa and beanbags were occupied and 'Rudolph the Red-Nosed Reindeer' tinkled through the sound system. Tracy, who had co-opted her two eldest children as wrappers and shelf-fillers, insisted that she could manage perfectly well for the rest of the afternoon as she knew Jemima had loads of other things to do.

486

Jemima sighed heavily. Saying goodbye to Matt was probably going to be exactly that—and asking her father about Christmas Day was going to be opening another can of worms—she was sure of it. The problem wasn't only Vincent's continued friendship with Maureen in Brian's absence—although, God knows, that was bad enough—but she was still convinced that there was something bothering him.

He had been shifty for weeks. And he had far too much money. Jemima was pretty sure that he was gambling again—but if he was, he must be using a completely different system. This one seemed to have a no-lose factor built in.

Waving gratefully to Tracy, she hesitated outside the shop. Which way to go first? Matt or Vincent? She opted for Matt and headed towards the High Street. Then at least if she got over-emotional at the parting—which she doubted, but you never knew what Christmas could do to you—she could go and cry on her father's shoulder. And, of course, she had to go to Peapods anyway with Poppy's present, so it wouldn't look as though she was checking up on Vincent, would it?

It took her five minutes to reach Matt's house. Since being incapacitated by the fall at Newbury, he had given her a front-door key. She'd been meaning to give it back now that he was fully mobile. She would leave it on the hall table this afternoon. She was pretty sure she wouldn't need it again.

Unlocking the door, she walked through the undecorated hall into the equally undecorated living room. Matt, going back to Devon for Christmas, must have decided to pass on the festive glitz. He hadn't even put up his Christmas cards.

To her surprise, Matt wasn't alone.

'Jem, love!' Vincent stood up as Matt, his shoulder unstrapped for the first time, tried to stagger to his feet from the sofa. 'I—we—weren't expecting to see you.'

That much was obvious. What the hell was Vincent doing here? He didn't like Matt much, did he?

'I was going to come and see you later, anyway, so it's quite handy.' She kissed her father's cheek before bending to kiss Matt in their usual fraternal fashion. 'So, what brings you round here? Getting some racing tips from the horse's mouth, so to speak?'

Matt blinked and looked uncomfortable. Vincent, who had half a tumbler of whisky beside him, looked even more so. She sat down on the sofa without being asked. Matt, who was obviously in the middle of packing, sat down again beside her. Neither of them said anything.

'Dad, I was joking—I know you've given up gambling. You didn't even look at the bookies at Newbury, did you? I was so proud of you. Gillian's giving up smoking as her New Year resolution. I wonder what I should give up?'

Well, not sex for a start—or men. Eating and drinking seemed favourites. Right at the moment breathing might be a good idea. They both stared at her as if she were demented. She fished around frantically for something else to say. Vincent and Matt seemed to be exchanging wild eye-meets. God—of course. It was probably some Christmas present conspiracy! One—or both—of them had bought her something and was seeking the other's approval. The gift was probably somewhere in the room and they were terrified that she'd spot it. She'd done that with her mother over Vincent's presents years ago . . .

Two suitcases were taking up most of the floor space, and clothes, neatly folded, were stacked on the table. There was a marked absence of wrapping paper, she thought. Maybe the Garsides weren't big on family present-giving. She could just see one long thin box wrapped in silver and gold paper peeping from a corner of the nearest case. Probably something for Matt's mum. Maybe, like most men, he would finish the rest of his shopping in a Christmas Eve rush in Exeter or somewhere tomorrow.

'You're all ready then, Matt?' She had to say something. Her voice sounded over-jolly. Like a nurse speaking to an elderly patient. 'I've left my key on the hall table—and here's your present. No peeking until Christmas morning!'

There—that had brought it out into the open. One or both of them were bound to laugh and be embarrassed and mutter about hers not being wrapped yet but there were still two days to go and—

'Er—right.' Matt took the robin-and-holly parcel and looked stricken. 'Thanks ever so much. Um—I'm afraid I haven't bought you a present. I haven't been able to get out and—'

'That's okay. I understand. No problem . . .'

That knocked the present theory on the head then. Feeling increasingly manic, she started to ramble about her shopping trip with Gillian. It was quite clear that nobody was listening. She wished Matt would offer her a drink, or that she felt sufficiently at home in his house to simply help

489

herself. And she was dying to know why her father was there.

'Gillian's invited us for Christmas.' She looked hopefully at Vincent. 'I said thanks—but I thought we'd be better on our own. I'll roast you a turkey portion to go with my nut cutlet. We just have to decide whether it's to be at your cottage or my flat.'

Vincent grinned sheepishly. 'Ah—I've been meaning to say something about that, Jem, love. Maureen has invited me to hers, actually. What with her Brian being on the Greek run—there's loads of business over Christmas for drivers who don't necessarily want to be at home, you see . . .'

Jemima stared. Bloody hell! So where did that leave her? Alone. Again. At Christmas. She wanted to cry.

Matt patted her knee. 'You'll be able to spend the day with Gillian and Glen and the boys, though, won't you? It'll be lovely.'

It would be absolutely appallingly awful.

'I can't wait.'

She hated them both. What the hell did they care? Both the men who professed to be important in her life had made plans that excluded her. Well, sod them! In two minds as to whether she should snatch Matt's book back and say it had all been a terrible mistake, she stood up. 'Well, I'm glad that's sorted out. I hope you have a lovely time, Matt. And happy Christmas. No, don't bother seeing me out. I'll find my own way.'

'Jemima—' Vincent was on his feet. 'I'll come round and see you later. I can always cancel going to Maureen's.'

She shook her head. He couldn't. She really wouldn't want him to. They'd both had a rough time in recent years. If her father was going to be happy—albeit with someone else's wife—who was she to deny him?

'No. You have a great time. I'll see you tomorrow anyway for the present-swapping and everything. And maybe you and Maureen could pop round to the flat on Christmas night for supper or something?'

'She'd like that.' Vincent sounded as though someone had just told him he'd won the lottery. 'We both would.'

'And I'll be back in the New Year.' Matt looked as though this would solve the world's problems at a stroke. 'Shame I'll miss the Nuke though. You'll have to tell me all about it.'

'I don't think anyone over sixteen is planning on going.'

'Charlie is.' Matt had kicked her present under the sofa. 'He's taking Lucinda.'

'I thought he'd be on holiday with Tina.' Jemima was still edging towards the hall.

Now what had she said? The atmosphere had changed again. Both Matt and her father were trying hard not to look at each other. 'Um—is that something we shouldn't talk about?'

'Of course not,' Matt said jovially. 'It's just that he's booked to ride in the King George on Boxing Day—and then again at Cheltenham on New Year's Day. He's jealous that I'm able to have a holiday and he isn't. He got really pissed off when I told him he'll have to stay sober on New Year's Eve.'

She supposed he would. Matt would no doubt be getting legless with his family on scrumpy or something. Vincent was smiling again too. She must have imagined the constraint. She crossed the room again and kissed Matt's cheek. ''Bye then. Have a good one.'

'You too.' He didn't kiss her back. 'And I'll see you next year.'

And that, she thought as she wandered outside, digging her hands deeper into her pockets and watching her breath spiral in plumes beneath the street lamps, was almost definitely that.

So Matt hadn't bought her a present—so what? Was she gracious enough to believe in the old adage of it being better to give than to receive? Not a bloody chance. Not in this case, anyway.

She was desperate to know why Vincent had been in Matt's house. And had been there for some time by the look of it. Relaxing by the imitation gas logs with a glass of whisky. Just what the hell was going on?

*   *   *

It was one of the first questions she asked Maddy when she was sitting beside the fire in Peapods' kitchen nursing a massive glass of Chablis in one hand and a plate of oven-warm mince pies in the other.

Maddy, absolutely enormous and looking stunning, managed to lodge herself in the rocking chair. 'Not a clue. Vincent has never seemed to like Matt much. I'd have thought, like you, that it might be a Christmas surprise they were planning between them.' She looked hopeful. 'Maybe it still is?'

'Absolutely not.' Jemima bit into a mince pie. 'God—how do you manage this in your condition?

I couldn't make anything half so good. I bet you could outdo Delia even in labour.'

'Don't you believe it.' Maddy hauled herself to her feet again and stretched. 'When I was having Poppy, cooking was the last thing on my mind. Vengeance and retribution were uppermost. I wanted to kill everyone—especially Drew. You wait until it's your turn.'

She'd be waiting a long time, Jemima mused as she relaxed back in her chair. Poppy had been taken to Fran's for the evening while Maddy and Drew pretended to be Santa's elves and decorated Peapods. Maddy's parents would be arriving in the morning ready to take over at the first twinges.

She looked around at the happy chaos: at the warmth and light and untidiness of busy family living. This was what she wanted. Maddy's contentment. She'd pass on the babies, of course, but she'd happily settle for the rest.

'You don't know how lucky you are.'

'I do. Believe me, I do. Still, you're not doing so badly, are you? You're over your dislike of racing, your shop is a stonking success, you've beaten Bathsheba Cox hands down, *and* you've got Matt. Not bad for less than a year in the village.' Maddy tucked Jemima's presents for Poppy into a box with several others on one of the dresser shelves. 'Thanks so much for these. It's very kind of you. I only hope my son allows me to hang around long enough to watch her opening them.'

'You know it's a boy?'

'Drew and I both think it is. Poppy thinks it's a dinosaur. She's pretty hooked on Godzilla at the moment. Finish up the mince pies. I've made dozens just in case. Another drink?'

She'd left Floss at the Vicarage—and was in no hurry to return to her empty flat—so she accepted happily. If only she could be spending Christmas—and the rest of her life—somewhere like this. With someone like Drew. Well, not Drew, of course. But someone who really and truly loved her.

Oh, God. What had happened to all her independent feminist principles? It was the Christmas syndrome, she supposed. All this happy togetherness and merry families and feel-good seasonal propaganda. It made her feel lonely every year. It was just a bit more acute this time.

'Are things all okay now? Oh, I know you and Drew are ecstatic, but with Peapods?'

'Bonnie winning the Hennessey has put a few more presents under the Christmas tree,' Maddy grinned. 'Complete survival depends on him winning the National, of course. I know Drew will have to give up the National Hunt side next year whatever happens. But a yard that sends out a Grand National winner can bank on getting plenty of interest from other owners. I suppose, putting it baldly, complete survival is all down to Charlie and Bonnie in April.'

Quite a responsibility. She hoped they'd win. Was that disloyal to Matt? She knew how desperately he and Kath wanted to win, too. And Bonne Nuit's triumph at Newbury may have helped Peapods, but it had caused quite a few headaches at St Saviour's. She smiled to herself, remembering Gillian's frantic coded telephone calls to the bank as she tried to move her money about without Glen discovering.

'Why the smirk?'

'Nothing—' Jemima shrugged. 'I was just

494

thinking about Gillian.'

'Being Bonnie's owner?' Maddy giggled. 'Yes, I do know. Drew told me on our wedding night. I wasn't sure if you knew.'

'I think it is one of the village's better-kept secrets. God knows what'll happen when Glen finds out.'

'Murder at the vicarage!' Maddy's eyes sparkled. 'Actually, more intriguing, is where she got the money to buy the horse. Drew says she's loaded—but even he doesn't know where it came from. Have you got any ideas?'

'Mad!' Drew's voice echoed through from the sitting room. 'Mad! I can't get these bloody fairy lights to work! Have we got another set?'

'Excuse me a sec. Drew's absolutely lousy with anything technical. He'll probably burn the house down. Help yourself to more booze . . .'

Jemima watched as Maddy waddled out into the hall, then closed her eyes. Saved by the fusing fairy lights. The way she felt tonight she'd probably have told Maddy about Bella-Donna Stockings. The dogs were wheezing in their sleep in front of the fire. The cats were holding a purring contest on top of the range. Somewhere, from a distant wireless, carols were playing.

The waft of ice-cold air as the back door flew open was like being drenched by a bucket of water.

'Mad! Any chance of a mince pie if I promise faithfully to live in the sauna until Kempton?' Charlie stopped and looked at her, then at the plate of flaky pastry remains. His eyes widened. 'Bloody hell—you haven't eaten all of them, have you?'

'Every last one.' Jemima eased herself upright in her chair, hoping that she hadn't smudged her mascara, or got crumbs caught anywhere. 'Maddy and Drew are playing with the fairy lights.'

'Better leave them to it, then.' Charlie sat in Maddy's rocking chair and shrugged out of his leather jacket. 'Drew's shit hot with practical things and horses but he's crap with electricity. Mad'll sort him out. Have you really eaten all the pies?'

'They're in the bottom oven.'

'Brilliant.' Charlie squatted down in front of the range. 'Do you want some more?'

Why not? She handed him her plate. She tried very hard not to stare at the lean thighs beneath the stretched denim, or the powerful shoulders under the sweater. 'Er—what are you doing for Christmas?'

'Eating nothing and drinking less and hoping I can make eleven stone wringing wet for Kempton.' Charlie plonked the piled plate back on her lap and retook the rocking chair. 'How about you?'

'No plans.' She tried not to mumble through the crumbs. 'Well, Gillian and Glen have invited me to spend the day with them, and Dad and Maureen are coming round in the evening.'

'Not seeing Matt?'

'He's going back to Devon.'

'Prat.' Charlie demolished a pie in two bites and reached for another. 'Are you and he still—you know?'

'Probably not. We'd reached a bit of an impasse. I think we might have finished tonight, actually.'

'You're not sure?'

She shook her head. She was never sure of anything in the relationship with Matt. She wasn't even sure there had been one. Charlie, she noticed, was smiling. Sod him. He probably found it really amusing that she couldn't even hang on to Matt.

'Can I give you some advice?' He leaned forward. His hair gleamed in the fireglow. His eyes were surprisingly gentle.

'As long as it's not a lecture on my fox-hunting cronies. I've learned my lesson.'

'If you and Matt pick up again when he comes back after Christmas, don't trust him too much. I'm not sure that he's ready for a permanent relationship.'

'And you think I am?' She laughed. 'You think I'm trying to tie him down to a house and a mortgage and a wedding ring and kids? God, Charlie. Get a life. I have far more important things to do with my future.'

He didn't seem in the least taken aback. 'I'm sure you have, lust keep an eye on him—and don't let him spend too much time with your father.'

Christ! There *was* something going on and Charlie knew!

Hello.' Maddy thumped back into the kitchen. 'I didn't hear you arrive. Drew's just finished the tree so we're going to have supper. Will you both stay?'

Sorry, I can't.' Charlie stood up. 'I only popped round to drop off Poppy's present. It's in the outhouse. I've got to fly over to Lambourn. Nicky Henderson's having a party. I'll be around tomorrow if you need hot water and towels and something to bite on. 'Bye, Jemima.'

*   *   *

Hours later, after she'd eaten an enormous Peapods supper and Drew had driven her home, Jemima curled beneath her duvet. She closed her eyes and started to drift, memories of the day flickering in and out of her semi-consciousness. The bustle and the laughter and the noise and the colour of Christmas had been everywhere. And people were different. More cheerful. And Charlie . . . She thought a lot about Charlie these days. And she really would have to ask him what he'd meant. Or maybe she'd ask Vincent. Oh, please God, don't let it be anything to do with gambling . . .

Jesus!

She was instantly awake. Among her replay memories was Matt's room. The suitcases, the neatly folded clothes, the single present for his mother . . .

Why the hell, she wondered, if Matt was going back to his family's farm in Devon, had his passport been on the top of his suitcase?

CHAPTER THIRTY-THREE

Vincent wrapped the last present and mummified it with Sellotape. They all looked the same—sort of long and lumpy. He'd never had a deft touch with a parcel—he'd always left that sort of thing to Rosemary—and latterly, of course, there had been no money for living, let alone gifts. This year, he thought with satisfaction, it was going to be different.

The radio was warbling 'White Christmas'. Vincent peered out of his window. It might just be. He hoped not. He didn't want Kempton to be snowed off.

Christmas Eve. He glanced across the cobbles

towards Peapods. It was racing's day of rest with no meetings anywhere, but the horses had been exercised and fed as normal, and he'd swept the yard. His fingers had been numbed by the biting wind as he'd clutched the broom and he'd been glad to defrost with a well-rummed coffee. Maddy was still at home, although her parents and Suzy had arrived a couple of hours earlier. He wondered if the baby would be born on time—unlike Jemima who'd had him and Rosemary on tenterhooks for three agonisingly long days after her expected birth date.

God, he'd been so proud on that day. So bloody happy. It was all very long ago. Another lifetime.

He pulled himself away from sentimental wallowing. He'd lost one good life—through no fault of his own, really—and he'd started to build another one. He had no intention of losing that. Perhaps what they were doing was morally wrong— but then he wasn't *forcing* Matt Garside to cheat, was he? Ned was doing that. Just as Ned was forcing his collusion. Nasty little phrases gleaned from *The Bill*—like accessory and collaborator and conspirator—all bubbled to the surface. Vincent pushed them down and slammed the lid. No point in thinking like that. What was done was done—he just had to make the best of it. And after the Grand National he'd confess to everyone and everything would be fine.

Having sorted out this dilemma, at least for the present, Vincent switched off the radio. The rest of the day stretched pleasurably ahead. Well, not all pleasurably. He was meeting Ned Filkins for a lunchtime drink in the Cat and Fiddle. He wasn't looking forward to that much, to be honest, but he never liked to cross Ned—just in case.

Still, at least Maureen's part of the day would be lovely. With Brian and his lorry in Greece, she'd invited him to call round for Christmas Eve drinks and stay over. It would be the first time. He hoped it wouldn't be the last. He knew she had no intention of leaving her husband, and he honestly didn't want her to. This arrangement suited them both nicely. He wasn't a hundred per cent sure what Jemima made of it, but even her disapproval wouldn't stop him.

And the Milton St John jungle drums had failed to pick up on the liaison—at least as far as he could tell. Maybe it was because he and Maureen were hardly Clark Gable and Vivien Leigh. Maybe the stout middle-aged weren't supposed to have desires stirring their sluggish hormones. Maybe it was simply that there were far more juicy titbits on offer.

Titbits like Matt. If that ever got out . . . Vincent groaned aloud and poured another dollop of rum into his coffee. He'd promised himself not to think about it until after Christmas. The whole thing had got right out of control. And Jemima walking in on them yesterday—Christ! He hadn't known what to say. And Matt, the cool, cruel bastard—Vincent stopped. No, he wasn't. Not either of those things. Not really.

Matt had been caught up in the web of his own deceit—exactly as he had. The more you struggled, the more entangled you became. Still, one thing was clear—the accident during the Hennessey had been precisely that. There was no way that Matt would have managed anything quite so spectacular. Ned Filkins had been jubilant over the Oscar-winning fall—but Vincent had been there. He'd been sure it was genuine. He'd been sure that Matt—against all orders and risking his reputation—would have gone on to win that race. And now he'd spoken to him, he *knew* that he would.

Now it was down to Charlie and Bonne Nuit to beat Dragon Slayer at Kempton. Kath Seaward had replaced Matt with Liam Jenkins again, who was nowhere near as good. Ned was convinced that Dragon Slayer would make a further poor showing, possibly be scratched from Cheltenham altogether, and be in the National at an incredibly good price.

There was of course one way out of all this. It was something he and Matt had discussed yesterday. It involved being very brave and very strong and risking everything—but at least they'd be free from Ned Filkins' blackmailing grip. If they both came clean about their misdemeanours to everyone who mattered, he would have no further hold. They'd decided against it.

Telling all. How could he? How could Matt?

Oh, God. Matt. Well, at least he knew what Matt's problem was now. It had sickened him to his stomach. Thank God that Jemima had no idea. Vincent had become very angry at this point, and demanded to know whether Jemima had come to any harm.

Matt had said that no, she hadn't. It didn't work that way. Matt told him everything. It had shocked Vincent rigid. He'd always considered himself to be a man of the world—but he had no idea that these sort of things went on. And among seemingly respectable people, too. He'd shuddered at the thought of the degradation. Bloody Matt. It was all his fault. If he'd kept his evil, corrupt habits under control, then he, Vincent, wouldn't be in this mess now.

Okay, so Ned knew about his own fiddles and the gambling and the debts. But that was positively *clean* compared to this other stuff, wasn't it? There was no comparison between his addiction and Matt's. No comparison at all.

Vincent had insisted that Jemima should be kept completely in dark—and that Matt must end their relationship as soon as possible. Then all he had to do was explain to Tina Maloret. Vincent winced. He wasn't too happy about that bit. Especially as Tina Maloret was also embroiled with Charlie. How long would it be before someone discovered what was going on? Christ! Still, Matt had assured him that he could handle it—and her. He'd just have to trust him.

And the Aintree scam? Well, as far as they both could see, that would go ahead. Matt was adamant on that point. He'd win the National. Even if it meant injuring Charlie to do it. Matt had a whole tree of chips on his shoulder. Winning the National was the only way he would ever hack his way free of them.

Vincent glanced at his watch. Nearly midday. He might as well go to the pub and get it over.

*   *   *

Ned was waiting for him, a pint of bitter at the ready. Vincent squeezed himself between the crowds—the place was packed with stable lads drinking themselves silly on their day off—and sat down. 'O Come All Ye Faithful' played in rap time made conversation impossible.

'Garside buggered off to the bosom of his family, has he?' Ned yelled in between verses. 'Did what you were told? Saw him on his way?'

Vincent nodded.

'Good on yer, Vince, mate.' Ned dug into the back pocket of his trousers. 'Here's your Christmas bonus, then. Don't spend it all at once.'

Vincent blinked at the wad of notes. Oh, God! He wasn't a saint. He couldn't give this up. Ned, despite being a ferret-faced bastard, had never let him down. This was so, so easy. He'd done his bit anyway, long before he realised it. He'd given away the information from Peapods that Ned had needed. This was simply the return. He couldn't do any more harm now, thank goodness. There was nothing left to do but to sit back and wait for the Grand National.

The juke-box burst into a reggae version of 'Silent Night'.

'Sorry.' Vincent grabbed at his pint and stood up. 'I can't cope with this. Coming through to the Snug?'

Ned trotted behind him. The Snug was also packed but the cannibalised carols were mercifully muffled.

'Got to be making tracks,' Ned said, draining his Guinness. 'I'm going to me sister and her family for Christmas.'

Vincent stared. It seemed incongruous—Ned, with all his unscrupulous fiddles, sitting down like everyone else on Christmas morning and unwrapping presents with his family, eating a massive celebratory dinner, and probably dozing in front of the Queen during the afternoon. Vincent hadn't really considered that felons had holidays

503

too.

'So,' Ned held out a skinny hand and pumped Vincent's arm chummily. 'Season's greetings an' all that, Vince, mate. Thanks for your backing. All we have to do now is sit tight until April and collect our dosh. See you in the New Year. And,' he tapped the side of his greasy nose, 'mum's the word.'

Vincent nodded like an automaton, wanting to wrench his hand free. As soon as Ned had gone he'd go into the gents' loo and scrub every trace of the bastard away. In the meantime he bought himself another pint, wondered what the hell Vicar Glen would make of Fizz Flanagan's version of 'Away in a Manger', and thought happily of Maureen.

*   *   *

Half an hour later he wandered back over Peapods' cobbles. He'd passed the bookshop—Jemima had waved to him from behind her still-busy counter, so they were still friends—and popped his head round the door of the Munchy Bar. Maureen, serving fry-ups to those who knew they had a week of cooking ahead of them, gave him a wink and a thumbs-up. He grinned to himself. The women in his life were well and happy. He'd go home and sleep for an hour, then start distributing his presents round the village. He'd given Maddy and Drew and Poppy theirs the previous day, so he'd start out at the James-Jordans' place and work inwards.

He was quite keen to glean whatever information was going about the New Year Nuke, to be honest. He'd never been to a rave before. The nearest he'd got was the Shepton Mallett Blues Festival in the sixties. He wondered if it was similar. Maureen might quite enjoy it.

'Vincent! Quick!'

Drew was belting across the yard towards him. Drew never ran. Not in the yard. He never shouted either.

'What's up?'

'The baby!' Drew grabbed his arm. 'She's started having the baby.'

'Wonderful—I didn't see you take her in—'

'I didn't. I haven't. She's in the kitchen!'

'You'd better get a move on then. You bring the car round and I'll go and see what I can do.' He tried to remember what had happened with Jemima. It was all pretty hazy. 'Er—have you phoned the hospital to say you're on your way?'

'Of course I fucking have! But there's no time! Come on!'

Vincent smiled to himself as they ran back across the cobbles and under the clock arch. Bless him. Drew was just as excited as he had been all those years ago. Still, this was his second. You'd think he'd be a bit more calm about it. He followed him through the outhouse and into the kitchen.

'Christ!' On second thoughts . . .

Vincent took one look at Maddy sprawled in the rocking chair and nearly fainted.

'Hi . . .' she panted through gritted teeth and a tangle of hair. 'Drew's-a-bastard.'

'Can't we get her into bed or something?' He looked at Drew. 'And where the hell is everyone else?'

'I'm-not-bloody-moving,' Maddy puffed. 'Don't-touch-me.'

'Maddy's parents and Suzy have taken Poppy

505

into Newbury to see Father Christmas.' Drew knelt by the rocking chair, holding both of Maddy's clenching hands and wincing. 'She said nothing was happening. She said she'd be fine for days yet. Not even a twinge . . .'

'It-wasn't-like-this-with-Poppy—Oh, shit!'

'Second ones are usually quicker,' Vincent said, remembering something he'd read in one of Rosemary's magazines. 'Um—shall I get Charlie?'

'No!' Drew and Maddy yelled together.

'He's gone to Newbury with the others.' Drew smoothed Maddy's hair away from her face. 'Remember to breathe. It's all right, darling. It's all right . . .'

'It's-not-bloody-all-right-you-bastard!'

Grimacing against the scream, Vincent belted out into the hall. Phone—where was the bloody phone? He punched out 999 and asked for an ambulance. Maddy screamed again from the kitchen. He felt very sick.

The calm voice on the other end said cheerfully that the ambulance had already been contacted and would be there as quickly as possible, but due to an RTA on the A34 there may be some delay.

'But the baby's coming!' Vincent howled. 'Get an ambulance!'

The calm voice asked questions which he couldn't answer, then suggested that maybe Drew would be more use.

Vincent swung round the kitchen door. 'Drew—speak to the woman on the phone! She's giving instructions! I'll stay here!'

'Piss-off!' Maddy spat. 'I-hate-fucking-men!'

When Jemima had been born he'd stayed outside the delivery room. He had paced up and down

506

with the other expectant fathers who were not yet new enough men to be standing at the foot of the bed with a camcorder. All his information on the techniques of childbirth had been gleaned from television. Mostly from Westerns. The women always seemed to have their wrists tied to brass bedsteads, wear a lot of petticoats, and still have their boots on.

Towels . . . hot water . . . something to wipe her forehead . . . No, possibly not. Maddy looked like she'd bite him if he tried that. He squatted beside her.

'You should be lying down.'

I-should-be—kneeling—in—a—birthing—pool—with—whale—music—so—sod—off. Oooh!'

Taking one frantic look, Vincent shepherded all the animals into the outhouse and slammed the door. As gently as he could, he lifted Maddy out of the chair and laid her on the floor beside the fire. He wasn't sure if it was hygienic—it just seemed that being doubled up in the rocking chair must only increase the pain. Surprisingly, she offered very little resistance.

He pushed cushions under her head and tried to avert his gaze from the bare legs.

'Thanks-and-I-think-I'm-going-to-be-sick.'

God—he flew back to the doorway. Drew, still on the phone, was writing things on the back of an envelope and muttering words like dilations and timed contractions and bearing down and pushing and not pushing and panting.

Shit. It was far too complicated. He ran back into the kitchen and knelt beside Maddy who'd stopped shouting and had her eyes closed. Oh, my God! Had she passed out?

507

Her eyes shot open and her teeth bared and she yelled. Just once. Vincent heard Drew drop the phone. Christ! The baby's head was there! Somewhere above Maddy's groans and laboured breathing he could hear 'Silent Night' playing as Drew belted in from the hall. At least it was the authorised version.

'Keep pushing.' Vincent closed his eyes and went in blind. He'd die if he hurt her. 'Maddy—don't cry—I think—I think I've got it—oh!'

He sat back with amazement, tears streaming down his face. The slithering, bloodied, tiny body was squirming in his hands. Drew, laughing and crying and still holding his notes, picked it up and laid it on Maddy's chest.

The room seemed strangely quiet. Then the baby yelled.

'It's a boy,' Drew was weeping unashamedly. 'A boy . . .'

Vincent swallowed as they cried together, and tried to stand up. His legs were far too wobbly so he sat on the hearth-rug again. It was the most amazing moment of his entire life.

'Do we have to cut the cord?'

'The midwife's about two minutes away.' Drew was stroking Maddy's hair and kissing her and telling her how much he loved her. 'She'll take over—and thank you. Thank you so much . . .'

Clutching at the table for support, Vincent hauled himself to his feet. Maddy smiled sleepily up at him. 'You were brilliant. Thanks a million.'

'You did all the hard work. No, no I'll leave you alone together. It's all right—'

Drew, still gazing at the baby and Maddy in complete disbelief, touched Vincent's arm. 'We'll never be able to thank you enough for this.'

Vincent sniffed. 'Don't be daft. You'd have managed fine without me. I'll go and see if the midwife has arrived—or the ambulance. Point them in the right direction . . .'

Vincent absent-mindedly patted the animals on his way through the outhouse, and watched as the midwife's hatchback screeched to a halt and she bustled under the clock arch. The ambulance wouldn't be too far behind. They'd all be all right now. Maddy and Drew and the baby. They'd be fine.

He wiped his hand across his eyes, feeling the tears trickle through his fingers.

*   *   *

'It was wonderful,' he said for the thousandth time, curled against Maureen's back, his arm resting comfortably across her ample waist. 'One of the most incredible moments of my life.'

'I'm glad you said one of them.' Maureen turned beneath the candyfloss-pink duvet and smiled at him in the semi-darkness. 'It's been quite a Christmas Eve, duck, what with one thing and another, hasn't it?'

It had. It truly had.

He traced the plaited ribbons in Maureen's peach nightie. 'I'll never forget today as long as I live.'

'Nor will I.' She snuggled against him, sweet-smelling, warm, comforting. 'I reckons this is what Christmas is all about, duck, don't you?'

Sleeping with someone else's wife? Hardly. Vincent blinked a bit in the low glow of the pink tiffany lamp. Maureen nudged him playfully. 'Not that! Just all the friendships, and the closeness, and being together. And the baby. That about put the icing on it.'

Vincent sighed happily. Daragh Vincent Fitzgerald was spending his first night under Peapods' roof. They'd taken Maddy and the baby into hospital for a check-up, and Drew had brought them home just after eight. He'd managed to poke his head round the door of the Cat and Fiddle, give everyone an update, say that the drinks were on him, and was kissed by every woman in the place before going home to his family.

Vincent cuddled a bit more into Maureen's billowy warmth. It was sheer bliss. She moved her face closer to his on the frilly turquoise pillow, the blonde hair splayed out like a manic halo. 'Jemima seemed really pleased to be coming to us tomorrow, didn't she, duck?'

Vincent nodded. She had. He'd thought that she might turn him down after the hoo-ha at Matt's, but she'd seemed rather pleased to have been asked. It would be lovely to be all together—Christmas Day was no time to be alone. He was going to collect her from the Vicarage really early and they'd all go to morning service—at Maureen's insistence—and then back to the Munchy Bar's flat for the rest of the day.

Maureen had a fibre-optic Christmas tree which glowed in a constantly changing rainbow, and the presents had been stacked under it. Cards were festooned round the walls like a washing-line, and the larder and fridge doors were straining at their hinges. He'd have Jemima and Maureen, food, drink, warmth, and happiness. Vincent couldn't have wished for anything more.

'Just one thing,' Jemima had said. 'Tomorrow I don't want to talk about Matt. I don't want to spoil Christmas. But there are things we need to discuss, Dad, aren't there?'

Vincent had fudged a bit and muttered about things not being all they seemed, and Jemima had stopped him with one of her looks.

'I don't know why you were at Matt's and I don't know where he's gone. I'm sure you'll have a really good explanation, won't you?'

He'd tried saying something about just popping into Matt's for a Christmas drink and Matt going home to Devon—which was true, as far as he knew—and she shouldn't be so suspicious. Jemima had smiled sadly and walked away from him.

He groaned softly in the darkness. He was going to tell her. Oh, not tomorrow. Not on Christmas Day. And not all of it—he couldn't do that. But before Matt came back to Milton St John, he'd let her know everything he safely could. Whether she'd ever speak to him again remained to be seen.

'What's up, duck?' Maureen asked drowsily. 'Not cold, are you?'

He shook his head and took a deep breath. 'If I told you that I'd lied ever since I came here, would you hate me?'

'Still married, are you?' Maureen gurgled. 'Well, that wouldn't bother me too much under the circumstances.'

'I'm not married. But everything I've told everyone since I arrived has been a fabrication. I've never been a gardener—I'm a bankrupt. A compulsive gambler. I lived in a bedsit on the Social because of my gambling. That's why Jemima didn't like horse-racing. That's why Rosemary left me.'

Maureen was silent for a while. Vincent touched the brittle hair and heard her sigh.

'Maureen?'

'I guessed you wasn't a gardener, duck. But you've done all right. No one suspects—'cept Maddy at first, of course, when you pulled up all them flowers—but since then you've worked hard for them at Peapods to put things right, and they're not ones to ask questions. They think the world of you, and everyone else thinks you're the real McCoy, duck. And as for the gambling—well, it's no big surprise. I knew there was something. There's a lot of unpleasantness behind the chintz, especially in a place like this. We've all got secrets we'd rather stayed out of sight.'

He hugged her. 'I've done some really bad things.'

'Show me someone who hasn't.'

He had to do it. He couldn't keep it a secret anymore. If Maureen blew his cover, then so what? It had been really good. He'd have the memories. 'All my money doesn't come from gardening...'

'Daft—' Maureen pulled herself up in bed and looked down on him lovingly. 'Do you think I didn't know that? If you and Ned Filkins are having a little bit of a razzle, who am I to blow the whistle? Ned's already told me that my Brian will be the first to know of our—um—friendship if I so much as opens me mouth about anything.'

Oh, Christ. He should have known.

'Should I go to the police, do you think? Should I tell Kath and Drew and everyone what's going on?'

'Is anyone going to get hurt—other than in the pocket?'

512

Vincent shook his head. They weren't. Well—of course, there was the Grand National and Charlie, of course—but that was too far-fetched for words. 'No one. In fact everyone seems to come out of it okay, actually.'

'Then let sleeping dogs lie, that's my advice. It's been done before in this village—and it'll be done again. There's fortunes made and lost in racing in ways that would make old Al Capone curl up and die.' Maureen slithered down beside him again and enfolded him with her marshmallow arms. 'Just listen to that wind. Fair howling across the Downs. And the sleet rattling against the window. And we're in here snug as bugs. Blooming lovely, isn't it? Happy Christmas, duck.'

CHAPTER THIRTY-FOUR

'Happy Christmas.' Matt walked up behind Tina and, putting his fingers beneath her ribs, encircled her naked slenderness.

'That was yesterday.'

'It feels like the rest of my life.' He bit her shoulder none too gently, his teeth grazing the skin stretched over the clavicle. 'Happy Boxing Day, then. So what *exactly* are we going to do today?'

'I have no idea.' Still in his arms, she turned to face him. They leaned against the white railings of the balcony. 'But then, you're the one with the imagination, aren't you?'

Imagination? Him? Stolid, solid, Mr Average? Except he wasn't. Not any more. Tina Maloret had changed everything. He'd hated her and it had

513

made everything perfect.

'You choose.' He stared at her body, still trying to believe that this wasn't a fantasy. Still trying to get his head round the fact that they were together; that Fate and mutual predilections had given them this—what? Happiness? Satisfaction? Love? 'As long as it doesn't involve getting dressed . . .'

God! Had he said that? Had he said half the things that had tumbled from his lips since he and Tina had been together? He was turning into Charlie Somerset. He laughed. No, he wasn't. Charlie hadn't been able to do this. For once he'd beaten Charlie hands down.

You mean,' he'd asked incredulously after that first time, 'that I'm *better* than Charlie Somerset?'

Better,' Tina had said, smiling at him, 'is subjective. It depends on what you want in the first place, doesn't it? You give me exactly what I want—and I have a feeling that it's a reciprocal arrangement.'

He'd eased his body away from her and, at that moment, had been sure that this was all that he'd ever wanted. Stuff the National; stuff being champion jockey, stuff Charlie; stuff his brother's superiority; stuff everyone and everything.

'And Jemima?' Tina had queried, pulling him back again. 'I take it she's Miss Missionary?'

He'd felt a twinge of guilt then. It hadn't seemed right to discuss Jemima—especially as they had never slept together. But he wanted to hear that he was better than Charlie. He wanted to hear it over and over again.

'I've no idea. I would imagine so.'

'So would I.' Tina had wrapped her legs around him. Her bones were sharp. 'Maybe we should get

514

her and Charlie together. They don't seem to like each other much, which means they're probably dying to rip each other's clothes off. Anyway,' she'd bitten his ear, 'Charlie is such a gentleman. He'd tell her she was wonderful—even if she wasn't.'

'Is that what he told you?' Matt felt jealous. 'Is that what he tells you?'

'He tells me very little these days. I try to wind him up, get him irritated, push him to the extremes of anger, but it merely seems to make him less interested, not more. No, sadly, Charlie, dynamic though he is beneath the duvet, is simply not my cup of tea. Nor am I his. Whereas you, Matt sweetie, definitely are.'

'Why do you stay with him, then?'

'God knows. He's got a pretty face and a dream body. He makes me laugh. And he's awfully good for my image. Every woman in the world would give her Amex Gold to be in my stilettos. It's a bit of an ego thing, I suppose. I don't really want him—but I'm buggered if anyone else is going to have him.'

For a moment Matt had thought about Lucinda, but had said nothing.

There had been another biting, scratching, hurting interlude then. Matt, rolling away, wondered if he'd died and gone to Heaven. He'd asked her about Charlie again. It was bliss.

'Charlie is fantastic stud value, sweetie. On performance ratings he's out of this world. Sadly, he has romantic and old-fashioned notions. And he's very straight—unlike you.' She'd looked at him with her smoky eyes. 'I'd never have put you down as an S and M devotee, Mr Garside. Never in a million years. Just think what I've been missing all this time. You've been riding Dragon Slayer for

515

ages—and never gave so much as a hint . . .'

He'd laughed into the skeletal ribs. 'We hardly parade around in rubber balaclavas and studded leather wristlets, do we? Anyway, I didn't like you.'

'And I thought you were the pits.' She'd slithered happily down his body. 'Which makes everything absolutely perfect, doesn't it?'

*　　*　　*

Matt looked down on to the pool and beach below. The morning sky was shimmering, the sun white-hot on his skin. The Caribbean Sea, like turquoise silk, wound itself around acres of silver sand. The marble floor of their balcony was already almost too warm for bare feet; and several holiday-makers were sitting at parasol'd tables just beneath them.

Tina stared at them over the railings. 'They look pretty bored, don't you think? Shall we entertain them? Liven up their breakfast?'

He closed his eyes in sheer pleasure as her nails raked his skin.

Afterwards, still naked, she sat cross-legged on the balcony and surveyed his injuries. It seemed to amuse her. 'When are you supposed to be riding again?'

'Two weeks.'

Tina shook her head. 'You'll never get past the MO. "Dear me, Mr Garside,"'—she adopted a gruff authoritarian voice, '"and where exactly did you acquire these bruises? How did you manage to accumulate this large abrasion? And these weals— where precisely did they come from?"'

'They don't ask those sort of questions.' He pulled her on to his lap. 'And I think they'd have

516

apoplexy if I told them, don't you?'

Tina kissed the tip of his nose. Gently. Her eyes were soft. Kind. She only hurt him now when they made love. Pleasure and pain. Such a fine line between the two for most people. A fine line smudged by deviation for him alone—or so he'd always thought.

He still couldn't believe it. None of it. If he felt any guilt at all it was over missing the Kempton meeting. Christ, Kempton was today. The King George would be run in subzero temperatures with typical Christmas sleet and everyone muffled to the eyebrows, and here he was in the Caribbean where wearing skin was even too much.

No doubt his family in Devon hadn't missed him. His telephoned excuse of being invited to a pal's place in the Virgin Islands for Christmas to let the sun heal his shoulder had been accepted without question. Even Jennifer hadn't seemed too disappointed. Mind you, as they spent their time together in much the same way that he and Jemima did, he wasn't surprised.

Jennifer and Jemima—and most of the other girls he'd met—he knew that they thought he was a bit of a sap with a low sex drive. It was only the women who had pocketed his money who knew the truth.

Until now. Tina's incredible nearly six-foot body lay supine on the balcony. She was stretched out on the marble, ignoring the deeply-cushioned loungers, allowing the floor's heat to penetrate her thin, blue-veined skin. She wore only Ray-Bans, a coating of Piz Buin, and his Christmas present. The gold-linked ankle chain with a tiny whip and set of spurs was their private joke. Tina had adored it.

She smiled and rolled over. He knew she wasn't sleeping. He'd watched her sleep. He'd held her while she slept.

Discovering that Tina and he shared the same interests had been a revelation.

That first night when Tina had suggested they spend the remainder of the evening together, had turned everything upside down. Had made sense of the nonsensical. And, while solving one problem, had thrown up a million others.

He'd been planning to see Jemima that night, planning to seduce Jemima, even while knowing that it probably wouldn't work. He knew her too well—and liked her. And, worst of all, he respected her. He'd known that any attempt to make love to her would either be a dismal failure—or terrify her. And he hadn't wanted to do either. But he was so frustrated. There had been no outlets for so long.

He thought Jemima might have guessed because of those books! He'd been outraged by the Fishnets that afternoon in the shop. He grinned to himself. Maybe, like that woman in Hamlet, he'd protested too much? He'd wondered if Jemima had sussed it then. She hadn't seemed to.

When he had read the book himself, he'd been stunned by the accuracy, the intimate details, the pleasure. That Bella-Donna Stockings knew a thing or two. He'd toyed with the idea of contacting the publishers and asking them if he could write to her and tell her how much he'd enjoyed her book. Deciding that she'd probably think he was some sad old pervert, he'd contented himself with buying the rest of her books and fantasising. If only he could find a woman like Bella-Donna Stockings in Milton St John.

Spanky Panky—the tide still sent shivers down his spine. And Tina had come into the shop that afternoon and said she'd read it—and he was intrigued . . . excited . . . wondering . . .

And then, when he and Tina had gone back to his house from the Cat and Fiddle, all the weeks of speculation came to an end.

*   *   *

He moved across the balcony and sat beside Tina, drawing his knees to his chin. The sun was healing his shoulder better than any physio could ever hope to. She turned her head slightly, and her pouty lips curled into a smile. She said nothing, but slid her hand between his thighs. It wasn't sexual, more proprietorial. Matt closed his fingers over hers and swallowed the lump of happiness his throat . . .

So—that evening—thousands of miles away in Milton St John, when they'd gone back to his house Tina had stalked around, looking out of place in her designer outfit, and criticised everything he'd ever done. He was a crap jockey. She expected better. She'd have better. She never settled for second best. Dragon Slayer should have won the National—and would win the next one. Understood?

He'd nodded, almost hating her. She was abrasive, angry. He'd watched her as she ranted; listened to her strident voice, demanding that he win on Dragon Slayer; demanding that he did what he was told; demanding that he proved that he was a better jockey than Charlie.

She'd stood in the doorway of the sitting room, staring dismissively at his unimaginative decor, his

519

average furnishings. At him. And he'd stared back. He was a bluffer, too. He recognised the signs. An outward shell protecting vulnerability and fear.

He'd called her bluff.

Grasping her roughly by the shoulder, he'd pulled her round, told her to shut up, fuck off, get out. She'd looked at him, angrily, challengingly. Her breathing had been shallow. Then she'd slapped his face. And he'd slapped hers—and he'd discovered that the fulfilment he'd paid so many hundreds of pounds for over the years was here— and his for free.

And after that, despite his intention not to, they'd been together whenever possible. Sometimes, because the excitement of potential discovery heightened the enjoyment, they'd managed some pretty hairy escapades in very public places. They'd always got away with it, although that night at Maddy and Drew's wedding reception, when Charlie had walked out of the marquee practically on top of them, had been a close call. It had been a hell of a turn-on at the time— and afterwards they'd nearly choked themselves laughing at the irony.

'Do you want a drink?' The sun was climbing higher in the sky now. 'Shall we be boring and use the minibar, or would you rather I telephoned for room service?'

'Room service.' Tina pushed the Ray-Bans on top of her head. 'I love it when they try not to stare.'

So did he. He still hadn't quite got used to it. His body, although tightly muscled and athletic by necessity, had never given him any visual pleasure. He certainly didn't pose in front of the mirror each

520

morning, flexing his pecs or admiring his biceps. Tina, however, had given him new confidence. He no longer looked at his reflection and wished he was Charlie. He didn't need to.

And when they did eventually dress and go down to the pool, or stroll along the water's edge, or, as they had done yesterday, eaten their Christmas meal in the dining room, people still stared.

'The supermodel and the jockey,' Tina had hissed, clinging to his arm. 'They recognise us both but don't like to say.'

It was fine for her—she was used to it. He wasn't. Fair enough, people might think his face was familiar because of the television or the racing press, but he wasn't as well known as Charlie. Everyone was used to seeing Tina and Charlie together, anyway. They were often in the gossip columns or splashed across the society pages.

But he was famous enough to have made his trips to London's high-class joints a major hazard. It had been his downfall, really. Not that any of the girls who had been so cruelly kind to him had said anything. They were used to dealing with far more celebrated faces—and bodies—than his. But notoriety cost. He knew he'd have to pay extra for the silence; fork out a fortune for the discretion.

It had just been a shame that he'd been broke at the time, and had borrowed money from Ned in a moment of desperation. He'd thought Ned might demand some stable information along with the repayment. But Ned had been far more clever than that. He should have realised that one of his scum-collectors would have been despatched to follow him and find out how the money was being spent; to find out exactly what sort of blackmailing leverage could be stored away for Filkins' future use. Times and places had been carefully logged and—even more terrifying—photographs had been taken.

His face was well enough known for it to cause a major scandal: to finish his career. Jockeys—like all sportsmen—had to be squeaky-clean. No drugs, no booze, and definitely no taste for bizarre sex. Ned Filkins had him—as he had poor Vincent—over the proverbial barrel.

He had still worried that he and Tina would be recognised as they left Heathrow. He didn't want Jemima to find out via the tabloids—and he didn't want Charlie to find out at all.

'If anyone asks why we're together, we'll tell them it's a business trip,' Tina had purred when they'd arrived at the hotel 'After all, I do own the horse you ride. What could be more natural?'

He rang room service, and pulled on a T-shirt. Tina laughed at him. 'Very suburban, Matt, darling, and a complete waste of modesty. After all, I'll only take it off again.'

He winced as he sat down. The floor was scalding now. He wanted to swim. He wondered vaguely if Dragon Slayer had won the King George. With the time difference, the race would probably be over by now. He mentioned it as the waiter bustled round with massive jugs of white rum and fruit juice and ice.

'He wasn't winning with you, was he, sweetie? So without you he doesn't stand a dog's chance. And his form has been pretty naff of late.'

Maybe, Matt thought, as the waiter placed the drinks beneath the awning, but did Liam Jenkins know he wasn't supposed to win? Had Ned Filkins managed to get the message across?

Tina sat up, uncurling herself with no regard for the waiter's blood pressure, and flicked ice cubes at Matt. They melted almost immediately and trickled down his thighs. She watched them appreciatively. Oh, God, he thought, please let her wait until the waiter has gone.

She did.

*   *   *

Slightly drunk from the rum, and smarting from Tina's expert attention and the chlorine in the hotel pool, Matt headed back to their room. Pushing the sopping hair from his eyes, he opened the door and looked around for her. He didn't have to search far. In her minuscule bikini she was jigging up and down on a sun lounger on their balcony, waving her mobile phone.

'Matt! He's bloody won!'

'Charlie? Bonne Nuit has won the King George?'

'No.' She pulled him down beside her, her voice quivering with excitement. 'Dragon Slayer. By a short head from bloody Bonnie Nuts! He must have come good again. Isn't that fantastic? Kath will be so pleased.'

And Ned would be fucking furious.

He nodded, rubbing his hair. He was going to tell Tina. He had to. It was something he'd discussed with Vincent, but they'd both decided against it, agreeing that certainly for Jemima's sake—if for no one else's—they had to keep quiet. And then, when Jemima had turned up in the middle of their chat, he'd not known what to do with himself.

And she'd given him a Christmas present which

523

he'd left behind in his rush to get to Heathrow, and he hadn't bought her anything at all. Not because he was mean or hadn't wanted to, but because he simply hadn't thought about it. His obsession with Tina had wiped out all other considerations.

Still, no doubt Jemima would meet someone else during Milton St John's round of seasonal parties, and when he came back they might even be friends again. He cared enough about her to want her not to hate him. He couldn't bear it if she pitied him for his sexual preferences. It would be even worse if she despised him for being a cheat.

Tina was applying an extra layer of Piz Buin to the ninety-five per cent of her body which was exposed to the sun. He took the bottle from her and massaged her back. Tenderly.

'Tina—can I talk to you?'

'Clean or dirty?'

'Seriously.'

'Bugger. Okay, go on.'

He told her quietly. All of it. How he'd been caught up in Ned Filkins' web; how Dragon Slayer wasn't supposed to win anything until the National; even how he was going to unseat Charlie at Aintree if necessary.

Tina said nothing. He couldn't tell from the set of her shoulders whether she was angry.

Without turning round, she sighed. 'And the Hennessey fall?'

'Was genuine. I'd have won that one and to hell with the consequences.'

Her hand reached for his. 'Good, you cheating bastard. Because nearly died when you fell. It was a bit of a sod, really. I knew then that I didn't want to lose you—and don't look so smug.'

He said nothing. He didn't know what to say. All his life he'd played in the reserve team—never expecting anything. This was as near to a declaration of love as Tina had ever got. It was far more than he deserved.

Tina curled her arms around his neck. 'You will try to win the National, though, won't you, sweetie? Not for Ned fucking Filkins—but for me? For us?'

'Yes,' he said, because he would. 'Even if it means hurting Charlie to do it?'

'Even if it means hurting Charlie—although actually I'd prefer it if you didn't.'

'And will you leave me if I don't win?'

She grinned at him. 'Would you care?'

Matt shrugged as he grinned back. 'What do you think?'

CHAPTER THIRTY-FIVE

The end of the year. Tomorrow would bring a fresh start, new hopes, new dreams. Jemima perched on the edge of her bed and wondered what to wear. Should she stick with the tried and tested and see the old year out in grunge? Or should she go for an entire change of image, raid the more avant-garde end of Gillian's wardrobe, and welcome in the new one as a stunna? She giggled. Somehow, she couldn't see herself rivalling Lucinda tonight. Not, of course, that she'd be going to the Nuke—but if she was—it might be nice to turn heads.

She wrapped her dressing gown more closely round her and drifted to the window. The icy weather had persisted, throwing biting winds and steel-grey skies across the Downs, and cloaking Milton St John in a perpetual veil of sleet. It hadn't been a white Christmas, but it had been satisfyingly cold, and she'd been delighted to crouch beside Maureen's real coal fire, with a large port and lemon—Maureen's favourite seasonal drink, apparently—beside her, and crack walnuts and watch a spine-chiller on the television.

In fact, it had been one of the loveliest Christmases she could remember.

Her father and Maureen had been very funny, trying not to touch each other, smiling at each other when they thought she wasn't watching. Their happiness had been tangible. She assumed they'd spent Christmas Eve night together—she'd never ask, of course. It was something she'd rather not think about. But if it made Vincent happy, and it obviously did, then who was she to moralise?

And then there had been the additional joy of Maddy and Drew's baby. Acting as emergency midwife had turned Vincent into a sort of folk hero in the village and, after church on Christmas morning, everyone was slapping him on the back and offering to buy him drinks. He'd admitted to her that it was the most terrifying moment of his life—but also one of the most wonderful. She'd hugged him and told him he was a star, and that Daragh Vincent had a lot to live up to.

While Maureen had been in the kitchen and tantalising smells of roasting turkey had wafted through the serving hatch, making Jemima momentarily regret—as she did every Christmas—that she was a vegetarian, she'd tackled Vincent gently about what Charlie had said.

He'd blustered for a split-second, then grinned

sheepishly. 'It was nothing, Jem, love. Nothing at all. You know what the gossips are like in this village.'

She did. But she also knew Vincent. 'Why were you at Matt's place, though? You don't really like him.'

Vincent had walked over to the fire and leaned on the mantelpiece. 'Well, let's just say that something had come up—a bit of scandal that I'd heard—'

'About Matt?'

'Sort of.' Vincent had looked mighty uncomfortable. 'I was just—well, making sure that it wasn't true. For your sake.'

She'd shaken her head. 'Come off it, Dad. I'm a big girl now. I don't scare that easily. What was it?'

Vincent had nearly lost the thread then. 'Er—well . . . that he was—um—seeing someone else.'

She'd laughed. 'Jesus! This isn't the Victorian era! Even if it were true—which I'm sure it isn't—I certainly don't need you to go storming in, flicking your coat-tails and twirling your moustaches on my account! Sorry, not believable. Try again.'

'That's all, Jem, honest. I didn't want you to get hurt.'

She'd sighed. She wasn't going to get any more from him. 'Matt and I aren't in any position to hurt each other. Just tell me it wasn't about gambling.'

Vincent had hesitated a fraction too long. 'No—definitely not about gambling.'

Then Maureen had come through and said dinner would be ready in twenty minutes and that Vincent should shift himself and get his carving arm limbered up, and they hadn't mentioned it again.

Naturally, she'd joined the other villagers in

the non-stop stream to Peapods on Christmas afternoon, just to have a peek, and say congratulations. The baby was adorable. Maddy looked radiant, and Poppy Scarlet had soon got over her disgust that Daragh was a normal little boy—and would never grow into a purple monster with a scaly tail—although Charlie, who appeared to be a permanent fixture and a dab hand at nappy-changing, had told her that if she was really good he'd take her into Newbury and buy her a fluffy Godzilla—which would be much less hassle than a real one.

She'd watched him with Poppy, turning into a child himself as he played with her mountain of Christmas presents. He was totally unself-conscious, and she'd thought what a brilliant father he'd make. It was such a shame that he didn't seem to want to settle down. Not, of course, that she was putting herself forward for the job of Somerset-taming—perish the thought—but one day, maybe, he'd find a woman who would turn his life around and stop the playboy bit dead in its tracks. Somehow, she didn't want to be around when it happened.

Charlie's mind must have been working along the same parental lines, because he'd carefully placed the sleeping Daragh in her arms and said she'd make the perfect mother. Looking down at the tiny face and the amazing miniature fingers clasped in sleep, she'd felt a rush of love, but no strong maternal tug. Motherhood simply wasn't for her—but it hardly seemed the right moment to mention it.

She'd managed to have a few minutes alone with Charlie in the mayhem, while Maddy's parents and the still-Lukeless Suzy were attempting to organise the chaos of half the village being in the house at the same time on Christmas Day.

'You know you mentioned about Dad and Matt? Well, you needn't have worried. It wasn't anything sinister. I asked him.'

Charlie had stopped twirling a snowstorm paperweight. 'Oh? And?'

'He said the only thing they'd ever discussed was Matt's bit on the side.'

Charlie had dropped the paperweight with a clatter. Neither of them bothered to pick it up. He'd looked quizzical. 'God—very brazen of them, considering. And you seem to be taking it well. Um—who is she?'

'No one,' Jemima had laughed. 'I know when Dad's lying. And Matt simply isn't in your league as a cheater, is he? No, whatever they say, I'm sure that it has something to do with horses.'

She wasn't sure why, but Charlie suddenly seemed different. Cagey? No, it had to be her. She was becoming paranoid. She'd looked at him again and knew she had imagined it.

He'd bent down to retrieve the paperweight at last. 'But Vincent doesn't gamble, does he? I've never seen him in the bookies.'

'No, you wouldn't. He used to have a—er—a bit of a problem. He's beaten it—but I'm sure it's like any addiction—the temptation is always there. He still likes to feel he's got some connection with racing.'

'I can understand that.' Charlie had grinned suddenly. 'I love temptation myself.'

She'd looked away, concentrating heavily on Bronwyn Pugh nursing Daragh. She felt very hot.

God, he was lethal. What was the cliché Gillian had used when she'd first mentioned him? Oh, yes— Charlie Somerset was sex on legs.

'Well, I thought I'd just tell you that I don't think we've got anything to worry about.'

Charlie had shaken the paperweight again and concentrated on the blizzard. Eventually, as the snow settled on the tiny houses and disproportionate fir trees, he'd looked up. 'So, which would bother you more? Matt cheating on you, or Vincent being involved in some insider dealing?'

'The latter, definitely. Matt and I aren't going anywhere. I hope he does find someone else, honestly. No, I'd far prefer it was that, rather than Dad getting hooked on betting again. Anyway, I'd better be going because Maureen's prepared tea for four o'clock, although I'm sure I won't be able to eat anything else for weeks. And, oh, good luck for the King George tomorrow.'

'Ta.' He'd grinned again, looking, she'd thought, far more cheerful. 'Will you be watching?'

'I shouldn't think so. Hopefully I'll be disgustingly drunk and curled up in bed.'

'Sounds great to me. If there's room for two, I could always cancel Kempton.'

*   *   *

They'd been lucky to run the King George at all, everyone had said, the weather being what it was. There'd been no racing anywhere in the country since.

Jemima had watched the meeting on television with Vincent and Maureen. They'd happily accepted her invitation to the flat and she'd cooked Boxing Day dinner in return for Maureen's Christmas hospitality. If her father and Maureen were less than ecstatic with refried beans and vegetable tacos, they certainly hadn't shown it.

And, as the tension built for the King George, she'd found herself clutching a cushion and trying to suppress the butterflies. Charlie, in Gillian's Fishnet colours, had looked totally devastating. They'd interviewed him outside the weighing room and, with his hacking jacket slung round his shoulders and his hair flopping into his eyes, her stomach had lurched. Too many refried beans, she'd told herself severely, a dose of Alka-Seltzer would soon sort her out.

Liam Jenkins, gangly and freckled, had then been asked about Dragon Slayer's chances in Matt's absence. She could have sworn that Vincent groaned—but, again, it may well have been the beans. They'd flashed a replay of the Hennessey fall on to the screen and she'd watched impassively. It was, of course, because she knew Matt was okay, she told herself; it wasn't lack of interest.

The final furlong of the King George had been spectacularly nail-biting. Jemima's cushion had been squeezed within an inch of its life. She'd willed and willed Charlie to win, but it hadn't been enough. Dragon Slayer's black nose streaked past the post merely inches ahead of Bonne Nuit.

'Oh, bugger.' She'd sighed and thrown the cushion to the floor.

Maureen and Vincent had exchanged raised eyebrows. Jemima had shrugged. 'Close, wasn't it?'

'Very, duck.' Maureen had patted Vincent's hand, interrupting something he was about to say. 'I didn't know you were so keen on racing. Oh, I know you've got over your real dislike, but I reckoned you'd settled for indifference.'

'I have,' Jemima had said quickly and stood up to refill the glasses. 'That was just a show of Milton St John solidarity.'

'But Liam Jenkins is from Milton St John,' Maureen had persisted. 'I didn't notice you being jubilant when he won. Something you haven't told us about young Charlie, is there?'

Jemima had paused, Chablis bottle poised. 'Absolutely nothing. Now, is anyone still hungry?'

*　　　*　　　*

She stared out across the Vicarage garden again. Everything was sugar-coated in ice, and cobwebs were suspended like gently moving doilies between the bare branches. It was so very beautiful. And lonely. The end of her first year in Milton St John and she was alone. Last New Year's Eve she'd been at a wild Oxford party with David or had it been Mark? Or maybe it was Hugh? They'd all merged into one. Still, this year, she definitely wouldn't be with Matt.

She wondered what this New Year's Eve would bring. Because of the Nuke there were very few parties arranged—most people who weren't going to be gracing the James-Jordans' marquee had decided to stay at home or, like Vincent and Maureen, join in the karaoke night at the pub. The convoy of cars and rave-goers on foot had been arriving in the village since the early hours. The Cat and Fiddle and the Munchy Bar must have done a roaring trade. Jemima, who wasn't reopening the bookshop until the second of January, felt she might have missed out on all the fun she was going to get that day.

'Jemima!' The door opened, and the twins, muffled in new combat gear, peered excitedly into the flat. 'Can we come in? Oh are you going to bed?'

'No, I've just had a bath and I'm trying to find something to wear for tonight. There's Coke and crisps in the kitchen.'

'Mega.'

There was an identical carrot-headed rush through the living room, followed by a lot of door-opening and rustling. Once equipped with vital supplies, Levi and Zeke collapsed on to the sofa. She knew that they'd taken their Christmas-present mountain bikes up to the outskirts of the rave field, and laughed at their chill-flushed cheeks and sparkling eyes.

'Good, was it?'

'Cool, or what? You wouldn't believe it!' Levi slurped through his Coke. 'There were ladies wearing furry bikinis—in this weather!'

Zeke nodded furiously. 'An' men in make-up! And a million policemen!'

What a pity, Jemima thought, that she would be listening to the chimes of Big Ben in the sober and eminently respectable surroundings of the Vicarage drawing room.

'It's going to be bloody boring for us, isn't it?' Levi sighed. 'We're not even allowed to stay up until midnight. Mum says maybe next year.'

'It's not that magical,' Jemima said, sympathising. 'Nothing changes. Nothing happens.'

Zeke quickly swallowed a mouthful of cheese

533

and onion. 'It does, Jem. An' not just the Nuke. I mean, there's an old man with a hooky thing who goes out when the bells chime, and a little fat baby comes in. Mum said so.'

'I stand corrected.' Jemima grinned. 'If I see either of them tonight I'll give you a shout.'

* * *

It was an extremely decorous New Year's Eve. Gillian and Glen and an assortment of the village elders and Parish Biddies, milling around the Vicarage sitting room with nibbles and sherry. Noël Coward would have adored it.

Eventually Jemima had settled on wearing the long, clinging wool dress she'd worn to Maddy and Drew's wedding. Smart grunge, she considered, was probably exactly right for the occasion.

Sitting as far away from Bathsheba Cox and her husband as possible—Gillian had invited them as an apology for her *faux pas* over Lucinda and Charlie at the wedding, and hadn't expected them to accept—she toyed with a plate of canapés and was bored.

This was no way for someone who wasn't yet thirty to be spending one of the big party nights of the year. God, only just gone ten o'clock. Two more hours before she could affect a yawn and escape to her flat. She thought of the mayhem at the Nuke and wished she was Lucinda and Suzy's age and could go without being stared at.

However, if she was far too young for the jam and Jerusalem brigade, there was no doubt that she was far too old for raves. But then, Charlie was older than she was, and he'd had no inhibitions

534

about being there. She sighed, watching Bronwyn and Bernie Pugh nodding in time to Mantovani. Charlie had no inhibitions about anything.

She tried to strike up a conversation with Petunia Hobday. It was very difficult on two counts. Firstly, because Petunia was scared of Bathsheba, and her fatwa against Fishnets in general and Jemima in particular was still in place; and secondly because she'd got the remnants of a cheese straw clinging to her whiskers.

Jemima stared at the offending flakes, trying not to giggle. God, this was really no place for her. She'd have been better off joining in with the crowd at the Cat and Fiddle. She trawled round the sitting room. No one seemed to be under sixty, and while Glen appeared to be happy, flirting with his ageing fan club, Gillian looked manic.

She was gliding between the guests in the silver-grey trouser suit from Dorothy Perkins looking as gorgeous as ever, but with a feverish light in her eyes. Poor Gillian! Having tried to lose all her Fishnets money by buying Bonnie, the horse was now increasing her bank balance with nearly every race. That night at Windsor when she'd first mentioned the horse seemed to belong to another lifetime. So much had happened. So much had changed. For all of them.

Suddenly Gillian clapped her hands. Oh, shit, Jemima thought, we're going to play charades—or even, worse—consequences. Bathsheba, Bronwyn and Petunia exchanged glances. Petunia, still flaky, leaned across and confided in a conspiratorial whisper, 'I think we may be going to have a Beetle Drive. Dear Glen's awfully good with them at the Tuesday Club.'

A what? Jemima blinked. A hush fell. All eyes turned expectantly. Gillian was obviously about to enlighten her.

'As this is a very special night—and the end of a very special year for me in particular—I'd like to make a little speech.'

Petunia sighed heavily. 'Buggeration. I really wanted it to be a Beetle Drive.'

Jemima shook her head. Please, no . . .

'If it's to do with that tribal affair in the James-Jordans' field,' Bathsheba brayed, 'there's no need to canvas the converted. Ted and I have already written a letter to *The Times*.'

'It's nothing to do with the Nuke, Bathsheba dear.' Gillian smiled sweetly. 'It's to do with New Year's Eve, and traditions, and resolutions.'

'I'm going to give up eating olives,' Petunia confided to Jemima. 'Actually, I don't like them much and they give me chronic indigestion, so it's no hardship, but I really couldn't think of anything else.'

Glen, Jemima noticed, had come to a halt behind Emily and Marjorie Campion, elderly spinster sisters from the new estate. He was clutching the backs of their chairs and looking extremely concerned. He'd obviously had more experience of Gillian tanked up on Harvey's Bristol Cream than most people.

'Resolutions!' Gillian's voice roared round the room, drowning out the strains of Pan Pipe Reflections. 'Resolutions are made to be broken, don't you agree?'

Oh, God, she's seriously pissed, Jemima thought. Everyone else nodded happily.

'However, I have no intention of breaking mine.

I'd like to share it with you—and then add a bit of spice.'

This had the Parish Biddies on the edge of their seats. Jemima closed her eyes.

'I'm going to give up smoking.' Gillian beamed. 'At midnight tonight I will smoke my last cigarette!'

There was a ripple of applause and a muttered 'about bloody time' from the far corner.

'And there is something else I would like to share with you all. If this is a time for turning over new leaves and—well, turning over new leaves—I'd like to let you all in on a little secret.'

Jemima wondered if she could dash to the loo and bolt the door for the next three hours.

'I know this will come as a surprise to most of you—and definitely to my darling Glen.' She waggled her fingers in his direction. 'But I'm not all I seem to be.'

'Not all-bloody-there's more like it,' the same voice muttered.

'Ladies and gentlemen, I'd like to tell you that I am the proud owner of Drew Fitzgerald's brilliant horse Bonnie Nuts.'

'Bloody liar!' The voice was indignant. 'Fizz Flanagan is.'

'No, it's one of the Saudi royal family,' Bathsheba corrected. 'Lucinda told me.'

'And she should know,' Petunia piped up bravely. 'Considering that she's sleeping with Charlie Somerset.'

Ritual disembowelling was only prevented by Glen using his twenty-third psalm voice. 'Gillian! Are you sure?'

'Perfectly, darling. Ask Jemima.'

Jemima, blushing from her toes, nodded

confirmation.

'But how? I mean—horses cost a fortune! Why didn't you tell me? How on earth can you have afforded to buy a horse? I know your writing is very profitable but—'

Gillian sashayed across the room and hugged Glen, almost unseating the Campion sisters. 'Darling, it's more profitable than you'd ever believe. Oh, look, I know you might be a teensy bit cross—but I don't want to keep it a secret any more. From you or from all our dear friends.' She took a deep breath. 'I'm Bella-Donna Stockings.'

'Fucking hell!'

Jemima blinked. Had Glen really said that? Bathsheba looked like she needed smelling salts.

Petunia grabbed a steadying handful of cheese straws. Everyone else sat rigidly, totally dumbfounded. Jemima, as always at moments like this, was terribly afraid she was going to laugh.

'Say you're pleased,' Gillian appealed to Glen. 'Tell me you don't mind.'

'Mind? You write pornography and you expect me not to mind!'

'It's erotica, actually.' Gillian looked a touch disappointed by the reaction. 'And no, I don't expect you to mind. You're a vicar.'

'It's because I'm a bloody vicar that I do mind, you daft bat!'

'Good Lord.' Bronwyn Pugh was on her feet. 'There's no call for that, Vicar. No call at all.'

Gillian gave a sob and fled from the room. Glen tore after her. All hell broke loose. There probably hadn't been so much fluttering and twittering and excitement beneath the post-menopausal Crimplene bosoms in years, Jemima thought. She very much doubted if they'd all be linking arms and singing 'Auld Lang Syne' tonight.

Bathsheba and the Campion sisters were tutting loudly that they'd always suspected as much. Bronwyn and Bernie helped themselves to another sherry. Several of the guests were searching for their hats and gloves.

'It's awfully exciting, isn't it?' Petunia nudged Jemima. 'Do you think there's any chance of us getting free copies?'

'I shouldn't think so. Anyway, I couldn't agree to that. It would ruin my profit margins—bloody hell!'

Everyone in the room was silent. The screaming from upstairs would have outdone the finale of *Fatal Attraction*. Holy shit, Jemima thought, he's stabbed her with a crucifix.

The sitting-room door flew open. A very un-stabbed Gillian belted in, followed by an equally distraught Glen.

'It's the boys! My little boys! My babies! They've gone to the fucking Nuke!'

CHAPTER THIRTY-SIX

'They do drugs, you know.' Bronwyn spoke up from Floss's back seat. 'Everyone knows that.'

'What, the twins?' Jemima nearly veered off the road. 'They're only children!'

'Not the twins, silly girl! No—these rave places—they do drugs. Vitamin E. I've seen it on the News.'

How, Jemima wondered, she'd managed to get Bronwyn, Petunia and Bathsheba in the back of her car, she really wasn't sure. Bernie Pugh, well strapped in, was sitting rigidly beside her. Ted Cox had been left open-mouthed on the drive. There was some scant hope that the Campion sisters may have picked him up in their Morris Minor.

Glen and Gillian had torn off in the elderly Triumph, leaving everyone else, teeth chattering in the subzero temperatures, staring blankly after it on the frosted gravel. Jemima had yanked open Floss's door. The scramble for the seats had been like the first day of the sales. Those not lucky enough to find accommodation in the leading cars, had tumbled into whatever transport was available. The resulting convoy was just like the chase scene in *Clockwise*.

She turned up the heater as she rounded the Peapods bend far too fast and winced. They'd all end up in the stream if she wasn't careful. To hell with the fact that she'd probably had too many sherries—every policeman in the Thames Valley would be patrolling the Nuke. They wouldn't, surely, be breathalysing anyone on the back roads of Milton St John. She'd just have to park Floss a decent distance from the marquee.

'You can hear the music from here!' Petunia piped from somewhere beneath Bronwyn and Bathsheba. 'Doesn't it sound lovely?'

It did, actually. It sounded bassy and sexy and primal and altogether exciting.

Jemima, trying to suppress total glee that she was actually going to the Nuke, attempted to remind herself of the potential severity of the circumstances. She kept failing miserably. She only wished she'd had time to change out of the wool dress and slip into something by Dolce & Gabbana.

'I always knew Gillian was up to no good.'

Bathsheba leaned across from the back seat as they hurtled along the single-track road in the darkness. The only signs of life were the Triumph's tail-lights streaking occasionally ahead of them and the Nuke's blue strobes dancing across the sky. 'Her being a porn writer comes as no surprise. No surprise at all. Devious so-and-so. Marching with us—pretending to be on our side! You and her were in cahoots, no doubt, young lady?'

Jemima smiled serenely. 'We were. And I'm very proud of her. And if you say anything detrimental about me or Gillian or Bella-Donna Stockings or Fishnets, then I'll stop the car and turf you out. Okay?'

After a moment's stunned silence, Bathsheba muttered mutinously, 'That's as maybe, but you tell me why her kiddies have run away tonight. Disturbed, that's what they are. No proper mothering at home. Why else would they want to be going to this—this—Nuclear thing?'

'Probably for the same reason as your daughter.' Jemima risked a glance in the driving mirror. 'Only, of course, Lucinda will be safely and chastely escorted by Charlie, won't she?'

'Attagirl!' Bronwyn trumpeted. 'And shut up about them damn Fishnets tonight, Bathsheba, do. There's more important things to bother about than Gillian writing a bit of slap and tickle.'

Bathsheba huffed a bit but said nothing. Jemima's smile edged up a few hundred watts in the darkness. Bernie Pugh patted her knee. 'I reckon she'll have enough trouble with the Vicar, my love. If she can win him round, then she shouldn't worry about a few mardy old women.'

There was a squawking explosion from the back

seat.

'Here we are.' Jemima squealed Floss to a halt on the outskirts of the field. 'Holy shit!'

The whole world must have been there. Not only was the music loud enough to jar her bones, but if the crowds outside the marquee were anything to go by, then inside must be total bedlam.

'Goodness! It's like the war years!' Petunia was first out of the back of the car. 'Look at all those bivouacs!'

Half a dozen additional tents had sprung up round the marquee. Each pulsed with a life and colour of its own. Locking the doors, and deciding to leave the Parish Biddies to their own devices, Jemima hurtled towards the entrance. If they hadn't slaughtered each other on the journey, Glen and Gillian must be somewhere inside. She was pretty sure she'd never find them. There must be thousands and thousands of people.

'Ticket!' A bald man in a tuxedo barked. 'Or arm-pass!'

Jemima stared at him. This was no time for niceties. She glanced over her shoulder. A stream of weirdly clad children were queuing behind her. She shrugged towards the nearest boy who was probably about twelve. 'Martin's got my ticket. 'Bye.'

She ducked beneath the momentarily distracted tuxedoed arm and belted inside. It was like nothing on earth.

The lasers pulsed to the bass line, and the bass line pierced her emotions. Jesus! An entire generation of children looking very grown up in heavy make-up and pantomime costumes were gyrating wildly. Tribal wasn't in it.

How would they ever find Levi and Zeke in this lot? Trying to get accustomed to the perpetual noise, lights, and motion, Jemima could see no one she recognised. There were probably hundreds of parents across the country tonight in the same state of despair as Glen and Gillian. But where the hell should she start?

Irritatingly, she wanted to dance. It was wildly infectious, although she'd probably never regain her normal hearing again. And she needn't have worried about the long woollen dress. People wore absolutely anything. And in some cases apparently nothing but body paint.

'Jemima! Hi!' The voice was at Concorde level. 'You are real, aren't you?'

She turned round. Lucinda, clutching two bottles of mineral water, was jigging on the spot beside her. Overwhelmed with relief at a familiar face, she tried to say hello and explain why she was there, but the music swirled her voice away.

Lucinda laughed, shrugged, and continued jigging. Jemima grabbed at her ski-tanned arm like a lifeline. God—she looked gorgeous. Jemima felt the recent bubble of optimism deflate inside her. Charlie, with the dual delights of Lucinda and Tina to entertain him, would never, ever, give her a second glance. Suddenly the conker-coloured dress and her glasses seemed to label her frump of the decade.

Lucinda, who was wearing what appeared to be a purple petticoat and nothing else, with purple and pink sequins attached to her eyelids, and fresh flowers entwined in the plait, looked like a dream. Her golden body gleamed beneath the lights. Jemima felt old and jaded and wanted to go home.

In a brief moment of relative hush, Jemima put her mouth to Lucinda's ear. 'Of course I'm bloody real! You haven't taken something, have you?'

'I reckon they've spiked the water,' Lucinda yelled back. 'I'm hallucinating! I thought I saw my ma just now! Spooky!'

The music changed and Lucinda slipped her arm away. Mouthing, 'Cool! Grooverider! I love this one! See ya!' she disappeared into the stomping sea —no doubt to be reconciled with Charlie.

Jemima closed her eyes. This was a completely pointless exercise. The Nuke was due to run until seven in the morning. It would have been far more sensible to arrive at kicking-out time and collect the twins then. But they were only eight—almost nine. Surely they couldn't have got past the doorman?

She forced her way back towards the entrance of the marquee. It had been so different the last time she'd been here. Then she'd laughed and danced with Charlie and wanted the night to last for ever. She'd hoped, really hoped, that he wouldn't go home with Tina. But of course he had.

'Arm-stamp if you're going into another tent!' a gruff voice barked in her ringing ear. 'Pull yer sleeve up.'

Jemima did. At least that was one problem solved. She wouldn't have to purloin another prepubescent for the purpose.

She shivered in the icy semi-darkness outside. It was still crowded with people cooling off, chilling out, smoking, dancing as they laughed and talked. The noise, although eardrum shattering was, by comparison to inside, almost bearable.

The field was awash with police. Several giggling children, still executing pretty neat dance steps, and obviously chock-a-block full of Bronwyn's Vitamin E, were being led away between officers.

'Thank God,' a familiar voice drawled in her ear. 'Someone of my own age to play with.'

She'd wanted to kiss Charlie many times—but never quite as much as at that moment. Wearing grubby white jeans and a navy polo shirt, he looked more sexy than any man ever had a right to.

'Lucinda said you were here.' He pushed his damp hair away from his forehead. 'But as she said she'd also seen her ma, I didn't believe her. Your mate Trev Perkiss is dealing in there like there's no tomorrow. I wondered if she'd taken something dubious.'

Trev Perkiss? Oh, Reynard. 'Is he a dope dealer as well?'

'He's just a dope. Tonight he's apparently calling himself Morpheus—the dream-giver. I'd like to give the bastard nightmares.'

'Didn't he stay in custody after the hunt, then?'

Charlie shook his head. 'Slippery sod. His mum cleans at the police station. She's probably got the Chief Commissioner's ear—or some other part of his anatomy. Cautioned and released pending social reports. Christ—' He looked along the row of slumped but still-dancing young boys in baggy combats and vests arrayed on the other side of Jemima. 'Are you with them?'

'God, no—I came with Bernie Pugh and the Parish Biddies.'

'I do love a woman with a sense of humour.' He squinted at her through the layers of multicoloured darkness. 'You haven't done anything, have you?'

Her? No, never! Her life had been orderly, decent, and practically blameless. Oh, right—he meant drugs. She smiled. 'Only OD'd on Harvey's Bristol Cream. Listen—'

She told him about Levi and Zeke's disappearance. 'Still I think they should be easy to spot—even in this crowd—after all, they're so tiny.'

He grinned at her. 'Jemima—this is Milton St John. Every bloody tent is awash with flat jockeys on holiday. Anyone over three foot nothing will stand out like a virgin at a white wedding.'

Of course, he was right. She shivered as the December temperature penetrated the blood-boiling heat from the marquee.

'Come on then, we'll give it a go.' He moved away in the direction of the satellite tents. 'Only another four to search.'

'What about Lucinda?'

'Lucinda's with a lot of her St Hilda's chums. It was very exciting for a while. A whole pack of eighteen-year-olds wearing ballet skirts.' He shrugged. 'Eighteen is probably their age *and* their waist size—but they all seemed as old as Methuselah to me. It's a very dedicated sport, this—all they wanted to do was bloody dance. What about you? Matt hasn't returned from Devon for tonight, has he? He's not waiting for you to join him for mayhem on the dance floor?'

They were halfway between the marquee and the first tent.

'Matt didn't go to Devon.'

'He did. Recuperation for his shoulder. He told me.'

'Not unless they've introduced passport control between Teignmouth and Newton Abbot, he didn't.'

Charlie raised his eyebrows but said nothing. He

indicated towards a tent surrounded by an ethereal orange glow and a thumping life of its own. 'We'll start here. It's Ragga.'

The rhythm reverberated. The guttural lyrics were so dirty that they made *Spanky Panky* seem like Rupert Bear. Jemima loved it. The girls were dressed in jungle prints and jewels and skin. Charlie, who seemed to know a lot about the club scene, raved about Beenie Man and Bounty Killer. She assumed they were horses.

There was no sign of Levi and Zeke.

They drew a blank in the other tents, too. Mind you, it had increased her education no end. Speed Garage was very flash with everyone looking like they should be at a Commem Ball and swigging champagne from the bottle, while Big Beat had an almost male clientele—it was hip hop and techno, Charlie screamed in her ear. Very laddish. Sort of seventies stuff with sex.

Handbag House was really bizarre. If she'd thought the marquee dressers were outrageous, then this lot beat them hands down. It looked like an explosion in a Julian Clarey clone factory.

'Ministry of Sound?' Charlie looked a bit shocked at her non-comprehension. 'Ibiza?'

She continued to shake her head. She thought she recognised some of the music from Radio One but she couldn't be sure. Whatever it all meant, it was a million times better than swigging sherry in the Vicarage.

'Back to the marquee, then,' Charlie said, shivering. 'God, it's cold out here. I wish we could get a proper bloody drink. I'm completely pissed off with water—and anything half decent has been tucked away behind the bar for the grown-ups to plunder later. I might have to bribe the barmen.'

Jemima stopped. The scything wind sliced through her woollen dress. Two minutes ago she had thought she'd never feel cold again. Now, with black clouds piling across the luminous black sky, it looked and felt like it would snow. Should she go home now? Did she want a re-enactment of dancing with Charlie in the marquee? Something else to add to the increasing pile of Charlie Somerset interludes which had developed an irritating habit of invading her sleep?

Charlie smiled at her. 'You might as well have a bit of a bop while you're here. There isn't much else we can do about the kids. No doubt Gillian and Glen will have told the police and they'll be able to keep an eye open for them.'

'Gillian and Glen aren't exactly on the best of terms at the moment.'

'Nah?' Charlie shouldered his way through a pack of kick boxers. 'Well, it must be a bit stressful for them.'

'She's told him about owning Bonne Nuit.'

Charlie stopped walking. She almost cannoned into him. She had to veer off to one side to avoid touching him.

'She also told him where the money had come from.'

'Bugger! And I missed it! Drew and I have been speculating for months!' He gave her a glimpse of the gloriously sexy crooked grin. 'So, go on? Where? Is she blackmailing the Mothers' Union?'

'She's Bella-Donna Stockings.'

'Fucking hell!'

'That's exactly what Glen said, actually.'

Charlie's eyes gleamed. 'Really? Truly? It's not a

wind-up?'

'No wind-up. I've known for ages. She was trying to lose some of her income by buying the horse. She hadn't expected you to do so well on it.'

Charlie still shook his head. 'God, I can't believe it. And I always fancied her in a sort of Madonna-ish way. Oh, not conical bras and stuff—I mean the real one. More kind of pure and untouchable. And she writes hard-core porn!' He sighed. 'I could have helped with the research. I wonder who did?'

'No one, apparently. She's got a very vivid imagination. And she doesn't write porn, she writes erotica,' Jemima corrected, wanting to giggle at his expression. 'And I'm very proud of her. She's very clever.'

'And devious. And so are you. How the hell did you manage to keep it quiet?'

'I always keep secrets.' She walked towards the marquee and flashed her invisible purple star under the scanner. 'Remember?'

Inside, it was once again wall-to-wall noise and movement. The dancers looked as though they'd be going until it got light. Reynard, or Morpheus, or whatever his bloody name was tonight, had obviously had a bumper selling spree.

She wondered if Charlie was going to try to find Lucinda, and tf he was, whether she should go back to the Vicarage. There wasn't much point in her staying—she hadn't even glimpsed the rest of the search party—and as far as she knew, Levi and Zeke could he snugly tucked up in bed.

'Fancy a drink?' Charlie's mouth was close to her ear.

She swallowed. 'Please—even if it's mineral

water.'

'I thought we could raid Gareth and Diana's more grown-up supplies. While the barmen are otherwise engaged.'

The barmen had balloons on their heads and were all dancing with each other. Three hundred people were climbing over the bar and raiding the bottles. Charlie elbowed his way through the throng. 'Whisky? Vodka? Gin? Or do you want to stick to sherry?'

'Anything but sherry.'

She watched him as he poured two generous measures of gin into half-pint plastic tumblers and added a threat of tonic water. She'd definitely have to walk home.

'Do you and Tina go clubbing?'

'Yeah. A bit. It's not my scene, really. But she needs to be noticed.' He downed a quarter of the glass. 'She's a bit scared of going off, you know. I mean half the catwalk models on the big agency's books are under seventeen. She's getting past her sell-by date.'

'Will she retire on her fortune and raise children then?' Jemima sipped the practically neat gin, not really wanting to hear the answer.

'God knows. I think she wants to go into advertising. We don't talk about it much. We don't talk about anything much.' Charlie stopped and looked towards the music end of the marquee where a massive crowd had gathered round the DJ. 'What's going on?'

The drum 'n' bass died away. The after-effects still rang in her ears. It was like being underwater. The echoes of a clock chime thundered through the marquee. Everyone started counting down.

Big Ben. Almost midnight. Seven-and-six-and-five-and . . .'

Charlie put his glass on the bar and took hers from her hand.

. . . three-and-two-and . . .

The marquee erupted. Everyone was screaming and kissing and hugging. Balloons cascaded from the ceiling.

'Happy New Year.' Charlie pulled her towards him. 'I'm so glad I'm a traditionalist . . .'

He kissed her. Gently. And then not so gently. And then she was kissing him back, and all the noise and colour and explosive vibration was inside her head and invading her body.

The DJ welcomed in the New Year with a blast mix of Roni Size and 'Auld Lang Syne'. Jemima simply didn't hear a thing.

March

CHAPTER THIRTY-SEVEN

He hadn't won the King George. He was pretty sure he wouldn't win the Cheltenham Gold Cup which was now only an hour away. And the Grand National? Forget it. And it was all Jemima's fault. Since New Year's Eve, Charlie simply hadn't been able to get her out of his mind.

It could have been so different. If only Gillian hadn't come belting up at what seemed like a split second after midnight, yelling that they'd found the twins bopping to Fizz Flanagan in the Ragga tent, and wasn't it a hugely tremendous relief? If only Lucinda hadn't shed her St Hilda's chums and said oh, hi, to Jemima, and then entwined herself around Charlie and said they had a lot of New Year's kisses—and the rest—to catch up on. If only Jemima hadn't looked at him shyly and sadly and said Happy New Year and walked away . . .

And he'd tried to follow her, but she'd disappeared into the throng outside. He'd stood in the icy early morning, the first snowflakes dissolving in his hair, and wanted to cry.

Charlie, who reckoned he'd performed every sexual equation known to man—and woman, of course—had been blown away by a kiss.

*   *   *

The snow had continued intermittently through January and into February. When it wasn't snowing, the temperatures plummeted to subzero again, and covered the Downs with royal icing. Now it was

555

March and a reluctant thaw had set in.

Drew and Kath, like every other National Hunt trainer in the country, were tearing their hair out over the disruption to their Blue Riband schedules. And, even more worrying, the weather in Ireland had been fairly mild by comparison, and the trials at Fairyhouse had thrown up some surprising, and extremely hot, competition.

Charlie had spent a lot of time sitting on the counter in the bookshop, or sprawling in Jemima's chair behind her desk. They'd talked—as they'd always talked—about everything.

They'd discussed the wave of gossip that had roared through Milton St John after Gillian's revelations. She had appeared on breakfast telly and all the local news programmes. Glen, after his initial shock, had been inordinately proud and supportive and, having received a rather censorious letter from the Bishop, had declared his intention of turning Baptist.

The Bishop, who had always had a soft spot for Gillian, Jemima told Charlie, had then battled his way through the Berkshire snowdrifts, and spent a weekend at the Vicarage. Gillian had shown him the classic works of other erotica writers such as Anaïs Nin, and pointed out that eminent writers such as D. H. Lawrence, and even good old Shakespeare, were not above hurling in huge chunks of pure titillation. The Bishop had left, convinced that God worked in mysterious ways indeed, with a parcel of Fishnets in his suitcase.

They'd talked about Matt's rather surprising suntan on his belated return from Devon. Jemima had said she hadn't seen much of him since he'd been back. Charlie hadn't been sure whether she meant she hadn't seen *Matt,* or she hadn't seen all of his suntanned body, and had been too scared to ask.

They'd talked about Lucinda's return to Southampton for the new term. They'd even discussed Tina's nation-wide television advertising campaign for a shampoo, which meant that they both saw her in their living rooms far more often than they wanted to.

Neither of them had mentioned New Year's Eve.

Bored to tears with the enforced lay-off because of the weather, Charlie had cleaned every bit of tack he could find at Peapods a million times; driven Maddy to distraction by picking Daragh up just as she'd got him to sleep; and started smoking again.

'For God's sake—tell her,' Maddy had insisted, falling over Charlie's legs in Peapods' kitchen yet again. 'Because if you don't, I will.'

'It won't make any difference, Mad.' He'd thrown his half-smoked cigarette into the embers of the range. 'She thinks I've got about as much depth as a puddle.'

'Charlie.' Maddy had dumped Poppy Scarlet and one of the new litter of kittens on his lap. 'You're absolutely gorgeous. You're kind and funny. You've never, ever failed to get any woman you've wanted. You've got Tina—well, not so much now, granted—but then she's working abroad a lot. And Lucinda in the vacs. And the postmen still get hernias from delivering your fan mail. Why the hell should Jemima turn you down?'

The kitten had turned round three times, purred, and fallen asleep on his knees. Charlie had buried his face in Poppy's dark, silky hair, curly like

557

Maddy's. It smelled sweet and fresh, and made him want to cry. For more than a decade he'd known that these surrogate babies were the nearest he'd ever get to having his own child. An accident had put paid to any chance of him ever establishing a Somerset dynasty. It had never been a problem. Until now. Because until now he'd never met anyone he wanted to spend the rest of his life with.

He lifted his head from Poppy Scarlet. 'Because I don't just want to go out with her.'

'Well, no, you wouldn't.' Maddy stopped in the middle of sorting out Daragh's Babygros from the tumble dryer. 'But I'm sure Jemima wouldn't mind going to bed with you eventually. It wouldn't be that much of a hardship.'

'I want to marry her.'

There. Now he'd said it. It had been hammering inside his brain for ages. Months. From long, long before New Year's Eve. For the first time in his life he had found the woman he wanted to marry—and he couldn't.

'Holy hell!' Maddy dropped the clutch of multicoloured towelling all-in-ones, and plonked herself in the rocking chair opposite him. 'Are you sure?'

He'd never been more sure of anything in his life.

Maddy picked up another kitten which was about to investigate the bottom oven. 'What about Matt? Are they still together?'

'No—yes. I'm not sure . . . I don't think so.'

'Then why the hell haven't you asked her out?'

'Because she has given me absolutely no reason to think that she wants me to.' He'd tickled Poppy Scarlet. 'Christ, Mad, you can always tell when

558

someone wants to take things further, can't you? She's still as cool as she ever was . . .'

'Except for the New Year kiss?' Maddy had cuddled the kitten. 'That didn't sound very cool to me.'

'Don't.' Charlie had groaned. 'It was the hottest thing ever. But now I think I might just have overamplified her response in my imagination—the way you do, you know? It may well have turned me upside down—but it probably didn't have the same effect on Jemima. And I've got absolutely nothing to offer her.'

Maddy had looked endearingly indignant. 'Of course you have. As well as all the attributes that are extremely well-chronicled, you'll also have a secure future here—either as Drew's assistant trainer if you and Bonnie win the National, or as a very much sought-after freelance jockey even if you don't.'

'I know. But that wasn't really what I meant.'

Maddy had wrinkled her nose. 'Wasn't it? Well, if you're asking for my advice, which I don't think you are, I'd say test the water. Ask her out. The poor girl might be longing to become a notch on the Wallbank-Fox for all you know. Oh—sorry, you want more than that, don't you?'

'I want her to be a permanent fixture in it.'

'She's never going to get past the duvet if you don't damn well ask her out to start with though, is she?'

'I can't.' Charlie had sighed. 'I can't—because I don't want her to say no. If she said no, then that would be the end of it, wouldn't it? I know she likes me—we've had some nice friendly times together.' think she thinks I'm incredibly lightweight. I don't

559

think she could ever—well—love me.'

Maddy had laughed and shooed the kitten away to find its mother. 'Charlie Somerset—I honestly think you're really and truly in love!'

He was. He wasn't sure he liked it. He had loved every single one of his girlfriends, however casual. It was the *in* bit that was a totally new experience.

And Maddy had asked about Matt. Well, Matt was another problem. Matt had thrown away the Hennessey—he was sure of it—especially now after the conversation he'd overheard at the wedding reception. Fortunately, the resulting injuries had prevented him from ballsing up anything else. And obviously, as the King George had proved, Liam Jenkins hadn't been in on Ned's scam.

'He's only on the end of a bloody phone,' Kath Seaward had said laconically in the Cat and Fiddle. 'No point in him kicking his sodding heels here when he can be getting himself into shape somewhere in the sun. Lucky bastard! Wish I could do the same. He'll be back in time for Cheltenham.'

And he had been. But he'd still been almost impossible to talk to. He'd worked Dragon Slayer every minute he could, spent hours in the sauna, and had refused all Charlie's offers of reinstating their double-act in the Cat and Fiddle on the grounds that he needed to be two hundred per cent fit after his lay-off.

Jemima hadn't seen much of him either, apparently. Or so she'd said. The fact that Jemima and Matt were no longer together as such, and therefore Charlie didn't have to worry about their blood-brothers pact, failed to lift his gloom. What the hell did it matter? His own reputation was his undoing.

Jemima would never take him seriously. She'd been with Matt for ages, even though he was a jockey and she hadn't liked racing, because he was well-read. Charlie Somerset, jump jockey and ladykiller. That just about summed him up. What the hell would someone like Jemima ever see in someone like him?

And then, of course, there was Vincent. If Vincent and Ned and Matt were in on some sort of fiddle together—and he was still sure despite Jemima's assurances to the contrary—then he'd have to let him know that he knew. Jemima would be devastated if she ever found out. She was so proud of her father—and she'd hate Charlie if he colluded with him, wouldn't she? Christ—it was so complicated.

And once that was cleared up—if it ever was— and he'd told Tina and Lucinda that they were both a thing of the past, which he felt neither would really mind about too much—he still couldn't offer Jemima anything. Well, nothing that he felt she wanted. And certainly not what she deserved.

*　　　*　　　*

And now it was Cheltenham. Gold Cup Day. The last day of the meeting. He'd had two winners on the previous days for trainers other than Drew, and a couple of seconds, and a third for Martin Pipe in the Champion Hurdle. Matt had been even more successful, having just won the prestigious Triumph Hurdle on Kath's Boating Party. The media were now revving up over Dragon Slayer in the Gold Cup—and the possibility of the most spectacular double of the decade.

'Don't worry,' Drew had said, patting his shoulder. 'I know Cheltenham is the punters' paradise, but I'd be happier with you winning the National. Bonnie will come good for the Gold Cup in future years if Gillian keeps him in training—although, sadly, not with me . . . Still, concentrate on getting him round safely. Dragon Slayer—and that bloody Irish raider are the ones we'll have to beat.'

Charlie had nodded and drifted back to the changing room to pull on the Fishnet colours. No horse had done the Gold Cup and Grand National double for more than twenty-five years. Garrison Savannah had been the nearest—and that had been ages ago. He knew he had very little chance.

The changing room, as always highly-charged with fear and excitement and the stench of sweat, was chaotic. Matt was sitting alone, already wearing Tina's colours. Charlie, getting cursed by everyone, yanked his stuff from his allotted peg and shoved his way towards him.

'Congratulations. Great win.'

'Thanks.'

Charlie fastened his stock, pulled on his breeches over a pair of laddered tights and picked up his jersey. 'Do you reckon you'll do the double?'

Matt seemed to flinch. 'Which double?'

'Today. The Triumph and the Gold Cup.'

'Christ knows. I'm bloody knackered now. I didn't think I'd feel so unfit.'

And that, Charlie thought, was the longest sentence Matt had uttered for months.

He pulled Gillian's shocking pink and black colours over his head. 'Tina will be rooting for you, anyway.'

There was a definite flinch this time. 'What? Has she said so?'

'Christ, no.' Charlie sat on the bench and tugged on the paper-thin riding boots. 'I haven't seen her for ages. I know she's flown in for today because it was all over Ceefax this morning. To be honest, I think me and Tina are a thing of the past. I'm pretty sure she's frying other fish.'

'Fucking stop talking about food!' an anguished voice howled from the far end of the room. 'I'm sodding starving!'

Everyone laughed. Matt didn't. 'Really? Does that bother you?'

'It's a relief, actually. I've now got all my required layers of epidermis. So—what about you?'

Matt practically jerked from the bench. 'What about me?'

'You and Jemima . . .' Charlie felt like he was wading through treacle. He hadn't got a clue what murky undercurrents were tugging at this particular conversation, but something seemed very wrong. Still, at least Matt was talking. 'I take it you're no longer together?'

'We're still friends . . . we've decided to call a halt on anything else.'

He tried not to beam too broadly. 'So Jennifer got an engagement ring for Christmas, did she?'

'Who?'

'Jennifer. Your faithful bit of Totnes totty. She must have been delighted to see you at Christmas— and the temperatures must have soared on the Torquay Riviera.' Charlie stood up and collected his whip, gloves and cap. 'That suntan could have come from the Caribbean . . . Although I'm no expert, I'd say it came from somewhere very like

563

the Virgin Islands.'

Matt glowered at him. 'Fuck off.'

Bingo! Charlie thought, pushing his way jubilantly through the weighing room. Bloody, sodding bingo!

Tina and Matt! It had to be. He wasn't sure why or how or even when—but it didn't matter. Not any more. Had it been Tina that Matt had been with at Drew and Maddy's wedding, then? Yeah—it must have been—it all made sense. He laughed. What an actress! No wonder she was getting so many offers of television work.

So, that was one problem solved. He wouldn't tell Jemima. Not yet. And even when he did, he'd fudge the timing for her. No woman liked to feel they'd been cheated on, did they?

Shit. He pulled up short at the door. *He'd* been cheated on, too. Bloody hell. No one had ever done that to him before—and with *Matt*? What the hell had Matt Garside got that he hadn't? What on earth had Tina found in Matt that he hadn't provided? And if Tina preferred Matt to him— then why shouldn't Jemima? Oh, God . . . Matt had Tina—and he'd had Jemima, too. Lucky, lucky sod.

He shivered in the biting wind that still prowled over the southern half of the country and was having a grand time playing havoc with the hats in Prestbury Park. This really was the most spectacular racecourse in the country. With its natural amphitheatre, and Cleeve Hill as a backdrop, it was no wonder that the whole steeplechasing world made the pilgrimage to Cheltenham for the festival.

The three-day meeting provided every racegoer with everything he or she could want: top-class horses jumping an incredible selection of obstacles over various distances; a classy social event a chance to spot the potential National prospects; and a party atmosphere to celebrate the end of winter.

It was a real rite of spring. Or at least, it should be. Charlie shivered. There had been Gold Cups run in blinding snowstorms—and although snow seemed unlikely today, it was still freezing.

The intrusive eye of the television cameras peered at him as he stood in the doorway. He wondered if Jemima was watching and smiled just in case. Milton St John had organised a coach, as always, and were putting up in various Cheltenham hotels for the meeting. Jemima wasn't amongst them. She wasn't in Milton St John, either. She'd gone back to Oxford to stay with Lauren or Louise or someone who she'd worked with, leaving Tracy in charge of the shop.

'There'll be no one in the village,' she said to Charlie. 'It'll be dead quiet. And I haven't seen any of the Bookworms crowd for almost a year. I'm looking forward to it.'

Charlie had hoped that she wouldn't be looking up old boyfriends—and then hated himself for the thought. He'd asked her if she'd be watching the meeting.

She'd smiled. 'Maybe. If I'm anywhere near a television set.'

He hoped she was.

The stir indicated that the Gold Cup was getting under way. The first horses were already in the paddock, and the watching crowds were yards thick. He could hear the clerk of the scales starting the weigh-in, and shrugged his shoulders. He hoped Bonnie was up to it.

                    *   *   *

The paddock was crammed full. Every horse
seemed to have countless connections, all milling
around, looking glamorous. He walked from the
weighing room, matching Matt stride for stride.

'About Tina—it's okay.'

Matt said nothing. Charlie, aware that the
television cameras Were on them, and knowing
that the most ardent armchair punters craned their
necks to read lips at this juncture in the hope of
picking up some hot tips, spoke through his grin.
'Honestly, Matt. It doesn't matter. Good luck to
you. Both of you.'

Matt looked sick. He always worried before a
race, but this was something different. God, Charlie
thought, why the hell do we do it? Starve and live
unnatural lives—simply to gamble with death. He
smiled again at the cameras. That was probably
why. The risk, excitement. The sheer undeniable
thrill of chasing a race.

They were very close to the horses. Charlie, still
smiling for the all-invasive electronic eye, touched
Matt's arm. 'You and Tina being together is fine—
but if you throw this race I'll go to the stewards.'

'Uh?' Matt looked even more sick. 'I don't know
what you mean.'

'I don't know why you're doing it—especially not
now you're with Tina—but I know you are. Matt, if
you're in some sort of trouble . . .

'Shut up!' There were tears in his eyes. 'Just shut
up. Christ, Charlie—we're mates. Please, please
keep your mouth shut.'

'You're cheating. Tina, Kath, the punters . . .'

'I'm fighting to survive.' Matt's teeth were gritted. 'And if you say anything—one word—to anyone, then I'm finished.'

Charlie could see the terror in his eyes. Shit. He couldn't say anything. He knew he couldn't. 'Play it straight then, for fuck's sake.'

Gillian and Glen and the twins were clustered round Bonnie, looking extremely proud. Gillian had got almost as much newspaper coverage as Tina over her ownership. She smiled vaguely at him, her long pale hair whipped from beneath the oatmeal cartwheel brim of her hat.

'Won't be a sec.' Charlie kissed her cheek. 'I've just got to talk to someone.'

He walked towards Kath Seaward, in her Cheltenham best of trench coat and beret, and the rest of Dragon Slayer's contingent. The cameras were following him, he was sure. Well, let them make what they wanted from it. Let Matt make more. Let Matt come to his bloody senses.

'Hi.' He Tipped his cap towards Tina. Matt, who was talking to Kath, glanced across, white-faced, and shook his head. Charlie touched Tina's arm. His voice was barely a whisper. 'Sweetheart, I know all about you and Matt. I just want you to know that I think it's great. We'd gone as far as we could, hadn't we?'

Tina, all in black which displayed her tan to perfection, nodded, looking rather surprised. 'Yeah, I guess so. Anyway, it wasn't love, was it?'

'God, no. It still isn't, I suppose . . .'

'It is actually.' Tina smiled gently across at Matt who was visibly shaking. 'I completely adore him. And it's surprisingly mutual. I'm amazed that you're not more shocked, to be honest. You were

567

always so straight . . . Brilliant, of course. The best. But Matt's just perfect for me.'

'Good,' Charlie said, feeling that he might have missed a nuance somewhere. 'Anyway, I know he's sick with nerves, but I've said much the same thing to him. No hard feelings . . .'

Tina laughed loudly. 'Oh, don't put yourself down, darling! We had dozens of those!'

'Charlie!' Drew's frantic hiss carried across the paddock. 'For Christ's sake—there'll be tons of time for that later!'

Charlie grinned, kissed Tina's cheek, shook his head sadly at Matt, and ran back to Bonnie.

'About bloody time.' Drew's eyes were laughing. 'You really do take womanising to the nth degree. Now, get up in the saddle.'

He swung himself on to Bonne Nuit's broad chestnut back. He'd done all he could. He hoped he'd scared the shit out of Matt. He couldn't do any more. The Hutchinsons were gazing up at him with delight. Even Glen. He hoped that he wouldn't be struck down by some celestial deity on the run-in.

'Don't worry if he's not going to get there,' Drew said quietly. 'Keep him safe. Matt's going to go at this one like the hammers of hell, no doubt. With the double being up for grabs for Lancing Grange, Kath will have told him to ride a hard race. Keep away from him. Just let Bonnie do what he does naturally. The National's only two weeks away. I don't want him crocked.'

'Okay. Understood. No problems.' Charlie touched his cap. 'See you in the winner's enclosure.'

*   *   *

568

You stupid bastard!' Charlie panted from the side of his mouth when they were three-quarters of the way through the race. 'You're not trying!'

Matt was scrubbing along on Dragon Slayer, keeping out of danger, looking as though he was working flat out. Charlie knew he wasn't.

'Mind your own pissing business,' Matt hissed. 'Ride your own race. Keep your mouth shut.'

Bonne Nuit was third, almost level with the easily-moving Dragon Slayer. Christ, but it was an artistic performance. Kath would never spot that she'd been cheated of the double. Tina would think both horse and jockey had worked their socks off. But Matt and Dragon Slayer wouldn't win. And they could have done it easily. Matt had buckets in hand. Charlie couldn't, for the life of him, understand why he'd want to throw it away.

'Sorry . . .' he muttered as Bonne Nuit lost the plot a bit. He couldn't worry about Matt. Not now. He had far too much to do. 'Sorry—just keep ploughing on, baby . . .'

He was exhausted. Every muscle ached. Cheltenham was a killer of a course. It really tested your stamina. And the Gold Cup, packed full of stars, was always run at a cracking pace. It had been a hard festival. Maybe he should be thinking of giving it up . . . But not until he'd won the National.

He thought briefly of Jemima watching on television in Oxford . . . Horses were crashing to the ground behind him. He didn't dare to look. He hoped they survived the carnage. He pulled slightly ahead of Matt at the fourth from home, Bonne Nuit meeting the fences just right.

Matt was falling further and further behind. Sodding hell. He'd thrown this one just like the

Hennesey. But why? In God's name, why?

Christ, he thought suddenly, as Bonnie surged over the notoriously difficult third from last, countering the dizzy downward slide, they might just win it. They might win the Gold Cup.

They didn't. But third was pretty damn good—especially behind a previous winner, and the well-in-form raider from Ireland. Drew and the Hutchinsons were jubilant.

Matt and Dragon Slayer came in last of the ten finishers.

April

CHAPTER THIRTY-EIGHT

So, Jemima wondered, what sort of masochist was she? Just over two weeks after Cheltenham and here she was at Aintree. Where she'd have the immense pleasure of being able to watch Tina and Charlie together all day. She'd managed to avoid him since Cheltenham, pretending to be busy if he called into the shop, and not visiting Vincent at Peapods unless she knew Charlie wouldn't be there. What was the point of prolonging the agony?

Gillian had been convinced there'd be an engagement announcement pretty soon—but maybe it would be after the National—not Cheltenham. She hadn't been too clear.

A lot of the villagers, including Vincent and Maureen, had travelled up for the full three days. Jemima had driven up to Liverpool in Floss that morning. She had avoided all the organised coaches, and even refused the offer of a luxury lift in Gillian and Glen's chauffeur-driven car—hired from Fernydown Limousines—especially for the occasion.

Most of the village crew were staying at the Adelphi. Maddy had even brought Poppy Scarlet and Daragh, having left Suzy, who was now irrevocably estranged from Luke, at Peapods to look after the animals. Jemima, who until the last minute had been refusing to go, had been practically coerced into it by Gillian.

'You don't have to watch the actual race if you're worried about the horses,' she'd said. 'I always used to keep my eyes shut and catch the replay later. But

I want you to be there to watch Bonnie and Charlie line up with me. We've shared this—all of it—right from the beginning, haven't we?'

Jemima had sighed and said yes, but she still thought she'd stay at home.

Gillian had persisted. 'Oh! But you've been brilliant about everything. No one else is half so important . . . At least, think about it.'

And Jemima had said it was a very kind thought but she looked awful in hats. She'd looked a complete fright at the Hennessey in that brown one she'd borrowed from Gillian.

'You don't have to wear a hat! I shall, of course, because I love them. But you don't have to.'

'I haven't got anything half decent to wear anyway . . .'

'Just wear what you want. Anything goes, apparently.' Gillian had waved her hands expansively. 'Help yourself from my wardrobe. Borrow whatever you fancy.'

Jemima had shaken her head.

'Just say you'll think about it.' Gillian had hugged her. 'I've got you all the necessary tickets and passes. Take them anyway. Just in case you change your mind. Go on, Jemima, please . . .'

She'd shaken her head more firmly this time. 'It's really kind of you—and I wish you all the luck in the world, of course. But I'll just stay at home and watch it on television.'

And so here she was, standing in the middle of Aintree, done up to the nines in Gillian's special Ghost collection, wondering if she needed certifying.

It was daunting. She needn't have worried about seeing Tina and Charlie together. She doubted if she'd ever see the same person twice. Thousands and thousands of people were jammed everywhere. It was akin to the Cup Final being held on a village football pitch.

The noise was amazing. It was like listening to the roar of the ocean. Incessant. Rising and falling. Always changing. And she could taste the excitement. The anticipation.

She'd never find Vincent or Maureen—let alone Gillian and Glen and the boys. Jesus. What the hell was she doing here? She jostled her way towards one of the many maps.

There were three courses! God! Being punched and pushed from every direction, she reluctantly decided that maybe using Gillian's pass would be a good idea. At least she wouldn't be trampled underfoot. She squinted at the map again. Not the Mildmay Course or the Hurdle Course then— although they both seemed to be joined to the National Course by a mind-boggling array of criss-cross lines like the London Underground. Jemima groaned. She had never been able to fathom that, either.

Clutching the necessary paperwork—proclaiming her to be Guest of Owner—she started to elbow her way in what she hoped was the right direction.

The sky was a sort of pale watered silk, with a matching pale lemon sun. It was reminiscent of a muted version of the Hampton-Hydes' decor— over a year ago . . . Over a year ago since she'd reluctantly rolled out of Simon Hampton-Hyde's birthday cake and changed her life.

The ground was surprisingly flat. She had expected the hills of Cheltenham or at least the undulations of Newbury. The flatness had the disadvantage of making the crowds seem larger than ever. She could see the tops of a million heads and the edge of several giant Star Vision screens, but very little else.

Eureka! By raising herself on tiptoe she could see the stands! And tents! And boxes! And even chalets! It looked like Butlins.

Jemima cannoned into a group of top hats and fur coats and apologised, then clammed up when she thought the fur might be real. Still, it meant she was probably heading in the right direction. Showing her pass to every steward she encountered, she entered a slightly different scrum. Here, everyone was practically manic, slapping backs, puffing on nervous cigarettes, calling to people who were completely hidden from view. And everyone seemed to be wearing sheepskin.

'Jemima!' A tall vision in shocking pink and black, courtesy of the combined talents of Nicole Farhi and Philip Treacy, moved through the crowd towards her. 'Oh, isn't this simply wonderful!'

She smiled at Gillian. It would be impossible not to smile. Happiness glowed from her and radiated in the cool grey air around her like the ectoplasm in *Ghostbusters*.

Glen and the boys are having a tour of the course with Drew—but I was far, far too nervous. Have you seen the size of the fences! Enormous! I can't ask Bonnie to jump those. The poor thing will faint with fright. You look wonderful. The colour really suits you. It looks far better on you than it ever did on me . . . And you're just in time for the first race.'

Jemima, feeling extremely wimpish, shook her head. 'Honestly, I'd far rather not watch. I know I was fine at Newbury—and I managed to sit through

Cheltenham on the telly —'

Oh yes, she thought. Cheltenham. Bloody Cheltenham.

*   *   *

In Oxford, Laura had turned on the television. It was no problem, she'd said. She always watched the Cheltenham Gold Cup herself—she'd got twenty quid on the Irish horse—and just exactly when had Jemima changed her opinion about horse-racing?

When? God knows . . . It had been a slow process. And Charlie? Just when had she changed her mind about him? Months ago. Long before New Year's Eve, anyway. Although, if she hadn't, that kiss would have definitely swayed things.

She'd touched her lips, remembering. Savouring the memory. It had been utterly blissful. But then Charlie was a genius, wasn't he? Lucinda had said so. And now she knew for herself. The man who had become her friend and ally, had changed her perspective on life and love and men. And it was too late.

She had pushed out of her mind what might have happened on New Year's Eve if the whole world hadn't suddenly decided to gatecrash their party.

'Jemima?' Laura had been staring at her across the room. 'You okay? I said—'

'Yeah—sorry. I—um—haven't changed my opinion,' Jemima had said, snatching her fingers away from her mouth, realising that Laura was grinning. 'Not really . . .'

Then Charlie's face had been smiling at her. She'd almost kissed the screen. Sod. Damn. Bugger. Just when exactly *had* he crept up on her?

577

They'd shared so much. Become friends despite everything. And now, when she would never want to be just friends with him again, it was too damn late. He and Tina were just about to announce their engagement. Probably straight after Cheltenham. Gillian had said so.

'He is sooo gorgeous.' Laura had draped herself over the arm of the sofa, ogling him. 'He's got to be the sexiest man in the whole world. I've even forgiven him for screwing up in last year's Grand National. And you actually know him? You lucky cow!'

Jemima had said, well, she sort of knew him, and hoped she wasn't blushing too much.

They had shared such a lot of things: thanks to Charlie Somerset she would never feel the same about trees again. She'd probably still be climbing trees way into her dotage and boring people rigid with the story of this beautiful man who had introduced her to the art.

She would see him around the village, of course. It would be impossible not to. Unless he and Tina moved away—she'd felt sick. Which would be worse? Seeing him with Tina—or not seeing him at all? She wasn't sure . . .

They'd discussed Matt. Not that there was a lot to talk about. Neither of them had seen him for long, but they'd spent a lovely hour speculating on the origin of his sun tan—and it had surprised her that she hadn't minded in the slightest that Matt had lied to her about where he was spending Christmas.

And hunting . . . They'd congratulated each other on the ill-wind effect. If the icy weather had meant Charlie couldn't work, it had also meant a halt to the fox-hunting brigade's jollies, as well. They'd even toasted each other in coffee in the bookshop's kitchen when Reynard/Morpheus, aka Trev Perkiss, had got a custodial sentence for dealing at the Nuke.

'Best place for him,' Charlie had said. 'Banged up. It leaves the way clear for people like Millie and Frank and Enid and us to get the anti-hunting message across, doesn't it?'

She'd raised her coffee cup to him, loving the reference to 'us'.

And they'd laughed, and teased each other, and it had been lovely. But he hadn't asked her out— and she was too afraid of rejection to ask him . . .

Back in Laura's parents' front room, the television cameras had Panned across the parade ring as the jockeys came out of the Prestbury Park weighing room—and there had been Charlie chatting to Matt, who looked so nervous, poor thing. She would always be fond of him. Probably more so now. So what if he hadn't fancied her? It wasn't really that much of a surprise. And after his holiday—she hadn't asked him where he'd been, merely told him the suntan suited him—he had been so much more relaxed. Nicer, somehow.

She had parted company with a fair few men in her time: as break-ups went, hers and Matt's had been among the most amicable. Pity, she'd thought, that Charlie hadn't seen it as an invitation. But then, why should he?

'Where's Charlie off to?' Laura had giggled, squinting at the screen. 'I thought you said he was riding for that vicar's wife you live with?'

'He is. He does.'

'Oh, God!' Laura had moaned, hugging a

579

cushion. 'Look at those thighs!'

Jemima already was. And then she had watched as he'd kissed Gillian briefly and walked over to Dragon Slayer's camp.

'Wow!' Laura had said. 'Tina Maloret! She's awesome! So stunning! Don't they make the most perfectly glamorous couple?'

Yes, Jemima had thought, her teeth clenched together. They did.

He'd been talking to Tina, his mouth close to her ear. Jemima had felt hot with humiliation, as Tina laughed straight into his eyes. Then, even worse, he'd kissed Tina's cheek and walked away.

Jemima had wished he would stop smiling at the bloody camera. She had been kidding herself that he was smiling just for her. She wanted to cry.

'I wouldn't mind living in Milton St John,' Laura had sighed. 'All those gorgeous men—and horses thrown in. Heaven.' She'd wriggled round on the sofa. 'If you're ever looking for an assistant, give me a shout.'

Jemima said she might well do that. The shop was doing extraordinarily well. Tracy didn't want to work full-time. And Laura had been Bookworms-trained. Why not?

'Jemima! You're not watching the race,' Laura had said later. 'Aren't you interested?'

She had shaken her head, averting her eyes from the screen. 'I told you I wasn't. Chuck me the *Oxford Times*—I want to see what's on at the cinema tonight.'

*   *   *

Gillian's voice wrenched her back to the present.

580

'Jemima! Wake up! I said, the first race is only a two-mile hurdle—'

'What? Oh, right—but I'd like to find Dad and Maureen. I mean, once the National starts, you'll be the centre of attention, won't you? I'll have to find another shoulder to hide my eyes in.'

'And I bet you hid behind the sofa in *Dr Who*, too!'

'I did not! That was years before my time!'

'Mine too—oh, goodness—look at the screen! The jockeys are coming out for the first race. That means only two hours to go to the National. There's Matt—looks very dour in dark green, doesn't he? I can't understand why more owners don't have bright colours—'

'Gillian!' Jemima practically stamped her foot. 'Please tell me where I can find Dad.'

Eventually, after much oohing and aahing about Matt as he forced his way into the parade ring, Gillian pointed her in the direction of the Owners' and Trainers' Bar. 'Arkle,' she said. 'I'm still not sure if that's the beer or the racehorse.'

*   *   *

Jemima found Vincent and Maureen sitting at a table overlooking the Chair and the Water Jump. The winning post was just visible if you leaned forwards. Jemima took one look at the jumps on the National course and felt sick. Gillian had been right. They looked big on television—in real life they were simply enormous.

'Jem, love!' Vincent was on his feet, hugging her. 'You look a picture! I didn't think you'd come. This is wonderful. Sit down, I'll get some drinks . . .'

She sat, still staring at the Chair. Last year, she'd ignored the Grand National coverage, dismissing it as cruel and a complete waste of time and money. Then she'd had absolutely no idea what it really entailed to be a jockey facing those obstacles. Charlie and Matt—and Liam and Philip and all the other men who she'd met in Milton St John—risked their lives doing this every day. And today more than ever.

'That outfit really suits you—oh, I say . . . You all right, duck?' Maureen, absolutely dazzling in black-and-gold lurex, leaned across the table. 'You've gone as white as a sheet.'

'Fine. I'm fine, thanks.'

'Right exciting all this, don't you think? And so kind of Gillian to get us into the toffs' enclosure.'

Jemima nodded. The jumps drew her back with horrifying fascination. What about the horses, though? They had always been her main concern. The jockeys had a choice—but no one asked the horses, did they? She'd spent enough time in Milton St John now to know that no one forced the horses to jump: it came naturally. And the horses entered for the Grand National were trained specially to cope with these mountainous fences. She knew how much training went into getting horses like Bonne Nuit and Dragon Slayer absolutely ready for today. She knew all this—but it still worried her.

'They're off!' Maureen roared along with about three million other people, craning her neck to see the start of the first race on the screen. 'Pull your chair round, duck, and get a better view.'

'No, thanks. Honestly, I'm fine here.' Jemima tried very hard not to listen to the commentary; she didn't want to hear the roars or the gasps or—

even worse—the shocked silence which obviously marked a tragedy. She closed her eyes and prayed that Matt got round safely.

Jockeys' wives, she reckoned, must die a thousand deaths.

'Here we are.' Vincent put the tray on the table just as the whole bar erupted. Maureen was practically hanging out of the window. 'Took a bloody age to get served. Just in time. Did you— er—have any money on young Matt, then?'

'No, of course not. And I hope you didn't, either.'

'Me? Not a penny.' Vincent sat down and squinted through the window. 'Which is probably just as well, because he's come in fourth of five . . .'

At least he was still alive.

'Have you seen the prices for the National, then, love?' Vincent sat back in his chair sipping his vodka-and-lime.

She hadn't. Somewhere, out of the corner of her eye, she caught a flash of gold. Looking up quickly she was just in time to see Maureen's vigorous shake of the head.

'Why? Should I? Is Bonnie favourite?'

'Ten to one and going in all the time.' Vincent clanked the ashtray across the table and span it round. 'The big Irish horse, Jack's Joker, is favourite. Probably the housewives' choice because of the name. Can't think of any other reason. He hasn't got much form to speak of. Maybe he'll be another Foinavon.'

'Who?'

'I don't think Jemima wants to know about Foinavon, Vincent, duck.' Maureen was quivering iridescently.

Jemima thought she just might. 'Who was he?'

'Oh—a horse. Rank outsider. Hundred to one. Won the National in 1967. Practically the only one left standing after a multiple pile-up at the fence after Becher's.'

Jemima felt sick again. 'What? They all fell? All the horses in the field?'

'Most of 'em.' Vincent's eyes gleamed at the memory. 'Just a couple left, I think. Foinavon was plum last, so he avoided the carnage, see? What?' He glanced at Maureen who was nodding towards Jemima like an automaton. 'Oh, right—but of course, that sort of thing doesn't happen nowadays. No—there'll be nothing like that today.'

'Of course there won't be,' Maureen said briskly. 'Now, who says yes to another tipple?'

Jemima pushed her glass forward. What would she do if that sort of thing happened again? How could she just sit and watch while horses and jockeys were trampled underfoot? How could she bear it if it was Charlie?

. . . so Bonnie could end up second favourite— or even joint . . .Vincent was still playing with the ashtray.

Again, Jemima was aware of Maureen almost imperceptibly twitching her head.

Gillian would be over the moon if he won. She'd put a lot of her Fishnets money on him already. She was bound to pile even more on today. And she didn't need to lose it again now that she'd come out, did she? 'What about Dragon Slayer?'

Vincent dropped the ashtray with a clatter. Maureen snatched it away and put it on the next table. 'Thirty threes,' she said tersely. 'And lengthening. Now go and get those drinks, duck.

I'm fair parched here.'

*   *   *

Jemima managed, by the same method of steadfastly not looking or listening, to avoid watching the following Red Rum Chase and the Aintree Hurdle. Neither Charlie nor Matt had been riding, and she'd clenched her hands beneath the table each time she knew from the intake of breath that someone had fallen.

'Up on their feet,' Maureen said, patting her hand. 'All safe and sound and hunky-dory.'

She still wished that she hadn't brought Floss and could have drowned her nerves in a gallon of gin-and-tonic.

'We making a move then?' Vincent said, as the tannoy announced that the jockeys had weighed in from the last race and that the Grand National preparations were now under way. 'We want to get down there and get a good view of them in the ring, don't we?'

Jemima didn't think she did, actually. But she was determined not to let Vincent out of her sight. Although, she thought as she pushed back her chair, he certainly hadn't had any money riding on anything so far. She'd recognise the signs if he had. She'd seen them often enough. Vincent had stayed calm and detached throughout all three races.

Not now though. He was simply buzzing. Firing on all cylinders. And why, she wondered, following them out of the bar, had Maureen been giving him semaphore messages throughout the discussion on the Grand National?

She shook her head. He was an old rogue. Well,

585

he'd have her to deal with if he thought he was going to go within sniffing distance of a bookmaker this afternoon.

*   *   *

They stood on the rails and watched the horses parading prior to the big race. Thirty-nine of them. Jemima hoped they'd all be alive at the end of it. Gillian and Glen, with Levi and Zeke, were standing with Drew and Maddy in the middle of the ring. Everyone waved.

Then the jockeys spilled out. Oh, they looked so glamorous! So young. Debonair. Like knights about to joust, Jemima thought. Matt was sauntering boldly towards the tall fiery black Dragon Slayer. Tina Maloret, again all in black, was smiling at him. So was Kath Seaward in her trench coat and maroon beret. Matt didn't turn his head. His eyes seemed to be fixed on Tina. Jemima wondered if he still disliked her as much as he had. She hoped not. It would be nice if they all got on. She hadn't expected him to look for her, of course. He had no idea that she would be there.

Still, she thought as she stared at Tina, her bets must be well and truly hedged. Matt riding her horse—and Charlie . . . Well, Charlie would be marrying her—or at least announcing his intention of doing so—probably right after the race. Jemima felt her hands tighten on the white rails.

She was, she realised, as jealous as hell of Tina Maloret.

'There's Charlie.' Maureen nudged her. 'Dead glam, isn't he?'

Oh, God. He was. Totally, totally, bloody

gorgeous. He was signing autographs all the way into the paddock, smiling, flirting, with no apparent trace of nerves. Jemima devoured him with her eyes. He didn't know she was there, either.

The horses were led into the centre of the ring by their lads. The tension was mounting. Adrenalin fizzed around the course like fireflies on an August night. Bonne Nuit, so much smaller than Dragon Slayer, with his sweet face, nuzzled up against Charlie. Charlie kissed his nose which brought a roar of laughter from the crowd.

Lucky, lucky Bonne Nuit, Jemima thought, sighing.

At some unheard given signal, the jockeys were all legged-up into the saddles. Everyone sucked in their breath and prepared to move to their allotted vantage points.

Not long to go now.

Jemima continued to stare at Charlie as Bonne Nuit plodded round the ring. Oh, God, she prayed, please, please let them be all right. I'll never lust over him again, or be jealous of Tina, or, well— anything—as long as you let them get round safely . . .

He was walking towards her now, leaning down, whip in one hand, adjusting his stirrups. As he straightened, he saw her. His grin was broad and beautiful and wildly infectious. He stared at her, still grinning crookedly, then winked and blew her a kiss.

Blushing from her head to her toes, she watched Bonne Nuit's gleaming quarters disappear towards the course.

'I'm going to break the habit of a lifetime,' she beamed at Vincent and Maureen. 'I'm going to put a tenner on Bonnie.'

There was a stunned and strange silence. All around them, people were rushing away, eager not to miss a second of the action on the course.

'I wouldn't, duck.' Maureen spoke softly. 'He ain't going to win.'

'What?' Jemima was still as high as a kite from Charlie's smile and the air-kiss. 'Are you psychic or something? He's got as good a chance as any.'

'No he hasn't, duck.' Maureen's blonde hair, tucked beneath the black-and-golden hat, was falling in brittle strands across her forehead. 'Has he, Vincent?'

Jemima looked at her father in complete bewilderment. 'Dad? I don't understand.'

'Tell her, Vincent. Tell her.' Maureen touched his arm with tenderness. 'Tell her what's going on. It's been keeping you awake at nights for too long. And Jemima's got a right to know.'

He told her.

She stood, transfixed, unable to believe it. She wanted to kill him. She wanted to kill Ned. And she definitely wanted to kill Matt.

Apparently some of it was news to Maureen, too. 'You never said that, Vincent. You just said Dragon Slayer would win the National. You never said he'd bump Charlie out to do it. I wouldn't have condoned that. And I've put all my holiday money on Dragon—'

'Sod your holiday money!' Jemima howled, grabbing Vincent's shoulders. 'What about Charlie and Bonnie? Charlie could be hurt—he could die—Bonnie could die! You stupid, stupid, greedy bastard! You've got to stop him! You've got to tell someone! Oh—if you won't, then I bloody well will!'

And gathering up the borrowed coat, she tore towards the course.

'Can't get through here now, madam.' The steward barred her way. 'They've all gone down to the start. Race'll be off in next to no time. You best find yourself a good viewing spot—if there are any left. Don't want to miss any of it, do you?'

Jemima stared up at the Star Vision screen as Charlie and Bonnie circled round with the other horses, taking a look at the first fence, then cantering back towards the start.

She had to warn him. To tell him what Matt was going to do.

They were lining up now. The starter had raised his flag. She had to tell him. She simply had to . . .

'They're off!'

A scream of excitement rocked Aintree as the tape flew away cleanly and thirty-nine horses cavalry-charged towards the first fence.

CHAPTER THIRTY-NINE

A year. A whole year on. And it was so different. Charlie sat, crouched over Bonne Nuit's burnished-conker neck, knowing that he was strapped aboard a rocket. If he'd thought Dragon Slayer was the best horse he'd ever ridden in last year's National, Bonnie, in this, had got the beatings of him hands down.

Having endlessly discussed various strategies, winning formulae, and plans of action, with Drew, and after watching hours of video tape, he'd elected

589

to start in the centre of the pack. This way, both he and Drew felt that if there were fallers ahead, it would give Bonnie two directions in which to swerve to avoid a pile-up. So far it had worked well.

One circuit completed. Half the horses already out of the race. The Chair—the most hazardous fence to occur only once on the circuit—had been successfully completed, and he still had bags in hand. Bonnie was a star.

Halfway round the course. Exhaustion was setting in. Muscles were aching. He'd have to pace himself for the final two miles if he was going to have anything left for that tortuous run-in.

Coming up to the twenty-first now, and several of the greener horses ahead of him who had survived the first round, belted away across the Melling road and immediately came to grief. Charlie winced. Bonnie met the fence just right. Up and over. They were lying about ninth or tenth and cruising. It was a brilliant feeling. Jack's Joker, the big Irish horse, was still thundering on up front, leading as he had from the start. Charlie was sure that if Bonnie got round safely, he'd have the beating of him for speed on the run-in. Dragon Slayer must be behind—perhaps he'd fallen—perhaps he'd pulled up . . .

Matt hadn't spoken to him. Charlie had asked cheerfully if he'd intended to chuck this race away too, and had been met with a snarl. He'd taken that as a no.

Concentrate. The end of the straight and Becher's Brook coming up for the second time. Nice position. Nice pace. Just right. Jump fast. Jump fast enough to clear the fence, clear the brook on the other side, be on course for the next two bends . . . Bonnie was well tuned in to the telepathy.

They were charging towards Becher's like a train. Now—and up . . . Charlie felt the wind punching him, felt it whistling . . . Perfect. Absolutely perfect.

Bonnie landed just right, seeming to cope naturally with the huge drop. Charlie wanted to kiss him again, but had to concentrate on the twenty-third, and then, almost immediately, the problems thrown up by the Canal Turn. The twenty-third fence—the seventh first time round—was the jockeys' spectre. It was the only fence of the Grand National's thirty that wasn't higher on take-off than on landing, built as it was into a natural hollow.

If you'd got a horse that could pace and jump the seventh, they always said in the changing room, then you'd got a horse that could win the whole race.

Bonnie had managed it twice in copybook fashion.

Charlie exhaled and swept round the sharp left-hand bend on the Canal Turn. This horse was an angel. Pegasus wasn't in it. A dream come true. Jack's Joker was still rampaging away, almost stepping over the fences as if they were pony-club cross-poles. A couple of the horses ahead of him went at the Canal. Tangling their legs on take-off, trying to co-ordinate turning a bend at speed and immediately taking off, proved too much. Charlie and Bonnie, in their central position, managed to avoid the mêlée, and jumping crabwise, landed safely.

Shit. Valentine's next. Last year's undoing. His swan-song fence . . . Still, he'd managed it once this afternoon—he could do it again. He almost laughed. He'd blown it last year because he'd been thinking of Tina. He hadn't been thinking of her this year. Maybe Matt had . . . He allowed himself one further brief delightful thought that Jemima was here, and watching him, and would be there to congratulate him afterwards . . .

Okay, fine. Now concentrate. No distractions. None.

Valentine's . . . He could hear horses gaining on him, but couldn't see them yet. Still no problem. He kicked Bonnie onwards, almost holding his breath. Lightning striking twice and all that . . . The take-off was perfect; the soaring, lung-bruising leap absolutely immaculate. The adrenalin rush was stronger than ever.

'Oh, please God let him stay on his feet . . .'

Bonnie slithered, pecked a little bit on landing, but regained his footing almost immediately and was racing again before Charlie had drawn breath. He lifted his head and looked. They'd kept their position.

Brilliant. Brilliant. Brilliant.

Three fences left in the back straight and then the sweep on to Mildmay and the last two. Then a charge to the elbow and that gruelling, killing, nearly five-hundred-yard final run-in—and the winning post. He was going to do it. He knew he was.

Four horses left standing ahead of him, and Bonnie picked his way fastidiously round the not so lucky balled-up jockeys and the sprawling equine legs. Jack's Joker made a mistake and lost ground. Another faller. Three to pick off. No sweat. He wondered if Jemima was watching him on the screen.

Stop thinking about Jemima.

A monochromatic flash to his right caught his attention. Matt, in Tina's black-and-white colours, was upside him. Great. They could have a real duel now—and Matt was obviously going all out to win. Thank God for that. Charlie grinned across. Matt was staring straight ahead.

'Great ride.'

Matt said nothing. He didn't even look at him. Charlie saw him pull his whip through, watched him yank at Dragon Slayer's reins. It was all done so quickly that he thought he'd imagined it.

Shit—now what was he doing? Dragon Slayer's pumping muscular legs were dragging the huge black body sideways, coming ever closer.

'Keep him fucking straight!' Charlie yelled, pulling his own whip through to keep Bonnie on course, the words almost too much effort. His lungs and his throat were screaming, 'Keep him away from me!'

Matt didn't appear to hear. Dragon Slayer was on a diagonal collision course with Bonne Nuit, matching him stride for stride. Charlie tried to steer Bonnie towards the rails, trying to increase his speed, looking for a gap. It wasn't ideal: the ground had been badly cut up on the first circuit—but it was better than trying to battle it out.

'Fuck off!' he yelled again, as Matt pushed Dragon Slayer ever nearer. 'You'll have me over the rails!'

Jesus—the horses' shoulders were almost touching now. Charlie could sense Bonnie's bewilderment and there was a fence coming up. He had no choice. There was no time to set him at the jump. Instinctively he gathered Bonnie up, felt the muscles tighten, felt him leap.

Airborne at the same time as Dragon Slayer, his stirrups and Matt's could have entwined.

'Get him off my line!' The words thumped out of him as Bonnie thudded over the fence. No artistic merit on that one—but at least they were still on their feet. One of the three in front hadn't been so lucky, and another was tiring rapidly. That left Jack's Joker still ploughing on. Just Jack's Joker to beat on the run-in . . . and Dragon Slayer.

There was no daylight left between Bonnie and the rails. If he'd looked down he'd have expected to see sparks. The crowd, unaware of any danger, were loving it—screaming their appreciation—and all the time Matt kept pressing Dragon Slayer even closer . . .

'Piss off!'

'Sorry.' Matt's voice was staccato with effort. 'You told me to win. Everyone told me to win. Sorry, Charlie . . .'

And yanking Dragon Slayer's head round again, he barged into him.

Bonnie staggered slightly, but didn't stop galloping. Another fence—he'd have to jump it with Dragon Slayer joined to him like a Siamese twin. Matt wanted to unseat him—he knew now. It was too crazy for words—the cameras would catch it all—wouldn't they?

Up—oh, please God . . . Bonnie, floundering, jumped. It wasn't close enough. The long chestnut legs were running in mid-air, scrambling. Charlie hung on and prayed.

The thump of landing jarred his body. He bit his tongue and could taste the blood. His eyes were watering. He couldn't see. It didn't matter. It didn't bloody matter. They were still on their feet.

Miraculously, so was Dragon Slayer—although they'd both lost a lot of ground. Jack's Joker was approaching the last.

Matt charged against him again. The crowd, still unsuspecting, were roaring their excitement. Charlie could just hear them above the thundering of his own heart and the rasping gasps of Bonnie's breath.

'Shit!' He tried to push Dragon Slayer away with his stirruped foot. No contest. Ten-and-a-half stone of knackered man against half-a-ton of race-fit horse. He spat blood. 'You're fucking mad!'

'I've got to win!' Matt's face was ashen. 'I've got to fucking win! Not you! Me!'

Jack's Joker had cleared the last and was rocking easily towards the elbow. Bonnie, still with nowhere to jump, lifted his head to place the fence, then took off. So did Dragon Slayer.

They landed together. Almost colliding. Almost falling.

Charlie could see the muddied turf, magnified, hurtling towards him, then, just as quickly, receding again. Bonne Nuit's head jerked up from the stumble and smacked him on the nose.

Shit. More blood. More tears. But they were standing. And still moving. Now, Charlie thought. It's got to be now.

He'd cleared all the fences in the National. He was lying second on the bravest, most brilliant horse in the world. If Matt had suddenly gone barking mad he'd have to worry about it later. With one regretful flick of his whip on Bonnie's shoulder, he managed to get a slight edge. They were no longer level.

'Go on, baby. Go on . . .'

Bonnie, obviously indignant about the sharp reminder, tore round the elbow like a Walthamstow greyhound. Charlie could no longer see the black-and-white colours. He could only hear the rhythmic thud of the hooves inches behind him. Jack's Joker, still ahead, was labouring.

He crouched low, hung on, and hands-and-heeled Bonnie forward. They were catching Jack's Joker! And Matt was catching them! The roar from the crowd was a living thing, organic, growing, pulsing. It picked him up and carried him.

They were level with Jack's Joker. Matt was still only half a length away. The black-and-white colours were flicking into his vision again.

Using only his knees and hands and prayer, flicking the whip in Bonnie's line of vision to keep him straight, they powered up the run-in. The big Irish horse seemed to be standing still. Then going backwards. They'd passed Jack's Joker! There were twenty yards left. Ten. Five.

Matt was upside him again. No—not quite. Not quite.

Where was the pole? Where the hell was the winning post? When would this race be over? Why were people screaming and cheering?

Charlie blinked behind his goggles. There was nowhere left to go.

Oh—holy God! He'd won the National!

Charlie tugged Bonnie's ears in delight, then standing in the stirrups, he punched the air, unable to see anything because of the blood. He shoved his goggles away and wiped his eyes. Jesus! The crowd were roaring, running, pushing, calling his name: everywhere a sea of grinning faces.

Wheeling Bonnie round, slowing through the

596

throng, Charlie grinned back. Olly, Bonnie's lad, grabbed the reins, tears pouring down his cheeks. Charlie leaned down and hugged him. Hugged Drew, too. They were both crying.

As if by magic, there was a uniformed escort, and television reporters, and still thousands of people crowding in on them. Everyone was shouting his name. Bonnie didn't flinch.

'Incredible,' Drew managed to mutter. 'Bloody incredible. We've done it. We've really done it . . .'

'Yeah—' Charlie's voice was barely audible. 'I think we have . . .'

The uniformed escort led them on through a veritable ocean of people, all pressing, cheering, wanting to touch him and Bonne Nuit. Drew had to hang on to the bridle to keep up. Charlie leaned down and hugged him again. His face hurt from smiling, and his smile must have looked deranged as his mouth was caked with dried blood. And all the time he was looking for Jemima.

He could see Tina, head and shoulders above everyone else, pushing her way towards them. And there was Gillian in her outrageous Fishnets outfit, waving as she barged through the throng. Perhaps Jemima would be with her. Hers was the only face he wanted to see now. Just let him get to the unsaddling enclosure—to that coveted winner's spot—and then he'd do a Frankie Dettori-style celebratory leap, and kiss Jemima. Everything was going to be all right . . .

The Tannoy crackled and hissed. The flash and staccato rattle of the camera shutters suddenly died away. The bristling grey OB mikes dropped out of sight, and the jostling sea of hacks was still.

Had someone died?

Something was wrong. Something was very wrong.

Gillian reached them, and was kissing him when the Tannoy's crackle bing-bonged into life.

Charlie and Drew stopped smiling at the same moment.

'Shit.' Drew's face was ashen. 'No!'

'What?' Gillian was blinking wildly. 'What's happened?'

Charlie knew. And he knew why. Oh, bloody, sodding hell. They couldn't do this—not now. The crowd knew, too. The roar of disappointment and disapproval swept across the course.

They'd called a stewards' enquiry.

CHAPTER FORTY

Drew had no time to find Maddy in the scrum. She'd have heard the announcement and would know what was happening, of course, but he still wanted to tell her himself. To have her squeeze his hand and wish him good luck. She'd always done it before when his runners had been the subject of an enquiry, and things had worked out fine. He needed Maddy as a talisman now more than ever. It was one of the drawbacks, he realised yet again, of being the product of two of the most superstitious races in the universe.

'Find Maddy,' he hissed to Gillian. 'Stay with her until it's over. Don't worry.'

'But why?' Gillian wailed. 'Why are they doing it? They can't take the race away from us, can they? Bonnie won!'

'Just stay with Maddy. She'll explain. We've been through this sort of thing before. Look, I can't hang about. They've got Charlie and Matt in there now. They'll probably be hauling me in in a minute. Bastards.'

Ignoring Gillian's further flutterings, Drew pushed his way towards the stewards' room. The bookies were already calling the odds on the outcome of the enquiry. Several hardened punters were reaching for their wallets, willing to gamble a fortune on Bonne Nuit losing the race. Vultures, Drew thought, angrily shouldering past. Picking off the flesh before the body's stopped twitching.

He'd seen, like the whole of Aintree, the collision course with Dragon Slayer. He had been going to ask Charlie about it later. After the presentation and the interviews. It hadn't been Charlie's fault, he was sure of it. There had been nowhere for him to go. Dragon Slayer had taken Charlie's ground—but so what? It happened. And it hadn't affected the outcome of the race. Bonne Nuit had beaten Dragon Slayer fair and square.

Bloody namby-pamby racecourse stewards! Any slight infringement of the rules and they hauled you up like miscreant schoolboys in front of the headmaster. Bloody hell!

Drew barged onwards, brushing aside the thrusting microphones.

'What d'you reckon'll happen, eh?'

'We'll keep the race.'

He said it a dozen times. A dozen times it was received with knowing smirks. God help him, he'd hit someone in a minute.

There was always a panel of stewards at racecourses, making sure that each race was run fairly, and Drew had considered them no more than a necessary evil. They kept racing on the straight and narrow. Or so he'd always thought. Maybe not now, though. Not if they robbed him of the race. Oh, God—they couldn't. Not when winning meant keeping Peapods.

There'd be three of them sitting at the enquiry. One of them would definitely be the steward who had been appointed to watch the television screen. Had he seen something that everyone else had missed? Something that would take the race away, take Peapods away?

Christ. He'd soon know.

There was a further clump of hacks outside the stewards' office. They asked the same questions. Drew barked the same answer.

'We'll keep the race.'

His confidence was ebbing away as he pushed open the door. It was like being randomly breath-tested. Even if you hadn't had a drink for weeks, you immediately felt guilty.

'Fucking debacle!' Kath Seaward was puffing furiously on a cigarette in the corridor outside the stewards' enquiry room. 'Don't know why they can't just leave things alone! This is the fucking National, for God's sake—not some seller at Chepstow! What the hell do they think they're doing?'

Drew shrugged sympathetically. He was sure Kath had more to lose than he did. 'What's Matt said?'

'Sod all. There wasn't time. I don't know what I'm supposed to say, either. What about you?'

Drew shook his head. 'Much the same. I didn't even have time to speak to Charlie about it. It looked like a problem on the straight—but nothing that hampered either horse.'

Kath snorted smoke down her nostrils and ground out the cigarette butt with her toe. 'Well, I certainly wasn't going to raise any objections, much as it galls me to have to admit it. Damn good race. Fight to the finish.' She scuffed the remainder of the grey ash into the liver-and-orange Wilton. 'We were lucky to snatch second. You did well.'

Drew almost smiled. 'Thanks. Does that mean you'll be paying over the grand you owe me?'

'Grand? What fucking grand?'

'The wager we struck last year? Charlie and my hopeless animal, I think you said, against Matt and Dragon Slayer?'

Kath fumbled for another cigarette. 'Yeah, I suppose so. I'll write the cheque later. Listen, off the record, and because I'll never admit it in front of the Vyella shirt brigade in there, I reckon you beat us hands down. I can't see them wanting to reverse the placings. I mean, I only saw what everyone else saw. No interference from your side. Bit of a coming together. Nothing more.'

Reverse the placings? Jesus. Drew felt sick. Not now. Not after everything they'd been through.

He stared at the oak-panelled walls and the collection of Stubbs and Munnings. The racing world's more recent stars were there, too: Desert Orchid; Red Rum . . . There was a huge No Smoking sign between the priceless equine paintings, but Kath obviously didn't care. He didn't blame her. This was a bloody awful experience.

The door swung open.

'Mr Fitzgerald? Miss Seaward? If you'd like to come in now?'

Kath ground out the half-finished cigarette

beside its fellow on the carpet, and strode through the door ahead of Drew.

Charlie and Matt, still in their breeches and jerseys, were sitting in front of the stewards on rather uncomfortable-looking straight-backed chairs. Matt was staring directly ahead, his back rigid. Charlie, his long legs stretched in front of him, looked slightly more relaxed. Neither of them looked up as Drew and Kath walked in.

Three stewards sat behind the table, all wearing the extremely appropriate Tattersalls checks and yellow waistcoats. Drew felt very sick.

The stewards' secretary smiled. 'If you'd like to take a seat. Just a few formalities. Won't keep you longer than is necessary.'

Drew sat next to Charlie, saying nothing. Kath muttered under her breath.

The oldest steward tapped a television screen. 'We've replayed the incident, and we've looked at the camera film from several different angles. Mr Somerset and Mr Garside have given their accounts. I wonder if either of you have anything to add?'

'About what, exactly?' Drew exhaled. 'I can't see any point in this. Our horse won going away. There was no interference. No suggestion of impropriety.'

'Interference in the straight.' The steward switched on the video machine. 'Maybe you'd like to watch . . .'

Drew watched. It didn't change his opinion. Charlie had the racing line. Matt seemed to have lost his way, and Dragon Slayer had strayed across.

'A bit of bumping and barging—but this is the National, for God's sake. It happens.'

Charlie turned his head then and looked at

Drew. He didn't speak, merely raised his eyebrows.

'So Kath leaned forward. 'What exactly is going on? What are we doing in here? My horse bumped Fitzgerald's horse. Fitzgerald's horse still won the race. Where's the problem?'

Drew bit his lip. He knew how difficult it must be for Kath to utter a whole sentence without an expletive.

'There doesn't appear to be one.' The younger steward shrugged. 'A bit of argy-bargy maybe . . .'

He was silenced by a frown from his more senior colleagues.

'Who else is giving evidence?' Drew shifted in his chair. He was sure the Aintree crowd would turn into a lynch mob if they delayed any longer. 'I don't see that Ms Seaward can add anything. We merely saw what you saw. And if you've taken all the relevant information from the jockeys involved—'

Again, Charlie raised his eyebrows. Drew shook his head.

'I don't think we need any further witnesses.' The senior steward pushed back his chair. 'We've reached our conclusion, haven't we, gentlemen? There certainly doesn't seem to be anything untoward. Both horses have been drugs-tested— with negative results. We shan't be sending any other samples away for analysis. Tack has been inspected for tampering. All clear on that score. I think we should just take the evidence of our eyes, the cameras, and Garside, here. Evidence which, I must say, was corroborated by Somerset's story.'

Jesus Christ. Drew wiped his sweating palms on his knees. For God's sake get on with it.

'So, unless either of you wish to add anything?'

Kath shook her head violently. Drew sighed. 'No.

603

Nothing.'

The stewards all looked at each other, nodded, and started shuffling papers.

'Get a fucking move on,' Kath hissed under her breath.

The stewards' secretary cleared his throat. 'The finding of this enquiry is that the placings should remain unaltered.'

*   *   *

The media was waiting in force outside the door. The crowd already knew the result. The Tannoy had announced it immediately, and the cheers were still ringing across Liverpool. Drew wiped the back of his hand across his mouth and hugged Charlie.

'You doing the press conference?'

Charlie shook his head. 'I haven't got enough strength to even lift the bloody trophy.'

'And you will tell me what happened in there?'

Charlie grinned. 'I haven't got a clue. I think Matt's the only one who knows the truth. Oh, shit— here come the hacks.'

Drew, who only wanted to find Maddy, put on his widest smile for the BBC.

'Congratulations Drew. Charlie. Bit of a scare there towards the end, eh?'

Charlie was beaming but remained silent. Bugger, Drew thought, he was going to have to go in blind. 'No, not really. We knew we'd keep the race.'

'Never happened before in the National, has it? A stewards' enquiry?'

'I haven't got a clue.' Drew stretched his smile. 'I'll have to check when I get home.'

The BBC weren't giving up on their viewers that easily. 'It looked as though Dragon Slayer lost his way a bit. Looked as though you were hampered.'

'Just a bit—'

'So, what did Charlie tell them in there?'

'You'll have to ask him,' Drew floundered. 'But not now. Sorry to cut you short, but we do have a presentation to get to. We'll both do a full interview later.'

The media were not going to be thwarted that easily. They started to jog alongside. Drew who by now was becoming seriously irritated. Calm down, he told himself, you've won the bloody National. Peapods will be okay. Everything will be okay.

Several statuesque blondes with corporate costumes and corkscrew curls had appeared from nowhere, and were leading them through the thousands of well-wishers. The noise was deafening. Charlie, Drew noticed with some concern, was completely ignoring the willowy blondes. Had he suffered some sort of catatonic shock? This was prime Somerset territory. Strange, he thought, that there wasn't the slightest flicker of interest.

'Clear a path! Keep clear!' The mounted policemen had now taken control. 'Stand well back!'

Drew, followed by Charlie, the curly girls, and the world's press, all crowded through the human tunnel. Maddy emerged from about six people deep and hurtled towards him.

Oh, brilliant. He caught her and hugged her. 'I love you. And we've done it. And everything is going to be all right—'

'Everything always was.' She snuggled against him. 'I'm dead proud of you, Drew. And Gillian is practically pawing the ground to get at the trophy. And Bonnie has been stuffed full of Polos.'

She glanced over Drew's shoulder and winked at Charlie. 'And he'll, no doubt, get his rewards later.'

'From Tina?' Drew found himself hoisted towards the podium. The clapping and cheering reached Richter-scale proportions.

Maddy, disappearing into the sea again, was smiling and shaking her head.

*   *   *

After the presentation, when the jubilation had died down a little, and all the hard-luck stories had been told a dozen times, and everyone had started to drift away to place their delayed bets for the remaining races, Drew and Charlie were buttonholed by the BBC.

They had already decided that Charlie should answer the questions about the enquiry. Drew had eulogised over Bonnie's training schedule, expectations, future plans, and general brilliance. It had been fine. He'd known what he was talking about. The clash with Dragon Slayer was definitely Charlie's territory.

Two dozen microphones were thrust towards them. Another two dozen spiral-bound notepads were unfurled.

'So, Dragon Slayer lost his way, did he? It looked as though you were badly hampered.'

Charlie shrugged. 'Matt lost his reins at the fifth from home. Just for a minute. But at that speed it could have been disastrous. No reins—no steering.'

'Like in a car?'

'Exactly.' Charlie beamed. 'An out-of-control

car criss-crossing lanes on a crowded motorway. Potentially deadly.'

'And you and Bonnie helped him out?'

Drew, who had been happily nodding, felt Charlie stiffen; heard his intake of breath; felt the infinitesimal pause.

'Yes . . .' Charlie's grin was a rictus. 'I—um— used Bonne Nuit to keep Dragon Slayer straight. As soon as Matt had regained control, we were able to ease away . . .'

The microphones pushed closer. 'We couldn't actually see the dropped reins on the screen. Is that what the stewards were querying?'

'They only saw the coming together.' Charlie nodded. 'They needed to know the reasons. And, of course, they accepted our explanation.'

'Matt has declined to be interviewed. Do you know why?'

'Probably still suffering from shock,' Charlie said lightly. 'I know I would be.'

'Anyway, congratulations to you both. A wonderful result—and a good race all round . . .' There were the same knowing media smiles. 'And Matt Garside no doubt owes you a pint?'

As they headed towards the changing room, Drew had a feeling that Matt owed Charlie a great deal more than that.

*   *   *

The changing room was quiet. The last two races on the card were an amateur handicap and a National Hunt flat race, so most of the jockeys were still closeted with their connections or already on their way to the party at the Adelphi.

607

'A gold star for the Oscar performance out there.' Drew grinned as he closed the door. 'Now are you going to tell me the truth?'

Charlie tugged the Fishnets jersey over his head. 'He barged me. I've got no idea why. He told the stewards he'd lost his steering—and I went along with it. I probably wouldn't have done if we'd been second—but where's the harm?'

'He deliberately barged you?'

'God knows. I don't know if he was trying to kill me or merely put me out of contention.' He shrugged. 'Look, Drew—I really would rather not know. I think Matt's got major problems. Problems that have just been made far worse by not winning the National. I don't want to make anything more of it.'

Drew shook his head. He was used to Charlie being so laid back as to be horizontal, but surely there were limits? He sighed as the door opened. Now he'd have to wait to find out exactly what had happened—Or maybe not . . .

'I saw you both come in.' Matt, changed into his civvies and looking like an insurance salesman, closed the door. 'I wanted to say thanks and sorry. Can we talk, or are you going to hit me?'

'Looks like someone's already done that,' Charlie said, standing up and tugging off the remainder of his clothes. 'Go on then. I've already heard the bullshit. Try it out on Drew.'

'Look, thanks for backing up my story. I didn't deserve what you said in the enquiry. I thought you'd drop me in it. I probably would have . . .'

'Thank your lucky stars that Charlie's a nicer bloke than you, then,' Drew said. 'I wouldn't have put my neck on the line to save yours. If that was

608

deliberate, you could have killed my horse and my jockey, and jeopardised your whole career.'

'I do know. I must have been bloody insane.' Matt sank down on to the bench. 'And I haven't got a career left. Oh, shit . . .'

After he'd told them, Drew still wasn't sure whether he believed it. Even Charlie, who obviously knew more than he did, had been stunned into open-mouthed astonishment.

Drew looked at Matt. Matt? He'd have sworn he was straight in every way. He was—so—ordinary. Boring, almost. He felt a slight rush of revulsion for the sexually sinister, then wanted to laugh. God—he wondered what Maddy would make of it! He somehow couldn't see Matt in scanty studded leather and thigh boots . . . Still, that probably wasn't how it worked. But Matt throwing races? Matt in on what would have been the biggest scam of recent years? It hardly seemed credible.

And Vincent! The conniving bastard. He should sack him—and he would certainly threaten to do so. But he knew Maddy would intervene. Anyway, how could they sack someone who had delivered their only son? Still, he'd put the fear of God into him.

Charlie was still looking shell-shocked. 'You mean—Tina . . . She enjoys being with you more than me?'

Matt gave a sheepish smile. 'Strangely, yeah. Sorry.'

'Fucking hell.'

Drew, trying to sort out the various strands, and not to imagine Matt striding around with a bullwhip, attempted to look solemn. 'You and Vincent must both go to the police. Blackmail is a

609

serious crime. You've got to tell them all this—and get Ned Filkins put away for a bloody long time.'

'How can we?' Matt spread his hands. 'We're both guilty. I threw races. Vincent paid to get them thrown.'

Drew shrugged. 'So? No one said it would be easy. It'll be bloody tough—but it still won't be the end of the world. Ned's the real villain. You'll be the victims as far as the police are concerned.'

Fair words, Drew thought. And probably true—whatever Vincent and Matt had been sucked into. He wasn't sure he could be quite so magnanimous. After all, between them, they could have wrecked his future.

'I'm not going to the police.' Matt scuffed at the dusty floor with the toe of his immaculately polished shoe. 'I'm actually jacking it all in. I'm going to America. I'm getting out of race-riding altogether.' He shot an apologetic look at Charlie. 'I'm going with Tina. She'll be doing most of her television work over in the States. We're leaving at the end of the week.'

Drew looked quickly at Charlie. Bloody hell. Didn't he mind? Apparently not. He'd never be alone for long. He had Lucinda in an on-off sort of way, didn't he? And, of course, everyone knew he was carrying a torch for Jemima. Apart from Jemima, that was.

'What about Kath?'

Matt gave a shrug. 'I've just told her. Oh, just the America bit. Not the rest. She blew my ears off as it was.'

Drew laughed. 'Christ! And you're scared of telling the police after you've faced Lady Macbeth? Get a grip.'

'I think Matt's right.' Charlie reached for his jeans from the peg. 'I think it would be far better to let things die down. And you can bet your life that Ned Filkins will have cleared out of Milton St John long before the first coaches get back to the Cat and Fiddle.'

Matt stood up. 'Christ, I hope so. I'd like to kill the bastard. Still, at least he'll be completely skint now. He had everything riding on me today.'

Drew smiled. Poetic justice. 'And Vincent?'

'Vincent, too,' Matt said. 'Poor bugger. He'll have to start his savings from scratch. Look, if I'm leaving the country and Ned Filkins is leaving the planet, and if you two can forgive me—'

Charlie sighed heavily, then held out his hand. 'Okay. Whatever. Drew?'

Drew sighed. He'd never forgive Matt for the disaster he could so easily have caused. But was there really any point in prolonging the agony?

'Yeah, well . . . if you're leaving, I don't suppose it'll make too much difference. However, if you change your mind and stick around I'll make sure you never ride for anyone again. Understood?'

'Understood.' Matt walked towards the door. 'And I won't be hanging about to find out. Thanks for everything—and well done, today. You deserved it.'

'Sanctimonious shit!' Drew exploded as soon as the door closed. 'Weirdo. You *knew*, didn't you?'

'Nah.' Charlie shook his head. 'Not about the rubber corsets. That's really freaky. I still can't believe that. No, I mean I knew the silly sod was chucking races—and I tried to stop him. I had no idea why. Poor bugger. So, that's two jump jockeys hanging up their boots then.'

'Two?'

Charlie grinned. 'You'll be wanting an assistant trainer of the highest calibre to get Peapods into flat-racing's celestial sphere, won't you?'

'Yeah, I suppose I will.' Drew chewed his lower lip. 'Can you think of anyone for the job? Hey— where are you off to?'

'I want to find Jemima. The do at the Adelphi won't be the same without her. I mean, we've got loads to celebrate and—hell, Drew—why are you looking at me like that?'

Drew shook his head. 'She's gone, Charlie. I saw her heading for the car park just as they announced the stewards' enquiry.'

CHAPTER FORTY-ONE

Jemima dragged a mug from the cupboard, tipped in a haphazard sprinkling of coffee granules, and thrust the kettle switch to boil.

Then she stood in the middle of the kitchen and burst into tears.

She'd been wanting to have a good cry all the way home from Liverpool, but her temper and the stupid sense of self-preservation, which insisted that Floss would negotiate the M6 far better with a dry-eyed driver, wouldn't allow her the luxury.

She wasn't sure if she was crying because watching Charlie win had been the most momentous occasion of her life; or whether it was because she'd died a million times while he and Matt had been battling against the rails; or simply because they'd called the stewards' enquiry and she couldn't stay and watch Charlie lose his dream.

Or maybe it was none of those things. Maybe it had nothing at all to do with Charlie. Maybe it was just because Vincent had proved himself to be only Vincent—the feckless get-rich-quick father he'd always been—and not some apple-cheeked, pipe-smoking, really good father from Pollyanna.

Anyway, none of it mattered now. She'd been to Aintree, and Charlie had won the National and kept the race, and Vincent had let her down. And there was no one in the Vicarage to hear her cry.

She blew her nose loudly on a piece of kitchen roll and removed her glasses. They always turned into little reservoirs when she cried. She really must remember to take them off earlier if she was going to turn into a habitual bawler—which of course she wasn't. Tonight though, she thought, a girl deserved a treat.

The kettle switched itself off. She wished she could.

Making the coffee, she trudged through to the sitting room and turned on the television. God—not another Grand National replay. She couldn't bear it. It simply wasn't fair. She jammed her glasses back on. Charlie, looking glorious, was even more everywhere because of the historic steward's enquiry.

'Get used to it,' she told herself, thumping down on to the sofa, spilling hot coffee on to her fingers and not feeling it. 'He's going to be ultra famous now. They'll probably be giving away little plastic models of him with the cornflakes.'

Models automatically threw up images of Tina. Jemima threw them out again.

She didn't want to think about Tina. Tina and

613

Charlie would no doubt be snuggling up together in the Adelphi's equivalent of the Wallbank-Fox at this very moment. And even if they weren't snuggling up in one of the well-appointed bedrooms, then they'd be bloody snuggling up on the dance floor. Oh, bugger! She'd never wanted any man half as much as she wanted Charlie Somerset—and he'd probably be grabbing the microphone and announcing his engagement to the stalking clothes horse right at that very moment.

She felt tears of indignation prickling her eyes and sniffed them back. One cry was acceptable: two was bordering on sheer self-indulgence. Trying to concentrate on the television, she watched, her heart thumping painfully, as Charlie and Matt fought it out for the final places. Everyone was cheering and screaming. Then, at the course, the atmosphere had been primal and frenzied: now that she knew the outcome it was some small relief to watch it clinically and calmly without the knot of terror grinding in her stomach.

There! Now Charlie was just beating the Irish horse and she exhaled heavily—that minute when he and Bonnie had actually passed the winning post had been like nothing on earth. Her legs had practically given way, and she'd bitten right through the finger of one of Gillian's borrowed leather gloves.

And Matt and Dragon Slayer had been so near! She'd thought at one point that they'd catch Bonne Nuit. But they hadn't—and Charlie had won—and she could hear someone very close to her screaming Charlie's name over and over again, and it was only when she'd shut her mouth that she'd realised the voice had been her own. And then they'd announced the enquiry and she'd felt his pain . . .

Well, that was quite enough of that nonsense.

She zapped the television channel over. This was better—a film about terminal illness by the look of the pale and anguished faces and the heart-tugging violin strings in the background. She thought she could just about cope with that.

She wasn't sure she'd be able to cope with anything else. Not just yet. She felt there would be an awful lot of mopping-up to do in the morning. Starting with Vincent.

She'd caught up with Maureen and Vincent in the post-National mêlée. Once her fury had dwindled a little, and Vincent had explained why he'd done it, she'd almost felt sorry for him. Well, there had definitely been pity mixed up in the anger. It must have been awful for him. He really had tried hard to build up a new life—but even so, he'd got sucked in because it was a gamble. And because he was a gambler whose life-blood surged with each taken risk. He would always be a gambler. It was like being on the wagon for years and having just one drink, she supposed. You never thought it would do any harm.

The film's terminal illness appeared to be infectious. Everyone on the screen was gasping and calling out in reedy voices. Wildly entertaining for a Saturday night. She wished she'd video'd *Blind Date.*

Then there had been Matt's involvement. That had really rocked her. Matt? Into submission and domination? When Vincent had explained how Matt had been drawn into the vortex of Ned's scheming, even Maureen had turned pale. It was almost impossible to believe that Matt had been

615

mixed up in something so tacky. Poor Matt. Or maybe he wasn't. If he enjoyed it, who was she to judge? It didn't seem that terrible, to be honest, when she thought about it. A bit unnatural, yes. And probably a killer for his career if the tabloids got hold of it. But it explained an awful lot, too. And it had given her a fairish dollop of satisfaction to know that it hadn't been her body that had repulsed him.

She had insisted that Vincent must go to the police the minute he got back to Milton St John. Ned Filkins should pay for what he'd done. Should pay for what he'd nearly done to Charlie and Bonnie—not to mention Drew's livelihood and Gillian's dreams, and loads of things. Ned Filkins was a bastard.

'And your Dad's not perfect,' Maureen had said quietly. 'But then, duck, who is?'

He was far, far, from perfect. And he'd blustered and said he'd think about telling someone when he got back—and she'd known he wouldn't. He never could face up to his responsibilities. Still maybe it had taught him something. He was flat broke again because of the scam. He'd lost every bloody illegally earned penny.

Maybe, she thought, as they carted out a couple of dead bodies and everyone else on the screen started wailing, he'd been punished enough by that. She hoped at least that he'd learned some sort of lesson from it all.

She clicked the television into silence, abandoned the coffee and the sofa, and wandering into the bathroom, turned on the taps.

*   *   *

616

A wallowing hour later and leaving a trail of Floris suds on the carpet, Jemima wrapped her dressing gown round her and headed for the kitchen. The Vicarage was actually pretty creepy. She had never been alone in it before. Her flat was fine, but she tried not to think about the dozens of empty rooms, and the surrounding shrubbery, and the dark staircases. Visions of Dickensian-style ghosts of previous clerical incumbents kept creeping into her mind. Maybe she should just pour herself a massive gin and go to bed and try to sleep.

Sleep! Bah! Humbug!

She'd probably never sleep again. No one needed amphetamine stimulation to keep them awake when they lived in Milton St John; she was sure of it. She poured the gin anyway, and switched on the wireless.

Nice. Bill Rennells being avuncular on TVFM. She sat at the kitchen table and listened to the comforting voice. Oh, God—it was no good. She couldn't rest. She needed to be doing something. If she was properly domesticated she'd take the squirty Jif to the kitchen cupboards or bleach her table linen or something. As it was, she could only think of one place she wanted to be.

Hurtling into her bedroom and dressing in record time, she skidded down the Vicarage staircase and out into the enveloping darkness. Jemima shivered, thinking of the village elders slumbering beneath their mossy headstones in the neighbouring cemetery. Why the hell had she watched that spooky film?

Shoving her hands deep in her pockets she headed for the High Street. The Cat and Fiddle

617

was rumbustious with excitement as they celebrated Drew and Gillian and Charlie's victory, even though all three of them were staying up in Liverpool. Absenteeism had never been a reason to skimp on a session in Milton St John. The karaoke machine was thundering 'We Are the Champions' out into the night. No one noticed her passing in the shadows.

She unlocked the door of the bookshop and closed it behind her. For a moment she stood in the gloom, then she took a deep breath and switched on the lights. The shop was lovely like this, Jemima thought, smelling of print and people, but quiet and comforting. A balm. But not for long. Being a great believer in the old adage about work being the only cure for heartache, Jemima headed for the chaos of the stock room.

Half an hour later and she'd refilled three sections of shelving, broken up boxes, and filed the invoices. May's Fishnets glowed in garish splendour at her feet. Oh, well she might as well get them out on the shelves. Gillian's fan club had probably trebled overnight and there'd be queues way past the Munchy Bar for the latest Bella-Donna Stockings.

She'd got the armful balanced under her chin when someone knocked on the door. Sod it. Probably the pub's overspill wanting to conga round the shop.

'We're closed!'

This time the knock was even louder.

'I said we're closed!'

'Jemima—let me in.'

She held her breath. Her heart was rattling a staccato tattoo.

'Jemima—it's me.'

She was overwrought. Imagining things. It sounded like Charlie's voice—but it couldn't possibly be Charlie, could it? Not unless he and Tina had belted all the way down from Liverpool to show her the engagement ring before she went to bed. The way the rest of the day had gone, she wouldn't be that surprised . . .

'Jemima?'

Bloody hell! It certainly *sounded* like Charlie . . . But it still couldn't be. It was probably some sort of Gotcha Oscar stunt. Possibly Gillian's idea of a celebratory joke. She'd probably hired Rory Bremner. There was only one way to find out.

'The door's not locked . . .'

With his dark red hair falling into his eyes, his trademark faded Levis, and his leather jacket pulled over his shirt, she thought that Charlie had simply never looked more devastating.

'What the hell are you doing here?' Jemima groaned silently. It was hardly the warmest greeting she could have issued. 'I mean—'

Charlie's witty repartee seemed to have abandoned him. So had his stock-in-trade grin. He looked anxious. 'I saw the light.'

God, she loved him. She really wanted to hurl herself into his arms. She had to clench her toes to keep herself rooted to the spot. She stared at him over the Fishnet pile. 'Did you think I was being burgled?'

Charlie grinned then. 'No. I saw you. I wanted to talk.'

Charlie seemed to be rapidly gaining his composure. She was equally as rapidly losing hers. Control yourself, you daft bat! She gritted her teeth. He'd probably just come to hand out the wedding invitations. Defensively Jemima hugged the pile of books. 'Why the hell aren't you still in Liverpool?'

'I was going to ask you the same question.'

'Oh, right—well, I came back because—um— well, because I did. After all, I was merely in the audience. The show was over, so I left. You?'

'Much the same.' He grinned again. She wished he wouldn't. 'Do you want a hand with those?'

She shook her head, clutching the Fishnets. 'Charlie—why aren't you still in Liverpool?'

'Because I'm here.'

'I suppose I asked for that. I keep forgetting your paradoxical side.'

'Paradoxical? Isn't that a disinfectant? Try to remember we don't all belong to MENSA.' Charlie grinned again. She really wished he'd stop. 'Have you got anything to drink?'

'Only coffee. I seem to be fresh out of champagne. Still, no doubt you and Tina are saving the Krug assault for later.' Bugger—she hadn't been intending to mention Ms Maloret.

Charlie shook his head. 'Drew and I had a hasty glass of Pol Roger after the presentation. I don't think Tina had a hell of a lot to celebrate.'

'Well, no, not about the outcome of the race, I suppose. Oh, and congratulations, by the way.'

'Thanks.'

God, he was so gorgeous. No, she mustn't think along those lines. No point. No point at all. She stared at the ceiling instead. She couldn't bear the temptation of the athletic body so close physically and yet as far out of reach as it was possible to get.

'Drew told me that you left Aintree straight after

620

they'd announced the stewards' enquiry. Was that because you hoped I'd lose the race. Hoped that Matt would win.'

'No, I didn't. Of course I didn't . . .' She took a deep breath. 'Charlie . . . today . . . this afternoon . . . when you won . . . It was utterly incredible. Really. Then I thought you might lose the race—and I couldn't just hang around and watch. I was being a coward, that's all. And I suppose I thought—well, that I was probably the last person you'd want to see. But watching you win, it was brilliant.' She stopped. Had she already told him that? There were superlatives practically punching each other to escape from her mouth. She clenched her teeth. 'You were brilliant . . .'

The Somerset crooked grin was instant. Charlie tried to look modest. 'I wasn't. Not really. Bonnie was the brilliant one. I just sat on and steered. And I—um—actually was dead pleased that you were there.'

'So was I. Why aren't you whooping it up in the Adelphi then? Why aren't you supporting Tina's wrist while she displays the Koh-i-noor to the world?'

Charlie shrugged. 'I wanted to talk to you. I needed to tell you something. Before you heard it on the jungle drums . . .'

'You could have phoned.'

'I couldn't tell you this on the phone. It wouldn't be fair.'

Jesus! Jemima closed her eyes. He was already married! He and Tina had got a special licence and had a quickie wedding in some Liverpool registry office! Or maybe the Adelphi was able to provide civil ceremonies for its guests?

621

'Look, Jemima. I don't know how much of a shock this will be to you, but Tina and Matt are . . . well, together.'

Her eyes snapped open. 'Matt? With Tina? He can't be. Matt doesn't even like her.'

'I think he might, actually. His little trip at Christmas . . . he didn't go alone . . .'

'He went with *Tina?* Jemima blinked. 'Oh, Charlie, you poor thing . . .'

'I'm fine about it. I was just worried about how you'd feel.'

'Me? Matt and I have hardly spoken since Christmas. I'm just glad he's found someone else— even if Tina was the last person on earth who I'd have thought . . .' she looked at him. 'Seriously— what about you? I know you're a callous sod where women are concerned, but even so, this is just a bit too cool.'

'That's not fair. I've never been callous.'

'Casual, then.'

'Slightly better.' Charlie leaned against the counter. 'But I've never deliberately hurt anyone. I've always made it clear that my relationships were not going to be of the lasting variety.'

'But, you and Tina, you were getting engaged this evening, weren't you?'

He blinked. 'Who the hell told you that?'

As she wanted to leap on him, Jemima gripped the Fishnets even more tightly. 'Gillian did, actually.'

'Gillian? And you believed her?' He laughed. 'Jemima, Gillian has never grasped the right end of a piece of gossip ever since I've known her. Tina and I never were—and never will be—plighting our troths.'

She restrained herself—just—from executing a victory jig.

One problem solved immediately. Only three million left to go. Charlie leaned further back against the counter. There were shadows of exhaustion under his eyes and a trace of dried blood on his lips. He looked like a valiant and wounded warrior. She had never felt so much love for anyone ever.

Still, what was the point in loving him? He'd just spelled out that he played relationships strictly as a fun game. Irritating thing, love. It tended not to stick to the rules.

'Okay, then.' Jemima studied the shop's uneven ceiling again; anything rather than look at him. She'd never be able to disguise the longing in her eyes. 'So, if you haven't come here to announce your engagement, why exactly have you come? Surely not just to tell me about Matt? Not tonight of all nights. I thought the Grand National winner was supposed to be fêted with Krug and laurel wreaths and lead the dancing at the ball, or is that Wimbledon?'

'No idea. I've never won Wimbledon. Anyway I couldn't lead the dancing without a partner, could I?'

There! He was upset about Tina. 'No, sorry. Insensitive of me under the circumstances.'

'Anyway, I've told you—I wanted to talk to you.'

'You're priceless,' she grinned. 'This is the biggest day of your life—the day you and Drew and half the village have been rattling on about ever since I arrived—and you're here, talking to me about Matt and Tina. For God's sake—'

'Do you know everything about Matt?'

623

She blinked again. 'Heavens—Tina's not pregnant, is she?'

'Not as far as I know . . .' He couldn't meet her eyes. 'Look, I don't want to sound like I'm telling tales, but there's something else. Matt has—um—come out of the closet.'

'What closet?' Jemima giggled. 'Oh, the block and tackle one? I know about *that*. About Matt's preferences. Dad told me all about it. I think he tried to score points off it, you know? My addiction's not as bad as yours, so there.'

'Sounds like Vincent.' Charlie pushed his hair away from his eyes and looked extremely relieved. 'And as Tina seems to be more happy to accept Matt's activities than mine, then it's probably a match made in heaven. Didn't you have any idea? About him being a—'

'I'd like to think he wasn't a real one,' she said quickly, smiling. 'More sort of helped out if they were busy. No, I didn't have a clue. Actually, it cheered me up quite a bit. Knowing. I thought he just didn't fancy me.'

Charlie's eyes widened. 'You mean—he didn't—you didn't—?'

'No, we didn't. And I don't want to talk about it.' Jemima shifted the Fishnets. Her arms were killing her. 'But I *knew*, you see, about what Matt was planning to do in the National. Dad told me all about it just before the race started—and I tried to get to you to warn you but there wasn't time. It was awful. I'm so very sorry that they were involved in what happened to you this afternoon. I just didn't know why until later. I was bloody terrified. You could have been killed.'

'Yeah, but I wasn't so it's no problem. It was

624

pretty hairy at the time, but it's all over—' There was a small silence, then Charlie scuffed at the lino with his boot. 'Look, I know you're probably still not all that keen on racing, or jockeys—but I wondered if you'd—um—come out with me?'

Was that what he'd wanted to ask her? Was that why he'd abandoned the celebrations and belted back to Berkshire? Was that what he couldn't say in a telephone call? Not just that Matt was into S and M on a part-time basis? He'd come all this way to ask her *out*? Oh, please God . . .

She bit her lip. 'No.'

'No? Christ. Why not?'

'Because it's dark and it's cold and I'm ever so busy stacking shelves.'

'Okay, then. We'll call a rain check on that one, shall we?' He moved towards her. 'Jemima—oh, shit . . . no, I can't do this.' He pushed his fingers through his hair. He wasn't looking at her. 'You think I'm a serial adulterer, don't you?'

'I know you are.' She smiled at him. It was impossible not to. 'It doesn't matter.'

'Of course it bloody matters. It matters a lot to me. And it matters what you think.' He moved closer again and sighed at the Fishnets armour. 'Can't you put those bloody books down?'

'No.'

Charlie's shoulders sagged. 'I'm actually very faithful—no, don't laugh. I want to be like Drew and Maddy. Like no one else exists. With no doubts, no fears, that the woman I love will leave me . . .'

'Oh, everyone wants to be Drew and Maddy. All that love and friendship and laughter. All that wall-to-wall happiness even when they're facing major problems. They've got what everyone wants . . .' She shrugged. 'If you—um—found—this perfect woman, how would she know that you wouldn't be unfaithful to her? How could she trust you?'

'Because she'd have my word. My love. Total.' He didn't smile. 'Does that sound really wet? I just think she'd know. I mean, I just think that there would be no doubts. Trust. Mutual trust and respect and love.'

He meant it. He was a hundred per cent serious. She tried not to smile.

'Don't laugh! You haven't heard the second reason.' His eyes were unblinking. 'What does marriage mean—to you—to any woman?'

For God's sake! This was hardly time to go into the Kinsey Report. She shrugged. 'Apart from two people loving each other, making a commitment, sharing, being friends—and lovers? Oh, I don't know!'

'Nor do I, and I'd like to find out. But—but there's a problem . . .'

Jemima's mind ricocheted back to the television film. Was he ill? Was there some appalling hereditary Somerset malady that would snatch him from his bride's grasp before the ink had dried on the marriage certificate? Or insanity? Or inbreeding? The possibilities were endless . . .

'Problem?'

'Children.'

Ah—she nodded slowly. So that was it. There were a string of Somerset bastards across the globe which he supported with Christmas cards and monthly maintenance payments. Well, that didn't surprise her. She could practically see them. A whole tribe of glorious looking children: miniature Somersets with trendy names like Seraphina and Spike.

'I haven't got any. I'll never have any. I can't—' He took a deep breath. 'That's my problem. That's why I've never stayed with anyone for very long. It's why I play the field. Apart from never finding the right woman, I'm irreversibly infertile. I was kicked by a horse when I was apprentice. That's why I can't expect anyone to want to marry me.'

'I'm sure—um—that the—er—right woman could manage—' Her voice was croaky. She cleared her throat. 'Um—manage very nicely with ponies and puppies and kittens and borrowing other people's children . . .'

'Do you think so?' Charlie attempted to hug her but the books got in the way. He sighed heavily. 'Please, please put those bloody things down.'

She did. They slithered into an erotic pink pile round their feet. Charlie pulled her into his arms and kissed her gently.

Wow! He really was a killer kisser. The gentle touch was equally as arousing as the slam-dunker on New Year's Eve.

He grinned down at her. 'Grab your coat then. I think we might have some celebrating to do.'

'Your place or mine?'

'Hussy.' Charlie switched off the lights and closed the door behind them. 'Yours of course. I've never made love in a vicarage before. But first I think we ought to down a glass of champagne or two, don't you?'

'Absolutely.' She snuggled against his leather jacket. 'And get a couple of crates in for breakfast.'

They shoved their way into the Cat and Fiddle

and stood, glued together, unseen for a moment at the back of the jam-packed bar. Charlie kissed the top of her head just as the karaoke machine exploded into 'Together Forever'.

'Oh, lovely,' Jemima grinned. 'I think they're playing our tune.'